NOT FOR SALE!

A Novel

RAJ AGRAWAL

Copyright © 2019 Raj Agrawal, Not For Sale!
www.rajagrawal.net
All rights reserved. Published in the United States by IJCA Press.
www.IJCAPress.com

ISBN-13: 978-1-7340810-1-5 (paperback) First Edition

Printed in the United States of America
1 2 3 4 5 6 7 8 9 10

In memory of my parents
Dedicated to my family

PROLOGUE

"Where am I?"

Dr. Ravi Kumar, a world-renowned aerospace engineer and the director of a prestigious aviation institute in Ithaca, New York, woke up in the middle of the night, sweaty and completely disoriented. He had no idea where he was except that he was on the run with his wife, Caitlyn. He turned over and felt Caitlyn—she was there in bed next to him. He let out a big sigh of relief and then slowly it all began to come back.

He was in a Riad in Casablanca, Morocco, which belonged to Dr. Larabi Hasan, his friend and old colleague from the Materials Research Institute in Ithaca, New York. Ravi had called him yesterday from Marseille, France, to ask for a place to stay for a few days where he and Caitlyn could keep a low profile and sort things out. At least two teams of professional hit men were after them, trying to bring them back to the States—willingly or otherwise.

So far, they had managed to stay just a step ahead. But Ravi had no illusion that it was only a matter of time before their luck ran out. They had been on the run for the last six weeks and it just could not go on. He needed a place where they could stay while he came up with a survival plan. He still could not believe that a person like him—that many would call colorless and nerdy—was involved in an international manhunt, running for his life. It did not make any sense.

It all seemed to have started six months ago when Ravi came up with the secret ingredient to a substance that had the power to change the future of the aviation industry—and the future of the planet itself.

CHAPTER 1

ITHACA, NEW YORK, FEBRUARY 1ST, 4 P.M.

Ravi was in his director's office at the Materials Research Institute when he received a call from his colleague, Dr. Marcel Giraud.

"Ravi, come down to the conference room in the lab!" Marcel exclaimed. "I've just gotten the test results."

Could they have found the missing element?

Ravi excitedly banged his fist so hard on his desk that he almost fractured his knuckles. Then he jumped up and headed downstairs to where Marcel and his colleagues were gathered.

It was not a long walk. The institute was in a cavernous building that used to hum with textile weaving and garment making machinery but had ceased production due to it, like many others in the country, not being able to compete against cheaper imports from China and other low-cost countries. It looked derelict from outside, with windows covered with grime and some of the bricks peeling off from the façade. Ravi and his nonprofit institute had acquired the building from the liquidators for almost nothing. Located just a few miles from the expansive campus of Cornell University, his alma mater, it was ideal for Ravi and his small team of scientists to conduct their research and advance the state of the art in materials technology—especially the very high-tech materials used in airplane engines.

For the last ten years, they had been laser focused on inventing a new super alloy—a mixture of two or more elements existing in nature, with at least one of them being a metal. Super alloys were mostly used in airplane engines, which allowed them to pack the power equal to ten train locomotives into a box the size of a couch. Most of the super alloys started with a nickel or cobalt-based material, which provided the strength at the exceedingly high temperatures these engines normally operated at. They were then alloyed or compounded with metals and non-metals, including chromium, which provided corrosion resistance; aluminum, which provided oxidation resistance; and others such as titanium, iron, carbon, and silicon. In addition, the alloying had to be conducted at precisely controlled temperatures, heating and cooling rates, and conditions. The super alloy Ravi's team was working on would allow planes to fly faster for longer distances, while burning less fuel and thus reducing climate-harming greenhouse gases—a scourge that Ravi had dedicated his life's work to fighting.

Two years ago, Dr. Marcel Giraud had entered the picture. A lanky Frenchman in his mid-thirties, he was an assistant professor at the Université de Marseille and a visiting associate at the Materials Research Institute. Over the following months he was joined by Dr. Larabi Hasan from Morocco and Dr. Riccardo Sperra from Palermo, Sicily. Larabi was a serious man in his early forties and talked in a measured voice. Larabi's light brown skin, from his Berber heritage—believed to be a cross between the Indians and the Arabs—made him uncannily look like Ravi, who also had remarkably similar skin tone from his North Indian heritage. Riccardo, a jovial, pudgy man in his late thirties, was always ready with a quip in English, which he usually got wrong. The staff at the institute loved the easy demeanor that masked the man's tough-as-nails personality.

All three foreign scientists were close to the end of their terms at the institute and were scheduled to return home within the next six months.

"Good afternoon," they greeted Ravi in a chorus as he entered the conference room.

It was a small room mostly occupied by a rectangular meeting table, with a glass wall on one side overlooking the shop floor and a large digital chalkboard opposite it. Another wall held a picture of the periodic table – a visual arrangement of all of the natural elements present on the planet - while the remaining wall was covered with a list of super alloy variants that Ravi and his team had explored over the last ten years. The variants had been both major—where the chemical composition of the super alloy had been changed from the previous versions—and minor—where the alloying process had been tweaked to obtain the desired material properties. The version that had been tested over the last three weeks was called MRI 297-10, meaning that it was the 297th major variant of the material, and the 10th minor variant within it.

"So, what do you have?" Ravi asked, pointing to the piece of metal on the conference table in front of them. It was one of the 20 sample pieces they had produced in the lab and was the last one available for display, the other 19 having been used for the myriad of tests the team was conducting. For the scientists assembled there, that piece of nondescript metal was a work of art, with its white-yellow hue that seemed to glow under the overhead conference room lights.

"This latest version appears to just about meet all our requirements, including high temperature strength, distortion, creep, and fatigue," Marcel said.

"What do you mean, 'just about'?" Ravi asked with anticipation and concern in his voice.

"We might be a little off on the fracture toughness and ductility," Larabi explained.

Ravi imperceptibly shook his head with disappointment. These were the two last key properties his team had been struggling to achieve over the last six months. The material in airplane engines needed to be tough enough to withstand the ingestion of many foreign objects, including birds, ice, pebbles, and dust particles, at an exceedingly high force. At the same time, it needed to be able to maintain its exceptional strength at the extremely high internal temperatures of airplane engines. Any shortfall in these properties meant that the material was still not ready for prime time and they had to continue their arduous and painfully long search for either the missing element or a further tweak of the alloying process.

"I think the cooling rate needs to be adjusted," Riccardo spoke up, trying to inject a sense of optimism. They could all see Ravi was disappointed at the news, even if he did not outwardly show his emotions. "If you like, I can have a new variant available for testing within the next two days. And I don't think it would violate any of the regulatory constraints since I would still not have knowledge of the entire process."

To meet stringent government and business constraints, the chemical composition and the alloying process were tightly controlled and could be disclosed only to U.S. citizens on a need-to-know basis. Even the regular members of Ravi's team had limited access either to the chemical composition or the process, but not both. Visiting foreign researchers could test the new material and learn about what it could do, but not how.

"I'm sorry, Riccardo," Ravi replied. "You may well be right, but I can't afford to take any risks in this area."

Ravi could see the disappointment on Riccardo's face, as well as on the faces of Marcel and Larabi. He felt bad for them. They had all become good friends and he could understand their frustration at not being able to fully participate in the invention of this groundbreaking material. He would have felt the same, but his hands were tied.

"In any case," Ravi continued, "I'm not certain we have the right chemistry. We may have to tweak it a little and make sure we have the right element."

Ravi continued to think about it long after his colleagues had left for the day. He was certain that the missing element belonged to the Lanthanide group of metals, also known as rare-earth metals—not because they were rare, but because it was difficult to separate them from the mixture of metal ores dug out from the earth. This group of metals had the highest melting points and retained their strength at high temperatures. Ravi's team had already tried Gadolinium and Thulium, which were close but not the ones. *Could it be Erbium or Holmium?* he wondered, scratching his head. These were the two elements next to the ones they had already experimented with. Feeling somewhat dejected and defeated at still not finding the right chemistry, he began to wonder if he would ever get there and if all their effort over the last ten years might have been in vain.

Just then a moth showed up from seemingly out of nowhere and landed, of all the places, on the rare-earth group of metals where the potential elements were located in the periodic table – specifically, on one of the two elements he was considering.

"That's it! It has to be the one," he screamed as loud as he could, looking up towards the ceiling and whispering under his breath, "Thank you."

Tests still needed to be done for absolute confirmation, but Ravi was sure in his heart that this element was the one. Success was so close that he could almost taste it.

Ravi had waited for this moment for a long time. The son of middle-class, small textile business owners in Varanasi, India, he had been in the top one percent of his graduating class at the Indian Institute of Technology. After a yearlong internship at Tata Steels, one of the leading steels and aluminum manufacturing industries in the country, and another as a design engineer, he found himself not fully challenged and fulfilled. He had grown restless and wanted more. He found himself awake at nights thinking, "This cannot be it. I know I can do more. I want to be at the leading edge of my profession. I want to be where the action is. I want to be where new inventions and discoveries are being made. And it is not here in India." He knew there was only one place on the planet that offered him the opportunities he was looking for, and that was the United States.

Over the next six months, he applied to all the major universities in the U.S. and was accepted at most of them. He decided on Cornell. It offered him a teaching assistantship, had a strong materials engineering program, and, more importantly, was the institution where Carl Sagan – one of Ravi's favorite scientists – resided and taught.

When Ravi left India, he could take only $300 due to the strict foreign exchange control by the government. He traveled for a few weeks in Europe and spent most of that money before he arrived in Ithaca, New York, the home of Cornell University. After paying the YMCA for a place to stay for the night, he had

$5 in his pocket. It seemed like a worn-out cliché, but he did come to this country with just $5 in his pocket.

What followed was a whirlwind of professional and personal achievements, but never in his wildest dreams could Ravi have imagined that at 47, almost 25 years after he had come to the United States, he was on the brink of making a discovery that could change the world and lift him, his family, and his beloved institute far from those struggling student days at Cornell.

And there was no one else he wanted to share this moment with more than his co-inventor and his life partner—and the only other person who knew everything about the super alloy—Dr. Caitlyn Mariko.

CHAPTER 2

ITHACA, NEW YORK, FEBRUARY 1ST, 7 P.M.

The first time Caitlyn Mariko saw Ravi Kumar was at the International Students Meet and Greet event at Cornell University. Born to a Japanese father and an Irish mother, she had come from Japan to pursue her post-graduate studies in the field of computer science and artificial intelligence. Although she grew up in Japan, she had spent many summers in her mother's homeland, and so was fluent in both languages. Financial aid was unheard of for her. In fact, it was cheaper for her father, the president of a subsidiary of Sumitomo Trading Company— one of the leading Japanese conglomerates involved in businesses ranging from banking to shipping—to send her to school in America than pay for her studies in Japan.

There was nothing about Ravi that particularly caught Caitlyn's eye, except that he was looking at her as if he had never seen a girl before. She knew that she attracted male attention everywhere she went, with her dark, uniquely shaped eyes from her father's side and blond hair and fair skin from her mother's side. Their eyes met for a fleeting second, after which Ravi simply looked down, but at that moment, in spite of her discomfort at being ogled by a stranger, Caitlyn had a tingling feeling with a gush of blood running to her cheeks. It was a feeling the like of which she had never had before and knew it in her heart that the two of them might have found something deeper and more profound than what they had both left their countries for.

Boldly, she went up to him and asked, "Do you normally stare at girls you don't know?"

Ravi could only stammer out, "I'm sorry, miss. I promise I won't look at you again and keep my stares to myself."

"Don't worry about it," Caitlyn said. "Now, tell me where you are from?"

"I'm an Indian."

"Oh, so where's your feather?" she asked teasingly.

"It's in my suitcase. Should I put it on?" Ravi replied playing along, having regained some of his composure.

Caitlyn burst out laughing, and that was the start.

Aside from Ravi, the only other thing that consumed Caitlyn's time at Cornell was her research work in artificial intelligence—or as the community called it, AI. Her focus was on the emerging branch of artificial neural networks, or ANN, in which science tried to emulate the working of a human brain. She was fascinated by how the brain's billions of neurons learned and modified instructions based on the results of their actions such that future results would be better than the past ones, and that even the most sophisticated machines with all their computing prowess struggled and failed at what humans did intuitively and effortlessly. ANN tried to understand the makeup of an individual neuron and how information flowed between that neuron and the neurons around it. Caitlyn was most excited about the immense potential that ANN held in its multitude of real-world applications, from cars to airplanes, from home to office, from banking to the stock market, and everything in between.

Now she was an assistant professor in the computing science department at Cornell and a part-time consultant at the Materials Research Institute. Her role in finding the super alloy was vital, as the process for creating and testing the variants was controlled by ANN and run under the AI software that she had developed. Without her software, Ravi and his team would have had to work through the literally millions of possible permutations and combinations of materials and process variables. Her algorithms had reduced that number to more manageable levels – still in thousands, but doable.

That evening she had returned home early from the university and was busy preparing dinner while video chatting with their eldest daughter, Lilly. Lilly was a sophomore at Harvard, studying environmental sciences, and as such was quite interested in her parents' mission of doing something about climate change.

"So, what's Dad up to these days?" Lilly asked. "Any progress on finding his new super alloy?"

"He's been working late," Caitlyn replied, without much elaboration. "What's new with you?" she asked, changing the subject.

"Well, I've met this guy, Jesse…"

"And?" Caitlyn asked, raising an eyebrow.

"He's from the Boston area and a senior majoring in environmental sciences," Lilly replied, not trying to hide her smile. "You guys will get to meet him soon, since he's coming to visit during spring break. I'm sure Dad will like him a lot."

"That's great, Lilly." Caitlyn was genuinely happy for her daughter, whom she suspected took after her serious, hard-working parents a little too much.

Caitlyn put in long hours at her job, and in recent months she and Ravi had been both so consumed with work that they had barely seen each other. Things hadn't been the same since all of their children had left the nest, she reflected—first Lilly, then their twin daughters, Sita and Reiko a year later. Caitlyn would never forget the day she found out she was pregnant with the twins, when Lilly was only seven months old. She had been planning to finish her PhD at MIT, but instead decided to stay home with her three daughters until they were in school and catch up on her career later. She quickly made up for lost time, and now that their children had left home, she hoped to finally get back on track. She also hoped she and Ravi would be able to spend more time together.

As she was putting the final touches to the three-course vegetarian meal she had prepared for dinner, she heard Ravi enter through the front door.

"I think I've found our missing element!" Ravi announced excitedly as he came barging in the kitchen.

While Caitlyn knew she should have been happy for Ravi, his words stung her a little. Why couldn't he ask how her day was instead of immediately talking about himself? And how many times over the past ten years had he come home with the same proclamation, only for her software to disprove it later? "That's nice," she replied, somewhat curtly.

"What's wrong, Caitlyn?" Ravi asked, knowing she was not in a good mood when she had that tone.

"Nothing, I've had a long day. I've fixed us dinner. Go wash and come down, and we'll talk after that."

Ravi was much appreciative of the elaborate meal she had prepared and had served with a two-year-old Merlot.

He was also genuinely apologetic for being somewhat self-centered. Caitlyn relented and said, "Tell me about what happened in the lab today."

When Ravi described the periodic table and the moth, Caitlyn's eyes widened. "Are you sure?" she asked.

"I'll need to run a few more tests, but yes, I think so. Compared to the other elements we've tried; it has a slight edge in fracture toughness and ductility without sacrificing its high temperature capability. I'm optimistic that it will get us over the edge."

"Do you think anyone else has a chance of figuring this out?"

"Caitlyn, it took us ten years using your software. No one else is going to come close."

It was only then that the import of Ravi's words sunk in. "You did it," she said. "After ten years, you finally did it."

"*We* did it," Ravi corrected, lifting his wine glass to hers.

"So, what's the next step?" Caitlyn asked.

"The next step," Ravi said, "is to over the next few months thoroughly test the material with the missing element we just found, and confirm it meets all the critical properties. Then we announce to the world about this major invention in aviation and see who comes knocking at the door as we decide how best to get it in the engines and airplanes of tomorrow."

CHAPTER 3

ARTICLE IN THE NEW YORK TIMES, SCIENCE AND TECHNOLOGY SECTION—MAY 24TH

On May 23, close to 10,000 aviation engineers, scientists, and researchers from around the world gathered at Madison Square Garden for the 50th anniversary celebration of the American Society of Aviation and Aerospace Engineers.

Attendees included experts from Cornell University and Caltech, the head of the aviation division at NASA and the regional director of the FAA, and engineering VPs from American Aviation, United, and Delta. Also present were the VPs of engineering at the top two aero engine manufacturers, Dr. Scott Carr from United Electric and Dr. Cheryl Adams from General Technologies. Dr. Adams is the first African American woman to hold the top engineering position at a major corporation.

It was a fine display of the American three-legged stool—academia, government, and industry—working in harmony to advance the state of the art and keep the American industry at the forefront of groundbreaking discoveries and inventions.

A Chinese delegation, led by Dr. Xi Ping, the head of the prestigious materials lab at the Beijing Institute of Technology, was also in the audience to attend the conference and hear about the latest invention in aviation materials technology from the keynote speaker, Dr. Ravi Kumar, the director of Materials Research Institute in Ithaca, New York.

Dr. Kumar reported on a new super alloy material created by his Institute that many believe will be a major disruptive force in the design of new aero engines due to its exceedingly high operating temperature capabilities which usually limits how well these engines perform. He noted that since the first jet engine was invented independently by Sir Frank Whittle in the UK and Otto Von Ohain in Germany some fifty years ago, the industry has been working on developing materials that would provide only small incremental benefits in key engine metrics. For example, during this time, fuel consumption has been reduced on average by one percent per year, with similar reduction in climate-harming pollutants.

"So, what limits these temperatures?" Dr. Kumar asked rhetorically. "Modern engines already operate at temperatures that are at the limit of their material capabilities, leaving little room for further increases," Dr. Kumar said. He went on to add, "That is, unless a new material, such as the one we have just invented with much higher temperature capabilities, becomes available. We have christened this new super alloy material MRI 297. With MRI 297 we can cut down the amount of gas we burn by almost half and those climate damaging pollutants by a whopping seventy-five percent. What that also means is that we can now begin to not only slow down, but also reverse the ravages caused by climate change."

"Quite apart from the benefits MRI 297 will bring to our planet, utilizing it in new engine designs will not just be an altruistic gesture," Dr. Kumar said. "I expect the bottom lines of all involved—the flying public, the airlines, and the airplane and engine companies, will all be positively impacted by this new material."

Due to government restrictions on dissemination of information related to high temperature aviation materials, Dr. Kumar was unable to reveal the composition of the new super alloy. However, he said that experts from MIT, Caltech, the Whittle Lab, and the Von Ohain Lab have all conclusively demonstrated the far-reaching benefits of this new material and deemed it ready to be incorporated into new engine designs.

And, fortuitously, he added, the commercial aircraft fleet was currently in its renewal cycle, which due to the extremely expensive cost of launching new airplanes happens only once every 10-15 years. Aero engine companies like General Technologies and United Electric currently have new engines on their drawing boards to power these airplanes. It would be an ideal time for them to be seriously exploring the possibility of incorporating MRI 297 into their designs and he expected to be talking to them in the coming weeks.

Dr. Kumar concluded his speech by thanking his associates at the institute with a particular shout out to his colleague and life partner, Dr. Caitlyn Mariko, whose expertise in artificial neural networks was critical to the discovery of the invention.

CHAPTER 4

CHICAGO, MAY 26TH, 8:30 A.M.

"Are you sitting down, Jack? I just came back from the aviation conference in New York and boy, do I have something to tell you."

Jack Stevens, chairman and CEO of American Aviation, listened intently to what his VP of technology had to say. A veteran of the U.S. Air Force, he had retired with a chest full of medals and ribbons, and flying was in his blood. His first flight from his hometown of Chicago to New York had instilled in him a love for planes. Sporting a brand-new bow tie, well-starched white shirt, and navy-blue slacks, he had climbed the stairs into the plane holding onto his parents' hands. Exhilaration and joy flooded his ten-year-old being when the jet took off from O'Hare and majestically climbed above the clouds to its cruising altitude of thirty-one thousand feet. He had peeked out the windows and saw nothing but gray blue sky and a school of cumulous clouds below them. They were soaring in the clouds, and young Jack was completely hooked. At that instant, he knew what he wanted to do with his life.

As the head of the largest airline in the country, Jack had weathered the shocks of the airline business for the past forty years. First, the oil crisis in the early seventies had taken a major toll on the airline's finances, offset by raising the ticket prices. Then, after the Carter-era deregulations, low-cost airlines gave the legacy airlines a run for their money as air travel became more accessible to the general public. While most legacy airlines had gone through bankruptcy, American Aviation managed to teeter on the brink. They had cut all so-called discretionary spending, such as free meals and baggage, and renegotiated labor contracts with the unions, but the one expense they could not control was fuel cost. Currently, fuel accounted for almost a third of the total operating cost of an airplane and more if the airplanes were older models.

Jack was well aware that 500 of American Aviation's fleet of 1,000 airplanes were the older models and needed to be replaced. They were the least efficient and accounted for more than seventy percent of the airline's total fuel expenditures. They were also at the noise and emissions limits imposed by many of the airports around the world and had to pay much higher landing fees because of it. American was looking for an airplane that was designed from scratch, or as the industry called it, a new center line airplane with the latest state-of-the-art engine that would become the work horse of its fleet for the next decade and beyond.

Before his retirement, currently slated for the end of the year, Jack was committed to finding this elusive airplane. It would be his swan song – the legacy he would leave to the airline that he had built and the industry that he loved. Thus, he was attentive when his VP of engineering told him what Dr. Ravi Kumar's team at the Materials Research Institute had discovered.

"Are you sure this material has been tested and is ready to go?" he asked.

"I have a copy here of the presentation detailing the results from studies conducted by independent institutes, including MIT," the VP of technology said. 'If this new material is incorporated in the engines currently on the drawing boards of United Electric and General Technologies,' the reports says, 'we can get a fifty percent reduction in the new airplane fuel cost and an overall thirty-five percent reduction for our entire fleet.'

After thanking and dismissing his VP of technology, Jack carefully considered his next step. First, he needed to get United Electric and General Technologies on board with Dr. Kumar's invention in their new engines. The CEOS of these companies needed to fully understand what was at stake and be ready to play ball.

Jack pressed the button on his phone for his assistant. "Get Bill MacMillan on the line."

CHAPTER 5

Twenty-five years ago, not long after Bill MacMillan had taken over the presidency of the plastics division at United Electric, he received a visit from the VP of human resources.

"Bill, can I talk to you for a few minutes? I have an urgent personnel matter."

"Sure, what's going on?"

"It's one of our bookkeepers. Or rather, her twelve-year-old daughter."

A year ago, this girl had been the captain of her soccer team and a long-distance runner. Her father having been lost to cancer; her mother was the only wage earner in the family. She was all her mother had and her mother was all she had.

One morning, the girl had gotten up with a splitting headache. Since she'd run a four-mile marathon the day before, her mother did not think much of it and gave her a couple of aspirins. The headache, however, did not subside and the girl had to be taken to the emergency room, where she was diagnosed with a rare bacterial infection that affected her brain, causing paralysis and loss of motor functions. This formerly athletic girl was now in a wheelchair and would require medical care for the rest of her life. She depended upon her mother's job for that care.

"That job is slated to be outsourced and eliminated," the VP of human resources said.

Bill had not blinked throughout the story. "And?"

"I know the global nature of our business and the need to cut costs, but can't we do it in a humane way and give people time to adjust?"

Bill nodded. "I understand. But we're not in a charitable business. United Electric pays our fair share of taxes to the government exactly for situations like this."

"These are real people we're talking about—"

"I'm sorry, but we're moving forward to make this corporation healthy and competitive in this very tough environment. I want people in this organization to fully understand that and be bought into it. I do not think you are one of those people and I'm afraid I don't see a place for you in our going forward plans. I'll have to let you go, as well."

The story circulated around the company and earned him the moniker of "Ruthless Bill."

Sometimes Bill wondered what his own mother would have thought of his rapid rise—and the ways in which he had made it happen—at United Electric. He had grown up in a small New England town, typical of those that dotted the Northeast. She was a single mother who worked two jobs to make sure her only child did not grow up in depravity and sent him to one of the best private prep schools in New Hampshire.

Following an undergraduate education at Harvard, Bill went to Harvard Business School, after which he was ready to take on the corporate world. His sights were set on United Electric, the industrial behemoth with a storied history that spanned more than a century, manufacturing everything from light bulbs to dishwashers to highly sophisticated airplane engines. There, he successfully applied what he had learned at business school—the significance of hard work, the power of outsourcing and automation, and, most importantly, not to throw in the towel when it looked like the game was lost. Above all, he learned that in big business, the bottom line was what mattered, and it was rewarded or punished by the emotionless financial markets on Wall Street. Human empathy had no place in the calculus of income statements, balance sheets, and cash flow.

After Bill got the call from Jack Stevens, he summoned his top executives from the UE aero engine division in Cambridge, Massachusetts, for a meeting the next day in his office in Manhattan. Among them was Dr. Scott Carr, who had attended Dr. Kumar's keynote address, and had prepared a Power Point slideshow summarizing the properties of MRI 297 and what it could do for the new engine design.

"As you can see," Dr. Carr said, "MRI 297 would make our new engine design as it's currently configured obsolete from the get-go. I've no doubt our competition will be jumping on it and, if they're able to get this material, they'll be far above us if we were to carry on with our current concept. I don't think we can afford to move forward without it."

"Then our mission," Bill said to his executives, "is clear. Go get this new material and get it exclusively for United Electric. I don't want General Technologies and Dave Ward to be anywhere near it. I hope this is fully understood."

Having received their marching orders—and the unspoken consequences of failure—the executives got up, and as they were leaving they heard, "Remember, I want this material exclusively for us and I want it *At Any Cost!*"

He was now alone in his large corner suite office. He had seen a call flash on his personal phone while he had been talking to his people. He had seen the word "Contessa" and was impatient to get back to the caller once the meeting had ended and he'd some down time.

The Contessa was ruthless Bill's one weakness if he had any. He called her Contessa and that is what she called herself, although it wasn't clear if there had ever been a count. With broad shoulders and a barrel chest kept toned through regular workouts, Bill knew he was in great shape for someone in his early fifties. But the Contessa was twenty years his junior, a Scandinavian national of Italian heritage with a full figure and a brunette bob that accentuated the features of her perfectly oval face. As the account's manager assigned to him by her brokerage firm, she had made it more than clear that she was there to take care of all his needs—financial and physical. Bill could not resist her offer. That had been three years ago, and Bill's desire and longing for his Contessa had only grown stronger.

His day's work done, Bill took the elevator down to the ground floor, and got into his chauffeured limousine. His wife was away on a business trip and, having their 3000-square-foot penthouse suite all to himself, he was going to make good use of it with his Contessa. The stress from his hard day at the office seemed to have melted away and a smile broke out on the face of ruthless Bill thinking of what the evening had in store for him. Any worries he had about Dave Ward and the new engine contract had seemed to fade away as his limousine slowly made its way through the crowded streets of Manhattan to his penthouse and his lovely young Contessa.

CHAPTER 6

CHESHIRE, CONNECTICUT, MAY 28TH, 7:30 A.M.

The last time Dave Ward had talked to Bill MacMillan was five years ago.

Dave had been a rising star at United Electric, having joined the company after completing his doctorate in aerospace engineering at MIT. He was just a few years younger than Bill, and aside from his full-time job at United, he was also a part time adjunct professor at the institute where his six-foot-tall frame and handsome face with a full head of dark hair made him quite popular with his students, especially young women who idolized and adored him and would go out of their way to curry his favor.

After twelve years he had risen to become the president of United Electric's aerospace division, the largest and the most profitable of its businesses. Under him, United Electric supplanted General Technologies as the primary supplier of commercial aero engines, delivering a near death blow to the competition. He knew that the presidency of the aerospace division usually was the road to the office of the CEO of the entire corporation, and that he had a good shot at it. His only real competition was Bill MacMillan, the president of the plastics division, whose cost-cutting methods had resulted in the company's stock nearly doubling. Wall Street had taken note of that and had recognized Bill's contribution and had showered him with much praise and accolades.

Dave did not have any illusions that it wouldn't be a steep climb to outrun Bill, but he was determined to do his best. There was still time before the current CEO planned to retire, and he just had to keep plugging away putting numbers that would be hard to ignore by his board.

It was nearing his twentieth year at United Electric when the CEO finally decided to call it quits and the competition for his job was truly on. The choice was still between him and Bill MacMillan, who was also making great strides in all his assignments.

It was a beautiful spring day when he finally received the much-anticipated call from the chairman of the board, Harry Daniels.

"Dave, I thought it was important that I called you personally and let you know of the decision of the board," Harry Daniels said without much preamble. Dave knew what was coming. "I am sorry that the board has decided to offer the next CEO position to Bill MacMillan and that it was the boards hope and desire that you remain with the company and continue to run one of our most important divisions as you have been doing so wonderfully thus far." Harry Daniels had gone on to talk about how difficult the decision was and so on, but Dave Ward was no longer tuned into him. While in his bones he had expected that result, he was still disappointed and had that heavy feeling of defeat and sadness. Bill MacMillan had won the battle, and it was time for him to think about his own future, which most likely was outside of United Electric.

The next morning, driving to work and still thinking about what lay next for him, he was taken by surprise to find an unexpected visitor waiting for him in his office. It was Bill MacMillan, the newly appointed CEO of United Electric.

"This is quite a surprise," Dave said, shaking his hand. "Congratulations on your promotion. I have no doubt you'll be a worthy successor to our retiring CEO." He had to muster all his civility to sound sincere.

"I'm truly sorry, Dave," Bill said in what seemed to be an earnest tone of voice. "It must have been a difficult decision for the board. I hope you'll stay on and help me move this company forward."

Did Bill really mean those words? Looking at the other man's easy smile, Dave couldn't tell. "You know I can't do that," he said.

Something in Bill's face seemed to slip, and for a moment Dave could see his true feeling which seemed to say -yes I have won the war, Dave, and you the loser need to move on. "Then I wish you good luck elsewhere," Bill said as he bid goodbye.

Before the week was out, Dave was approached by the leading executive search firm in the country for the open CEO position at General Technologies, United Electric's main competitor. They wanted him to resuscitate General Technologies' aero engine division and position it to win the next major engine competition, which was expected to be the largest single contract in the history of commercial aviation.

It was an easy decision for Dave Ward to accept the offer and take on the challenge. And this time he swore to himself that he would not let Bill MacMillan win again. It was personal and he was going to do all in his power to bring home to General Technologies the biggest prize in the history of commercial

aviation – the new engine contract, and he was going to get it
At Any Cost!

That was five years ago. And ever since, Dave Ward had
been positioning General Technologies to take on the new
engine challenge. Finally, the time had come, and he was ready
to respond to the call from Jack Stevens.

He asked his secretary to get Andrew Wheeler, the president
of the aerospace division of General Technologies, and Dr. Cheryl
Adams, the VP of engineering for an urgent conference call.

"I need to talk to you about a call I got from Jack Stevens
and our new engine design," he began, "Cheryl, I understand
you were at the conference where Dr. Ravi Kumar talked about
the new material he and his team at MRI have invented."

"I was," Dr. Adams replied in the measured and clear voice
that was her hallmark.

"Did you speak to him about how he planned to license
the technology?"

"No, he didn't take any questions and didn't stick around
to talk to anyone. But I had our people run some numbers
for our new engine using this material, and they've concluded
that the projected improvements in fuel burn and emission
reductions could be even better than what Dr. Kumar and his
team have estimated."

"Did Dr. Kumar talk about how he achieved these
groundbreaking properties?" Wheeler asked. "Did he give any
hint of the chemistry that made this invention possible?"

"No, he did not. I suspect they're going to closely guard
the chemistry and the alloying process until we have a signed
contract. And even after that, I doubt he'll disclose anything,"
Dr. Adams replied.

"Well, I want to have exclusive rights," Dave said. "And if
Dr. Kumar isn't willing to give them to us, we may have to invent

this new material ourselves. If he can do it, I'm sure we can, too. Remember, folks, we can't afford to lose this competition."

"That will be all. Cheryl, can you hang on for a few more minutes?" Dave asked Dr. Adams. "You used to know Dr. Kumar quite well, didn't you?"

"Yes, he reported to me as director for materials engineering. That was just before he left to start the Materials Research Institute."

"Then I want you to extend a personal invitation to him to come to General Technologies and meet with us. I'm sure United Electric will be doing the same, and we need to use whatever advantage we have with him."

Dr. Adams nodded in understanding. "I'll do my best."

CHAPTER 7

BEIJING, CHINA, MAY 29TH, 8 A.M.

"Zhang Min-Chung?"

Min-Chung Zhang knew well the gravelly voice on the other end of the line when he answered his phone and did not have to ask for the identification of the caller. He had just arrived at his office in a high rise on the outskirts of Beijing that housed engineering and backroom staff of many Chinese companies, one of them being the China Aero Engine Corporation. Min-Chung was the director of strategic planning, as well as the security chief and the all-around fixer, at this company.

"Yes, sir," he answered with deference.

"I understand you were recently at a conference in the United States where a groundbreaking invention in aero engine technology was discussed," the gravelly voice said.

"Yes, sir, I was there along with Dr. Xi Ping and several other scientists and engineers from the institute and our company."

"Zhang Min-Chung, we need to get that material or something close to it. I know about the restrictions on the export of aero engine technologies, but we simply must find a way to get this information. Our long-term strategic plan calls for China becoming a leading country in aero engines. High temperature materials technology is one of the few areas where we still do not have indigenous capabilities and need to get it from abroad. If we cannot get this latest material, we can make a start with materials that may not be as advanced but would still be better than what we currently possess. Our engines may not be able to compete in performance, but we will undercut on price to get a part of the market. This will get our foot in the door, just as we have done with other products."

"Yes, sir, I understand," Min-Chung replied.

"I am counting on you, Zhang Min-Chung. And remember, cost is not an issue. You have authorization to commit whatever resources you need to complete this important mission." With that, the man with the gravelly voice and Min-Chung Zhang's superior hung up.

CHAPTER 8

CAMBRIDGE, MASSACHUSETTS, JUNE 3RD, 8 A.M.

It had been ten days since Ravi had given his lecture at Madison Square Garden. Since then, he'd been contacted by Dr. Scott Carr at United Electric and Dr. Cheryl Adams at General Technologies, inviting him to attend an all-expenses paid meeting at their offices. The two companies were major corporate sponsors of the Aerospace Industries Association (AIA), the nonprofit industry team that supported the work at the institute and was also one of its major customers. Having worked for both companies as well, Ravi welcomed the chance to revisit the places he'd developed his career.

United Electric's Cambridge office was his first stop. This was where Ravi had cut his teeth transitioning from academia to a real-world business. It was his first job, and just like first love, it had a special place in his heart.

When Ravi joined United Electric, the aero engine division was one of the largest in the world, employing close to 8,000 engineers and scientists. He worked on the turbine component system in aero engines, undeniably the most challenging part of the machine.

These aero engines were based on the Brayton Cycle, where the engine swallowed ambient air through fans mounted on the underside of the wing or on the body, technically known as the fuselage of the plane. Through a series of rotating curved wing shaped plates called airfoils, the air would be compressed by as much as forty times the normal atmospheric pressure. Moving on to the combustion system, it would be mixed with fuel and ignited, its temperature rising to levels that would melt most metals. The high temperature air-fuel mixture would then move to another series of airfoils in the section of the engine called the turbine component system. There the air was expanded, dropping some of the high pressure it had acquired in the front part to supply the internal power requirements of the compression system. It then exited from the turbine section at speeds exceeding 650 mph—approaching speed of sound at that height—and moved the airplane forward.

Ravi soon learned that the turbine component section was the most profitable part of the machine. The engine manufacturers generally did not make any money on the sale of new engines. They got their investments, which could be in billions of dollars, back and began to make profit by servicing these engines and selling spare parts, which might be marked up five to six times relative to what it cost to make them. Altogether, turbine spare parts accounted for nearly half the total profit of not just the aviation engine division but the entire United Electric conglomerate.

His first project was upgrading the engine materials for a mid-size commercial plane, with the relatively modest goals of a five percent reduction in fuel consumption and a ten percent reduction in engine weight and emissions. Ravi was eager to tackle the challenge of cutting down the amount of fuel airplanes burned, and, more importantly, reduce the climate-damaging greenhouse gases they produced. This cause had become foremost in his mind now that he was the father of three young daughters.

Ravi was still reflecting on that mission from all those years ago as he walked into the conference room at United Electric for the first time in fifteen years. Waiting for him there, around a shiny mahogany table were Dr. Scott Carr, the president of the engine division as well as its CFO. Ravi had not been expecting such high-level executives to attend what he thought would primarily be a technical meeting. It was obvious that they wanted to talk about more than just the technical details of the new super alloy.

"Dr. Kumar, we're glad you were able to take the time from your busy schedule to come down to see us," Scott said.

"Thank you for having me," Ravi replied. "I'm happy to be here to talk about MRI 297."

"We're quite excited about this material and see an important place for it in our new engine currently on the drawing board. Of course, as a major sponsor of AIA and your institute, we expect to get favorable terms for licensing it."

Ravi cleared his throat. "As you know, the charter of the AIA consortium is quite explicit in that any discoveries made by the many institutes and universities it sponsors would be the property of the institution that discovers it, and that the members of the consortium would have the rights to license it for their use. So, like any other member of the consortium, United Electric would have the rights to license the technology from MRI on mutually agreed upon terms and conditions."

The president leaned forward and asked, "Understood. So, what are those terms and conditions?"

This was Ravi's opportunity to talk about his greater objectives for the new material. "I will come to that. But before I get into the specifics, allow me to give you some background to our licensing conditions. I'm sure you already know that this new super alloy is expected to provide significant reduction in the consumption of fossil fuels along with the climate damaging emissions produced by commercial airplanes. And although there is debate about the extent of the impact of these airplanes on climate change and how much fossil fuel the planet holds, there is no debate that it is finite, and that it is adding to the greenhouse gases in our atmosphere. I believe it's our responsibility to future generations to look for ways to leverage any new technology to its fullest extent to preserve this precious non-renewable resource and begin to arrest the runaway increases in climate damaging pollutants."

"That's all well and good," the president said impatiently, "but what does that have to do with United Electric?"

"I need to make sure that this game-changing material is used in as many new engine designs as possible, spawns more future inventions, and keeps our industry healthy, vibrant, and competitive."

"In that case, why don't you make this an open source and have the chemistry and process for manufacturing your new super alloy available in open literature to all?" asked the CFO.

"We did consider that, but that would mean violating the extremely stringent regulations enforced by the United States government regarding the dissemination of information related to high-temperature super alloys."

"Point made," the president said. "So, what are your terms and conditions?"

Ravi summarized them: a two percent license fee from all new engine and spare parts sales incorporating the new material, and a four percent license fee, again, on all engine and spare parts with MRI 297 that would go to an environment defense trust fund. The trust would be managed by trustees drawn from academia, the government, the industry, and MRI.

"Is that all?" the president asked.

Ravi considered what came next to be the most crucial part of the terms and conditions. "To ensure as wide an adaptation of this new material as possible, MRI will not exclusively license this technology to any of the engine manufacturers. We will license it to any of the major and smaller engine manufactures that are legally allowed by the U.S. government to use this new material."

This came as a shock to the corporate attendees. This was not the industry norm. Usually, any new invention was exclusively licensed to the highest bidder, which was how companies maintained an edge over their competitors.

Dr. Carr was the first to speak. "Your honesty is appreciated, Dr. Kumar. But, as I mentioned before, we are expecting an exclusive license for the new material. We have no problem accepting the licensing fee requirements. And, to sweeten the deal, we are willing to pay a onetime fee of ten million dollars to MRI."

Ravi hoped no one noticed his quick intake of breath at that last number. It was a generous and tempting offer and could independently fund MRI for years. It would also allow him to expand the mission of his institute to discover other groundbreaking technologies to combat the rapid deterioration in the climate. He had been thinking about inventing portable devices that could recapture CO_2 from the atmosphere and convert it into fuel, or a fleet of autonomous drones that would fight fire and flood by adding or removing moisture from the surrounding air. His expertise in materials technology combined with Caitlyn's extensive knowledge in AI would be the key enablers, with his institute providing the required infrastructure for their inventions. What they lacked now was the funds to do all that. The $10 million dollars offered by United Electric would go a long way.

"Thank you, for your generous offer," he told his hosts. "Let me think about it. I will get back to you with my response in forty-eight hours."

CHAPTER 9

CHESHIRE, CONNECTICUT, JUNE 4TH, 8:30 A.M.

Ravi's next stop was the offices at General Technologies. That company, too, was a major part of his career and his life. It was his five years at General Technologies that eventually led him to start MRI.

He had been well settled in his job at United Electric, where he had learned the reality of the business world—that unlike academia or government-funded research institutes, private corporations needed to have objectives with short rather than long-term payoffs. He also understood that he had responsibilities to his family, even if at times he felt professionally unchallenged; he needed to keep going biding his time until a suitable opportunity came along.

So, when his old professor from Cornell contacted him about a call he had received from Dr. Cheryl Adams at General Technologies saying that she was interested in bringing him on board as the director of material engineering, he was intrigued to say the least. General Technologies, she had said, was planning a major expansion of their materials engineering group, including an experimental laboratory aimed at getting some of their lost aero engine market back, and she wanted him to head that initiative. Ravi had heard of Dr. Adams and her work from her graduate days at Caltech, where she had invented the process for depositing multi-layer protective coatings on turbine airfoils. She had gained the respect and admiration of the engineering community for that pioneering development, and also for her achievements at General Technologies. A shiver ran through his body. This was the opportunity he had been waiting for. He was excited at the prospect of working for someone like Dr. Adams.

But first he had to discuss it with Caitlyn and get her buy in for this major change and disruption in their lives. The girls were in school now, and Caitlyn was finally ready to get back to her studies and her career, which she had put on hold while the girls were still small.

"You should accept it," Caitlyn had said firmly with finality when she heard about the offer from General Technologies. "I can transfer to Yale or the University of Connecticut in Storrs. Both of them are within driving distance from Cheshire and have excellent computer science programs." And that was that. Their time in Cambridge had ended.

That summer, with much apprehension and uncertainty, they had said goodbye to Massachusetts to start the next chapter of their lives in a new city and new institutions.

At General Technologies new materials engineering laboratory, Ravi worked specifically on thermal barrier coating, a layer of paper-thin, non-metallic material that was deposited on the surface of the turbine airfoils. It acted as an insulation, protecting the bare metal from the exceedingly high temperatures those airfoils were exposed to. The more effective the insulation, the less the damage to the underlying metal and the longer the airfoils lasted. The increased service life meant these expensive aero engine parts did not need to be replaced as frequently, translating into lower maintenance costs. With the help of a manufacturer, Ravi had created a thermal barrier coating machine that allowed him and his team to not only produce state-of-the-art coatings, but also to experiment with the process and the constituent elements of those coatings.

It had been almost ten years since he had left the university. He was well recognized and respected in his field, and his work was challenging and interesting, but something was still missing. Everything he was working toward in the corporate world felt short term. He would often lie awake in the night thinking about the revolutionary and disruptive discoveries waiting to happen – that *needed* to happen. He was especially concerned about climate change and the impact humans in general and his industry were having on it. "There must be a material out there that will allow the engines to run at higher temperatures. We just need to find it," he used to say to himself. "If only I could work on it, I know I can do it."

But the corporate world was not the place for such long term and risky projects. He yearned to start an independent institute where he could work on a mix of projects – some short term to keep the lights on, and others dedicated to the advancement of science and engineering knowledge and groundbreaking inventions. He had tossed around the idea with Caitlyn off and on, but nothing had come out of it.

He could not ask Caitlyn to disrupt her career again and had just bid his time for the right opportunity. Once again it was Dr. Warren McQuinn, his old professor at Cornell, who gave him the opportunity. Dr. McQuinn was aware of Ravi's dream of starting an independent Materials Research Institute and strongly supported it. So, when he heard about an old textile factory, not far from Cornell's Ithaca campus, which had been shut down and was now available for next to nothing, he called Ravi to see if he was interested.

"Yes, I am. Very much. But let me talk to Caitlyn first," Ravi had replied to his mentor excitedly.

"Ravi," Caitlyn had said that evening when he told her about Dr. McQuinn's call, "you have been dreaming about it, and I know you can do it. We're going to be okay, even if it takes time to get the institute up and running. You need to take this chance."

He needed to hear that and have Caitlyn's support and encouragement. She had once again decided to put her own career and ambitions on hold. He wanted to say how important those words were and how grateful he was, but all he could do was look at her with a sense of love and gratitude that required no spoken words.

With Caitlyn behind him, he was ready—ready to take the plunge—ready to launch an organization whose work would make the world a better place for not only his generation, but that of his daughters and the generations that followed. He could feel the exhilaration from the thought of finally being able to do something that had concerned him ever since he had become a parent of his three little girls. A drop of salty water had trickled down his cheeks.

With much regret, he had submitted his resignation to Dr. Cheryl Adams, who wished him the best of luck and asked him to keep her informed about his work at the institute. "I look forward to working closely with you as you help advance the state of the art," she had told him.

Now, ten years later, he was back to see his old boss.

Ravi arrived at the engineering building located in the middle of the large General Technologies aero engine complex. It was an environmentally friendly, modern structure with solar panels completely covering its roof and double-paned windows, giving it the look of a greenhouse. A glass-topped atrium in the center of the five-story edifice allowed in copious sunlight, giving it the feel of an open-air complex.

When he stepped into the conference room, Dr. Cheryl Adams was the first to greet him. "Ravi, how are you?" She clasped his hand with the welcoming but firm grip that he remembered so well. "How are Caitlyn and the girls?"

As Ravi murmured a reply, he looked around the table to note the presence of Andrew Wheeler, the president of the aero engine division; the CFO of the division; and the director of the materials engineering lab, Ravi's former position.

"Dr. Kumar," Wheeler said, "we are about to share with you some very confidential and proprietary information about our new engine that should not leave this room. I hope I have your agreement on that."

"Absolutely," Ravi replied.

"Then let's begin," Dr. Adams said. She took him through the many studies the team at General Technologies had performed to try to optimize their new engine design. The new engine would indeed be significantly better than any of the current engines. "But" she emphasized, "it would still not be able to compete with an engine that incorporates MRI 297. Ravi, this new material would indeed be a paradigm shift in the evolution of aero engines."

"Dr. Kumar, we understand that as a founding member of the consortium that supports your institute, we have the rights to use MRI 297 on terms and conditions that are mutually agreed upon," Wheeler said.

"Yes, that's true," Ravi acknowledged.

"We are aware of your terms and conditions and intend to abide by most of them. However, we would like exclusive rights contract for MRI 297. And for that, we are prepared to pay a one-time signing bonus of twenty-five million dollars to the institute."

Ravi wondered if he had heard correctly. This was more than double the offer United Electric had given him. He had already begun dreaming of all the new inventions he could make with the $10 million figure he had heard from them. This higher amount would certainly accelerate those discoveries by allowing him to hire more qualified staff and expand the scope of their research.

His response, as it had been to United Electric, was to get back to them within forty-eight hours. He had a lot of thinking to do, and a lot to discuss with Caitlyn.

CHAPTER 10

AVIATION WEEK AND SPACE TECHNOLOGY REPORT FROM THE PARIS AIR SHOW—JUNE 5TH

At the Aviation Industry CEOs breakfast meeting this morning, CEOs from the leading U.S. and European aircraft manufacturers announced their plans for new centerline airplanes in response to the airlines' need for new work horses to replace the current fleet of fuel-hungry, older models. Jack Stevens, the CEO of American Aviation, committed his airline to be the launch customer for these new airplanes, with an order of 500 spread over the next decade. At list price, this would be worth more than $100 billion dollars, making it the largest order in the history of commercial engines. He challenged the engine companies to come up with new engines for these airplanes that would provide a major reduction in the amount of fuel they burn and the climate damaging pollution they create. He set a goal of fifty percent reduction in fuel consumption, which based on the latest news reports appears to be achievable with the latest material technologies.

Dave Ward, the CEO of General Technologies, indicated that his company had already begun work on an engine design that would meet or exceed these goals.

"Our new engine," he said, "will be a game changer and help General Technologies once again become the premier engine supplier of commercial airliners."

They expect to announce a hard launch for the engine in September, which should comfortably meet the FAA certification schedule of the new airplanes.

Bill MacMillan, the CEO of United Electric, spoke after Dave Ward and also committed his company to provide the new fuel and environmentally efficient engines.

"I have a lot of respect for Dave Ward and his team, but I'm confident that my team at United Electric can do whatever they can, only better," he said, somewhat facetiously with a broad smile on his face.

It looks like the big engine war is on.

CHAPTER 11

BEIJING, CHINA, JUNE 6, 7:30 A.M.

"Zhang Min-Chung."

"Yes, sir."

"I assume you have seen the announcement from the Paris Air Show about the launch of the new engine," the gravelly voice said.

"Yes, sir, I have."

"I believe we have a joint venture partnership with one of the two companies. Would that allow us to get access to the new material?"

"No, it would not," Min-Chung replied. "The high-temperature aero engine materials are strictly controlled by the United States government and cannot be exported without a license from the state and defense departments. Even then, it is only to countries that are on the approved list. China is not on that list."

"What would we need to make this material ourselves?" the gravelly voice asked.

"We would need the chemistry, which means we would have to know what all the basic elements in this new super alloy are. There is an element that has thus far not been used in previous alloys, which has enabled this new material to operate at much more severe conditions. We have no idea what that element is, and Dr. Kumar did not give any clues at the conference."

"Is there any way to get a sample of this new material and work out the chemistry from that?" the gravelly voice persisted.

"I am not sure how. And even if we knew all the ingredients, we would have to know the exact process of mixing them to get the right properties. There would literally be millions of possible combinations of the many factors that control the alloying properties."

"But, Zhang Min-Chung, as I said in my previous call, China must get the know-how to make this aero engine material. You are resourceful and have come through in many similar situations before. There is an old Chinese proverb—*get the potter if you cannot get the pottery*. Think about that, and remember money is no object. China must have this."

"I understand, sir."

"And, Zhang Min-Chung, I also wanted to remind you that this may be the best time to make our move. You may already know this from your time in the United States, that country appears to be losing its focus on excellence by sacrificing meritocracy in the name of diversity, by hollowing its industrial core through mindless outsourcing and by submitting to the demands of Wall Street for short term results at the expense of long-term strategic plans. It is now up to people like us to fully exploit this opportunity and make it work to our advantage."

"Yes sir, I understand" replied Zhang Min-Chung as the man with the gravelly voice hung up.

CHAPTER 12

ITHACA, NEW YORK, JUNE 8

The third major engine company, European Engine Corporation, had decided to sit this competition out. They had recently made a large investment in another one of their projects and were fully stretched –too much to undertake another large project. They were, however, interested in acquiring the know-how to the new super alloy, but did not have the same urgency and criticality as the two US based manufacturers.

With the European company sitting out, it had now become a two-horse race for the very lucrative and large new aero engine that would dominate the commercial aviation business for the next two decades. Amongst the two American companies, one was the incumbent and the other was fighting hard to become relevant again. Both were run by executives groomed by the same company, with one of them having lost to another for the top spot and now running as the underdog and determined not to lose again. It was shaping up to be an epic battle between two powerful titans of the American industry with Dr. Ravi Kumar, a technocrat engineer, caught in between. He had to be extremely careful as he navigated the dangerous minefield that could blast his entire institute and his career along with it.

What he did not know that there were equally powerful forces working in the dark that were going to be as insidious as the two he knew about and was trying to prepare himself for.

Dr. Kumar got back to both United Electric and General Technologies and informed them of his decision. Both Dr. Carr from UE and Dr. Adams from GT were expecting that response and it did not come as a major surprise to them. They promised to discuss the status with their respective corporate bosses and get back to him.

Dr. Kumar did not have to wait long to hear back from the two companies. He was invited to New York and Cheshire for high level meetings with the Chief Executive Officers of United Electric and General Technologies. He was quite surprised to get these invitations and found it unusual for the top executives of such powerful conglomerates to be meeting with a technocrat such as himself on a business that affected only one of their many divisions. He accepted their invitations knowing he would be subjected to great pressure and financial incentives which may be hard to resist. He needed to be fully prepared for these meetings, and he had little time to do so.

CHAPTER 13

MANHATTAN, NEW YORK, JUNE 10, 8:30 AM

UE sent their latest Bell Helicopter to bring Dr. Kumar from his Lab in Ithaca to Manhattan and their corporate offices. Bill MacMillan was there personally to greet him at the Helipad on the 76th floor of the UE building and escorted him to the main conference room which could easily accommodate 50 participants. It was UE's showcase room with deep mahogany wall paneling and an oversized solid teak oval table. The room was lined with portraits of the past chief executives of the fabled company who appeared to be quietly observing the proceeding as the current crop of leaders gathered around and conducted the business. The entire United Electric executive council had been invited to the meeting and were already seated at their assigned places. Bill MacMillan was going to take his place at the head of the table on the right, and Ravi was going to be seated at the other end facing the current CEO of the largest aero engine supplier on the planet.

The symbolism of this was not lost on Dr. Kumar. He could feel the enormous weight of one of the most powerful corporations being brought to bear on him. His forte was research and a dogged pursuit of discoveries and inventions that would make a meaningful difference to his industry and the society at large. He found himself intimidated at the setting, but it was his deep-rooted belief in his principles that gave him the temerity and audacity to stand up to someone like Bill MacMillan and hold his ground, on Bill's turf surrounded by Bill's people.

He was quite surprised to hear Bill MacMillan describe in some detail the discussions he had in his meetings with the UE Aero Engine Unit president and his staff at their Cambridge, Massachusetts office. Clearly, Bill had spent some time with them and was prepared to bring the full weight of his mighty corporation on him.

Bill, the consummate marketeer, cleared his throat and opened the meeting,

"Dr. Kumar let me welcome you to United Electric headquarters and tell you how very thrilled we are to be talking to you about the revolutionary super alloy you and your team have invented and are now making available for engine companies like ours. We are grateful to you and your community for continuously exploring opportunities for improving our industry and in turn the world we live in. Thank you, very much for that."

He then went on to catalog, in some detail, the contributions of UE to address the environmental damage being caused by humans in general and the aviation industry. United Electric, Bill noted, was a leader in the continuous improvement of the aero engine performance and was fully aligned with the goals of the Materials Research Institute as articulated by Dr. Kumar at the meeting with his executives at the Aero Engine division.

Bill MacMillan was clearly trying hard to make a case for an exclusive license arrangement with United Electric. Ravi had anticipated this when he was invited to meet with the CEO; he had come fully prepared with his response and wanted to interject but held his tongue as Bill MacMillan continued with his pitch.

"United Electric," Bill MacMillan emphasized, "is the leading manufacturer of modern aero engines and has greater than 70% of the commercial engine market share. We are fully committed to maintaining or increasing that market share with our new engine design. It is therefore only logical for MRI to work with United Electric to get the biggest impact of the new super alloy on what is personally important to you – minimizing use of the non-renewable fossil fuel and reducing the climate damaging pollutants emitted by aero engines."

"The design, development and certification of a new aero engine," Bill added, "is a long and very capital-intensive endeavor typically taking 48 months or more. Engine companies do not recover their investment on new engines for many years and only start making money when there is a sizable installed base of these engines in service. This can be anywhere from 15 to 20 years and depends on the number of aircrafts sold with that new engine."

"The engine companies," Bill MacMillan continued, "therefore, have a big hurdle to cross before a new center line engine design can be economically justified and even then, it is a big gamble. It is because of this large economic hurdle that the launch of a new center line engine design is a relatively rare event. In fact, since the invention of the first commercial jet engine some 50 years ago, there have been no more than a handful of brand-new centerline engines. The majority of the so-called new engines are the evolution of engines already in service and provide only incremental rather than step improvements in their performance."

He then added, "Right now the industry is at one of those rare junctures in its history where the airlines are scheduled to massively renew their fleet of legacy aircrafts with modern designs. These new, high-performance aircrafts will have significantly reduced fuel consumption, emission, and noise. The airline industry needs these new highly efficient airplanes for a business model that has drastically changed due to the advent of the low-cost airlines. It was now a matter of survival for the big legacy airlines and they were exerting immense pressure on the aircraft and engine manufacturers like UE to meet the extremely ambitious goals for these high-performance aircrafts with most of those performance gains coming from our engines."

"The UE board has authorized this large investment on the condition that we field a product that would not only be the best in its class but has a significant advantage over the competition to position UE to win most if not all the new engine orders."

"I am told," Bill added, "that your new super alloy will provide that differentiator. Now, I have heard of your conditions Dr. Kumar, and UE accepts all of them except the one related to exclusive licensing. As I have been explaining, the business case for launching our new engine is only viable if we get most of the market and the only way we can convince our board to make this large investment is if we get an exclusive right to this new super alloy."

"And Dr. Kumar, for the exclusive right, the UE board has authorized me to offer a signing bonus of $15 million to your institute and an additional $10 million to you personally as the lead inventor of this new material. I urge you to carefully consider our offer and please understand that UE must have this new material for our new engine and that we are committed to get it and to get it *at any cost*."

It was too much for Dr. Ravi Kumar to take in. The offer was extremely attractive and guaranteed the ascension of the boy from a middle-class family from Varanasi, India to the privileged 1% class of his adopted country. Between Caitlyn's job at the university and her part time consultation at MRI and Ravi's remunerations from the institute, they had a comfortable life. But with Lilly, Sita, and Reiko all at good schools, money was tight, and this generous offer from UE would certainly go a long way in making their life much easier, even providing a nest egg for the girls and for their own retirement.

It would also position his beloved institute on a firm financial footing, ensuring it could continue to do research work which may not have a short or even long-term payoff. This would be like the type of research that used to be conducted by government and other non-profit establishments before "Return on Investment" became the key currency – the type of research that allowed scientists and engineers to venture into the realm of the unknown, encountering dead ends that were as important to new discoveries as were finding the way forward. Dr. Kumar worried that the dearth of such knowledge advancing fundamental and applied research was sure to lead his adopted country to the same fate as many of the great civilizations in history. He was committed to do his part, small it might be, in not letting that happen. The creation of the Material Research Institute was geared towards that end, and the funding promised by UE would ensure MRI could continue to conduct groundbreaking work and advance the state of the art in his field.

The temptations were great for Dr. Kumar to accept the offer. It was also impossible to miss the emphatic closing phrase from the CEO "***At Any Cost.***"

He had to muster all his will power and determination to resist and not accept the offer on the spot. He thanked Bill MacMillan for the time he had taken to talk to him and for his generous offer. He promised to get back to him within the next 72 hours. He needed to discuss this with Caitlyn and the girls. He also needed to talk it over with his associates at the institute to make sure they were all aligned with him and their response, whatever that ended up being. He knew where Caitlyn and his associates stood before, but he needed to make sure they were still there with this latest extremely lucrative and tempting offer – and the not-so-veiled threat from one of the most powerful men in their industry.

Dr. Kumar headed back to the helipad to take the return flight to Ithaca. Bill accompanied him and just before he was to board the helicopter, Bill reminded him once again about UE's commitment to get exclusive rights to the new super alloy and to get it ***at any cost***.

Bill did not have to remind Ravi of that phrase again since he had already internalized it from Bill's earlier closing statements, except, at the time Ravi had no idea what "At Any Cost" meant and how far Bill was prepared to go to get what he wanted to win the great engine war.

It was to become clear a week later.

CHAPTER 14

CHESHIRE, CONNECTICUT, JUNE 11, 9:00 AM

Dr. Kumar's next meeting was with Dave Ward, the CEO of General Technologies, Bill MacMillan's counterpart. Unlike Bill, Dave was himself an expert in Aero Engines and specifically aero engine Materials Technology. Before his promotion as the president of the United Electric aero engine division, he directed the UE Materials Engineering Lab and had intimate knowledge of the subject. He had taken Dr. Kumar under his wings when he had joined UE out of Cornell and had been his mentor and friend ever since. Dave had always found time to talk to Ravi about his work and was happy and ready to provide his advice, which Ravi much valued.

Ravi had not had much contact with Dave lately and was excited at the prospect of meeting his old mentor and friend.

"Ravi, welcome back to your old haunts. It is really good to see you again." Dave Ward greeted Dr. Kumar as he was escorted into his corner suite by his secretary. Unlike the UE meeting where Bill MacMillan had his senior staff present, Dave Ward was all by himself. He was going to have a one on one meeting with his former protégé and now friend. Dave had decided to keep the meeting informal and use his personal connection to try and achieve his objectives. His board had signed a blank cheque to be used at his discretion and he was going to make an offer that Ravi would find hard to refuse.

He also had a backup plan but for that to succeed he needed to exploit one of Ravi's weaknesses – he did not like to be second guessed. Ravi got flustered and angry when someone – especially those in authority – questioned him on his technical knowledge and challenged his recommendations. He prided himself in being detail oriented and expected his results and conclusions to be accepted without arguments. He would go to any length to defend his position. Dave Ward remembered that well and had often advised Ravi to soften his approach, but he admired his honesty and had just chalked up his stubbornness to one of his quirks. He hoped the intervening years had not mellowed Ravi out too much. He needed to pick his brain, and for that he needed to get him rattled.

"So, Ravi, I have heard a lot about the new material and am quite intrigued by its claimed capabilities. Can you tell me a little more about it?" Dave Ward said, using words that he knew would get Ravi excited and rattled.

"Well, Dave, I am sure you must have also heard that the properties of this new material have been verified by experts in our field. It is not just claimed but real. And due to the proprietary considerations, I cannot tell you much about it except that after almost ten years of trial and error, we were able to find the missing element that allowed us to achieve our target goals of a step increase in the temperature and strength," Ravi said, trying to not sound offended, but not succeeding well.

"I am sorry, if I offended you, Ravi. I was just trying to make sure you have fully examined all potential alternatives and have not left anything on the table. This could be one of the most disruptive changes in the aviation industry, and I am sure we all want to try and extract the most out of it," Dave Ward said, trying to mollify his visitor and clearly achieving his objective of getting Ravi all worked up. He then pulled out a 11"x 17" copy of the Periodic Table. The Periodic Table was developed by a Russian chemist about 150 years prior and listed all of the elements known to mankind – currently standing at 118. The elements were listed in periods and groups – based on their atomic structure and their chemical properties. Hydrogen was the first element with an atomic number of 1, and Oganesson the last with a number of 118.

Chemists and materials engineers around the world used the Periodic Table to understand the behavior of individual elements but more importantly when the elements were combined to create an alloy or super alloy.

Dave Ward and Ravi had often used the Periodic Table to discuss and better understand the materials and coatings that were being developed in the lab and how to squeeze additional capabilities out of it.

It felt like old times when Dave pulled out the Periodic Table. He had already crossed out many of the elements such as those in the Radioactive group, or those that were primarily in gaseous phase or those that were already in the current generation of super alloys. Clearly Dave Ward had spent time getting ready for this meeting.

Ravi was quite surprised to see the preparation Dave had done but did not suspect any foul play from his friend and mentor. He went on to describe in some detail the work they had been doing over the last ten years and some of the elements they had eliminated. He was careful not to divulge the identity of the element that finally enabled the new super alloy, but Dave Ward got a fairly good idea of what it might be and which group it most likely belonged to. He had succeeded in picking his friend's brain so he could, if necessary, execute his backup plan.

He was going to win, and win at any cost, even if it meant betraying his old friend's trust.

For the next hour, Dave Ward took Ravi through the considerable work his team had done on the General Technologies version of the engine that was slated to power the new generation of aircrafts. He also showed Ravi results from the assessment of their engine with the MRI 297 and just as was the case with the United Electric, this new material would make the engine as it was currently configured obsolete from the get-go.

"Ravi, I hope I have given you a good appreciation of where we are and how important we consider your material is for our new engine. General Technologies is committed to getting back in the commercial aviation arena and reclaim our position as the premier supplier of aero engines. We are going to invest several billion dollars on this new engine program, but to justify this level of investment, we need to position ourselves to win most, if not all, of the new aircraft business. We therefore must have an exclusive right to MRI 297, and for that my board has authorized me to accept your terms and conditions and offer a signing bonus of $15 million to the institute and a $10 million dollars bonus to you personally as the lead inventor of this material. Additionally, General Technologies will retain you as a consultant for the next ten years at an annual fee of $1.0 million. I sincerely hope you will seriously consider our offer and help your old company become healthy again and provide a legitimate competition in this extremely important business," Dave Ward said.

It was uncanny, but perhaps not surprising, to get a remarkably similar lucrative and tempting offer from General Technologies. It almost appeared that two companies knew of each other's bids and were trying to outbid the competition. Of course, that was not the case, but listening to their increasingly more generous and tempting offers, it sure appeared that way.

What Dr. Kumar found even more perplexing was that the GT CEO also let him know that General Technologies was committed to get an exclusive right to the new super alloy and was committed to get it at any cost.

He did not know then, but if he would have known what was to come later, it was not surprising that the two companies had the same message for him – after all, they had both gotten the same call from Jack Stevens, the wily boss at American Aviation. Jack's message was unambiguous – the engine company that gets MRI 297, the new super alloy, gets his contract and would basically own the most lucrative engine program in the history of commercial aviation.

The stakes could not be higher for UE the incumbent and GT the underdog and the two men that ran those two conglomerates. It was business, but it was more than that – it was personal – Bill to keep his winning streak alive against Dave, and Dave to avenge his loss to Bill. They were both in it to win and win at any cost.

"Dave, I am at a loss of words at your generous offer. It is very tempting, indeed, and I would be lying if I did not say that I would like to accept it right now. But I need to talk it over with my associates at the institute before I give you my answer. I promise to get back to you within 72 hours with our response," Ravi said as he left Dave Ward's office and headed back to Hartford, Connecticut's Bradley International Airport to take the short turboprop flight back to Ithaca.

CHAPTER 15

ITHACA, JUNE 11, 6:00 PM

"Caitlyn, Dave Ward has made a very tempting offer and I am thinking of accepting it," Ravi said as Caitlyn walked into the house from the University. Lilly was also at home preparing for her trip to Japan to spend some time with her grandparents. She would be attending a summer program learning Japanese at Tokyo's Sofia University. She was in the other room busy packing her suitcase.

"Oh, really. What is it?" Caitlyn said as she made her way to the foyer bathroom to freshen up and get ready for the dinner that Ravi had laid out on the dining table.

"It is similar to what Bill MacMillan had offered – accepting our terms and conditions and a $15 million signing bonus for the institute. But Dave's offer to me personally as the lead inventor is much more generous – amounting to $20 million over the next ten years. You were worried about us not having saved enough for our retirement and the years ticking by. This will take care of that and will also provide a decent nest egg for the girls," Ravi said, trying to sell the offer to Caitlyn.

"So, what is the catch?" Caitlyn asked.

"They, like United, want exclusive rights to MRI 297," Ravi replied.

"I thought you wanted it available to all engine companies legally allowed to use this new material to get the maximum possible reductions in fossil fuel consumption and production of greenhouse gases. Are you backing down on that?" Caitlyn said, with a noticeable concern in her voice.

Ravi then took Caitlyn through the arguments both Bill MacMillan and Dave Ward had used about the very large investments required for new aero engine programs and the need to have most if not all of the market to justify those investments, adding, "The engine with MRI 297 will put it in a different class and will have no competition. That means the new airplanes from either the US or the European company must be built around this new engine, ensuring all future aircrafts will burn less fuel and produce reduced level of emissions. We would therefore have achieved our goal of MRI 297 being used in all future engines and also have our family receive a much needed and well-deserved compensation. It is a win-win situation for all."

"I guess that should be OK and as we had discussed, we do need to start saving for our retirement and for the girls," Caitlyn said, reluctantly accepting Ravi's arguments.

"Dad, did you not say that there needs to be a healthy competition to make sure that the Technology continues to advance?" Lilly, who was listening to her parent's conversations from the other room, chimed in. "You were quite emphatic that if any one of the major companies got this new material, they would essentially capture the whole market and will drive competition out that would dis-incentivize the continual advancements in the state of the art. And without that, future reductions in fossil fuel use and production of greenhouse gases would be jeopardized. Are you backing off on that?" Lilly asked, with concern in her voice.

"No, we are not. But we do have to think about our family's future, as well," Ravi replied defensively.

"You have given us a solid foundation and education at the top schools in the country. I have talked to Sita and Reiko and we all agree that we will be fine and would not need a lot of support from you. You can correct me on that, but I also think your jobs at the institute and the university should provide retirement living that would be better than the majority of people in this country. I don't think you should compromise on your principle and determination to do all you can to fight the scourge of climate change. You know how important it is to control the unabated increase in the greenhouse gases, not just for our generation, but the generations that come after us. I don't think you should let greed and personal gratifications dictate your actions now," Lilly said earnestly and forcefully

The Kumars had brought up their daughters to stand up for what they believed in and not be afraid to speak out when necessary. Lilly was making sure her voice was heard as their parents were in the process of making a critical decision that would have a long-lasting impact on aviation and its contribution to the global climate change.

"She is right, Ravi. I have to agree with her. We do not need to give up on our beliefs. We did all right when we had a lot less and I am sure we will manage fine in the future. We cannot let this opportunity pass by to give back to society and the future generations. I don't think you should sign an exclusive rights contract for MRI 297 with any of the engine companies and keep it available for all those who can legally use it," Caitlyn said, changing her stance and agreeing with Lilly.

Dr. Ravi Kumar was both exasperated but at the same time relieved listening to these two people who were so important to him and whose advice he much valued. But he still had to think about how best to balance his commitments to society and his family. The companies were offering him a once in a lifetime opportunity to get his family and his institute on a firm financial footing that would ensure they would not be continuously worried about making the payroll, creating a carefree retirement. But not at any cost? Not an easy decision.

"I hear what you are saying and appreciate your concerns. Let me sleep on it," Ravi said as they began clearing the dinner table.

CHAPTER 16

AVIATION WEEK AND SPACE TECHNOLOGY – JUNE 12 ISSUE - NEW ENGINE UPDATES

Both United Electric and General Technologies announced today the thrust class of their new engines. As expected, the engines will be designed to cover a thrust range of 30,000 to 40,000 lbs. The lower thrust engines are sized for the 150-passenger class and the higher thrust engines for the 175 passenger versions of the new single aisle airplanes on the drawing boards of both the US and European aircraft companies. The engine companies did not commit to the fuel consumption, but both indicated it would be at least 25% better than the current generation of engines. Hard launch for both engines is still scheduled for September, just about 12 weeks from now.

Confidential sources tell AW&ST that both United Electric and General Technologies are in advanced negotiations with the Materials Research Institute and its director, Dr. Ravi Kumar, for licensing of the new super alloy MRI 297. It appears both companies have offered very lucrative terms but would prefer to have exclusive rights to the material. No word on whether Dr. Kumar has accepted either company's offer.

In a related development, AW&ST has learned the Chinese are also actively working on their version of an engine in the same thrust class. It is not clear if they plan to collaborate with one of the Western engine companies or go it alone. AW&ST's understanding is that the Chinese currently do not have the super alloy technology that would be competitive to the west, but it is possible that they may try to acquire it from the west or field an engine that may not be competitive in performance but would be significantly lower in cost. The Chinese Government has openly declared its goal to be a leading player in aero engines within the next decade. This needs to be taken seriously as aero engines are one of the few remaining high tech and high value-added products that the west still has a lead in and should be protected at any cost. AW&ST plans to actively monitor and report on the developments in this area.

CHAPTER 17

ITHACA, NEW YORK – JUNE 13, 12 WEEKS TO LAUNCH DATE...

Ravi had made his decision and was now ready to relay that to the two chief executives. He knew it was going to be a difficult and gut-wrenching conversation requiring all of his resolve and will power to stay the course.

His first call was to Bill MacMillan.

"Mr. MacMillan let me start by thanking you for your very generous offer. My associates at the institute and I are humbled and grateful that your company has decided to use MRI 297 in your new engine. It is, indeed, an honor. Your offer is extremely generous, and I would be remiss in not admitting very tempting. But, after careful consideration and discussions with my family and my associates, I must regretfully decline your request for exclusive rights to the new super alloy."

Ravi then went on to say that he was declining not because of some altruistic reason, although it was a consideration, but to ensure the new material will be available to all engine manufacturers, large and small, to maximize the reduction in fossil fuel consumptions and the climate harming emissions from aero engines. He added MRI was ready to work with UE and transfer the know-how for the new material if Bill were to accept the non-exclusive right clause.

Bill MacMillan was not used to being turned down and wanted to lash back at Dr. Kumar. But he contained himself and tried to reason with him. He made the same argument that Ravi had heard before trying to convince him that there was no conflict between assigning UE the exclusive rights and meeting his laudable and altruistic goals.

Dr. Kumar carefully and politely listened to Bill's argument and replied,

"Yes, while I agree with you that assigning exclusive rights to your company will in the near term ensure that the majority, if not all of the next generation of engines would indeed have the significantly better fuel consumption and emissions, my concern is that assigning exclusive rights to any one company would almost certainly eliminate competition in this business." He then went on to underline the need for a healthy competition that he had made before and that was so passionately re-iterated by Lilly. He added,

"The aviation industry has been extremely good to me, my family, and my associates, and I cannot consciously do anything that would jeopardize its long-term health and vibrancy. I therefore cannot accept your demand for exclusive rights and hope you understand my reasons, even if you do not agree with them."

Bill had heard enough. His true ruthless character that had gotten him to where he was now came out. He was angry and even on the phone call, Dr. Kumar could sense his anger and was not surprised when just before hanging up, Bill told him about his disappointment and reminded him once again that United Electric was committed to getting the new super alloy, getting it with exclusive rights, and it would do so *at any cost*. He then gave Dr. Kumar his private phone number and asked him to call if he changed his mind.

With that, Bill MacMillan hung up.

After hanging up with Dr. Kumar, Bill called in the Chief of Security at United Electric to his office. The Chief, a retired FBI agent, was personally hired by Bill and had his full confidence. His loyalty was to Bill MacMillan first, and then to the company that paid his six-figure salary and a very generous expense account, most of which well-hidden under many layers of accounting obfuscation. The security chief had a lot of latitude in carrying out his assignments, some of which required undocumented help from characters that he, in his earlier life as an FBI agent, would have worked hard to put behind bars.

Bill briefed his security chief with the essentials and without explicitly instructing him what to do, he asked the chief what he thought needed to be done. The UE security chief had worked with Bill MacMillan for a long time and knew exactly what he was being instructed. Shake down hard but do not break, unless breaking was the only alternative left to ensure the other party did not get what UE considered theirs. He also understood that the boss did not need to know the details and that their complex international web was to be deployed to fully erase any traceability to UE and the man running it.

The UE security chief left the room to make necessary arrangements and to bring the full weight of his multi-national corporation on an unsuspecting and mostly defenseless academic researcher. He was looking forward to it and was going to enjoy making him understand something clearly at last and bring him and the priceless know-how he possessed back to his master. But he, like his boss, had underestimated the seemingly meek and nerdy researcher.

CHAPTER 18

ITHACA, NEW YORK – JUNE 13TH, 12 WEEKS TO LAUNCH DATE...

Dr. Kumar's next call was to Dave Ward, the Chief Executive Officer of General Technologies.

"Ravi, I was just about to call you. I have been thinking about our discussions about MRI 297 and can still not wrap my head around as to how you and your team were able to get the fracture toughness and the high temperature capabilities at the same time. You remember we tried that when you were at United Electric and we could get one but not both properties simultaneously. We could not find any element or group of elements that would satisfy all the requirements. Are you sure that MRI 297 has been extensively tested to show it does meet all of the requisite specifications of an aero engine super alloy?" Dave Ward asked as he answered Ravi's call.

It was a continuation of his effort to get as much information from him by exploiting his weakness of reacting adversely to being second guessed. Dave Ward had a feeling that Ravi would not be accepting his demand for exclusive rights. He was working on his back up plan. He needed to find out the identity of the element or elements that had enabled this new super alloy. He had spent the last 48 hours going over his notes from his earlier meeting with Dr. Kumar and had narrowed the possible elements to a small list. His hunch was that it was a single element – most likely from the Rare Earth Group, also known as Lanthanides. But that group contained 14 elements – the first 10 of which could be eliminated since they did not have high enough melting points. It had to be one of the last four – his bet was on Erbium, element number 68 and or Thulium, element number 69 in the Periodic Table. These two rare earth elements had the requisite properties, but he needed some confirmation from Dr. Kumar as he had extremely limited time to execute his backup plan. He needed to trap him and get the information, but he knew it was a trade secret that would be hard to get out of his old friend. He had also been working on that trap and now he was ready to spring on the unsuspecting and naïve scientist.

"Dave, I thought we went over this at our meeting and I had answered all of your questions. I was calling to talk about your offer," Ravi replied with an edge in his voice.

"I am sorry, Ravi. But as an old Materials engineer, I have been troubled by what you had told me and have been curious to find out how you managed to achieve the two contradictory properties and wanted to get educated on it. But let us talk about our offer. I hope you are going to accept it," Dave said, simultaneously stroking Ravi's ego and trying to pry the identity of the missing element.

"Dave, I am sorry, but I am afraid I cannot accept your requirement for exclusive rights to MRI 297," Ravi replied, and then went on to explain his reasonings just as he had done with Bill MacMillan.

Although Dave Ward had expected that response, he was still quite disappointed to be turned down. He and his team had been counting on the new super alloy to get them back in the business. But unlike Bill, he maintained his external veneer of calm.

"Well, Ravi while I understand and admire your motives for turning us down, I am nevertheless extremely disappointed. We had spent a lot of time together and I was hoping you will take that in consideration as you and your team deliberated our very generous offer. But if you do change your mind, call me directly on my cell. Our offer will be open for the next 30 days and you can call me any time to talk about it. Now before you go, I still am curious about how you solved the problem of getting the fracture toughness at those exceedingly high temperatures. Was it the Lanthanides?" Dave Ward was clearly fishing.

"I should not really be talking about the chemistry of our new material. But I know at heart you are still a Materials engineer and I do owe you much from our time together. Yes, it is an element from the Lanthanide group," Ravi answered reluctantly.

"Is it Erbium or Thulium?" Dave Ward persisted.

"I cannot tell you anything else, Dave. I am sorry. And even if I told you the exact composition of the new super alloy, it would not help since as you know the properties of the material is dictated by the very precise process we must follow. Development of that process is what took us close to ten years, and even, then it was as much luck as our hard work that finally got us there. I hope that helps assuage your curiosity and puts some of your concerns to bed. We do have the material and we would be happy to license it to you, just not exclusively," Ravi replied as he came to the end of his call.

Dave Ward was taking copious notes as Dr. Kumar was talking.

"Ravi, thank you for that fascinating background. I wish I were part of the team working on it. It sure looked like a fun journey, and I am truly glad you and your team finally nailed it down. And thank you for candidly answering my questions about your new invention. It has been troubling me for the last few days, and I am grateful that you have put my doubts to rest. I once again appeal to you to carefully think about our offer and call me any time you like," Dave answered as he ended the call.

Dave Ward had not gotten to where he was without nerves of steel and with the streak of ruthlessness required to climb the dog eat dog world of corporate culture. He was in the game to win as much as Bill MacMillan was. He was certain that Ravi would not have signed the exclusive contract deal with United Electric, either so he would not have given any ground to Bill. He had backup plans, in fact, several, and was confident that he had a leg up in the race, especially after what he had learned in his phone call with Ravi. He had a smile on his face as he got to work on executing his plans. He was not going to lose again. He was going to win and win *at any cost*.

CHAPTER 19

Dave Ward's next several calls were to his vice president of human resources, vice president of engineering, and the chief of Materials Engineering. He summoned them to an urgent meeting at the corporate headquarters in Cheshire.

The three executives were quite apprehensive as they gathered in Dave's sumptuous corner office around his large desk. He had intentionally invited them to his personal office to keep the meeting informal and impress upon them the urgency of their assignment.

He instructed the VP of Human resources to dig into the backgrounds of the key researchers at Materials Research Institute and find out from the published papers, patent filings, and other public – and maybe non-public – sources the names of those who might have worked on the new super alloy. Dave Ward knew that Research Institutes such as the MRI, who depended upon funding from major industries and government, must publish results from their research to constantly be in the focus of their peer group. He knew the well-known axiom – publish or perish, and was confident that given enough hard work, they should be able to find the key MRI researchers involved with MRI 297 – the new super alloy.

The VP of human resources was authorized by Dave Ward to hire those researchers at whatever it took to have them jump the ship and get them over immediately, even if it meant GT had to buy out their contracts. He was counting on another axiom – "we all have a price at which we would sell ourselves" – unless we encounter someone like Dr. Kumar who were not for sale – at any cost. Fortunately, for people like Dave Ward and Bill MacMillan, these were exceptions rather than the rule. Dave Ward had no doubt he would find the right people at MRI and bring them over to GT.

Dave Ward, then turned to Dr. Cheryl Adams, the vice president of engineering and Dr. Ravi Kumar's old boss. Cheryl Adams was at the conference as was the chief of Materials Engineering and had already heard about the development of the new super alloy. They, therefore, did not need much of a background from Dave. Dr. Adams had also met Dr. Kumar in person after the conference when she was trying, unsuccessfully, to get him to sign the exclusive license contract. The chief of Materials Engineering was also at the meeting with Dr. Kumar. They were both fully up to speed with the latest status.

They were, however, quite curious, about this urgent call from the Chief Executive Officer of their parent corporation. Such calls were infrequent and usually meant a high-level assignment critical not only to their aero engine division but also to the whole conglomerate.

Dave did not waste much time. He handed a copy of his notes from his phone call with Dr. Kumar to each one of them and addressed Dr. Adams and the Materials chief.

"Cheryl, I have been talking to Dr. Kumar and have not been successful in getting the exclusive license to MRI 297. I have given him 30 days to get back to me if he changes his mind. But we cannot count on that. Getting MRI 297 or equivalent material in our new engine is critical to GT getting back in the commercial engine market and it is imperative that we win the majority, if not all of that business, to justify the exceptionally large investment the corporation would be making."

"In my one on one meeting a few days ago with Ravi and an extended phone call that just finished," Dave Ward continued, "I was able to almost get him to reveal the missing element that enabled their new super alloy. I say almost because Ravi admitted it was from the Lanthanide group but did not take my bait when I asked him if it was Erbium or Thulium – the two most likely elements that have the needed properties. My hunch is on Erbium. Any questions so far?"

The two executives did not have any. They were still waiting for their assignment.

"Now you already know that even if we have the chemistry of the new super alloy, the environmental conditions and the alloying process are critical to getting the desired material characteristics and therefore need to be tightly controlled. You also know from what you heard at the conference and confirmed by Ravi again during our phone call that it took him and his team close to 10 years to go through a painstaking process of trial and error and a large dose of Artificial Intelligence and Neural Networks to finally discover this new revolutionary super alloy," Dave Ward continued his briefing.

"Cheryl, I intentionally used the word MRI 297 or equivalent. GT must have this material and if we cannot get it from MRI, I plan to develop it inhouse and I am counting on you and your team to make it happen."

He emphasized the importance of this assignment saying, "You may already know this, but let me remind you that the future of not just the Aero Engine Division but, indeed, the entire General Technologies Corporation depends upon us being able to field the planned new engine that would meet or exceed the capabilities of an engine with MRI 297. We do not have another option."

And it had to be done, Dave Ward had added, in less than 3 months - an infinitesimally small time in the field of new materials development. The 3 months deadline was dictated by the latest date the new engine needed to be launched to meet the very tight schedule of the airplane manufacturers. They would, of course, have the help of the researchers from MRI that he had just instructed the human resources vice president to bring on board, but even with that he acknowledged,

"I know it is an extremely aggressive schedule for developing, testing, and certifying the new material for use in a new center line aero engine design, but it has to be done and it must have some identifiable difference from MRI 297 to get around the MRI intellectual rights and patents. Although, at this point it is more important to get the properties and if it ends up being a clone, we will let the lawyers sort it out. You have a carte blanche from me to get whatever you need to get you to your goals, and this is your and your team's highest priority task"

Dr. Adams and the chief of Materials Engineering simply nodded. They now understood why they had been summoned to this meeting and what was being asked of them. They had no illusion about the challenge and how heavily the odds were stacked against them. They also understood failure was not an option and they had to give it all they had and let the results follow – something Dr. Adams had heard from Ravi – a well-known quote from Gita, the Hindu holy book – that Ravi used to mouth whenever he was faced with situations like this.

After the trio left, Dave Ward took a deep breath. He now had one of his backup plans in motion. For the backup to the first backup, he took out his private unlisted phone. He dialed another unlisted private number which was promptly answered by a woman in Cambridge, Massachusetts, Dave's old company. It was Veronique Pena, the head of metallurgy at United Electric.

Dave and Veronique went way back to when Dave was the head of the Materials Engineering at United Electric. Veronique, a native of Medellin, Columbia was in the final year of her PhD program at MIT. She was in the US on a student visa and was required to go back to Columbia after she had finished her studies unless she could find a job and a sponsor at a US company for her permanent residency application.

Veronique did not want to go back to Columbia.

Dave Ward was an adjunct professor at MIT and was one of Veronique's thesis supervisors. He was impressed by the sincerity, dedication, and keen intellect of the young Columbian and had no hesitation in offering her a position as a research engineer at United Electric and to sponsor her application for a green card.

Under the mentorship of Dave Ward, Veronique flourished at United Electric, steadily climbing the engineering ladder. By the time Dave Ward had decided to leave United Electric, Veronique had risen to the position of Chief of Metallurgy, a position second only to the Director, in the large Materials Engineering group at UE.

Veronique owed all what she had in this country to Dave Ward.

She was also completely smitten by her young dashing professor and mentor and had become his secret lover; would do anything for the man she loved more than anyone else in this world.

After he had left United Electric, his calls to Veronique had always been to arrange for a rendezvous in some inconspicuous location to be with each other, if only for a few hours. Both Dave and Veronique were married with families and were respected members of their community, so they needed to keep their relationship out of the prying eyes of the world around them. They had thus far managed it well.

Dave's call this time, though, was about MRI 297. He was going to ask his lover to betray the confidence of the company that had been so good to her, and he hated to do that. But he was at war, and he justified his actions falling back on one of the oldest clichés – *all is acceptable in love and war.*

He asked Veronique if she was at the conference and if she had heard of the new super alloy. Veronique was at the conference and was well versed with Dr. Kumar's presentation and the new super alloy. She also told him that UE was currently not working on a competing material, that they were in negotiation with MRI, Dr. Kumar's institute for exclusive rights to the new super alloy, and that Dr. Kumar had not agreed to provide the material with exclusive rights.

Veronique promised to keep Dave informed if the situation at United Electric in relation to the new super alloy changed.

Dave Ward had gotten the information he needed and was pleased to hear that his assessment of Ravi had been right. Bill MacMillan was still banking on the highly unlikely possibility of breaking Ravi down to get the new material and win the war of the engines. He was feeling good as he bid goodbye to his friend and lover, "Veronique, I cannot say how grateful I am for what you just told me and am sorry to have to ask you to betray the confidence of your employer. Thank you for that."

And to assuage any guilty feeling Veronique had, Dave Ward, the smooth operator had added, "It has been too long. Let us find an opening in our busy calendars and spend some time together."

"I would like that, Dave," Veronique replied as they ended their call.

Dave was relieved to hear Bill had not gotten the rights to the new super alloy and that the new material was still up for grabs. He was pleased with the move he had made to launch the inhouse initiative. He was confident he was ahead of Bill MacMillan. It was now Bill MacMillan's move.

CHAPTER 20

ITHACA, NEW YORK – JUNE 19TH, 11 WEEKS TO LAUNCH DATE...

It had been almost a week since Dr. Kumar had talked to both Bill MacMillan and Dave Ward and not much had happened. He was beginning to wonder if the two companies had lost interest in the new super alloy, but that seemed highly unlikely given what the disruptive benefits this new material would bring to aero engines. He knew the airlines were at the conference and had heard his talk including the independently validated reduction in fuel consumption and emissions that MRI 297 promised. He also knew the airlines were operating on razor thin profit margins and could not afford to pass the large reductions to their fuel bills which would directly show up in their bottom lines. They were not driven by any altruistic motives, although some in the airline industry might as well be, but rather by cold, hard business realities. They were going to bring substantial pressure on the airplane and engine manufacturers to incorporate the new revolutionary material in their new airplane and engine designs. He was confident it was only a matter of time before he would hear from the engine companies.

It had been a hectic life for Ravi and Caitlyn with little down time to reflect upon their journey thus far and some of the more memorable milestones. It was coming up to close to twenty-five years since he had left his native country and had come to Ithaca. His life had taken many twists and turns, leaving indelible imprints on his long-term memory bank, and as he waited to hear from the two engine companies, his mind wandered back to one particular spring day in Ithaca and the year that followed.

He had been at Cornell for four years and his work at the University was just about done. His PhD thesis was reviewed and accepted and only the final defense was left. After that he would be a full-fledged Doctor of Philosophy in Materials Engineering. He had been in contact with hiring managers at both United Electric and General Technologies and had kept them abreast of his progress. They had invited him for a visit and meet and greet at their Headquarters in Cambridge, Massachusetts and Cheshire, Connecticut. He had planned to take them up on their invitation as soon as his defense was over and had also asked Caitlyn to join him. They planned to explore the area and get to know the two neighborhoods which would play an important role in their decision.

But before that he had another major life event planned. He wanted to keep his promise and change that marriage license into a proper marriage certificate – sounded like semantics, but for both Caitlyn and him, it was as important if not more as the piece of paper which legitimized and authenticated their academic achievements.

They had decided upon the date for their big day and had gotten the reception hall at the condominium complex of their friend Pradeep free of cost. They had invited some of their associates from the engineering and computing science departments. Dr. McQuinn and Dr. Squires were to be the guests of honors. Caitlyn's roommate, Hilde, was to be her bridesmaid and her husband, Harold, the best man. He had bought a 10ct gold wedding ring – the most he could afford, for the occasion. He was also going to tend the bar. Caitlyn's friend, Cathy, had tailored her wedding gown from some fabric she had bought at a local fabric store. They had splurged and had arranged for a caterer to take care of the dinner.

Caitlyn's Dad was planning to attend the wedding, but her Mom could not make it due to problems with her knees. His parents could only send their best wishes; they could not come in person due to what looked like insurmountable visa problems and the high travel costs.

The big day had finally arrived. Caitlyn was dressed up in her bridal gown and looked beautiful and radiant. He had bought a suit for the occasion, as it was in the budget, and looked quite presentable as well with his head full of thick black hair and his 120-pound frame. Caitlyn's Dad was also staying with them. They all piled up in their old Vauxhall which had sustained a few more bruises since they had bought it used from a Persian diplomat but was still in good running condition. Hilde and Harold were already in town having driven the night before from their home in Syracuse where Harold worked for the big Air Conditioning Corporation, part of United Electric. The reception hall was only 3 miles away from their apartment and they did not expect any surprises. But halfway into the trip, the Vauxhall began to badly veer. Caitlyn was driving and she knew they had just blown a tire.

There was no time to waste, as the reception was only an hour away and the guests would be arriving soon. Fortunately, the spare did have air and there was a working jack. He had fumbled through the trunk, gotten the jack out and somehow managed to get it in place while Caitlyn in her bridal gown had begun to jack up the car. Meanwhile, Caitlyn's Dad, a well-placed executive in his home country, undid the nuts and removed the flat tire. It was a real team effort. They got the tire replaced in less than fifteen minutes and were on their way to reception. But Caitlyn's Dad was worried. He still remembered the look on his face – pleading to his daughter, as if asking in unspoken words,

"There is still time. Do you really want to marry this guy?"

And he also remembered that crack of the smile from Caitlyn – one that he had become so familiar with – replying to her Dad in the same unspoken language,

"Yes, Dad he is the one!"

Caitlyn's Dad could only wish them a long lasting and fulfilling union as they said their vows and begun the rest of their journey as life partners.

In August of that year, almost four years after they came to the United States, as unattached single students from different parts of the world, they said goodbye to Ithaca and moved to their two-bedroom apartment in Cambridge, Massachusetts as husband and wife and ready to face the future.

Summer of that year had slowly made way for the fall, as they settled in their modest apartment. Caitlyn had made contacts with the faculty at MIT and was enrolled as a transfer student in the Computer Sciences department. She had also obtained a part time position in the AI lab at the university. She could do most of her assignments from home and only needed to go there when she had to meet with one of her professors.

This worked out well and gave her enough time to get their small apartment organized while he was busy at UE, where he spent long hours coming up to speed and becoming a productive member of his team. They had organized themselves to limit their work to mostly the weekdays and kept the weekends for themselves. There was lot to do and see in their new town and the nearby metropolis of Boston.

Caitlyn had also stopped taking her birth control pills.

Almost exactly to the day when Caitlyn had stopped her birth control pills, she brought into world their first child, a baby girl. They named her Lilly, after the beautiful flower that Caitlyn had grown up with in her family's garden in Japan.

In anticipation of the arrival of Lilly, they had already begun looking for a small house and had settled on a neat, three-bedroom, 1500 square foot bungalow not far from his office. The house had a small backyard and enough room for Lilly to run around and spread her wings as she grew up.

Lilly now became the focus of their lives. Caitlyn was already doing most of her university work from home and with a very understanding lab supervisor, she could bring most of her lab assignments with her and complete them at home. On occasions when she had to be present at the university, either he took some time off from work or they could leave Lilly with their friends and neighbors, Victor and Grace.

Life had taken a familiar albeit quite tiring turn. They were happy and content.

It was the weekend; Lilly had just turned 3 months and was progressing well. Caitlyn had her checkup done with her OBGYN the day before and was given a clean bill of health. She was still off her pills and the Doctor had warned her to take precautions to avoid unplanned pregnancies. The chances of getting pregnant were small but not zero. Caitlyn was not worried; she had full confidence in herself and him and that they could control their emotions and passion. They had planned to leave Lilly with Victor and Grace and take a well-deserved night out on the town. He had already bought a pair of tickets to the new show in Boston and made dinner reservations at one of the more expensive restaurants. The budget would take a big hit, but it was well worth it, and for that one night they were not going to worry about it and enjoy themselves.

And that is what they did. They came back home, feeling good with a few too many of that very tasty cocktail. Lilly was still with Victor and Grace and was going to stay with them for the rest of the night. They had the night to themselves and it had been a long time….

When next month Caitlyn missed her regular period, she did not think much about it. Her doctor had told her that it was common for women to miss their period or have irregular periods immediately after childbirth. But, when she missed her period again the second month, she knew something was not right. She went to the nearby clinic and submitted her blood and urine samples for testing and was asked to come back the next day.

All night she had been worried and quite apprehensive. She was all set to resume her PhD work – mostly from home and on days when she had to be at the University, either he would take some time off or Grace, who also just had a boy of her own and was staying at home, would take care of Lilly. But if she got pregnant again, it would be almost impossible for her to look after two infants and be working on her degree.

He remembered joining her on the visit to the clinic the next day. He was carrying Lilly. The nurse at the counter got the results and sympathetically looked at Lilly and announced, "Positive." Caitlyn was pregnant again.

He and Caitlyn had just looked at each without saying anything. They had driven home in their five-year-old Ford Pinto in total silence – still recovering from the news – wondering with no family to help in this distant land, how they were going to manage the responsibilities of two almost same aged children.

As they got home and got out of the car, he remembered gently putting his arm on Caitlyn's shoulder and smiling. Caitlyn had simply looked back at him and saw a trace of moistness in his eyes and the dam broke loose. With his arms around her and Lilly trapped in between, the three of them had just stood there for what seemed like an eternity before he whispered, "Caitlyn, I love you, don't worry, we will be just fine." She had looked back at him and had given him that familiar crack of her smile before running inside to get cleaned up.

Caitlyn's Gynecologist, Dr. Bourne, was an old school doctor from the Virgin Islands. She was now getting on to the sixth month of her pregnancy and was beginning to show the baby bulge. The experience with Lilly was still fresh and she knew what to expect, except this time it felt different. She was bigger and felt more discomfort than with Lilly and was not sure if it was normal or she should be worried. She made an appointment with Dr. Bourne and almost exactly at the six months mark she went to see him.

Dr. Bourne conducted the usual exam and found nothing out of the ordinary or at least that is what he had told Caitlyn. He did make an appointment for her with a Radiologist for an ultrasound – a procedure not quite common or definitive at the time. The appointment was in three weeks, and the baby would be almost seven months along.

He had accompanied Caitlyn for the ultrasound and had brought Lilly along. Dr. Hakim, the Radiologist prepped Caitlyn and conducted the tests. He was in the room during the tests.

Although he was quite familiar with the ultrasound technology – it was widely used in his field of Materials Engineering, he could not quite make out what he was seeing on the monitor. To his untrained eyes, it looked like there were two hearts beating inside Caitlyn's body, but he was not sure and anxiously waited for Dr. Hakim to interpret the results. Dr. Hakim carefully examined the pictures on the monitor and smiled and cheerfully announced, "Congratulations, you are going to have twins and although I am not absolutely sure they both look like girls."

They were going to have twins and most likely twin girls.

They were going to be parents of three girls – all in one year and with no support system in place. They were not sure what to think – was it the fate being cruel to them or were they being blessed, and the person up there was rewarding them for their good Karma in the life before? What they were sure about was that life was not going to be as they had planned and there were going to be major course corrections in the journey ahead. They looked at each other again, but this time there was a sense of calm and resolution that they both felt and communicated through that look as if saying, "Hey life, we are ready for you, and we are going to do whatever it takes to do right by our three daughters…."

The twins were born one month premature, 2 days before Lilly's first birthday. They named them Sita and Reiko in honor of their parents. Caitlyn stayed at the hospital for three weeks. He would visit her every day after work with Lilly. Most days, Grace would look after Lilly while he was at work. One day Grace was visiting her mother in another part of the city and could not take Lilly in. He had taken Lilly to the local daycare. She was crying when he left,

"Don't worry Dr. Kumar, this is normal, and she will quiet down after a while," the daycare lady assured him. In the evening, when he came to pick her up, Lilly was still crying. Her eyes were red and swollen.

"I am sorry, Dr. Kumar; Lilly has been crying all day and has not eaten or drank anything," the daycare lady told him. "I don't think she is ready for daycare, at least not this daycare. I am afraid you need to make other arrangements," she had continued.

Lilly was in the nursery room when he picked her up to bring her home. As soon as she had seen him, she had stopped crying and clung to him with all the might her little body could muster. She had then looked at him with her Caitlyn-like eyes with a mix of relief and perhaps anger as if she was asking, "What have I done to deserve being abandoned by you guys?" and then she was fast asleep on his shoulder.

He had no answer except to feel the salty water trickling on his lips. He made a promise to himself that whatever happened, Lilly was not going back to daycare and neither were Sita and Reiko.

That evening at the hospital, they had agonized over how best to manage their lives with three infant girls, and with both their families in faraway lands, the two immigrants had to face a heart-wrenching decision. One of them had to stay at home to look after the girls. Should it be him and was he ready to do it? Should it be Caitlyn, who had already put her career on hold? But he already had a job and they needed the income to support their expanding family. Caitlyn could probably find a job but that could take time and it would in any case put her studies on hold. It was not an easy decision, but in the end, Caitlyn had decided that for the next few years until the girls were ready for schooling, she would be staying at home. She knew she might have to take a refresher course or two but there was always a second chance. There was not a second chance when it came to the precious formative years of her girls. He knew she resented that decision but had told him not to feel bad about it and had given him her familiar reassuring crack of the smile telling him they were going to be fine. He did not have to say it, but Caitlyn knew how relieved and grateful he was for putting the welfare of her family before her own ambitions to get them through this critical milestone in their lives. And as their life unfolded, it was only the first of many times that Caitlyn had decided to take the back seat for his and their family's sake. Sitting there alone in his office on that summer day, Ravi once again felt the salty water trickling down his face as he mouthed "Thank You" to the person above.

⸻

"Ravi, have you got a minute?" It was one of his senior associates knocking on his door as he came out of his trip down memory lane and back into the present.

"Yes, come on in," Ravi said as Dr. George Allen entered his small but neat office.

CHAPTER 21

ITHACA, NEW YORK – JUNE 20TH, 11 WEEKS TO LAUNCH DATE...

Dr. George Allen, an unassuming Texan, was a renowned expert in chemistry. After getting his PhD from the University of Texas in Austin, he had worked in several Government Laboratories but had been looking for something more challenging when he heard about the new Materials Research Institute and its mission. And even with all the uncertainties associated with this non-profit, he had not hesitated to take the plunge and was one of the first researchers to join Ravi's small team. He had proven to be an invaluable member over the years and had played a key role in nailing down the missing element that had made MRI 297 possible. He held a special place in the organization and Ravi had a lot of respect for him.

Dr. Allen had a folded paper in his hand.

"Ravi, I am so sorry, but I am afraid I have some bad news," he said as he handed Ravi the paper. It was his resignation letter. He went on to profusely apologize to Dr. Kumar for leaving the institute after so many years but, he continued, he had received an offer from General Technologies that he just could not refuse. He asked him for his understanding and to waive the 2-week notice requirement in his contract since GT would like him to start his new job immediately.

The resignation had come out of blue and was completely unexpected. It took Ravi by surprise and he was quite disappointed and saddened to see him leave. He also understood that it was for the best for one of his loyal and valuable colleagues. His nonprofit institute did not have the wherewithal to match the offer from a deep pocketed corporation such as General Technologies. He was, however, intrigued at the timing, but did not suspect any foul play on the part of his friend and mentor Dave Ward.

He wished his associate the best of luck in his new endeavor and accepted his request for waiver of the 2-week notice.

But when two of his other key associates also submitted their resignations and informed him of their significantly better contracts from General Technologies and asked him for the 2-week notice waiver, he knew this was no coincidence.

Dr. Kumar now had a mini crisis on his hands, with three of his most senior and trusted associates bolting from his small staff of scientists and engineers. He had no doubt that his friend and mentor, Dave Ward, had put their personal relationship aside and was orchestrating these moves. It did not surprise him much – he knew in his own polished way, Dave was as ruthless, if not more, as his nemesis Bill MacMillan. And that he would be doing whatever it took to either get him on his side or develop a competing material himself. It now became clear to him that the penetrating questions Dave was asking during their last phone call were not a part of casual conversation but were carefully planned to milk him for as much relevant information as possible. But he also knew, even with the three key researchers Dave had poached from MRI and all the milking he had done, he did not have much of a chance to come up with an alloy that could compete with MRI 297. General Technologies might have deep pockets and deep bench in their lab, but they did not have him, and they sure as hell did not have Caitlyn, the computational brain behind the discovery of this new super alloy. They also did not have the time. He knew they had to launch their new engine within 3 months, and even with the best of brains and all the resources, new material development required a minimum gestation period to fully characterize and certify it for man carrying airplanes – and it took years, not months, to make it happen.

He was not worried and knew Dave Ward would be back and would play ball. But he needed to be vigilant and be careful of the man whom he had considered to be his friend and mentor. He needed to watch his back, not just from Bill MacMillan but also from Dave Ward.

He also knew about Veronique Pena and he would not hesitate to play that card if he had to. If Dave Ward were going to play dirty, he was ready to reciprocate and hit hard where he knew it would most hurt his now former friend and mentor. He did not want to go down to their level, but he would if that is what it took to stand his ground. He was not going to be bullied.

But as it happened, this was just a start of the showdown with the two powerful captains of industry. The next salvo came in the form of both United Electric and General Technologies withdrawing from the consortium that sustained Dr. Kumar's nonprofit institute. UE and GT were two of the main funding sources, and their withdrawal meant the institute's revenue would go down by close to 70%. Although with the departure of three of his key researchers the institute's expenses were reduced, it was not enough to offset the reduction in revenues. Dr. Kumar had a quick huddle with his staff and Caitlyn to map out a survival strategy while the issue with MRI 297 played out.

Caitlyn agreed to completely forego her retainer as the institute's part time consultant and manage on her salary from the university. Dr. Kumar also agreed to take a 50% pay cut, as did most of the remaining four full time employees. It was agreed by all of the fulltime employees that the stipends for the four interns and graduate students – which were modest to begin with –should be maintained at the current levels.

The team hammered out a budget for managing this emergency – the primary income coming from the balance of the funding from the consortium and the royalty payments the institute received for licensing its various metallic and thermal barrier coatings for aero engines manufactured by all three major engine companies. The institute would suspend many of the non-essential research work to conserve cash and would focus on the complete characterization of the new super alloy. Dr. Kumar was confident that at the right time both United Electric and General Technologies would accept his terms and would be back at the table. He was counting on the accountants and the market forces to convince Bill MacMillan and Dave Ward that their new engine designs had to be based on the new super alloy and that they really did not have a choice if they wanted a share of the most lucrative opportunity in the history of commercial aviation – and that half a loaf was better than none.

He was also counting on the clock – the two companies had to launch their engines within 3 months to meet the very tight aircraft development schedule. And he was counting on the likes of Jack Stevens – the wily and powerful chairman of American Aviation – to make Bill MacMillan and Dave Ward see the futility of fighting Dr. Kumar. Yes, Ravi was counting on a lot, but then again, he had been doing that all his life and so far, he was still standing, fighting, and moving forward.

CHAPTER 22

ITHACA, NEW YORK – JUNE 27TH, 10 WEEKS TO LAUNCH DATE...

Dr. Kumar was still waiting for the other shoe to fall. Dave Ward had made his move and was going to try to come up with his own version of the new super alloy – MRI 297. Good luck to him, Ravi thought with a smirk. But what was Bill MacMillan going to do? Although he was no longer sure about that, Ravi considered Bill MacMillan to be more ruthless and knew he had much more to lose than Dave Ward – United Electric had the market and their stock price to a large extent was propped up by the Aero Engine business. Lose that and the stock tanks along with the fortune of Mr. MacMillan. Ravi knew he was not going to let it happen and he had told him so – Bill was going to get MRI 297 and he was going to get it any cost. But what was Bill's next move?

He soon got his answer. Ravi had just packed up after a long day. Caitlyn had also come down from the university to dial in the numbers from the latest material characterization tests that Ravi and two of the interns had just completed on the new super alloy. The results were looking good and provided additional validation of the properties of the new material. The team would continue populating the database with more test points tomorrow.

Ravi and Caitlyn bid the two young interns – one from Caltech and other from Cairo University in Egypt – good night and got in their Toyota Prius Hybrid for the drive back home on a local two-lane country road.

The sun was beginning to set, and the traffic was light. Ravi and Caitlyn had taken this road ever since they had moved to Ithaca and they knew it like the back of their hands. It was usually a boring drive with the car almost on auto pilot, and not much happened. They would engage in some small conversation or just sit back and unwind and enjoy the beautiful Cayuga Lake hugging the two-lane road as they drove by. But today was different. They could feel it in their bones.

Ravi had just completed the long straight stretch of the road and was on a gentle curve which followed the contour of the lake, which was on his right side with less than 10 feet of embankment and a three-foot-tall protective rail. Suddenly a white unmarked old van travelling in the opposite direction swerved into Ravi's lane. There were no other cars on the road and Ravi knew this was no accident. It was a calculated move to drive Ravi off the road into the embankment, and if his reaction was not fast enough, into the lake.

Caitlyn screamed as she saw the van approaching, "Ravi, watch out." Ravi's survival instinct was fast enough to duck the oncoming van and collide head on into the embankment rail.

The van did not stop and got back on the road and sped away. Ravi and Caitlyn were badly shaken but not hurt and could still open the doors of the car. They got out and stood by the side of the road, shaking, and still trying to understand what had just happened. They looked at their almost new Hypersonic Red Prius. It was totaled.

"Did you get the license number?" Ravi asked Caitlyn.

"No, I was just trying to duck my head while you were running into the guard rail," Caitlyn replied, sounding quite annoyed at Ravi's question.

"Excuse me for not having a head on collision and getting us out alive," Ravi answered, equally annoyed. But they quickly calmed down as they normally did when an argument, or worse still, a fight might be in the offing. One thing was certain, neither of them had had the time nor the wits to take down the plate number of the van. They did, however, see the face of the driver, but were not sure how much help that would be when they reported the incident to the local law enforcement.

They were thankful to have escaped with only property damage and no injuries themselves. Their priority right now was to get back home and think through what had just happened, make some sense of it, and then come up with a going forward plan. They had a nasty feeling that this was not a random accident but was related to their dealings with the two engine companies. But they were scientists and did not want to jump to any conclusion until they had had the time to fully analyze the information available to them. The only caveat - they had to do it fast, it could not be paralysis by analysis - their lives may well depend upon it.

Ravi and Caitlyn hitched a ride back home in one of the police cruisers that had arrived at the scene. The officers had taken down the details of the accident which were not much beyond the color of the van and what they could remember about the face of the driver – a light colored man with mustache and a big rotund face. Not much for the police go on, but they did promise to get back to them as soon as they found something out about the accident and the perpetrator. Ravi did not mention his suspicions about the possible involvement of the engine companies. He wanted to think through it before he made any allegations.

It was late in the evening when Ravi and Caitlyn got home and said goodbye to the two officers who had given them the ride. They called the girls and were relieved to hear their voices and that they were doing all right. Ravi and Caitlyn had discussed the lucrative offers with the girls and had gotten their buy in before turning them down. The girls therefore did have some idea about what was going on. They did not, however, know that their parent's refusal to accept the offer could turn violent.

Caitlyn and Ravi did not mention the harrowing experience they had just gone through. The girls could sense there was something wrong, but they knew their parents well enough not to push. They knew their parents would get back to them at the right time.

It was then time to reflect upon the events of the evening. Ravi took out his trusted notebook to take notes about the events of the last 10 days as he said,

"Caitlyn, a lot has happened over the last few days. Let us try and make sense out of it to map our going forward plan. I will take some notes. Can you go back and tell me what you remember about what we just experienced? Even the smallest detail may be of significance, so don't skip anything."

"It was a white van that almost certainly did not accidently come into our lane. It had to be a deliberate action since there was no traffic on the road and therefore no need for the van to take us over by coming into our lane," Caitlyn replied.

"Also, it looks like the driver selected a section of the road where there was a decent sized embankment to the lake. The van therefore did not intend for us to go into the lake, but only give us a scare and maybe cause damage to the car," Caitlyn continued.

"I agree. The guy came at me really slowly, giving me enough time to react and avoid a head on collision, which could have almost certainly crushed our little Prius and could have been fatal for us," Ravi said. "What else?"

"I did not see any markings on the van. It was white with no distinguishing features. I also think it was an American made the likes of which we see plying the Finger Lake region in abundance. And although I am not sure, to me the driver looked like a foreigner – probably an Eastern European," Caitlyn said.

"I think that pretty much captures this evening. I will add to it if we remember something else. Now, let us summarize some of the major developments from the last 10 days after I talked to both Bill MacMillan and Dave Ward. Let me start," Ravi said.

"Three of our senior researchers who had been with us almost from the beginning resigned in succession to work for General Technologies at significantly higher salaries and benefits, and they all asked for waiver of the 2-week notice clause," Ravi continued.

"And you lost funding from both United Electric and General Technologies almost at the same time, reducing the institute's revenue by 70%," Caitlyn said.

Ravi then added to his notes the gist of his phone call with Dave Ward where Dave had tried to milk as much information as possible about the trials and tribulations of developing the new super alloy. At the time, Ravi had considered it to be a benign and stimulating conversation with his old mentor and friend. He was not sure about that anymore and wondered if Dave Ward might be doing an end run to try and come up with the new material himself with the help of the three researchers he had just poached from Ravi. It was highly unlikely, but possible, for

Dave and his team to come up with a comparable material, and if so, there would be less of a reason for him to terrorize Ravi.

Finally, he summarized the takeaways from his phone call with Bill MacMillan. Bill was not so sanguine when Ravi had turned down his demand for an exclusive contract. He had let Ravi know of his intentions to get the new super alloy and get it at any cost. Could that include violence? It was hard to accept the top man at one of the leading and storied corporations will stoop down to that level, but then again Bill MacMillan was not like any other CEO's; and he had not acquired his reputation and his exalted position by playing nice and by the rules.

But they did not want to jump at any conclusions. They both spent the next ten minutes looking at the notes and analyzing their observations when Ravi broke the silence and asked,

"Caitlyn, what do you think?"

"I am not really sure because the obvious conclusion is quite unbelievable. I have to say, in all likelihood it must be Bill MacMillan and his henchmen that are trying to shake you down and scare you into submission. But he knows you well enough to realize that is not going to happen. It will take a lot more than just trying to run you off the road. Could it be just his first salvo, and more is yet to come?" Caitlyn said.

"Look, it could be Bill, but we cannot rule Dave Ward out. He may be more polished, but he can be equally ruthless as Bill, and he has much more at stake. He has already lost out to Bill once and his company is in the fight for its life," Ravi said.

"Or it could be someone completely different and unconnected to either of the two rivals and even the new super alloy – although I cannot think of why anyone would want to attack two academic researchers like us. But we cannot rule that out, as well," Caitlyn added.

Ravi needed some answers and more data. He did not have to wait long to get both – more data but instead of answers, more questions as to who really was behind the attack and why.

CHAPTER 23

AVIATION WEEK & SPACE TECHNOLOGY – JUNE 28 ISSUE, NEW ENGINE UPDATES

With the new engine launch date just 10 weeks away, confidential sources tell AWS&T that Dr. Kumar has refused to sign exclusive rights contracts with either of the two engine companies, insisting on making the new super alloy available to all who can legally use it. Both Bill MacMillan, the CEO of United Electric and Dave Ward, his counterpart at General Technologies, are reported to be frustrated and angry at the Materials Scientist and have vowed to do all in their power to get the new material in their engine exclusively. General Technologies have poached three of the senior researchers from the Materials Research Institute in what appears to be making an end run around Dr. Kumar's invention and presumably developing their own version of the super alloy. AWS&T considers the probability of success to be extremely low and believes this may only be a ploy to bring Dr. Kumar back to the negotiating table and also get a leg up on the competition.

AWS&T does not have any news on what Bill MacMillan and United Electric's next move is except that he cannot allow

Dave Ward and General Technologies to own this new material exclusively.

AWS&T will continue to follow and report on this critical program that will determine the course of future commercial aircrafts for a long time.

AWS&T has nothing new to report on the Chinese engine program. Our Beijing bureau is actively monitoring developments at the China Aero Engine Company and will be providing updates as they become available.

CHAPTER 24

BEIJING, CHINA – JUNE 29 PM – 14 HOURS AHEAD OF ITHACA, NEW YORK

"Zhang, Min-Chung." It was the gravelly voice calling again. It was late in the evening, but the director of strategic planning and the all-around fixer for the China Aero Engine Company did not work regular hours and was available any time of the day, especially to his mentor, a high ranking official in the Chinese Government.

"Yes, sir" Min-Chung Zhang replied with deference.

"I just read the latest story in AWS&T about the new material and that neither of the two American companies have acquired it. That gives us an opening. You understand that, right?" the gravelly voice said.

"Yes sir, I do. But our options are limited. Export laws prevent us from getting it legally and simply throwing money at it does not appear to open up other avenues as well," Min-Chung Zhang answered.

"Zhang Min-Chung, old Chinese saying. There are many ways to scale the mountain. Think about it." The gravelly voice said as he hung up.

CHAPTER 25

**ITHACA, NEW YORK JUNE 28 – 8:00 AM,
10 WEEKS TO LAUNCH DATE…**

A t his office next day, Ravi found an unopened letter on his desk that his secretary had marked urgent. Usually she would have opened it, but it was boldly marked "To be opened by Addressee only." It had no return address and it seemed to have been mailed at a post office near the institute. There was another letter that his secretary did open. It was from his friend and old colleague – Dr. Xi Ping from the Beijing Institute of Technology. Except for the brief encounter at the conference, Ravi had not heard from Dr. Ping in quite some time and was surprised to get this unexpected letter from him.

With mounting anticipation Ravi opened the letter addressed to him. It was printed on a plain white bond coat paper in the common Ariel font and simply said:

"*This is only the beginning. Do the right thing for you and your family at any cost.*"

And that was it. It was unsigned and provided absolutely no clue except the last three words – *at any cost.* Could it just be a coincidence that the code words used by both Bill MacMillan and Dave Ward on more than one occasion were part of this cryptic note? Ravi did not believe in coincidences, but then again, he was not about to accuse one of the captains of US industry of trying to physically harm him and his family through a low-level stunt used by thugs and common criminals.

But he could not rule it out, either, given their reputations. What got him especially worried was the mention of his family. Were they now going to go after his family to get him to surrender? It was blackmail and he was determined not to give in to their bullying and terrorizing. He had to do something – but what?

He then picked up the second letter from his old colleague and friend Dr. Xi Ping.

Xi summarized the status of their new engine – a competitor to those planned by both United Electric and General Technologies. It was in planning stages at the Chinese Aero Engines.

Ravi was aware of the desire of the Chinese Government to get in the high tech and very lucrative aero engine business. They had been investing heavily in research and development at the many universities and industries in China. Dr. Ping's institute was one of them and was founded and funded by the government to catch up with the west and close the very substantial gap that existed in the field of Materials Technology. His sabbatical at Ravi's Materials Research Institute in Ithaca was part of this long-term strategic plan and since returning to China, Dr. Ping had significantly advanced the state of the art in his country. However, in high temperature super alloys that were critical to high performance aero engines, his country was still significantly behind the west. They did have the basic tools required to manufacture the alloys; they just did not have the detailed know how.

Dr. Xi's letter went on to describe some of the key characteristics of the new Chinese engine and the performance goals they had set for it. Not surprisingly, they were remarkably similar to what Ravi had outlined as the potential capability of a new engine with the new super alloy – MRI 297.

Dr. Xi then admitted that with the capabilities they currently possessed, they would be well short of the targets and would essentially have an engine that would not be able to compete in the marketplace. The missing link, Dr. Xi continued, was the new material that Dr. Kumar had developed. He then went on to say that he was authorized by the Chinese government to offer Dr. Kumar and his institute whatever terms he deemed suitable for licensing the new super alloy.

Dr. Xi concluded his letter hoping to hear back from Ravi, expediently adding:

"Dr. Kumar, as your friend and old colleague, I want to emphasize that the Chinese Government is fully committed to this project and intends to get this new super alloy at any cost. I hope you will consider this offer very seriously."

Ravi read the letter several times and each time the same dreaded phrase jumped out at him – ***at any cost***.

Again, was it just a coincidence that two letters landing on his desk after the harrowing experience he and Caitlyn had gone through the night before would use the same threatening phrase that he first heard from Bill MacMillan and then from Dave Ward? He knew of collaboration between United Electric and the Chinese Aero Engine company on various legacy engine programs, but he could not imagine a scenario where they would use gangster tactics to scare an academician into submission.

And even assuming they could scare Ravi, what would be the business arrangement and how would they ever get around the extremely strict export control regulations related to high temperature super alloys? It just did not make any sense. Having spent a year in the US with access to the readily available US government export control documents, Dr. Xi must know what he was purportedly asking Ravi could not be done without him criminally violating the laws of the United States which would result in harsh consequences. He knew there was no possibility of Ravi ever accepting his or the Chinese Government demands, whatever the threats may be. So, why would Dr. Xi send him this letter – or did he?

There had to be some other plausible explanation – coincidence could be one of them, but somehow his gut just did not accept it. He needed to let the problem brew in his head and see if he could come up with a better answer, but in the meantime, he had to assume the threats were real and make some defensive moves to protect himself and his family.

CHAPTER 26

ITHACA, NEW YORK – 10 WEEKS TO LAUNCH DATE...

Ravi was well aware that both United Electric and General Technologies had to launch their new center line engine within three months if they wanted to meet the very tight schedule of the new airplane's certification. And that was two weeks ago. He also knew that the airlines would exert enormous pressure on both the airplane and engine companies to meet the paradigm shifting aggressive performance goals which could only be met with the new super alloy. He was certain that the engine companies would be back at the negotiating table and that they were going to scare him into submission and may even hurt him in the process, but they were not going to kill him. How the Chinese fit into all this, he had no idea, but he had to assume that the Chinese, if they were involved at all, would also want to keep him alive.

He therefore had to devise a survival plan for himself and his family for the next ten weeks and wait out the two engine companies. It was like running the time clock off in the big game – except the game here was not the Super Bowl, but the game of life for Ravi and his family.

As it happened, all three girls were out of the country for the summer. Lilly was in Japan enrolled at Sofia University in an intensive Japanese Language course. She was also using her time in Japan to prepare for the MCAT exam she was planning to take some time during the year. She was hoping to get in a good medical school next year after she had completed her Baccalaureate at Harvard. Sita was in France at the Sorbonne enrolled in an advanced French Language class and Reiko was in the UK attending a special, semester-long, multi-discipline seminar at the London School of Economics.

He had been keeping them informed, except for the incident with the van yesterday. But it was time now to tell them about the attack and their decision to go underground and what the girls needed to do. It was late evening in Japan when Lilly answered her phone.

"Lilly, please listen carefully," Ravi said, trying to keep calm, but not succeeding in hiding his true emotions.

"Dad, what is up. Is everything all right?" she asked.

"Well, not quite," he replied, and then gave her a quick summary of the events of last evening and the two letters he had just received. He told her how much he and Caitlyn loved her and assured her things would eventually workout. He then added,

"Lilly, for the next three months you need to be extra vigilant and careful. Please keep a low profile and restrict your movements. Limit your interactions with people you do not know and make sure you always let your grandparents know where you will be at all times. I also want you to discard your current cell phone and get a new one from the local phone company and restrict your calls to only contacts you know well."

"I understand Dad. I hope you and Mom will be safe and know that we are fully behind you and proud of what you are doing. Please do not worry about us." Lilly said.

"Thank you, Lilly. We are counting on you," Ravi said. He then gave her his unlisted cell number and asked her to text him at least once a day and anytime if there were an emergency. He then called Sita and Reiko and gave them the same message.

He then took a deep sigh and mouthed a quick prayer for their safety and wellbeing. He could not imagine what he and Caitlyn would do if something happened to their girls, and he was going to do everything in his power to keep them safe.

His next call was to Caitlyn,

"Hi Caitlyn, listen it looks like we would need to go underground outside the US for the next three months. I will fill you in when I see you, but can you please apply for a leave of absence for the next three months and let me know if there is a problem. I will see you at home, but in the meantime can you pack a few things? We will be leaving tonight and need to travel light. And, oh, please do not talk about our plans with anyone. If someone asks, just tell them it is for family reasons. We really need to keep it under the radar."

Caitlyn understood the urgency and applied for the leave to her head of department, who had no problem in granting her request. The University was in the summer semester, and Caitlyn had a relatively light workload – mainly in the Artificial Intelligence Lab – which could easily be rescheduled without much impact.

Dr. Kumar meanwhile fished out his unlisted cell and dialed a number in Marseille, France. The call was answered on the third ring by a familiar voice with a southern French accent. It was his old friend and colleague – Dr. Marcel Giraud – Head of the Materials Engineering Department at Marseille

University. Dr. Giraud had spent a year in Ithaca with his wife Sophie and had become close friends with Ravi and Caitlyn. He had only recently returned to France and was in fact was one of the three researchers at the Materials Research Institute who had spent many days and nights testing and characterizing the new material. He was the one who had called Ravi to let him know that they had found the missing element.

Dr. Kumar knew Marcel would do anything for him and Caitlyn, just as he had done for him and Sophie when they were in the US. He also knew Marcel was good with keeping secrets and could be completely trusted. He gave Marcel a short background and the essentials of what had transpired thus far, finishing with the event of last evening where he and Caitlyn were almost driven off the road in the lake. He also told Marcel about the two notes he had received and the direct and implied threat to him and his family.

He then briefly described his plans for the next ten weeks and the need for him and Caitlyn to go underground outside the US. Marcel, as expected, was shocked to hear, and could not believe that one of the leading companies in the world could be behind acts that were more in the domain of despot warlords and chieftains of drug cartels. He was equally surprised and intrigued by the letter from Dr. Xi and had difficulty in accepting the Chinese government could be involved in such a nefarious and outlandish scheme that could well bring a diplomatic showdown between the two governments. But, just as Ravi had concluded, for now the threat had to be taken seriously until they had more facts to help them sort through what was turning out to be an international scandal.

He agreed with Ravi's plan to go underground until the smoke had cleared and offered to arrange a secluded place for him and Caitlyn in the Southern French region of Provence, not far from Marseille, its major port city, and the provincial capital.

Ravi thanked Marcel and requested him to be extremely discreet about their visit. He told him that he would be in contact again with his travel plans and if all went as per the plans, should be in Marseille the next day. He would then rent a car locally and travel to the location Marcel would have selected. Before hanging up, he once again thanked Marcel profusely and repeated his request,

"Marcel, thank you for doing this for us. Caitlyn and I really appreciate it. But, before I go, let me reemphasize the importance of keeping our visit completely secret – Caitlyn's and my lives may well depend on it."

He then logged into his personal laptop and made online bookings for himself and Caitlyn for the late evening Air France flight out of New York. It was a four-hour drive from Ithaca to the NYC John F. Kennedy airport, but even with traffic they should have enough time to make it if they left around noon time. He called Caitlyn and summarized his discussions with Marcel and asked her to meet him at the institute with their luggage – one 22-inch roller board for each of them with a few changes of clothes and only the most essential personal items. They were going to be on the move and needed to travel light.

Ravi's next call was to Bill MacMillan's private number. Bill had told him that he would accept his call any time of the day from wherever he was and would answer promptly. Bill had received a text late last evening which simply said:

"At Any Cost in motion."

Bill answered Ravi's call on the second ring and said,

"Dr. Kumar, good to hear from you. I hope you are calling to accept our offer and work with us to get your new invention in our engines."

Ravi did not have any time for perfunctory conversations and came right out and said,

"Mr. MacMillan, I am sorry, this call is not about MRI 297 but to talk about what happened to me and my wife yesterday evening and the note I received this morning." Ravi then went to summarize the events of the past 24 hours and asked Bill directly,

"I was wondering if you or your staff had anything to do with these incidents."

Bill had asked his security chief to not share with him any details of his actions. He could then truthfully deny knowing anything about it. So, after feigning surprise, anger and disappointment, Bill admonished Ravi,

"Dr. Kumar, I am offended at your audacity to imply that I, the chief executive officer of one of the leading and most iconic American corporations, could be involved in what clearly appears to be a criminal act. Please be warned that if you ever call me again for anything else but to talk about your new material, I will have my legal team launch a defamation suit against your institute and you personally." With that, Bill hung up. He still had a smile on his face as he leaned back in his plush executive chair, confident that United Electric would soon have the exclusive contract to the new super alloy.

Bill's response and his admonishment did not completely come as a surprise to Ravi. Even though he had no evidence, in his gut he felt Bill was behind the attack and at least one of the letters and maybe both. He tried hard to sense something – perhaps a tenseness in his voice that might support his suspicion, but clearly this was not Bill's first rodeo and Ravi was just an amateur. He did not have a chance.

Ravi was going to make a similar call to Dave Ward, but decided against it. He knew Dave well enough and although he could be as ruthless as Bill, he could not see him going down to this level. He was much too cerebral and polished for that. Ravi admitted he might well be wrong about Dave, but for now, he was going to let it pass.

That evening Dave Ward had also received a text from his security chief:

"Eyes on At Any Cost."

As for Dr. Xi and the Chinese connection, this was a completely unexpected development and he needed to think about it and talk it over with Caitlyn before deciding how best to handle that.

Ravi then called in a quick meeting of his staff and informed them that he was going to be away on some personal business for the next three months. For the safety of all concerned, he could not tell them of his plans and that he would be mostly out of direct contact and would only get in touch when it was absolutely necessary and safe. He asked them to be extremely vigilant and report any unexpected developments to the local law authority.

As he was wrapping up the meeting, Caitlyn walked into the room. They wished their colleagues good luck and goodbye and left for the drive to JFK and a journey into the unknown, running for their lives from the greed and power of a pair of mighty industrial juggernauts and maybe a powerful and odious foreign government.

CHAPTER 27

MARSEILLE, FRANCE – TEN WEEKS TO LAUNCH DATE...

They landed at the Marseille Provence Airport the next evening. Ravi had taken a circuitous and torturous route through the streets of Queens to get to the airport in New York to make sure they were not being tailed. He did not think he was, but only time would tell.

Marcel and Sophie were waiting for them at the airport, and after a warm hug and French greetings – kisses on both cheeks – they whisked Ravi and Caitlyn into their waiting van and were on the way to Remoulin, a small village about two and a half hours from Marseille and close to the famed town of Avignon.

The village of Remoulin, Marcel's birthplace, was a tiny French hamlet in the heart of Provence with about 250 permanent inhabitants and 10 times as many tourists. It had a long and interesting history which made the village a tourist hot spot in its own rights, but it was also only about half an hour away from Avignon – the old papal seat and the origin of the famed nursery rhyme:

"Sur le Pont d'Avignon on y danse on y danse tous a rond (On the Avignon Bridge we dance we dance in a circle.)"

Ravi did not know the rhyme, but Caitlyn, growing up in Japan, had learned it in her childhood and was excited to hear that they would be staying in the area at least for a few days. Hopefully, they would be able to explore the rich history of the region while maintaining a low and inconspicuous profile as tourists.

Marcel's brother Pierre had bought an old eleventh century house with a silo like tower. The original owner of the house was a rich landlord who had used the tower to fortify his residence with guns against invaders and looters from other villages. Pierre had converted it into a Bed and Breakfast. It was as discreet a place as one could find. Marcel had arranged with Pierre to rent out his biggest suite to Ravi and Caitlyn for the next few weeks.

Pierre was also a retired officer of Surete Nationale – the French National Police – and was well equipped to protect the friends of his brother.

Ravi and Caitlyn settled in their new residence hoping to stay there for as long as possible before they were discovered. Ravi had no doubt that with all the resources at their disposal, Bill MacMillan, Dave Ward, and the Chinese, if they were involved, would locate them and they would need to find another venue for their hide out. But for now, they were going to keep a low profile for a few days and if it looked safe would take in the many historical and beautiful sights Provence had to offer. They were determined that although it may appear to be foolhardy to risk venturing out and expose themselves to whoever was after them, they were not going to be kowtowed and were going to make the most of their time in this beautiful part of France, rich with history and traditions of old Europe.

They had been in Remoulin now for the last three days and not much had happened. They had spent their days admiring the countryside and the eighth century Catholic church that had been built by the local warlord. Pierre was an excellent host. His breakfast of freshly baked French baguette and croissants, coffee, and juice ensured they would have more than enough energy to get out for their occasional walk around the small village. But they were getting restless and frustrated.

On the following day, Caitlyn and Ravi were in the middle of a heated argument about what to do next – Caitlyn wanted to go out and explore the region, but Ravi wanted to play it safe and not venture far from their well protected hideout under the watchful eyes of Pierre, when Ravi got a call on his unlisted cell. It was his secretary calling. He had given her his number with instructions to call him only if there was an emergency.

"Dr. Kumar, I am sorry to call you, but I got a strange call that I thought you should know about," his secretary said. His secretary, Helen, had been with him since the start of the institute and he had utmost trust in her judgement. He also knew she would do anything for them to protect their safety and would not be calling unless she thought it was critically important for them to know what she had to say.

"Helen, it is all right. So, what did you want to tell us?" Ravi said.

"Well, this man called who would only identify himself as *At Any Cost.* He said you would know what that means and that he wished you a pleasant stay in France. He said he hoped you had gotten his letter and were going to do the right thing. He then added that Provence is a beautiful region to explore including Avignon, Salon de Provence, and Pont Du Garde and that he might also be visiting those places; if you were interested in meeting him and getting to know him, you should go there. He looked forward to seeing you. And then before he hung up, he said he also knew where everyone was and that it would not be advisable to involve the authorities."

Ravi tried to remain calm as he listened to his secretary. But she could still sense his nervousness as he said,

"Thank you, Helen. Did he say anything else and did you try and find out where he was calling from?"

"No, he did not say anything else and I could not trace his call. It was from an unknown number. I also did not call the police and wanted to ask you if you wanted me call them. I was concerned about the caller's warning."

"You did the right thing by not calling the police. Let me think about this and I will get back to you if I need you to do anything. In the meantime, please be extra vigilant and call me if you remember or find out anything else," Ravi said as he hung up.

Caitlyn was listening to their phone call and already had a good idea as Ravi summarized the conversations with Helen and then said,

"I guess we are going to Avignon after all. It is risky, but we have to find out who is behind this. Looks like they already know we are in France and most likely are keeping an eye on us here in Remoulin. So, it cannot be any worse in Avignon than it will be staying here."

"I agree. I am especially worried about the implied threat in the message. Looks like they are also watching the girls. I suggest we let Pierre know about our plans and get in touch with the authorities if we are not back within four hours. I hope my black belt in karate is finally going to be of some use," Caitlyn said.

It was ironic that the hunted had now become hunters. Ravi and Caitlyn were determined to find out who was after them even if it meant they would be making it easier for their attackers by leaving their secure habitat in the old tower and venturing out to historical spots dotted around Remoulin.

Avignon was the natural choice for their first big outing. Caitlyn was somewhat of a history buff and was fascinated with the cultural and historical wealth of the region. She took pleasure in giving Ravi lessons in the subject – Ravi was a good student and lapped it all with growing respect for Caitlyn at the depth of her knowledge.

Avignon was located close to the mouth of River Rhone, one of the major rivers in Europe draining the clean fresh water from the melting glaciers in the Swiss Alps to the Mediterranean Sea. Besides the bridge, which spanned the river, Avignon was famous as having been the Papal seat in the 14th century. During the Papacy of Clement V, a Frenchman who refused to move to the Vatican, Avignon served as the Papal residence and the center of the influential Catholic Church. For the next 67 years and through 7 Popes, all French, it was the only Papal city.

Gregory XI moved the Papal government back to the Vatican in 1376, but after his death in 1378, the French Cardinals wanted to bring the Papacy back to Avignon which the new Pope in Vatican refused and thus began what was known as the Western Schism which lasted for the next 40 years until the two Papacies united again in Vatican to become what we have today.

Ravi and Caitlyn spent almost a whole day at the old Papal palace which looked more like a fortress, and indeed it was built and used as such. After the last Pope moved out of Avignon, the palace was used variously as a prison, army barrack, regional government seat, and now mostly a museum.

Ravi found the whole story fascinating as Caitlyn patiently took him through the Papal history and the 14th century fort that was still standing strong as a witness to its colorful past.

Although Caitlyn had read about the Papal wealth, both she and Ravi were struck by the opulence of that place and had difficulty in reconciling what they saw with what they believed was the dogma of Catholic church – the vow of perpetual poverty. They agreed they had still a lot to learn about the real world.

Ravi was intently listening to Caitlyn, but he was also carefully examining the people around them. The palace was crowded with tourists from all over the world and he could hear a Babel of languages, some of which he could understand while others were completely foreign to him. There was a large contingent of Chinese tourists, many from Italy, and the ever-present conspicuous group of Americans talking loudly and being stared at by the rest of the crowd. There were very few loners or even couples that could fit the bill of *At Any Cost*. And there were a pair of middle-aged nuns in their neatly pressed habits. He was sure he had caught them stealing a glance at them but did not think much about it. He was searching for someone who looked like the Eastern European man he had seen in the van in Ithaca, but no one stood out and nothing happened to them.

So far, so good, and no sign of any trouble. They were ready to take a longer drive – this time to Salon de Provence – about an hour and half south of Avignon and an hour north of Marseille. Salon de Provence was another one of the places the caller had mentioned to his secretary.

They left their bed and breakfast early in the morning in their rented Peugeot. Their ride to Salon – as the locals called it, would take them through the lush countryside that was the southern France. They decided to bypass the highway and instead travel the small, two-lane country road which wound through the many small villages dotted along the road. It was indeed an exhilarating ride, and for that morning they forgot why they were there in that part of the world and were simply happy to be there.

Salon de Provence was the home of the 16th century occultist Nostradamus – who prophesized the future in his famous book "Les Prophesies" or The Prophesies. The book, written in French and filled with 4 verse quatrains, was still in publication and was the bible for a vast number of believers from all over the world. By profession, Nostradamus was a physician, but his claim to fame were his prophesies which were followed with almost with religious fervor by many of the noble houses of the time which included Catherine de Medici, wife of King Henri II of France.

It was said by Nostradamus fanatics and believers that he predicted the rise and fall of Napoleon, of Adolf Hitler, the Challenger Explosion, the 9/11 attack and the assassination of JFK. Caitlyn had bought a copy of his book and was understandably skeptical about the predictions which were deliberately written to be vague and subject to interpretations by the experts in the field. She could not find clear reference to any of these events but then again, she was only an amateur and a non-believer scientist.

Nevertheless, it was an interesting experience to visit his house and the town where he had spent his later years and where he wrote his prophesies. The house had been mostly renovated, but there were still some sections of the building that were from his time, and both Caitlyn and Ravi had the eerie feeling of hearing his voice talking to them about their own predicaments.

"Did you hear that?" Caitlyn asked Ravi.

"Hear what, I didn't hear anything," he replied.

"Well, I think Dr. Nostradamus has a prophecy for us. I can hear him clearly. He is prophesizing a sunny and fulfilling future for us. Can't you hear that?" Caitlyn said teasingly.

They looked at each other and Ravi just smiled. He was only perfunctorily looking at the displays on the wall chronicling the prophesies. His main focus was on the people around them. *At any cost* could be here but had not made any moves or was not readily identifiable. He was surprised to spot the two nuns from Avignon. It was too much of a coincidence. He ratcheted up his courage as he approached them and said,

"Hello, we must have similar taste. I remember seeing you ladies in Avignon at the Papal Palace."

"Oh yes, we were there. We are visiting from Paris and my friend, Sister Anne, is a fan of Nostradamus," one of the nuns replied and then added,

"I don't remember seeing you there. Did you see him, Sister Anne?" she asked the other nun.

"No, I do not remember. But there were many people there and it is possible we were there at the same time. We are easy to remember because of our habits, but it is difficult for us to remember everyone we see," Sister Anne said in her soft lilting French accent.

"Well, sorry to bother you. It was a pleasure meeting you both. Please enjoy your visit and have a pleasant day," Ravi replied as he made his way back to Caitlyn who was in the last room of the building and then back to their car.

The sun was setting as they got in their Peugeot for drive back to Remoulin and their bed and breakfast. It was a good day made better by no sign of any trouble. But they were still no closer to finding out the identity of their attacker. They would just have to keep looking.

Pont du Gard was their next adventure out of their 11th century tower. It was almost on the outskirts of their village, just 20 minutes away. Like everything in the region, Pont du Garde had a long history, this time going back to the Romans. It was also one of the places mentioned by *At Any Cost*.

Pont in French meant Bridge, so it was a bridge on the River Gardon, one of the many tributaries of River Rhone. But this was no ordinary bridge. The Romans in the 1st century AD, that is more than 2,000 years ago, had built the bridge to carry the aqueduct they were building to bring fresh water from the bubbling springs in Mount Uzi to the city of Nimes, some 35 miles away. The Roman Civil and Water Engineers of the time had to work with the relatively small drop in elevation from the mountain to the plains and had to precisely lay the ducting, which at some places had almost an imperceptible slope. Pont du Garde was one such section of the aqueduct system with a gradient of less than 1 in 18,000 – a drop of 1 foot in a span of 18,000 feet!

Ravi and Caitlyn, both engineers by training, could only marvel at the ingenuity and brilliancy of the engineers who had designed and then managed the construction of the bridge and the entire aqueduct system, some 2,000 years ago with no modern technology at their disposal.

The bridge was still standing tall and the aqueduct system, if cleared of the silt and accumulated debris, might well be used in a pinch to transport the fresh spring water still bubbling in the Uzi mountains to the populace in the villages and towns below.

Walking through this UNESCO World Heritage complex, taking in the sights and sounds of the place, it was hard not to wonder aloud if the wonderful edifices man has built today would still be there as a witness to our times 2,000 years from now.

Ravi and Caitlyn were lost in their thoughts as they came out of a tunnel about fifteen feet above the ground level at the exit. They had almost forgotten about one of main reasons for their visit – to find *At Any Cost and* had let their guards down.

The tunnel used to carry water and was part of the aqueduct system. There were a set of stairs at the exit to allow visitors to get down to the ground level with a small landing area at the top aligned with the tunnel mouth.

It happened as they had just exited the tunnel. Ravi was on the small landing area and Caitlyn was just behind him. There were several other people around them crowding the platform. Ravi was about to descend to the first stair when suddenly someone bumped into him, tripping him over. He fell on the ground and would have tumbled down had it not been for the lightning quick reflexes of Caitlyn which she had developed over many years of karate training and in which she was now a level three black belt. Caitlyn grabbed Ravi from behind, breaking his fall. He was on all fours suspended between the landing area and the first and second steps of the staircase. Caitlyn, with the help of other bystanders, pulled Ravi back onto the platform. He was scraped and bruised but otherwise all right and was steady on his feet and could stand up.

They knew it was not an accident and a deliberate push. They looked for the man who had bumped into him but in the confusion and the ensuing melee he was long gone. All they could remember of him was that he was a short and stout Oriental man.

They quickly descended the stairs. Ravi went in one direction and Caitlyn ran in another to see if they could see the man who had just pushed Ravi. It was clear that the man had chosen a discreet and strategic spot for the accident, ensuring he would have the time to get away, and that even if Ravi tumbled down the entire flight of stairs, he would only be injured and that the injuries would in all probabilities not be fatal. It was clear that this was a continuation of the terror tactics that had begun back in Ithaca. And it was not the same man.

At Any Cost was here and were it not for Caitlyn's quick reflexes would have hurt him badly. They were no closer to finding out who he was except this time he was an Oriental looking man. And what did he want? Ravi got the answer to that question when he put his hand in his wind breaker pocket and came out with a piece of paper. Printed on that were those same dreaded words:

"Do the right thing – At any cost."

Their fear of being found out was confirmed and although they were not sure running away would help, it would buy them some time before those chasing them got close again. They had to run the launch clock down and keep moving. They had managed to burn 2 weeks, leaving eight more weeks to go. The cycle of hunted becoming hunter becoming hunted again had to continue, but in a different place. Their stay in the South of France was over. It was time to move.

CHAPTER 28

MARSEILLE, FRANCE – EIGHT WEEKS TO LAUNCH DATE...

Dr. Ravi Kumar and Dr. Caitlyn Mariko made their way back to the Peugeot. They knew there was not much point in reporting the incident to the local police. They did not have any evidence or any witnesses and even if they did, the perpetrator must have been a professional to have bumped into Ravi, slip the piece of paper in his pocket, and then vanish out of their sight before they had gathered their wits. He must, by now, be long gone, having done his job of doing enough to terrorize and cause some injury to the target but to not make it life threatening or fatal. The police report would only make the already difficult situation messier without any tangible benefits and they would have to explain the whole story to put the incident into proper context. They were also worried about the warning they had received about not involving the authorities for the safety of their girls. No, they could not take the risk with little reward. They had to tackle it on their own and decided to take a pass on the complaint to the local police.

But they were puzzled by how they were found out. They had maintained a low profile not contacting anyone on the outside through email, phone, or text. On the rare occasion they wanted to follow the news from stateside, they had gone to the local Internet café and browsed through Google news. They had basically shut themselves off from the world.

It could not be anyone at their office since no one knew of their plans and they could not imagine Marcel or Sophie could be involved in anyway, or could they? No, they quickly discarded that thought, even though Ravi had sensed Marcel's frustration and perhaps anger at being shut down from much of the inventive work down at the Institute due to the very stringent government regulations. He had come to accept it as the terms of his employment and did not appear to hold it against Ravi or the Institute, or if he did, he had successfully masked it.

Pierre, Marcel's brother, and the retired French Surete National agent, had given them good vibes and even if he could have betrayed them, how would anyone know how to contact him in this remote village? No, it had to be the long tentacles of the multi-national corporations or the Chinese government or both. They had used their international contacts to locate them – an Indian man with an Oriental woman - and deliver the threat and let Ravi know they were being watched. The attacker this time around was an Oriental man pointing to Chinese involvement. Ravi still did not accept that his old friend and colleague, Dr. Xi Ping, was involved. But circumstances change, and he had to find a way to either eliminate him or include him in his going forward survival plans.

They drove straight to their lone village Internet café. Ravi sent out an email to Dr. Xi Ping from the public computer with a brief note:

"Did you recently send me a letter? Please urgently reply Yes or No at my email address back home. - Ravi"

It was possible that the email could be traced back to him here in Remoulin, but he was not much concerned. He had been outed in South France and was already served with the threatening notice. Come tomorrow, he would have moved on to the next stop in what was turning out to be a deadly game of international hide and seek.

Ravi then took out one of his several cheap burner phones that he had bought at a discount store in Manhattan after his first meeting with Bill MacMillan. He dialed his friend Dr. Larabi Hasan, an old colleague of his who had spent a year as a postdoctoral fellow at his institute. Larabi was from Casablanca, Morocco and now was the head of Materials Engineering department at the Universite de Casablanca. Larabi, his wife Rabia, and their twin sons had stayed with Ravi and Caitlyn while looking for a place in Ithaca and had become close family friends.

Larabi had answered on the second ring and was surprised and happy to hear his old friend's voice. But from Ravi's tone, he knew this was not a social call and was listening carefully as Ravi summarized the events of the last six weeks, and the attack on them yesterday at Pont du Gard. Dr. Hasan was angry but more concerned about their safety, and immediately offered his Riad in Casablanca for as long as they needed it. He was also going to look for a safer and more discreet place in the hinterlands of Morocco, somewhere in the Atlas Mountains, as their hide out at least until they were found out again, which both Ravi and Larabi agreed would be only be a matter of time. The only silver lining in all this was that the clock for the launch of the new engine was winding down, and Ravi was confident that if they could survive for 6 more weeks, both Bill MacMillan and Dave Ward, assuming he was also involved, would be back at the table. That left the Chinese. Ravi was expecting to hear from Dr. Xi soon to help with that mystery and how to handle it if the Chinese were indeed one of the groups chasing after him.

But that was tomorrow's problem…

In Beijing, in the offices of the Far East Headquarters of a multi-national company, the chief of security received a text:

"At Any Cost Moving Along."

In Cheshire, Connecticut, another security chief received another text:

"At Any Cost on the move."

CHAPTER 29

CASABLANCA, MOROCCO –
EIGHT WEEKS TO LAUNCH DATE...

Ravi woke up from the nightmare he was having in his friend's Riad in Casablanca. It took him several minutes to focus and get oriented again. All he remembered from last night before crashing, was the red eye he and Caitlyn had taken from Marseille to Casablanca and being driven to the Riad by his friend and old colleague, Dr. Larabi Hasan.

The Riad was a beautiful old house with an open courtyard and rooms all around it. It was tucked away behind the sprawling main bazar – called a souk in the local Berber language of the Moroccans. They had driven through what looked like a maze of small lanes and gulleys to get to the house. Larabi and his family occupied one wing of the Riad. The other wing Larabi normally rented out as a bed and breakfast. Fortuitously, it was vacant when Ravi had called. Larabi reserved it for them for an indefinite period.

Ravi did not know much about Casablanca and Morocco. His only knowledge of the city came from the Humphry Bogart movie of the same name. Ravi was a big Bogie fan, as he had been one of the few Hollywood actors he had known about even in his native India. He had always dreamed of visiting the city and the famous Rick's Café, albeit not under these circumstances.

That evening, he sat down with Larabi to map out a plan for their stay in Morocco. They agreed that it was not safe for them to stay in Casablanca for more than a few days, and that they needed to travel to the hinterland of Morocco. Larabi had located such a place, close to both the Sahara and the Atlas Mountains in a remote town called Ouarzazate.

In Ouarzazate, Larabi's friend owned a Moroccan Kasbah - an old fortified building used by the local Arab and Berber landlords of the day to house their families and protect them against the marauding gypsies and invaders from the desert. It had been fully updated with all the modern conveniences and was now rented out to tourists from all over the world. The Kasbah was vacant and was available for immediate occupancy.

Ouarzazate was about six hours south east from Casablanca and although it was also a tourist spot, they figured it should be safer than Casablanca as a hide out. Ravi and Caitlyn thought they should be able to blend in with the tourists and not be overly conspicuous. Larabi had also arranged for a local security company to provide around-the-clock protection, although they were not sure how effective that would be against the professional hit teams that seemed to be after them. But it was better than nothing.

Caitlyn and Ravi spent the next few days in Casablanca, not venturing out much and staying mostly in the Riad. The only trips they took were short visits to the Souk which was almost in the backyard of their Riad - just a fifteen-minute ride on a horse cart – a common mode of transportation used to negotiate the narrow and winding gulleys of the old town. The souk teamed with people of all persuasions and had almost anything one could imagine available in one of the small shops tightly packed in the two-football fields sized plaza. It reminded Ravi of the bazaars of his hometown in India, bringing back many nostalgic memories from his childhood, with his parents taking him there to buy fresh fruits and vegetables. For Caitlyn, having grown up in Japan, it was a new and fascinating experience. She could have easily spent another few day trolling the souk, but they knew it was not safe and they needed to get out of Casablanca before they got caught.

They left Casablanca early in the morning in their rented Renault Station Wagon and made it to Ouarzazate just around lunch time. Caitlyn had bought a book on Morocco and was fascinated with its colorful history. Ravi was attentive as she shared some of it during their drive through the scenic Atlas Mountains full of Argon trees laden with green berries that produced the famous Argon oil – a major foreign exchange earner for the country.

Caitlyn gave him a thumbnail sketch of the long history of the country which spanned more than ten thousand years and still had a lot of unanswered questions about the origin of the Moroccan people. What was not in question though, she had added, was that they were a mixture of many races and had skin color and facial features that resembled fair colored Indians from the North, not very much unlike how Ravi would appear to a foreigner. It was an interesting observation, one that Ravi had himself made during his stay in Casablanca and had wondered if the Moroccans and the Indians did not in fact share the same genetic code. It was an idle thought, but little did he know that it would become quite significant as the events unfolded.

Caitlyn's story about Morocco and its people was interesting and helped pass the time on the relatively sparsely travelled three lane highway. It also kept Ravi awake. Caitlyn wrapped up her story talking about the more recent history and about the King who was currently in power.

"The current king, Mohammad VI is a well-loved ruler and has liberalized the social fabric of the country," Caitlyn said. "He has also invested heavily on upgrading the vast infrastructure and modernizing the education system. The road we are driving on is part of the new highway system that covers the majority of the country and extends into many of the neighboring countries. With its fertile land, Morocco has become the granary of North Africa, feeding a large swath of the continent. The highway system is critical to supporting the extensive trade between the countries of the region and providing Moroccans a standard of living that is comparable to the countries of Europe and the Middle East."

Caitlyn could have gone on, but they were approaching Ouarzazate and Ravi needed to concentrate on the road and look for their Kasbah which Larabi had told them was located on the outskirt of the town tucked into the foothills of the mountain, where it seemed to rise from the desert. He asked Caitlyn to take a break and continue with her story about Morocco after they were settled in their Kasbah.

Larabi's friend Muhammad was waiting for them at the Kasbah with one of the security guards. Larabi had already briefed Muhammad about Ravi and Caitlyn and the need for them to be protected from one or more teams of professional hit teams. The hit teams were trying to terrorize them by engineering deliberate accidents which thus far had not been fatal but could be in the future if their employers concluded they had reached a dead end with Ravi.

Muhammad had retained around-the-clock surveillance of the Kasbah. The guards were all retired police officers, were licensed to carry small arms, and had worked on protection details before. Ravi and Caitlyn were given a tour of the residence – a 3,500 square foot building fortified with 10-foot tall walls around an almost half acre compound. The Kasbah was fully furnished and stocked with provisions and fresh groceries to last at least a week. There was a main entrance to the building and a back entrance which was normally kept secured but could be used for a quick exit in an emergency.

Muhammad provided a map of the town and showed them the many eateries spread all along the main road which was about a mile from the Kasbah. His suggestion was for Ravi and Caitlyn to settle down and mostly remain indoors for a few days and then if it looked safe, they could venture out to the nearby restaurants and tourist sights, many of which were within a 5 miles radius from their Kasbah.

He then asked them to call him any time if they needed something or if there was an emergency. His house was only a few miles away and that he was generally at home and could be at the Kasbah within 10 minutes. Just before leaving for the evening, Muhammad handed Ravi a small wireless device and said,

"Dr. Kumar, if you need anything at all or sense any danger, please press this button. It will buzz the security guards who are stationed across the Kasbah to remain inconspicuous. They will be making rounds of the premises in their unmarked vehicle and will respond to your call immediately."

Ravi and Caitlyn understood the instructions and spent the evening exploring their residence and checking out the pantry and the kitchen. They fixed themselves a light meal and settled down in the old but well-appointed living room with a short history and guidebook for Ouarzazate and it environ.

Ouarzazate, which in the Berber language means "without noise," was by Moroccan standard a small town of roughly

60,000 permanent inhabitants. At about 3,800 feet above sea level, it was in the foothills of the Atlas Mountains, which stretched from the South West port of Morocco on the Atlantic to the North-East city of Tunis in Tunisia. The mountains, rising to close to 14,000 feet at their apex, were the rocky backbone of North Africa that separated the Mediterranean Basin from the Sahara Desert. Ouarzazate was an important trading post for African traders on their way to northern Morocco and Europe. South of the city was the western end of the great Sahara Desert, making Ouarzazate a natural stop for travelers from the desert to the fertile and prosperous cities and towns on the other side of the mountain. Even today, itinerant vagabonds often made the trek from the poorer neighboring desert communities to the town in search for better lives and to find conveyance to the western ports on the Atlantic and northern ports of the Mediterranean.

Ravi and Caitlyn were fascinated with the story of the town and the region and looked forward to getting out and experiencing it for themselves once it was safe to do so, hopefully in the next few days. For now, they were happy to be there and thankful to their good friend Larabi, who had arranged for them to come and see some of the remote areas of this beautiful country that they would have otherwise not known about. He had helped them make the best of what was turning out to be a run for their lives, which had already taken them through three continents and was far from over.

They settled down into a routine, staying mostly within the Kasbah and venturing out only to the main drag of the town to take in the local cuisine called Tajin – a delicious mix of vegetables, rice or couscous, local spices, and sauces all steam cooked in a conical ceramic pot. There were also the Moroccan versions of common Middle Eastern fare – couscous, falafel and all manner of kabobs barbequed on wooden and metal skewers. For the vegetarian Ravi, the restaurants, and eateries of Ouarzazate offered a much larger and more enticing selection of dishes than he could find at home in Ithaca, and it was all very reasonably priced. Caitlyn teased him about being in seventh heaven and not wanting to go back to the real world. He had to grudgingly admit that there was some truth to it.

It had now been more than a week since they had come to Ouarzazate and not much had happened. It looked like they may have dodged their pursuers, although they had no doubt it was only temporary. Ravi had texted the girls on his burn phone and they were all doing well with no evidence of anyone trying to harm them. It was a big relief. They were now ready to explore some of the other sights in and around the town. They called Mohammad and he suggested a day trip to Ait-Benhaddou – the site of an old traditional mud brick city on the edge of the high Atlas Mountains. The city, more like a village, had a string of 17th century Kasbahs surrounded by desert. With the Atlas Mountains in the background, it had a biblical feel that made it look like Jerusalem. It had been featured in many well-known Hollywood movies from *Lawrence of Arabia* to *Gladiator* to *Jewel of the Nile* and a whole lot of others in between. It had been declared a UNESCO world heritage site and was a good place to get some training for climbing the steep hills and ramparts of the Kasbahs.

Caitlyn was a big fan of "Old Hollywood Movies" and was all excited at the prospect of visiting the location of one of the classics – the *Lawrence of Arabia*. They made arrangement with Mohammad for the transport and planned to visit Ait-Benhaddou on the weekend when there would be a greater number of tourists, providing them a good cover and making them less conspicuous.

It was late in the afternoon that day. The sun had just set, and they were getting ready for dinner and a quiet evening with their favorite book and the strains of John Coltrane's "Love Supreme" playing on the CD. And as they did every night, following the instructions of the security guard, the drapes were drawn, and the house appeared completely dark from outside. The photo sensitive flood lights covering the outside compound would activate only if they detected movement in their arc of vision; otherwise, except for the natural light from the moon, it was all pitch dark.

Caitlyn was in the kitchen, when she suddenly detected a faint rustling sound coming from just outside the window which faced the rear of the building, away from the main entrance. It appeared as if someone or something was trying to make its way from the rear to the front. Caitlyn put her finger on her lips and motioned to Ravi outside towards the kitchen window. He quietly moved towards the fireplace and picked up the iron poker. The wireless buzzer for alerting the security guard was on the coffee table. Ravi pressed it and made his way to the front door on the tip of his toes with the poker in his hand. Caitlyn also crept into position on the other side of the door.

They could now see someone trying to use a tiny pick to work the lock tumblers and open the door. They were breathing hard and the hair on their necks were standing with terror. They had been found out, and there was little chance of escaping this time. Even with Caitlyn's third-degree black belt in karate, they knew they were no match for professional hit teams. Their only hope was the security guard. But he was all alone, and even if he called for backup it will take some time for the help to arrive. They had to hold the fort until that happened. They were determined not to give in without a good fight.

Finally, it looked like the intruder had picked the lock and the door handle was beginning to move. The door was about to be flung open when they heard the siren from the Guard's SUV. Ravi stiffened with the Poker in his right hand ready to strike as soon as the door opened. Caitlyn's side of the door had a glass pane covered with a drape. She moved the drape slightly with her left hand, still in position to jump with her karate kick. They saw the front yard brightly lit up by the flood lights and the Guard rushing to the door with his weapon drawn. They could hear footsteps noisily retreating from the front towards the rear of the building. And then they heard a gunshot and a loud scream. There were other SUV's also pulling up the driveway with their headlights blazing. Looked like the help had arrived much sooner than Ravi had expected.

They could now hear several sets of footsteps rushing to the back from where the gunshot had come. They should have remained inside, but their curiosity got the better of them. With the poker still in his hand, Ravi rushed toward the back of the house with Caitlyn just behind him. They could faintly make out the shadow of a man lying on the ground surrounded by a bunch of guys, most likely the guards. The man was softly moaning. One of the guards was bending and appeared to be examining the man on the ground. As they got closer, they could now clearly see the man on the ground, bleeding from his leg. The bullet from the guard's gun had hit him and knocked him down.

Ravi's fear was now replaced with concern for the fallen man. It was not hard to conclude that this was no professional hit man.

The man on the ground was young, maybe in his twenties, and was dressed in what looked like a robe with a headcover – a typical middle eastern outfit worn by people travelling through the desert. The guard had lifted the robe to expose the wound from the gun shot. It was bleeding, but to their untrained eye it did not appear to be a major injury. The man was crying in pain and saying something in the local language that the guard translated for them. He said he came from a nearby village in the desert looking for a ride to get to the port city Casablanca where he was hoping to find a job. He had been travelling all day and tried to hitch hike, but no one stopped. He saw the dark Kasbah and thought it was empty and was trying to get in to rest for the night and then be on his way to the town, hoping for a ride from some charitable person. He had no money and a family to feed and there was no work in his village. He did not want to harm anyone and begged for their understanding and mercy.

Ravi and Caitlyn looked into the man's eyes and knew he was telling the truth. They brought him inside the Kasbah. Caitlyn got the First Aid kit, that Mohammad had left for them in case they needed it in an emergency and cleaned up his wound and bandaged it to stop the bleeding. Ravi fixed a quick sandwich for the man, gave him some local money, and asked the guard to take him to the nearby hospital. He knew the socialistic and mostly free medical system in Morocco would take good care of him. He told the guard to make up whatever story he felt might fly with the local authorities and that he did not plan to file any official charges against the man.

They closed the door as the men left and breathed a deep sigh of relief. Ravi fixed a stiff shot of Scotch on the Rocks for Caitlyn and another one for himself and sat down on the expansive couch to unwind. They were relieved that it had turned out to be a false alarm; with all that was going on in their lives, they surely did not need this, but they were glad they could help. Over the last two weeks since they had arrived in Morocco, they had taken a genuine liking for the country and its people. They felt indebted not only to their old friend and colleague Dr. Larabi Hasan, and Mohammad the gracious owner of the residence they were living in, but also to the many Moroccans whom they had met during their stay and whom had gone out of their way to make them feel welcome and part of the family. This was the least they could do.

Their planned day trip to Ait-Benhaddou was still a few days away and although their nerves were all jangled from the episode with the itinerant man from the desert, they had decided to carry on with it. They called Mohammad the next morning and briefly summarized the events of the previous evening. He was, as expected, quite concerned about it, and wanted to report the incident to the local law enforcement but deferred to Ravi's decision not to press any charges. Mohammad tried hard to persuade them to cancel their plans for the visit and stay in and around their Kasbah in Ouarzazate, but it was to no avail. Caitlyn was beginning to show house fatigue, being mostly cooped up inside. She needed to get out even if it meant taking risks.

Ravi told Mohammad of their decision to carry on with their planned trip to Ait-Benhaddou but asked him to book it as part of a guided group excursion rather than for just the two of them. That would provide some cover against whoever was after them and make it more informative and interesting.

It was a beautiful day when the tour bus arrived at their Kasbah to pick them up for the trip to Ait-Benhaddou. It was a small bus with nine other tourists. The guide, Farah, was a Berber Moroccan about the same age as Ravi and had an uncanny resemblance to him; he could have been easily mistaken for Ravi by a foreigner.

Ravi and Caitlyn got into the bus and introduced themselves to the group. It was an interesting group of mostly retired, well-educated people. There was a semi- retired physician couple from New Zealand, a retired school administrator couple from Long Island, a mother and daughter pair from Spain, a gay middle-aged couple from Toronto, and an eighty + year old retired teacher of Swedish origin from Austin, Texas. They were all travelling through Morocco as independent tourists and had gotten on this day tour from various pick up points in Ouarzazate. Ravi and Caitlyn were the last ones to be picked up. The group was now on its way to Ait-Benhaddou.

Farah turned out to be an entertaining guide with a lot of tribal knowledge of the region. He appeared to be particularly well-informed about Ait-Benhaddou, its history and anecdotes, and some of them no doubt had a little Arabian Night feel to them. One of those was about Sir Peter O'Toole, the "Lawrence" in *Lawrence of Arabia*. It immediately piqued Caitlyn's ears – she was a diehard fan of "Lawrence."

Continuing his story about the movie, Farah came to the scene where they were going to film the Arab uprising and capture of Aqaba, the port city from the Turks. Lawrence was going to lead the rebel army of Prince Faisal on a camel. The problem was O'Toole did not how to ride a camel and kept falling off, much to the annoyance of Director David Lean. When after several tries and misfires, he finally got the hang of riding the camel, the beast took off. O'Toole could not hang on to the saddle and fell and would have been trampled by the horses of his Arab army had it not been for the same camel standing over him and shielding him from the stampede. Peter O'Toole was shaken up but not injured, and promptly got up to resume the shooting, adding to his already legendary status within his filming brethren.

Farah did qualify the story by saying he was not sure how much of it was true, but in this business, truth was only marginally interesting if it made for a good story – and this one sure did.

The minibus pulled up to the huge entrance gate to the Ait-Benhaddou village. It was a good half mile walk to the main Kasbah and the stairs and ramps that climbed to the top of the fort like building. They walked in a group, with Farah leading the way and giving a running commentary about the village and its surroundings. The village did not have a large population – about 50 families, and most of them were paid by the government to live there and make it look like an inhabited community. It almost felt like one of the communities in the US where people dressed in period costumes for the benefit of tourists and visitors.

For the hike to the Kasbah and the climb to the top, Ravi and Caitlyn had intentionally separated – Caitlyn was with the guide upfront and Ravi was bringing up the rear with the senior citizen retired teacher from Texas, giving her a hand in negotiating the steep climb. The Kasbah was fairly crowded, with several groups like theirs climbing on the stairs and ramparts of the building.

They finally made it to the top, all huffing and puffing. From down below, what looked like an easy, benign walk turned out to be quite a workout, but they were finally there. They were all standing on the narrow landing with a steep drop of more than fifteen feet to the next landing. There was just a single iron railing at about waist level to provide some level of safety. The scene below of the vast, open desert lined with the small and medium sized houses and Kasbahs of the villagers transported the visitors to times when camel caravans would routinely ply through the Sahara with their cargo of goods, merchandise, and sometimes slaves to the ports of the Atlantic and Mediterranean. To say it was dreamy and out of this world would be no hyperbole.

Farah was in his element as he was describing that beautiful landscape.

"So, ladies and gentlemen, here we are at the crossroads where the mighty Atlas Mountain meets the great Sahara Desert. For centuries, camels have brought travelers who have suffered through a long and tiring journey through the Sahara to this village for some well-earned rest and recharging of their batteries. It is a unique location and because of that has been the setting for many big budget and not so big-budget movies from Hollywood to Bollywood and many other movie studios from all over the world."

Caitlyn was just next to him eagerly taking everything in. Suddenly, Farah, without any warning, went all limp and was going to slide through the gap in the railing to the landing below. Once again, Caitlyn's quick karate reflex saved him from going down. She grabbed Farah by the tail of his long flowing robe and hung on to him while one of the gay men from Toronto grabbed his torso and pulled him back. Farah's face had turned all white and eyes dilated as they laid him down on the floor. The retired physician couple from New Zealand quickly sprang into action to check his pulse and heart. They asked everyone around to disperse and give Farah some room. It looked like he was unconscious. Ravi immediately called in the Moroccan emergency from his cell.

The doctors were not sure what had caused Farah's illness. His pulse and heart rate looked to be OK and he was breathing. They did notice a small prick mark on one of his arms that was red and was beginning to swell. They did not think much about it at the time. Someone handed them a bottle of water. They poured some of it in his mouth and he seemed to be gulping it. That was a good sign. There was not much more anyone could do except to wait for the emergency help to arrive. That is when Caitlyn noticed a piece of paper sticking out, almost falling off, Farah's robe. She picked it up and thinking it might give her some relevant information about their guide, she opened it and read the note. It was printed and had just two sentences:

"We are watching you. We all need Electricity. Do the right thing for yourself and your family at any cost. Our patience is running out."

A shiver went through Caitlyn's body. She knew the note was for Ravi and her. The attacker must have mixed up Farah with Ravi since they looked so much alike. Caitlyn looked around to see if she could recognize anyone in the crowd – an Oriental man or a European man that looked familiar. She could see no one like that. She had to warn Ravi about it and let him know they had been discovered. She had left the note in Farah's pocket but had memorized the content. Something about it looked different and bothered her. She could not quite place what it was but needed to share it with Ravi as soon as they were alone again.

What was not in question was that their time in Morocco was over. It was time to move again.

CHAPTER 30

Bill MacMillan had just gotten off the phone with the President of the Aero Engine division of United Electric. He had asked him for a weekly, or if necessary, more frequent update on the new engine program. That was an urgent call.

"Bill, I need to talk to you about the new engine. We need to have a firm decision for my team to move forward. We are getting awfully close to the launch deadline and I need your guidance in how you would like us to proceed."

The president of the aero engine division of United Electric then went on to summarize the status of the program. He reminded the CEO that the launch was only six weeks away and that a great amount of prelaunch conceptual design work had already been completed to give the team a head start in what was a very tight schedule for a new, center line, fully certified aero engine design. They needed a firm decision on the new material and needed it as soon as possible. Although they could still wait for the next six weeks, that assumed a fully success-oriented program with no unexpected problems. With the new material and the extremely aggressive performance goals, the design team considered this high risk and would like to get whatever extra time they could get. They had, therefore, implored the senior management to decide on the way forward as soon as possible and not wait until the last-minute.

Bill promised the President to get back to him within the next 48 hours, hopefully with a definite direction for going forward. He had gotten a cryptic text last night from his chief of security that simply said:

"At any cost moving along – await capitulation."

Bill texted back:

"Move faster at any cost – cap window shrinking."

The security chief acknowledged and sent out two texts of his own. They both read:

"Need Results now at any cost."

CHAPTER 31

In Cheshire, Connecticut, Dave Ward met with Dr. Cheryl Adams, the Senior VP of Engineering at General Technologies, and her Chief of the Materials Engineering Group. The chief provided a summary status of the inhouse effort on the development of a material comparable to MRI 297- the new super alloy developed by Dr. Kumar and his team at the Materials Research Institute.

The inhouse General Technologies Materials team, which now included the three senior researchers poached from MRI, had experimented with nine new elements from the Periodic Table as potential candidates. They included Erbium, Thulium, and Holmium the three elements, from the Lanthanide or Rare Earth metal group that Dave Ward had managed to coax Ravi in admitting could be one of the missing elements in MRI 297.

All three had looked quite promising in their initial results but did not match the creep strength and fracture toughness – two of the many critical properties required of materials suitable for aero engines. The team also tried elements from other groups in the Periodic Table, but so far none of them met the requirements.

It was most likely, the chief had continued, due to the team not being able to precisely define the extremely sensitive and rigorous process required to control the mixing of the many base metals needed for a super alloy. The team had fully leveraged the experience of the three MRI engineers, but they did not have the benefit of having an expert, such as Dr. Mariko, who had utilized latest developments in Artificial Intelligence and Advanced Neural Networks to reduce the almost infinite number of permutations and combinations of temperature, chemical composition of the surrounding environment, rate of heating, rate of cooling, and so on to a manageable level. Even with the reduced number, the MRI team still had to test hundreds of thousands of variations in the process before they could come up with the final solution. And it had taken them more than 10 years to do so.

To expect to get it done within 3 months, the chief had continued, was a task that was close to impossible. And although as engineers, they would never say it was impossible, and it was possible that they might luck into the final solution tomorrow or the day after, the probability of that was close to zero.

The chief had finished his summary and was now looking at his feet. He said he was extremely sorry to have failed the organization and assured them that he and his team would continue working on it, but he implored Dave Ward and Dr. Cheryl Adams to not bank on his success and develop a backup plan.

Dave Ward asked for Dr. Adams' expert opinion on the subject, and she fully backed the conclusions and recommendations of her Materials Chief.

Dave was not surprised at the seemingly bad news. He already had a backup plan, in fact two – a backup to backup. He was determined not to lose out again to his nemesis at United Electric and was going to use all means at his disposal, some legitimate and some not so much that might well be illegal or at least immoral. But he was not going to worry about that – in his own mind, his actions were justified. He was doing what was best for the company that had put their faith in him when they brought him over from his old company – United Electric.

He asked the Materials chief to summarize the results thus far in a report and send it to him. He then thanked Dr. Adams and the chief of Materials Engineering and asked them to continue working on the new material. He also promised to get back to them within the next 72 hours with a firm and decisive going forward direction for the new engine design.

After his visitors had left, Dave Ward took out his private unlisted phone and sent out two short texts. Both read:

"Please Call asap – dw"

Victoria Panini received the first text. She was about to leave her office at Sicily Airfoils in Palermo, Sicily. Although Victoria had kept in touch with Dave Ward over the years since she had left the United States after completing her Masters in Materials Engineering at MIT, she was quite surprised to get this unexpected and cryptic message. It brought back a lot of memories….

Victoria came from a well-known industrial family in Palermo. She had completed her bachelor's in engineering degree at the local Palermo University with the Italian equivalent of Suma-Cum-Laude. She was the only child and was slated to take over the family business. But before getting involved with the business, she wanted to spend some time abroad. Her father had agreed and even encouraged, thinking she would make new contacts in the biggest market in the world which should be good for the business. And although Victoria had some inkling, she did not know much about her father's other business – which in fact was his main business – the boss of the biggest and most powerful Panini Cosa Nostra family of Palermo. She was slated to take over the reins of that side of the business, as well.

Victoria fell for the young dashing adjunct professor, Dave Ward, as soon as she first saw him. She was already engaged to be married to the son of another major Palermo family, a marriage arranged between the head of the families, with neither Victoria nor her fiancé having much say in it. But that did not stop her from falling for the American. She would try to find any excuse to get some personal time with Dave in his office at the University. Dave was married and had his ring prominently on his finger, but that was no deterrent to Victoria. Her glowing olive skin, dark brown eyes, and beautiful Sicilian features made her irresistible to men. Dave Ward could not resist her, either. They became secret and passionate lovers – both knowing full well that that is all they were – lovers and nothing more. And that was OK with them.

They genuinely enjoyed each other's company – Dave used to love discussing about the projects he was working at United Electric, bouncing off ideas that were still not fully clear in his mind, taking full benefit of Victoria's keen intellect and understanding of the subject.

Victoria went back to Sicily after completing her master's degree. She took over the businesses, both of them, after her father died and by all accounts was quite a successful businesswoman. They had kept in touch, but over the years, it had become more of a business contact than personal. Victoria wanted to expand her business and become a certified supplier of Airfoils to United Electric but had so far not succeeded due to the very stringent supplier qualification requirements at UE. She had since addressed most of the shortfalls identified by UE and was confident that her company could now meet all the requirements to be certified as an Original Equipment Manufacturer or OEM for the largest aero company in the world. It was going to be a major victory for her company and a big feather in her cap. And although she did not ask, she did expect and hope that Dave Ward, who was now running the Aero Engine Division of United Electric, would help or at least put in a good word for her and her company.

She was quite disappointed to hear that Dave did not get the top job at UE and had left UE for General Technologies, the other major US Aero Engine Company that Victoria was also trying to become a supplier to. But when she heard that Dave was the new CEO at General Technologies, she was elated and sent him a congratulatory note letting him know how happy she was for him and that she and her company were willing to help Dave in any way they could to succeed in his new position.

That was quite some time ago, and she had not heard back from Dave until now and this cryptic text.

Victoria called Dave back on his unlisted private cell, the same number she had been using when he was at United

Electric. He was, as always, happy to hear her voice, which after all these years still gave him the same sensations as when they were together at MIT. But this time it was serious, and Dave needed her help.

"Victoria, thank you for getting back to me so quickly. It is really good to hear your voice after so long, and I am sorry that I did not call you before or right after I left United Electric. I just had a lot on my plate. But even though I did not call, you were always in my thoughts and all the fond memories we had made together," Dave, the polished and cerebral adjunct professor, said in his baritone voice.

He then asked her if she had heard of Dr. Ravi Kumar and the new super alloy he had just developed. Victoria was in the business and was keeping up to date with the latest developments in the field. Although she was not at the conference, she had heard about Dr. Kumar's presentation and the groundbreaking new super alloy his institute had developed.

Victoria also knew about the new engines on the drawing boards at both United Electric and General Technologies for the two new airplanes which were expected to become the largest selling commercial airplanes in history. And she had heard that the European engine company, due to other major investments they had recently made, had decided not to field an engine for these new airplanes, leaving the field to the two US aero engine manufacturers – Dave Ward's previous and current employers.

She expected an all-out bidding war between the two aero engine companies for the new material and their desire to have exclusive rights to it. This would guarantee the winning company the majority, if not all of the new airplane business, and perhaps put the losing company out of the commercial engine business. She expected it to be a good fight between two industrial giants of the biggest economy in the world.

What she did not expect was how personal this fight had become between the two chief executives and the extent to which they would go to win. But she had been through some nasty and often violent fights of her own and was ready to provide whatever help her old lover and future business partner needed.

Dave Ward was relieved to hear how much Victoria already knew and did not require a long preamble and background to the reason for his call. He succinctly summarized the status of his discussions with Dr. Kumar and his insistence on not signing an exclusive contract with either of the two companies. He emphasized to Victoria the underdog status of General Technologies and how he needed this big engine contract to make GT relevant again in the commercial engine market or face extinction, leaving United Electric in a virtual monopoly situation. He made the case for healthy competition between equals to ensure a continuous advancement in the state of the art and the capabilities of engines and airplanes of the future. Absent such healthy competition, he had continued, the industry was bound to get on a downward spiral of increasing cost and reducing capability, causing irreparable damage not only to their business but also the society at large.

Victoria was intently listening to Dave and mostly agreed with his arguments for a healthy competition. She was still not sure why Dave had called her and what he wanted from her. That became clear as Dave continued.

He then told Victoria about what he had learned from his people who were following Dr. Kumar and his wife, Dr. Mariko. He had asked his security chief to assign around the clock surveillance of the husband wife team until they had come to an agreement with General Technologies about rights to their new super alloy. He had instructed that they be only followed and that no harm should come to them.

His surveillance team had informed him of the attack on them starting with their hometown of Ithaca. They had been on the run for the last several weeks and had since been to Marseille and Morocco. He did not know who the attackers were, but he suspected they might well be orchestrated by United Electric, although he had no proof of that.

It looked like, Dave had continued, Dr. Ravi Kumar and Dr. Caitlyn Mariko had been outed in Morocco and were on the move again. He believed, based on what he had learned from his people, they were now heading to Palermo, Sicily.

It was his belief that Dr. Kumar was aware of the launch schedule constraints for the new engine and was trying to run the clock down. There were now only six weeks left to the drop-dead date by which the two engine companies must launch their new engines if they had any chance of meeting the extremely tight schedule for certifying a brand-new engine and airplane.

He asked Victoria if she had any questions on what he had summarized thus far. She did not, except she was still waiting for Dave to tell her what was it that he wanted from her. She did not have to wait long.

Dave had known about Victoria's "other" business. Without specifically coming out and saying what he wanted from her, he said, "So, Vic, can you think of a way we can encourage Dr. Kumar to sign the contract with us? As you can see, it is critical for the future of not only our aero engine division but also the entire corporation. I, of course, do not want to bring any harm to Dr. Kumar or his family, just persuade him to work with us and let us exclusively use his new material. I am now at a point where I have run out of other options and am looking for your help to make it happen. I will be eternally grateful and will not forget you and your company in the future."

Victoria now fully understood the reason for Dave's call, what was being asked of her, and what was in it for her. This was her city; she had the resources and she wanted the business. She also still had the soft spot for that dashing young professor that she had madly fallen for.

She promised to do what she could and get back to Dave when she had something to report. Dave did not need to remind her of the delicate nature of their conversation and the need to maintain total discretion. Victoria understood – this was not her first rodeo....

As soon as Dave hung up with Victoria, his private cell phone rang again. It was Veronique – the recipient of his second text. She confirmed that not much had changed about the new material at UE, but she could sense panic had set in. The launch date was only six weeks away and the headquarters was being pressured to provide a firm direction. She was expecting something big was in the works; what it was, she did not know, but it must be related to the new super alloy as she had been getting a lot of questions from Dr. Carr, their VP of Engineering.

"Veronique, I cannot over-emphasize how important it was for me to get this update and that I really feel awful about having to ask you to betray your company's trust. I promise to make it up to you and find an opening to spend some time together as soon as this panic is over. Please let me know if there are any developments in this matter," Dave said with a sly smile on his face. His ex-lover had once again come through for him, and he had once again justified his action as all is fair in love and war, and he was definitely in a war and determined to win it this time and win it at any cost.

He was relieved to hear that Dr. Kumar had yet not succumbed to Bill MacMillan's "persuasions" and that the new material was still very much in the game.

He then took out the little bottle of scotch that he had locked in his personal desk drawer, poured himself a stiff drink and downed it. He desperately needed it.

CHAPTER 32

AWS&T, AUGUST 1 ISSUE – NEW ENGINE UPDATES

With the new engine launch date approaching fast – just six weeks away, there is still no news if either or both of the engine companies have acquired rights to the new material. When approached by AWS&T, both companies reiterated their plans to launch the new engine on schedule and meet the aggressive goals which can only be achieved with MRI 297. AWS&T can only assume that the companies must have undisclosed plans to acquire the new material in time for the launch.

AWS&T has also learned from confidential sources that the Chinese Aero Engine Company has significantly ratcheted up their activities on what appears to be a competitor to the western new engine program. Except for hot end materials, the Chinese do possess most of the technologies required to design and manufacture an aero engine in this thrust size. It is not clear how the Chinese plan to get around the very stringent export control regulations of the West and get the critical materials technology, but AWS&T would not put it past the Chinese to get what they are missing by means that might not be completely above board. They have done it before in other key technologies and can certainly do it again.

With only six weeks to go, it has all come down to the new material and the man holding the key, Dr. Ravi Kumar, appears to be on the run from what AWS&T has learned have been attacks on him and his family. AWS&T will continue to actively monitor the developments and provide updates as they become available.

CHAPTER 33

MOROCCO – SIX WEEKS TO LAUNCH DAY...

Dr. Ravi Kumar and Dr. Caitlyn Mariko were on their way to Palermo, Sicily. Ravi had called his friend and old colleague, Dr. Riccardo Sperra the night before and asked him for his help with their flight to safety. Dr. Sperra, like the other international friends of Ravi, had spent a year at the Materials Research Institute as a visiting fellow from the University of Palermo. He had come with his wife Jenny and had been a guest of Ravi and Caitlyn, while the young couple looked for their own place in Ithaca. Jenny, who was also in the Computing Science field, had found a lot in common with Caitlyn, and had become a good friend of hers.

Even after Riccardo and Jenny had found their own place, they were frequent visitors of the Kumars and got to meet their three daughters and became good, trusted family friends. Ravi was confident in his friend to be discrete and do all that he could to provide them a safe haven and help them weather this storm. Riccardo was in a unique position to do so. His was from a well-entrenched and very well-connected family. His grandfather had been the mayor of Palermo and his father ran one of the largest olive oils producing companies in Sicily. Dr.

Sperra himself was a full professor in the Materials Engineering Department at the University of Palermo, and Jenny was the Chief Information Officer at her father-in-law's company.

Ravi gave Riccardo a brief summary of the events of the past weeks starting with the conference in New York and his meetings with the Chief Executive Officers of the two US industrial giants and their demand for an exclusive rights contract to the new super alloy. Dr. Sperra had been following the development of the new revolutionary material and was happy and proud of his friend for advancing the state of the art in this critical field of engineering. He also understood why the two companies would want to get exclusive rights to this game changing material.

Riccardo had known Ravi well and was not surprised to hear Ravi had turned down their extremely lucrative offers and was prepared to accept the consequences. He fully agreed with his plan for running down the three-month clock for the launch of the new engines that the two companies had on their drawing boards and try to keep a low profile during that time.

During the phone call the night before, Ravi had gone through their time in Marseille, France and Ouarzazate, Morocco and their efforts to stay underground. But by means still befuddling to them, he had added, they had been found out and had been physically attacked and warned of more serious consequences to them and their family if **"they did not do the right thing."**

He told Riccardo that he did not know who was behind these threats and could only guess it might be one or both engine companies. He did not mention the letter he had gotten from Dr. Xi Ping and the possible involvement of the Chinese Government. He was still waiting for a confirmation from his friend from China about the authenticity of that letter and considered it highly unlikely for the Chinese to be behind this given the insurmountable export control rules and regulations.

Dr. Sperra had a fully furnished apartment in the beautiful town of Monreale, not far from Palermo, the capital city of Sicily. He and Jenny used it for their weekend getaways and to unwind from the busy and hectic life in the city where they both worked. He offered it to Ravi and Caitlyn for as long as they needed and assured him that they would be safe there with its discrete location in Pellegrino, the mountain that ringed around the city of Palermo and its surrounding towns and villages. For additional safety, he was going to arrange for around-the-clock guards for them from his father's company's security department. He would also alert his vast network of local law enforcement contacts in the city of their arrival and ask them to do whatever they could to keep them safe while they were in town.

Ravi thanked his old friend and arranged for him to meet them at the Palermo International Airport. Caitlyn was in the room during his call and had heard everything; she was quite excited to be spending some time with her old friend, Jenny. They were both relieved to hear about Riccardo's apartment in the mountains and the protection from his father's company's security team. But they did not have any doubt that it would only buy them some time before the long reach of the two US aero engine companies and their ruthless chief executives got to them again.

After they had gotten back to their Kasbah in Ouarzazate from the harrowing trip to Ait-Benhaddou and the near miss that could have easily resulted in a major injury and maybe even death, Caitlyn thought about the note she found in Farah's pocket. It was clear to them the note was meant for Ravi, and it was fortuitous for him and a bad break for Farah that the two of them looked alike to a foreigner and the hapless Farah had to take the fall for him. Caitlyn had memorized the note and wrote it down for the benefit of Ravi:

"We are watching you. We all need Electricity. Do the right thing for yourself and your family at any cost. Our patience is running out"

They had so far been attacked three times – in Ithaca just before they left, in Pont du Gard, France and most recently in Ait-Benhaddou, Morocco. The three notes were all anonymous and mostly identical with no explicit demand except to do the right thing. The notes could be from one of the two engine companies or from someone else like the Chinese Government. The last note had increased the threat level with the phrase "***Our Patience is Running Out***" and for the first time gave a clue of its origin – ***We all need Electricity***. Was it pointing to United Electric, and if so, how did the Oriental Man in Pont du Garde fit in? He could well be working for UE or General Technologies, or was he sent by the Chinese Government? If he was part of the Chinese Government, was his friend Dr. Xi involved, and why had he not heard from him so far? Was he in some trouble back in China? He had seen him at the conference, and although he had not gotten a chance to talk to him except to say a brief hello, he had appeared to be fine. So why had he not replied to his email? He had known his Chinese friend to be quite sincere, and it was unlike him to not respond to him even after several days. Ravi was getting quite worried about Dr. Xi and could only hope that no harm had come to him and his family.

And what exactly did "Do the right thing" mean – did it mean sign the exclusive rights contract? He could not think of any other reason why someone would be after him and his family. After all, he was just a researcher in what most people would consider a boring and unglamorous field. It had to be the new super alloy and the exclusive rights contract. If so, it had to be one of the two engine companies. The Chinese, if at all involved, would need to collaborate with one of them to get access to the new material, and even then, it would be close to impossible to get around the very stringent US export control laws.

Caitlyn and Ravi convinced themselves that it was one of the two US engine companies, and their bet was on United Electric and its chief executive officer – Bill MacMillan. The phrase "*We all need electricity*" had been added in the last note to point Ravi in the direction of UE without explicitly implicating the company or its chief executive but leaving no doubt who was behind it. Ravi could call Bill MacMillan again and confront him, but he knew even if Bill took his call, what his response would be and if he were not behind it, Ravi would have made an enemy of one of the most powerful men in his industry. He could not afford that. He needed more evidence. He needed more data....

For now, his only choice was to keep running, stay under the radar, rundown the launch clock, and bring them back to the negotiating table. That they would be back at the negotiating table was not in question – the question was how to stay alive for the next six weeks. Their hope was that Palermo would be good for at least a few weeks before they must be on the run again. The city and its surrounding region were rich with history dating all the way back to the Greeks and before that era. And even with the restrictions imposed by the need for them to be inconspicuous, Caitlyn and Ravi were determined to explore and experience as much as possible the rich culture of the Sicilian Island. Once again, they reminded themselves that although it might appear to be foolish for them to be acting as sightseeing tourists with people constantly trying to harm them, they were not going to be scared of whoever was behind these attacks. They were determined to hold their ground and stand up to the bullies who were after them. They also needed to become hunters again and find out who was after them. There were still six weeks left and the attackers were clearly becoming more desperate, ratcheting up the screw, and could get to the girls if they did not succeed in getting them to capitulate. They could not let that happen and had to smoke them out even if it meant they were going to be the bait themselves.

In a weird, fatalistic way, the Kumars were looking forward to this trip and were ready to face whatever tomorrow brought.

CHAPTER 34

PALERMO, SICILY – SIX WEEKS TO LAUNCH DATA...

They landed at the Palermo International Airport just before noon. Riccardo and Jenny were there to greet them and drive them to their apartment in Monreale, about hour and half drive from the airport. Vincenzo, one of the security guards that was going to be with them during their stay, was in the other car. He would be rotating with two other guards to provide them around-the-clock protection during their stay in Sicily and would travel with them wherever they decided to go. The local Monreale Carabinieri, a unit of the national police force, would also be providing extra surveillance of their residence which was about a mile inland in the hills from the famous Monreale Cathedral, a major tourist attraction for visitors to Palermo and Sicily. It would provide a good cover, at least for some time, to Ravi and Caitlyn and not make them overly conspicuous amid the mostly Italian population of the village.

Riccardo and Jenny had well stocked the apartment so that they did not need to go out until they had settled down and felt safe in the neighborhood. They gave Ravi a local, unlisted phone to call them at any time if there was an emergency. The guard would be checking on them but would try and remain inconspicuous to not attract any unwanted attention. He had Ravi's unlisted phone number and would be calling him every half hour to check on them. The guard was on the phone's speed dial and would respond promptly and would also alert the Carabinieri if he got a call from Ravi.

Ravi and Caitlyn then got down to making this place in Sicily their home – their third since they had left their real home in Ithaca. Their hope was that this would be their last home before their flight was over and they could safely get back to the States. Somehow, they were not so sure about it and had the uneasy feeling that this was just another stop in their worldwide run to stay alive. They were getting tired but had no choice but to take it one day at a time.

For the next few days, they stayed at home, venturing out for a walk in the neighborhood not far from their apartment. They could see the guard following them. This they expected. What they did not expect, and it could well be just their imaginations, was that they were being watched by someone besides their guards and the Carabinieri who periodically patrolled their neighborhood in their marked, Italian-made vehicles. But so far, their time in Monreale had been without any incident. They had learned a few words in Italian – Buongiorno, Grazie, Prego – Good morning, thank you, please – and were pleasantly surprised how far these few words with copious use of hand gestures could get them with the people they met during their walks.

The locals and the occasional tourists who happened to venture near their villa were curious about the foreign looking couple but were friendly and welcoming. There was, of course, no chance of Ravi and Caitlyn blending in and if someone were looking for them, it would not be hard to find them. They would be the proverbial sitting ducks for a professional hit team. But so far nothing had happened, not even an obtuse threat. They felt emboldened and were ready to see more of Palermo and the Sicilian Island starting with the famous Monreale Cathedral next door. They also wanted to ferret out anyone who may be following them and provide some clues of their pursuers.

Monreale, a corrupted word from Monte-Reale or Royal Mountain was home to what many calls the most beautiful Cathedral in Sicily or perhaps all of Italy. Its history dated to the Normans who came after the reign of the Arabs in Sicily ended in the late 12th century. While the external edifice and dome of the Cathedral were impressive and massive, the true beauty of this monument was inside the walls which showcased the harmonious existence of the many cultures and religions of the time – Arab, Byzantine, Jewish, and Catholic. The murals and frescos on the walls narrated stories from the Old and the New Testaments, bringing many of their characters to life in mosaics, which the legend had it were done by artisans from Constantinople in pure gold.

Ravi and Caitlyn were awestruck to explore this UNESCO World Heritage site literally a stone's throw away from their apartment in the hills. They spent a whole day taking in the Cathedral and its gardens without any incident and no obvious sign of anyone following them. Vincenzo was shadowing them, maintaining his distance, keeping his trained eyes on the crowd. So far, so good. Time to go explore Palermo, and it happened to be a good time to do so. Riccardo had talked about the once a year festival in honor of the Patron Saint of Palermo – Saint Rosalia – and the tall chariot built to look like Noah's Ark that the citizens of Palermo dragged through the streets of the city with the statue of the saint sitting on the top.

The procession would start late in the evening from the Palermo Cathedral and would make its way through the old streets, many of which dated back to the Phoenicians – the original inhabitants of the city. On that night, Riccardo had said, it looked like the whole town of Palermo had come out to celebrate the festival and partake in the merry making that was now part of it.

For Ravi and Caitlyn, it was a unique opportunity to get out and experience the sights and sounds of this old historical city, but they needed to be extremely vigilant. The large crowds provided them some protection but could also make it easy for the hit teams to attack and then get lost in the sea of people.

They thought hard and long about taking the risk. In the end their adventurous spirits and their curiosity, combined with the determination of exposing their attackers, got the better of them. Ravi called Vincenzo and told him about their intentions to attend the festival.

"Dr. Kumar, I don't think that is a good idea. There would be thousands of people at the festival and it would be extremely hard for us to keep an eye on you and also look out for any attackers. Please think about it again," Vincenzo pleaded with them. But Ravi and Caitlyn had made up their minds and were going to go with or without him. Vincenzo had no choice but to reluctantly go along with their decision.

They were apprehensive about the evening, but not scared, and were determined to fully participate in this once in a lifetime opportunity, keeping an eye out for any sign of trouble. They slowly and carefully made their way to the big Noah's ark shaped float mounted on a large wagon. Saint Rosalia's statue was mounted on the top and there were several ropes attached to the float. A line of young and old men and women were going to drag the "ark" through the streets of the city. Anyone and everyone were welcome to join and lend a shoulder. Ravi and Caitlyn joined the procession, also taking their turns on the rope, feeling like locals and not afraid of being attacked. It was as if they were under the protection of the patron saint of that historic town and she would keep them safe.

But their survival antennae were still fully extended, their sixth sense warning them that they were being watched and followed as they traversed with the crowd. The security guard was constantly shadowing them but maintained a respectable distance, trying not to make them too conspicuous.

The procession soon ended, and the crowd slowly began to disperse. Their pulses were racing with anticipation, but nothing happened; no one was following them, no one gave them a shove, no one tried to inject them with a needle, absolutely nothing – it was quite anticlimactic. Yes, Saint Rosalia was indeed looking after them….

They each felt relieved. It looked like they had gotten through another day of their flight unharmed. But they were also no further in discovering anything about the people who were behind the attacks. They reminded themselves not to be complacent but at the same time not to live in terror. They would be on guard, but they would not be cooped up in their apartment. There were still four weeks left until the launch date and they were certain neither them nor the girls were safe yet and they had to get the perps before they got them. Their time in Sicily had not yet ended and they were ready to explore more of it.

Caitlyn had heard much about a historical town, Agrigento, almost due south of Palermo, a 2-hour train ride on the other side of the Sicilian Island. They decided that would be their next destination….

4,000 miles away from Palermo, Dave Ward received a text from Victoria:

"Watching and moving as planned. Waiting for an opening to encourage. Others here too."

3,000 miles away in Beijing, China, at the regional headquarters of a multi-national, the security chief received a text:

"At any cost here. Will deliver message imminently. Others also watching."

4,000 miles away the United Electric security chief got a text that read:

"Eyes on at any cost. Others watching too. Will be moving soon."

CHAPTER 35

AGRIGENTO, SICILY - THREE WEEKS TO LAUNCH DAY...

Ravi and Caitlyn had been in Sicily for more than 2 weeks and thus far they had only met Sicilians who could not be more different than their preconceived notion about them – an island filled with gangsters and crooks belonging to the infamous Mafia. Like most Americans, their knowledge of the people who inhabited this island was based on movies like the "Godfather" and "Valachi Papers." They had found the reality to be more like the two sisters they met on a local train who in spite of the big language barrier had hugged them and using copious hand gestures had urged them to visit the "belle" city of Agrigento. They were pumped at the thought of finally visiting that "belle" city as the train to Agrigento rolled away from the platform at Palermo.

It was a beautiful fall day – a little on the hot side for this time of the year, but a perfect day to travel through the lush olive groves on the nearly half empty local train. Vincenzo was riding with them. He had contacts in the Agrigento constabulary and had alerted them about their trip to the city. Riccardo also knew the mayor and had sent him a note about his friends and asked for his help in keeping them safe.

Caitlyn, as usual, had studied the colorful history of this old city and was giving Ravi a crash course as the train rolled by the fertile Sicilian countryside.

"Agrigento was founded in the 6th century BCE by the Greeks and quickly became one of the leading cities in the Mediterranean Sea. The city was located on a high plateau overlooking the sea and the surrounding area providing a strategic military location for the rulers of the day which included 6th century BCE Greek tyrants Phalaris and Theron. It became one of the oldest democracies after Theron's son was overthrown. Around 400 BCE, the city was seized by the Carthaginians, who defeated the Greeks and dissolved its democratically elected government, turning the city and the province into an autocracy."

"The Romans came next after about 150 years," Caitlyn continued, "capturing Agrigento and making it a part of their ever-expanding Roman empire. Agrigento prospered and remained part of the Roman empire, its citizens acquiring Roman Citizenship under Julius and Augustus Caesars."

"It was ransacked again in the 9th century CE by the invading Arabs until the Norman conquest in the 11th century CE.

The city, like the rest of the island of Sicily, became part of the modern-day Italy only in 1860 with the arrival of Garibaldi from the mainland as an emissary of King Victor Emmanuel of the unified state of Italy."

Caitlyn paused just for a moment to look outside the window of their slowly ambling train and took in the sights of the copious olive trees in full bloom at this time of the year. Despite their current predicament, she was enjoying the beautiful sights and sounds of this ancient land as their train rolled by.

"Throughout all this constant upheaval," she continued, "and change of the ruling empires, the city and the province of Agrigento kept its ancient Greek culture and civilization and many of the monuments built by the Greeks some 2,500 years ago.

The ancient Greek monuments, with many in ruins but many others still standing tall, are the magnets that attract people from all over the world and are now on the UNESCO world heritage register."

"Most of these monuments were in the *Valle dei Templi* or the Valley of Temples," Caitlyn continued with her narrative to the very attentive Ravi and now Vincenzo, as well, who admitted he did not know much about Agrigento and was happy to get this history lesson from her.

Caitlyn was now in full swing with her story and felt gratified by her attentive audience.

"There are seven temples," she continued, "dedicated to the various Greek Gods and deities and were all built in the same style as the Parthenon of Athens – the Doric style. One of these seven temples – the temple of Concordia, built about the same time some 2,500 years ago – is still standing as it was then with all its 78 columns and the temple roof intact, unlike the Parthenon which is now mostly in ruins. It is a UNESCO world heritage site and ranks as one of the finest examples of the ancient Greek Civilization. Then there are temples dedicated to the Greek God Zeus, Heracles, or Hercules as we know him, to Juno, and to Vulcan."

"The Carthaginians destroyed many of these monuments and left them in ruins, and that is how we find them today except for the Temple of Concordia."

"The Valle dei Templi," she added, "was a small acropolis or town of the ancient Greeks and had in addition to the temples, large amphitheaters for public gatherings and festivals."

Caitlyn then talked about an interesting Google news article she had read just the day before about the open-air super-secret conference held at Agrigento in the Valle attended by the who's who of Silicon Valley. The tech world royalty, the news item reported, had been meeting at this remote and historical site to get inspirations from those that lived here 2,500 years ago. They had been doing it for the last several years for unstructured brain storming that lasted over the weekend, the latest one being just this last weekend.

Ravi, who at the best of times was only a reluctant partner to Caitlyn when it came to ancient monuments and museums, was all excited about visiting Agrigento and the Valle dei Templi. The fact that the Silicon Valley titans had just been there only the day before made this visit even more interesting for him. So, as the train pulled up to the station, he was ready to take on this historic site and all that it held in store for them.

Dr. Sperra had arranged for a Limousine to pick them up at the station. The car would be with them for the rest of the day and was cleared to go inside the Valle complex. Although they were not famous or celebrities like those who had been there on the weekend, Dr. Sperra had used his contacts at the local constabulary to assign a patrol car to them during their visit to the temple. Vincenzo was going to ride shot gun with the Limo driver.

It was a pleasant drive from the train station to the Valle. The driver had taken the city road to give them a tour of the historic Agrigento city, much of which dated back to the Greeks and Romans. They got to the Valle just before noon for a quick bite at the site cafeteria. Then it was on to the ancient monuments and the tour of the Valle itself where crew had begun taking down the elaborate set up for the weekend gathering of the Silicon Valley elite.

Caitlyn and Ravi felt goose bumps when they saw the stage on which the modern-day philosophers - Gates, Page, Brin, Pichai, Cook, Zuckerberg et al. held court with 300 or so of their compatriots from that other "Valle" – the Silicon Valley. It was not hard to imagine the spirits of the philosophers of yester years - Socrates, Pluto, and Archimedes, also present on that same stage listening to and counseling their modern brethren.

It was a weekday and the crowds were thin. Spread across the vast area, there were few people at each of the temple sites. Ravi and Caitlyn discreetly studied the crowd and did not recognize anyone they had seen before. There was an Oriental man, but he was older and was with an Oriental lady. Nothing like the man they had seen back at Pont du Gard. There were several white European men, but they all were older and most likely part of an excursion that had come in at the same time as them. Nothing and no one appeared to be suspicious. But then again, they reminded themselves, if there were professional hit teams after them, they did not expect them to be conspicuous. They needed to be cautious and on guard as they toured the Valle and its memorable sights and sounds.

Their first stop was the Temple of Heracles. It was one of the oldest temples at the site and was mostly in ruins, with only a few of the original Doric columns still standing. The temple was located on a high plateau providing a magnificent bird's eye view of the old town below. Ravi and Caitlyn mostly remained together, with Vincenzo following them close by. They could also spot the two constables from the local constabulary in the distance keeping an eye on them and the surrounding area.

From there it was on to the other temples, most of them in ruins but still standing after all these years. Then they arrived at the main temple – the Temple of Concordia. It was going to be their last stop.

It was the most preserved of all of the seven temples in the Valle. Caitlyn had given a sneak preview of what they were going to see when they got to this temple, but it could not have begun to capture the glory and magnificence of the edifice that stood in front of them.

The Greeks had built this temple in the 5th century BCE in honor of Concordia – the goddess of Harmony. It was, like the rest of temples of the day, a place of worship for the Pagans who before converting to Christianity believed in celestial supremacy and worshipped all that represented both the physical and abstract forms of the universe. Harmony was one of those abstract forms. Many of the Pagan statues discovered in the temple were subsequently removed by the 6th century Christians who converted it into a basilica and used it for conducting regular mass and services.

The engineer in Ravi was simply awed by the dimensions of the temple and how the Greeks would have built it. At about one third the size of a football field and 2 stories tall, it had 78 columns each 20-foot-tall and intricately carved with 20 flutes that covered the entire length of the column. The diameter of each of these columns provided a large enough area for a person to hide and wait, if they so desired.

Caitlyn was taking her own time carefully studying the engraving on the columns and the arched roof of the temple. Ravi had separated from her and was almost at the end of the building. Vincenzo was somewhere in the middle trying to keep an eye on both, but just barely able to. That was when he heard a volley of shots coming from the direction where Caitlyn was. Ravi also heard the shots from the other end of the building. He sprinted faster than he ever had. They got there about the same time and saw Caitlyn lying on the floor and a bloodied man just besides her.

She looked unconscious but still breathing. Ravi put his right ear on her chest and although not a doctor, he knew enough to conclude her heart was pulsing at the normal pace. He then saw the two police officers from the local constabulary, who had also heard the shots, running towards them. Vincenzo was on the phone calling the Emergency Services. The man laying besides Caitlyn was a white man and had gunshots on his back. He was lying face down and most probably dead. Ravi was busy trying to revive Caitlyn by sprinkling water on her face. Her face twitched ever so imperceptibly but it was enough to give Ravi the hope that she was all right. He did not know what had happened, but he did see an object that looked like a white cotton swab in the man's right hand. He was still holding it. He then noticed a loose piece of paper near Caitlyn about to flutter off into the wind. Instinctively, he grabbed it and shoved it in his pocket.

A small crowd had gathered around them, keeping their distance – curious, but not wanting to get too involved. The two police officers soon arrived at the scene. The older one put on his gloves, checked the man, and found no pulse. He gestured to the younger police officer with his hand on his throat – the man was dead. Vincenzo was talking rapidly in Italian to the police officers and telling them about Ravi and Caitlyn and what he knew about the incident.

He did not actually see what had happened, as Caitlyn had been hidden behind one of the 78 columns and Vincenzo did not have her in his sight. He had no idea where the shots came from or who fired the shots. The police officers had radioed for back up and were taking down Vincenzo's statement. The older police officer took the cotton swab out of the dead man's hand and smelled it and nodded knowingly. He then motioned to Vincenzo and asked him to smell the swab. Vincenzo was in the security business and immediately recognized the smell as that of a mild form of anesthetics used as a tranquilizer to immobilize a person. Its effect typically lasted for 30 minutes to an hour depending upon the person, giving the perpetrator enough time to do their business and get away. The business could be anything ranging from robbery to kidnapping to simply delivering a message….

Caitlyn was beginning to stir from her sedation but still on the floor. Two more cars from the local police precinct and an EMT van pulled up at the base of the temple. They all rushed to the column where the crowd had gathered, and the two constables were talking to Vincenzo. Just as the two police cars and the EMT van was pulling up, a white box truck with the *Valle dei Templi* livery on its sides was pulling off the curb. Ravi had noticed it parked there when they were coming into the temple and had thought nothing of it. He screamed, "Stop that truck!" Vincenzo heard the scream and stopped talking to the police officers and ran towards the truck. But it was a long run and the truck had had a head start and was getting away fast. Vincenzo tried taking the license number down but could not get it from his position. The white truck was soon out of his sight.

The police officers began to interview the crowd to see if anyone had seen anything but got nothing from the mostly foreign tourists who either had truly not seen anything or did not want to get involved with the notorious Italian law enforcement. They dismissed the crowd from the area and turned their attention to the still panting Vincenzo who had come back from his chase, Ravi, Caitlyn, and the man who was pronounced dead by the two EMT technicians.

Vincenzo repeated the same story he had just finished telling the first two police officers while the EMT technicians finished examining Caitlyn. He also told them about the white box truck. The police officers had also seen the truck and the livery on its side and had not suspected it to be part of the attack. They were not so sure anymore.

Caitlyn was now awake and blinked her eyes while the technicians gave her some more water, which she drank thirstily. Ravi held her hand tightly and was almost in tears, relieved to see she was OK. The technicians confirmed the initial findings of the first two police officers and Vincenzo that Caitlyn was administered a mild form of anesthesia to temporarily immobilize her, the effect of which lasted about 30 minutes.

The police officers searched the dead man and found no identification. The technicians had brought the stretcher with them and began to load the dead man for transporting him to the city morgue and autopsy. The initial conclusion was that he was shot from behind by multiple rounds and had died on the spot. The police officers conducted a walk-through examination of the site but did not expect to find any clues or evidence. They had been through many similar incidents and knew that this was the work of a professional hit team and the dead guy with no identification was also part of a professional hit team. They also knew their chances of finding the killer or killers or the identification of the victim was slim to non-existent. They had seen that many times, too.

Caitlyn was now fully awake and whispering to Ravi and the lead police officer what she remembered. She was behind one of the 78 columns studying the vertical flute engravings and admiring the superb workmanship of the ancients. It was hard to believe the engravings, which were most likely done manually, were so precise and uniform – exactly 20 flutes equispaced around the circumference. She had her fingers on the column to get a feel of the texture, when she felt a hand come from behind and douse her with a swab. She knew it was some form of anesthesia – she had experienced that during a recent colonoscopy procedure. She remembered her instinctive karate response and trying to take her attacker down, but the effect of the drug was too powerful. She remembered going limp before losing consciousness and she had been about to fall, but her fall was broken by a hand, and then she heard the faint sound of gun shots – appearing to come from a distance. It all went black after that as she went down and awoke to see Ravi sprinkling water on her. And that was all she remembered.

The lead police officer had taken down her statement.

"Can you stand up?" Ravi asked Caitlyn, feeling relieved but still quite concerned.

"Yes," she nodded.

Ravi and Vincenzo helped her get up. There was nothing more to do. Vincenzo gave the police officers his contact information and asked them to give him a call if they had any more information about the attack. The lead police officer promised he would get in touch if they had new information and if they wanted to talk to Caitlyn and gave Vincenzo his card to call him if she remembered anything else that may help solve the case.

Vincenzo summoned the Limo driver to the temple and asked him to drive them back to Monreale. They did not have the strength to take the train back and needed to put Agrigento behind them as soon as possible.

Ravi and Caitlyn knew their time in Sicily was over. Time to move again. Three weeks to go, another attack and still no further in finding out the identity or the motive behind the attacks. And the attacks were becoming deadlier. They had to keep running but not hide. They had to keep being the prey and keep the gun aimed at them. They had to protect their three girls at any cost.

CHAPTER 36

CHICAGO - THREE WEEKS TO LAUNCH DATE...

Jack Stevens was going through the latest trade publications – Aviation Week & Space Technology and Flight International and did not see any updates on the new engines. With the launch dates of such a major program getting closer, the trade publications should have been filled with stories – some true and some just rumors. But he found nothing and found it to be quite unusual.

In previous new engine programs, the engine companies would normally let out snippets with claims of superlative performance of their engines, just to keep the readers and decision makers from airplane and airline companies interested. But this time around, with what would certainly be the most expensive engine programs in the history of commercial aviation, not much was being reported. Jack found this odd and troublesome.

His airline needed these new engines to reduce the average fuel burnt by his fleet of aircrafts, many of which were old and inefficient. The ticket prices had not gone up, and in many cases due to stiff competition from low cost no frill airlines, were in fact coming down. The increasing fuel cost, which was now becoming the largest single component of the overall aircraft operating costs, was eating into the profits, making the airline business not quite attractive to Wall Street and the large institutional investors. Several legacy airlines had already given up, declaring chapter 11 bankruptcy, and a few of them had done so more than once. Thus far he had managed to keep American Aviation afloat, but it was becoming harder and only a matter of time before he might have to go the same route. He was not going to let it happen, not on his watch.

He absolutely needed to refresh his fleet with the new fuel-efficient airplanes powered by the revolutionary engines that were currently on the drawing boards of the two major US engine companies - United Electric and General Technologies. He needed to talk to Bill MacMillan and Dave Ward, their CEOs, and get a firsthand status report on their new engines. United Electric was the current supplier of most of the engines in his current fleet. He called Bill first on his private number.

Bill MacMillan answered on the first ring – a call from the CEO of one of his largest customers demanded that. He had a good idea why Jack was calling, but he wanted to hear it from him.

"Jack, good to hear from you. How are things going at American Aviation?" Bill asked, sounding cheerful.

Jack Stevens immediately got to the point,

"Bill, how is the new engine going?"

Bill did not know that Jack Stevens had started his career as a young aerospace engineer in the aero engine business working for General Technologies. He had gotten the flying bug as a General Technologies test engineer assigned to the flight program of the first generation of airplanes powered by the new turbofan engines as opposed to the turbojet engines which powered the airplanes of the time.

Bill was not an engine man, but he knew the turbojet engines produced thrust by sucking in a relatively small amount of air at the front and then ejecting that air at extremely high jet velocity from the rear – hence the name jet engine. Newtons third law of motion – "every action has an equal and opposite reaction" – then came into play propelling the airplane forward in reaction to the speeding jet coming out from the back. This worked but was not a very efficient process. The fuel consumption for these engines was remarkably high; comparing them to automobiles, these engines were gas guzzlers with low miles per gallon.

The turbofan engines, he had learned, unlike the turbojets, produced most of their thrust by the large fans attached in front of the engines to suck in a large amount of air. They then only needed to eject this large amount of air at smaller jet speeds to produce the same amount of thrust as the pure jet engines. This significantly increased the efficiency of the engines, giving a much better fuel burn or more miles per gallon. The larger the fan, the better the mileage until it reached a point where the fan became too heavy to carry, offsetting the fuel burn gains.

The engine that Jack Stevens had worked on many moons ago was still considered a historical milestone in the annals of aviation, having provided a large step improvement in the fuel burn relative to the turbojet engines it replaced. Jack was understandably proud of his contribution to the aero engine industry and even after leaving the engine business for the flying gigs, first in the air force and then in a commercial airline, the aero engine was his first love.

So, when he asked Bill, how things were going, he was expecting to get a detailed low down on the design of the new engine. Bill told him what he knew and confessed that he was not an engine man and could only talk in generalities and mostly about the strategic and business side of the new engine program.

"Jack, the program is moving along as planned. My preliminary engine design group has been working on it for the last 18 months and have accelerated their work significantly over the last three months. The full-scale launch is planned for 3 weeks from now with a target to fully certify the engine in 48 months."

"Are you going to use MRI 297?" Jack asked.

Bill had received a cryptic text from his security chief late last night informing him Dr. Kumar and Dr. Mariko had gotten away from his team and were still on the run. He was seething and was going to rip the security chief for his failure to make ***Dr. Kumar do the right thing***. Jack's call had interrupted him, and he had to think fast to come up with credible answers.

"We are negotiating with Dr. Kumar for licensing MRI 297 but have not yet signed a contract." He then tried to bluff Jack by saying, "In any case, we have back up plans for the new engine if for some reason that falls through."

Jack was not buying it. He knew Bill was bluffing. He knew that with the current state of the art, the other levers designers had – increasing the size of the fan, increasing engine temperatures, increasing engine component aerodynamic efficiencies, were not enough to achieve the step change in performance the new material would provide.

He called Bill's bluff and asked, "That is good to hear, Bill. Can you tell me a little more about your backup plan?"

Bill did not have an answer and tried wiggling his way out,

"Jack, I am sorry this is not my field of expertise and I cannot give you details of our backup plans. But we do have them. Let me get back to you with the details and with my experts in the room to answer your questions." But before hanging up, Bill reiterated that United Electric's primary path for the new engine was with the new material and that he would find a way to bring Dr. Kumar on board.

Jack did not need to know, and Bill was not going to tell him how he planned to do that, but Jack had been in the game long enough and had known Bill well enough to know what "find a way" meant. He was a firm believer and practitioner of the mantra "Don't Ask, Don't Tell" and knew you did not climb to the pinnacle of major corporations by being a "Play by the Rules" kind of person. And that was all right by him so long as Bill delivered....

CHAPTER 37

CHESHIRE, CONNECTICUT –
THREE WEEKS TO LAUNCH DATE...

Dave Ward was about to wrap up for the day when his private, unlisted phone rang. It was Victoria from Palermo, Sicily. Dave was quite apprehensive when he answered the call; it was close to midnight in Sicily, and if Victoria was calling him at this hour, it must be urgent and most likely not good news.

"Dave, you did not tell me it was a dangerous assignment," Victoria said frantically, without any preamble. She had been through some rough battles before, but in all those she knew the enemy well and was usually over prepared to stack the odds in her favor. She did not like to lose.

Although Dave had briefed her on the situation with Dr. Kumar and that both his company and the competition were trying to get the rights to the new material, he had not fully shared with her the dangerous and potentially deadly nature of her assignment. He had given her some indirect hints about the dangers involved when he talked about the Kumars almost being broadsided and run off the road in Ithaca and the incidents in France and Morocco, but he had left it to Victoria to draw her own conclusions and make the necessary preparations.

"What is it, Victoria? You sound frantic," Dave said, trying hard not to sound frantic himself.

"I just lost one of my key operatives. So, yes I am frantic and angry at not getting the entire picture from you and that what you were asking me to do could get one of my people killed."

It probably was Victoria's fault that in her zeal for the new US business and the soft corner she had for Dave, she had not fully anticipated the danger of the mission and prepared accordingly. Although her people had reported seeing others watching the Kumars, she had not expected there would be shooting. She had selected the site carefully, a public and tourist place, to temporarily knock one of the Kumars out, deliver the message, and slip out stealthily. Now she was down a man and not sure if the message got delivered. In her books, this was a botched job and she was furious with Dave for not telling her everything – but even more furious with herself for not being fully prepared.

"I am terribly sorry to hear that, Victoria. I must admit that I knew that the job could be dangerous and in fact I did tell you that, but I did not expect it to result in anyone getting killed. Can you tell me what happened?"

Victoria gave Dave a detailed run down of the events in Monreale and Palermo looking for and not finding a suitable opening to deliver his message. She then came to the Kumars' visits to the Valle dei Templi in Agrigento.

"Agrigento," she said, "looked like an ideal place, being an exceptionally large complex frequented by tourists and many opportunities to find an isolated place where my people could carry out the mission. And they almost succeeded. One of my men, who has been with me for more than 20 years, was the look out and his partner while another one of my experienced operatives administered the sedative to Caitlyn and broke her fall by catching her just as she was going down. He was tasked to leave the piece of paper with the printed message on it on Caitlyn and surreptitiously slip out and mingle with the crowd."

"The look out," Victoria continued, "was standing at the other end of the temple when suddenly he heard a volley of shots. He could not see where the shots came from or who fired them. All he saw was a box truck with the Valle dei Templi livery marked on its sides leave immediately after the shots were fired and the Kumars' security guard and the local police rushing to the scene. He knew his partner was either dead or severely injured. His instructions were to leave the area and not risk being apprehended. None of them had any identification on them and could not be easily linked to me and certainly not to you."

"Now, the lookout man did see his partner attempting to give the piece of paper to Caitlyn before she went down, but he was not sure if she got it and what happened to it in the ensuing confusion and panic. He did take down the number of the box truck, which he was almost certain was the getaway vehicle for the shooter with a dummy license plate number," Victoria added.

Dave Ward was relieved to hear that he or General Technologies could not be linked to what was certainly going to be a messy investigation into the attack on the Kumars and the shooting.

"Victoria, let me say one more time about how sorry I am about your man. I will make sure that his family is well taken care of and thank you very much for doing it for me. I should have warned you about other groups also following the Kumars, but I never thought it would come to this and result in shootings and loss of life. Please, forgive me." Dave's soothing words sounded genuine and helped Victoria calm down. He then asked her what the message was and if that could in any way identify him or his company. Victoria assured him the message:

"Do the right thing, Technology will rule the future"

would not mean much to anyone else unless they knew the full background. Dr. Kumar would understand, but for anyone else it would be musings of some technocrat fanatic attending the just concluded gathering of the Silicon Valley aficionados at the Valle.

Dave had already heard much of this from his security chief who had hired a private investigating firm to track the Kumars. They had been providing reports on their whereabouts ever since Ravi and Caitlyn had left the US. Dave had in passing mentioned about the surveillance to Victoria when he had asked for her help in their first call on the subject. However, he had not gone into any details and the logistics of how the surveillance was done. In fact, he himself did not know all the details and had left it to his security chief to work it out with the private security firm. He did know that the security company constantly rotated the detectives on the job, selecting them to look and act like normal tourists and blend in with them.

The old lady from Austin, Texas that the Kumars had befriended in Ait-Benhaddou was one of the firm's operatives, as were the two Sisters in the Papal Palace in Avignon and Salon de Provence, and the Oriental couple in Pont du Gard. The short, professor looking man roaming around the Temple of Concordia while Ravi and Caitlyn were there was also one of their detectives. He had discreetly witnessed the episode with Caitlyn as part of the crowd and had reported back to the General Technologies security chief. The short, professor looking man's report generally supported what Dave had heard from Victoria. The man had added one more important detail in his report.

He had seen the Indian man pick up the piece of paper that the man who was shot was trying to slip to the Oriental woman.

Dave did not share this information with Victoria. He wanted Victoria to think her mission was not complete and to use it to extract other favors from her and minimize his obligations to her in the future. He was being "Dave Ward – the polished and cerebral man who in many ways was more dangerous than his United Electric nemesis."

He once again thanked Victoria for all her help and reiterated his condolences for her lost man. He told her that he would let her know if he needed any more help from her and assured her that whatever happened in the future, his commitment to help her qualify as one of the certified suppliers to General Technologies stood and that he would do everything in his power to help her expand her business in the US.

Before hanging up, he extended a personal invitation, hoping to assuage her anger and grief at the loss of one of her trusted lieutenants,

"Victoria, I would love for you to find some time to come over. I so very fondly remember our time together and the special relationship we had. All those evenings and nights we spent lying on the oversize bed in our hotel and talking about our projects and our lives and the many accessories we used to make our short time together memorable. I still have some of them and would like nothing better than to recreate some of those magic moments with you in my private cottage in the Vineyards."

He could feel Victoria blushing and hot as she accepted his invitation….

CHAPTER 38

CHESHIRE, CONNECTICUT –
THREE WEEKS TO LAUNCH DATE...

Dave Ward still had the smile on his face and a tingle in his skin thinking about Victoria and all the passionate nights they had spent together. He could feel her smell in his tiny office at MIT, where she would come to see him with one excuse or other. He had quite enjoyed being an adjunct professor at the university and the adulations from his students, specially the female students – most of them foreigners – and from some of them, a little more than adulation. But that was then, now back to the present. There were only three weeks to the drop-dead date for the launch of the new engine, and he was no closer to getting Dr. Ravi Kumar to sign the contract. His attempt to "encourage" him to do the right thing had so far not been successful. He could continue on this path and double down on his "encouragement" medicine or just accept Dr. Kumar's conditions. Time was running out and he needed to decide. He was deep in thought when his private cell phone rang again.

It was Jack Stevens, CEO of American Aviation and the launch customer for his engine that will power the new aircraft and slated to become the biggest single airplane model in the history of commercial aviation. Maybe this was an omen and his conversations with Jack would help him decide which way to go with Dr. Kumar. Dave had known Jack for a long time and enjoyed his in-depth conversations with him about the aerospace industry in general and aero engines in particular. He had not had the occasion to talk to him in depth since he had taken over the reins of General Technologies and was happy to take his call on the first ring.

"Dave, how are you doing? It has been a long time since we talked; in fact, I don't think we have connected since you left United Electric," Jack Stevens said.

"Yes, you are right, Jack. It has been quite a while since we last talked. I still remember, you were in the middle of getting your long-term plans finalized and you wanted to talk to me about where the engine companies were going. How did that come out?"

"I remember that, too, and we did put together our comprehensive strategic plans; it depends a lot on where the engine guys are heading, specifically with your new engine design." With that, Jack got to the point right away and just like he had done with Bill MacMillan, he asked Dave how the new engine was coming along and if General Technologies had obtained rights for the new material from Dr. Kumar.

Dave began by reviewing with Jack the several concepts his preliminary design team had been exploring, all of which increased the fan size and the proportion of thrust produced by the fan, thus improving the engine's ability to convert fuel energy into useful work – which in the case of aero engines was the forward thrust. This, in the business was called propulsive efficiency. Ever since the days of Sir Frank Whittle, the co-inventor of the modern jet engines, the propulsive efficiency had been gradually increasing, mainly by increasing the size of the fan.

Jack was quite familiar with this definition. He also knew there was a limitation to how far the size could be increased due to the need for the fan to run at lower speeds to maintain its aerodynamic performance. The lower fan speed meant that the turbine driving that fan would also run at reduced speed, which was not good for its performance. So, there was a conflict between what was good for the fan and that for the turbine driving it. This was not new and not limited to aero engines. Designers of high-performance machinery such as an aircraft engine had faced this dilemma ever since the time of Wilbur and Orville Wright and had successfully solved it by balancing and optimizing the conflicting requirements. He asked Dave how General Technologies was addressing this in their new engine.

Dave was in his element now.

"Jack, I will be happy to talk to you about our studies and the directions we may be heading. But this is our company confidential and proprietary information and I would be grateful if you kept it to yourself." He then jumped into the discussion of the major trade studies GT had done involving Geared Fan and Direct Drive Fan. In the Geared Fan, Dave continued, a compact gear system was introduced in between the fan and the turbine driving it. The gear allowed the fan and the turbine to run at different speeds – the fan slower and the turbine faster. The fan and the turbine could now both run at their desired optimum speeds. The gear thus addressed the conflicting speed requirements of the fan and the turbine if they were connected directly – as would normally be the case – in what was known as the direct drive configuration.

Jack, being an aero engine designer at heart, was fascinated with what he was hearing from Dave. He asked him the next obvious question – if that were the case, what would limit the size of the fan, and what were the trades? Something had to give. Gear systems had been around for long time, so why was it that only now they were being considered seriously?

Dave expected this question. This was why he so enjoyed talking to Jack, knowing it would be a stimulating discussion to say the least. "The trade," Dave continued, "was the weight of the fan and the higher drag force– which was the measure of the resistance the air imposed on the engine as the airplane passed through it. The bigger the fan, the heavier it was and the higher its drag was, which reduced the overall propulsive efficiency benefits the big fan would provide. There was thus a sweet spot for the fan size and the challenge was to find that sweet spot. And I think my designers have found that sweet spot."

As to why the Gear System was only considered now when they had been around for long time, Dave added,

"Jack, your question about why use gears now when they have been around for a long time, well the gear technology not only at General Technologies but in the aerospace and automobile industries in general has gone through an order of magnitude of advancements. What it means is that the capability, reliability, compactness, and weight of gear systems have now reached levels where they could be used in high performance applications such as commercial jet engines."

"But," Dave continued, "even with the sweet spot for the fan size, the larger fan in the geared configuration has still become heavier, the frontal drag has gone up, and the gear system even if more reliable and capable has added one more very complex part to the engine. And anytime we add a new part, we increase the chances of something going wrong which means the reliability of the overall engine is reduced – not a good thing."

Jack understood all that. His next question showed a bit of impatience as he asked Dave if GT had converged on a going forward configuration for their new engine. Dave hedged his answer by saying the two designs – geared and direct drive were remarkably close in their overall performance and that GT was going through some additional studies to finally decide upon their chosen design.

Jack then asked about the fuel burn improvements and if either of two configurations would meet the targets of reducing it by close to 50%, a target that could potentially be achieved using the new material invented by Dr. Kumar and his laboratory.

Dave's answer was again not very satisfying to Jack when he heard that without the new material, the best they could do was a 25% reduction in fuel consumption, still huge, but nowhere close to the 50% target reduction that could be achieved with the new material. Dave quickly went on to add that his team at GT were working around the clock to squeeze additional performance benefits from the new engine. He then summarized the work his Materials Engineering group were doing in coming up with their own version of MRI 297, talking about the encouraging results they had had thus far and that he was hopeful that the technical issues with the GT version of MRI 297 would be resolved by the time they were due to formally launch the new engine.

Jack had carefully listened to Dave's detailed and well thought out commentary on General Technologies new engine and said before hanging up,

"Dave, I understand that and thank you for sharing your thoughts. But I am not convinced you can come up with your own version of MRI 297 in time for the new engine. You need to carefully think about it."

Dave had those concerns himself and did not argue with Jack. He assured Jack that he personally and his company – General Technologies - were committed to delivering on the new engine metrics and he was in the process of negotiating with Dr. Kumar and encouraging him to sign on with his company. He promised Jack to keep him informed of the developments.

The code word "encouraging" was not lost on Jack. Dave, just like his archrival, Bill MacMillan, was telling Jack that the Kumars could not be running for ever and that he, Dave Ward, was going to bring them back to the table by means which were better left unsaid.

Dave now knew what he had to do. Jack had helped him with his dilemma, and he had a go forward plan. He had to double down on his efforts to bring Ravi on board. Time for a final show down with Bill MacMillan....

CHAPTER 39

PALERMO, SICILY – THREE WEEKS TO LAUNCH DATE...

Dr. Ravi Kumar and Dr. Caitlyn Mariko arrived back from Agrigento, shaken but not yet broken. Ravi still did not have a clear idea of who was behind these attacks. He could once again only infer from the cryptic notes he had received that it must be the engine companies trying to pressurize him into signing the exclusive contract. It was frustrating and exhausting. This last attack on Caitlyn had truly shaken his nerves and he was ready to give in, but Caitlyn was not. Her Japanese Irish heritage had ingrained in her a stubbornness and defiance against injustice that compelled her to get up and fight. The greater was the hit, the greater her spring back. She convinced Ravi that they were almost at the end of their flight and that if they gave up now, all the running they had been doing for the last two and a half months would have been in vain.

She also reminded him why they were running in the first place – to fight the deleterious effect of burning fossil fuel on the climate. She argued, "Ravi, we cannot just be bystanders while our planet is being irreversibly damaged. Tell me, what are we going to say to our girls? How are we ever going to justify to them our surrender to the bullies and not do all what we can to preserve the planet they would inherit? No, we cannot back off now."

An exclusive rights contract with either of the two companies, Caitlyn had continued, would almost certainly eliminate the losing company from the commercial engine arena and would destroy competition which drove the industry to strive for higher and higher goals. "No." Caitlyn said with finality, "We will not give in. We will fight."

Ravi took a deep breath and nodded. He was happy to see Caitlyn back as her usual, feisty self. He knew Caitlyn was no bleeding-heart liberal; she was just like him – middle of the road, he on the red side and she on the blue side. They had their differences when it came to the important societal issues – he passionately believed in meritocracy and opposed lowering the standard of excellence simply to satisfy optics of equality through diversity. She, on the other hand believed it was necessary to accommodate diverse people, especially those who had been left behind due to historical injustices. And this was just one of the many issues they did not always agree completely about.

But on the issue of climate change and the impact humans were having on the climate, they were as close as two peas in a pod. They were not the extreme fanatics wanting to halt all human activities to save the planet but believed that they had the moral and ethical obligation to do what they could to arrest if not reverse the change humans were causing to the climate. They could see the evidence of this change in the climate even in their own lifetime with the polar ice caps receding, ozone layer being pierced, and the cycle of hot and cold temperatures becoming more extreme and more unpredictable, causing draught, food, and water shortages impacting an ever-increasing area of the planet.

Caitlyn had gotten Ravi back on track. He was not going to capitulate. The question now was where to next. How could they best dodge the bullet for three more weeks?

But first, they needed to go over the events at the Valle and that was when he remembered the piece of paper he had found next to Caitlyn at the Temple and had instinctively shoved in his pocket before anyone else could see it. Maybe it was not the right thing to do – tampering with the evidence – but he had to find out if that piece of paper offered any clues about their attackers. Trying to get it back through the legal Italian system would have been an exercise in futility. In his mind, it was a legitimate justification for his actions.

Ravi fished the paper out of his pocket and straightened it. As with the other notes he had received over the last three months, this one had a cryptic printed message:

> **Do the right thing. Technology will rule the future.**

And just like with the other notes, there was no signature or any clue as to who sent that note. What they were sure about was that the note was for them. Although it did not say so, **Do the right thing** most likely was pointing to the contract and that Ravi and his institute should sign the contract with the right engine company. The second phrase – **Technology will rule the future** was a new one. It was different than the last note which said **Everyone needs Electricity.**

What were these notes trying to tell them? Was the new word *Technology* pointing to *General Technologies*, one of the two engine companies and the *Electricity* in the last note – was that for *United Electric*, the other engine company? Assuming that to be the case, who was the person who got shot, and who shot him? Was the dead man, a GT man, and the shooter a UE person? That made the most logical and obvious sense. And where did the Chinese fit in – assuming they were in it? And if they were not – how could the note from his friend Dr. Xi be explained?

Ravi was no further now getting answers to his questions, here in Sicily, then he had been in Morocco or Marseille or Ithaca. The only thing that he was further in, was time. They had managed to survive for 10 weeks and now they were just three weeks away from running the launch clock down. He and Caitlyn needed one more stop in their worldwide hide and seek from the two ruthless and all-powerful captains of the aviation industry. They had survived so far, and he made a mental redetermination to surviving the next three weeks, with the assurance Caitlyn was with him. And this time it was Ravi who had a crack of a smile as he began to narrow down their next and hopefully final stop.

"Caitlyn, we just have three weeks left before the launch clock runs out. We need one more stop before we can think of returning back home. Any thoughts, where we should go next?" Ravi said.

"You know, I have been wondering how we were found out. Now, I know that these multinational corporations have long reach and resources and would have eventually located us. But the ease with which they could do that is perplexing. Could it be that an Indian man with an Oriental woman made us an easy target for our pursuers? If so, we should find some place where we will not stand out so readily," Caitlyn replied.

"I think you may be on to something here. I have been thinking about it as well and have just such a place in mind where we should be able to lose ourselves with the local crowd," Ravi said.

"Where is that?" Caitlyn asked.

"Darjeeling, India," Ravi said with a smile on his face.

"That sounds interesting. But why do you think we will be safe there?' Caitlyn asked.

"Well, I am not sure there is any place on earth where we would be completely safe from professionals such as those who had been after us, but with my Indian and your Oriental looks we should be able to blend in with the local population who are a mix of Indians and Nepali Gorkhas who look like you. We will not stick out as foreigners as we did at our earlier getaways," Ravi replied.

"Sounds good. Let us do it," Caitlyn said.

Darjeeling/Kalimpong – north of the well-known Indian megapolis Calcutta or Kolkata as it was now called, was a famous town at the foothills of the great Himalayan mountains. The population mix there was Indians – like Ravi, and Gorkha Nepalese who looked much like Caitlyn. Darjeeling, famous for its Tea Plantations, was also the seat of several well-known educational institutions with Kalimpong, its sister city, about 20 miles from Darjeeling, home to one of the premier research institutes in the region. The region was remote and could be accessed only by car or bus from the closest airport, about 60 miles from Kalimpong. It should be an ideal location for Ravi and Caitlyn to hide and hopefully run down the final clock. It also had a lot of history, giving them time to explore without being conspicuous foreigners.

Dr. Shiavats Pradhan was the director of the institute and an old colleague and friend of Ravi and Caitlyn from his days at the Materials Research Institute. Ravi had sent him an urgent text and had received an immediate response with an invitation to be Dr. Pradhan's guests for as long as they needed to be there. Dr. Pradhan would make all of the necessary arrangements.

Dr. Pradhan, a Nepali Gorkha, came from a long line of Gorkhas well-known for their bravery and fearlessness. They had shown their metal in the Second World War and many wars before that, as part of the British Army, and had earned a reputation as a fierce fighting force. The Gorkhas now made up a large part of the Indian Army, many of its soldiers coming from the towns and villages of the Himalayas like Darjeeling and Kalimpong.

Before flying out to Kalimpong, Ravi had called Shiavats from Sicily's Palermo airport and had brought him up to speed with the events of the past 10 weeks, emphasizing the dangerous and potentially fatal nature of their run. Shiavats assured Ravi that that they would be safe there and that he would arrange for a team of experienced Gorkha fighters to be with them during their stay in India and that he would himself try and be with them as much as possible to help make their stay safe and enjoyable. Ravi and Caitlyn were grateful at their friend's generosity and relieved to know that they would have one of the finest group of fighters protecting them and helping them run down the new engine launch clock. But they were not naïve enough to think that they would be able to hide there without ever being found out by their pursuers and were eventually going to be discovered no matter where they hid.

Their only wish was that they would have enough time before the hit teams got to them to take in the beautiful Himalayan sights and sounds. And just like their other hideout locations, they were not going to be scared into simply biding their time inside their residence, but were going to explore the region, albeit carefully and well protected by their security team. This was the home stretch and they were ready for the final sprint, still hoping to find out who was after them and their family and what exactly it was that they wanted. They were once again going to play the dangerous game of the hunted becoming hunters and spring a trap with themselves as the prey as they ran down the clock at the foothills of the Himalayas.

CHAPTER 40

KALIMPONG, INDIA - TWO WEEKS TO LAUNCH DATE...

Their plane landed at the Bagdogra airport in the afternoon. It was an hour flight from Kolkata International airport, where they had arrived the night before and had stayed with one of Ravi's cousins for the night. Ravi had blended in well with the rest of the 10 million inhabitants, many of whom also looked like Caitlyn, Oriental women of Nepali heritage. They did not stick out as they had done at their previous stops and if they were being followed, which they were sure they were, it would have been close to impossible to track them amongst the throngs of Indians at the airport. Ravi's cousin had whisked them off to their residence in the city and had dropped them back at noon for their flight to Bagdogra. Ravi was confident they had not been followed or at least not followed by someone who could do them harm.

Dr. Shiavats Pradhan was waiting for them with a contingent of six Gorkha fighters suitably equipped to provide them protection at the levels normally reserved for visiting dignitaries. Their procession of three vehicles took them through the narrow and winding roads from the plains of the mountains, through the many hamlets scattered all over the route to their destination of Kalimpong, about 60 miles from the airport and 4,000 feet above the sea level. It was a slow but scenic drive through the hills and valleys of the lower Himalayas. It took almost three and half hours to make the 60-mile trip. They all felt relieved when they safely reached Dr. Pradhan's residence in the gated compound of his institute with around-the-clock security. Ravi and Caitlyn were going to be staying in the guest apartment attached to Dr. Pradhan's house. The Gorkha fighters would be guarding their apartment – in teams of two, rotating every six hours.

Ravi and Caitlyn settled down in their new residence enjoying the fresh mountain air and the view from their balcony of the Kanchenjunga – the third highest peak of the great Himalayan mountains - right after Mount Everest and K2. They enjoyed the hospitality of the Pradhans and the simple home cooked Indian/ Nepali meals. They did not leave the premises of the institute for almost a week, well protected by the campus security and the Gorkha fighters. They were trying to run the new engine launch clock down and they were succeeding. No attack so far, and no sign of any intruder. But just like at their other stops, Ravi and Caitlyn were becoming restless with their virtual imprisonment. They had to get out and explore the beautiful hill side, the tea gardens, and the many historic monuments and ruins scattered all around the Darjeeling/ Kalimpong region and the neighboring states of Sikkim and Bhutan. Both Caitlyn and Ravi had been voraciously reading the fascinating history of the region and its people and could not wait to learn more about them and experience them firsthand. It meant taking some risks. That evening at dinner, they expressed their wishes to Shiavats and got his enthusiastic support. He also understood the risks and was going to make sure the six

Gorkha fighters assigned to protect Ravi and Caitlyn were fully briefed about the plan and were ready to take on the mission.

They would start with exploring the old town of Kalimpong first.

Although Ravi's birthplace of Varanasi was only 500 miles from Kalimpong, growing up, that was a very long-distance travel and it might just as well have been on another planet. He did not know much about the region or the towns scattered around the Himalayas. It was all new to him, as he learned that before being part of India and the old British empire, Kalimpong was part of the autonomous region that comprised the kingdoms of Tibet, Bhutan, and Sikkim. In fact, the name Kalimpong, by one account, was a Tibetan word meaning "Assembly of King's Ministers." There were other meanings of the word as well in the Nepali Lepcha dialect, but they all referred to a tribal meeting place.

The strategic location of the town, close to two natural passes or gateways, through the Himalayas, between India and Tibet, made Kalimpong an important stop on the old Silk Road that connected the Orient to Europe, and was an important trading post for furs, wools, food grains, and of course silk. The remnants of the old Silk Road had seamlessly merged with newer roads and spawned a modern version of the old trading post, becoming one of the major draws for the visitors to this hill station city.

For Caitlyn, the history buff, this was the natural first stop in their exploration. It would also be a good test of the security system Dr. Pradhan had put in place, and a way to check if they could detect any obvious tails on them.

As they were making their way to the Silk Road and the bustling markets surrounding it, Caitlyn talked about its fascinating history, which was as old as the written history itself.

It had been in existence, in one form or another, for more than 2,500 years, even before the time of Alexander the Great. The old road, which was still in use in some parts of the world, spanned three continents, starting from the Chinese planes, travelling westward through the Himalayas, the Hindukush mountains, the rugged plateau of the Pamirs in central Asia, winding its way through what was now Iran, then Egypt, and the northern African countries.

From there it made its way to Europe and the countries around the Mediterranean Sea. Alexander and his conquering Macedonian army travelled on this road as did many others that followed him in search of the riches of the East. But the main purpose for the road was intercontinental trade in the many goods that flowed between East and West.

From East came silk, fur, spices, and food grains which the west paid for with gold, precious stones, and horses. And it was not just goods that travelled on this road, it was also the main artery for communication and interchange of knowledge and culture between the civilizations that existed and thrived along its route. Key inventions like paper and gun powder were exported from China to the countries along the Silk Road, while advanced mathematical concepts such as Algebra were brought back from Egypt to the East. The Silk Road, Caitlyn had added, was the precursor of the modern Information Highway – a fact that made their visit to the remnant of this old highway even more interesting and contextual for her.

They spent most of the day exploring the endless rows of small and large kiosk like trading posts, selling everything one can imagine. The market was bustling with people of all persuasions milling around, many just looking and taking in the history that was the Silk Road. Caitlyn and Ravi generally stayed together, with the six Gorkha fighters making an invisible protective circle around them. They were on guard, as well, looking for anything or anyone out of the ordinary or suspicious. They were certain they were being watched, just not certain by who and by how many.

Their first day out of Dr. Pradhan's campus had been quite enjoyable, educational, and uneventful. The security detail Dr. Shiavats Pradhan had put in place seemed to be working. Ravi and Caitlyn were now ready to venture out further.

As they were discussing with Dr. Pradhan where they should be visiting next, Ravi's unlisted phone rang. It was his secretary again,

"Ravi, I got a call again from At Any Cost," Helen, his secretary, said.

Ravi's heart almost missed a heartbeat as he heard that dreaded message. He was sure they had been found out and were being watched.

"What did he say?" Ravi asked.

"He hoped you had enjoyed your visit to the Old Silk Road and that time was quickly running out. That you needed to think about your ladies, all four of them, and that this time they will not miss," she answered, and added she did not quite understand what he was talking about.

"I know what he was talking about. Did he say anything else?" Ravi asked.

"Only that at this time of the year the Tea Gardens in Darjeeling and the Peace Pagoda are the places to be and that he will be waiting for you there," Helen said.

"Anything else and did you try and find out his location?" Ravi enquired.

"Yes, he cautioned you again to not get the authorities involved and no, he seemed to be calling from a burner phone, and the phone company could not tell me anything about his location," Helen replied as Ravi ended the call.

Caitlyn and Dr. Shiavats had listened to the phone call since Ravi had placed Helen on the speaker phone. Ravi was clearly shaken, but at the same time, relieved to know that the three girls were still safe and that he had another shot at finding out who their attackers were. Dr. Pradhan was not fully convinced if it was safe for them to visit Darjeeling, but he understood their dilemma and the need to keep the focus on them rather than on their three daughters.

They all agreed they would be going to Darjeeling and would visit one of the better-known Tea Gardens there before making their way to the Peace Pagoda – a magnificent Buddhist temple just on the outskirts of the city.

Darjeeling, the famous tea city, was also was the home of Peace Pagoda, and was a natural draw for both, the Buddhist/Christian Caitlyn, and Hindu Ravi. After all, Buddha was a Hindu prince before he renounced his kingdom to attain enlightenment and become the Buddha living the life of an ascetic and giving birth to the new religion of Buddhism.

They were apprehensive, but just as was the case at their earlier stops, had begun looking forward to their visit to this fascinating hill station town, about 7,000 feet above sea level, just on the foothills of the great Himalayas. The launch clock was slowly but surely winding down as well, with just one week to go before the two engine companies had to launch their new engines if they had any hope of getting them certified in time for the new airplanes. Ravi could not wait for their flight for life to be over and to get back to doing his normal, boring, and routine tasks at his beloved Materials Research Institute. Still, even with only a week to go with the light at the end of the tunnel, but Ravi could not shake off that uneasy feeling he had in his bones, a premonition of something terrible awaiting them at the next turn. Perhaps it was nothing, just his tired and fatigued brain and soul playing tricks on him. The call from his secretary had not helped and had only heightened his anxiety. He could only hope for the best, pray, and wait.

CHAPTER 41

DARJEELING, INDIA - ONE WEEK TO LAUNCH DATE...

Darjeeling, from their compound in Kalimpong, was less than 30 miles away. But these were 30 miles in the lower Himalayas with just a single winding road, with the mountain on one side and a deep ravine on the other. The road was designated as a National Highway, but one would have to really expand the definition of highway for this and all the other highways in the region with potholes galore from the incessant avalanche of boulders dropping on the road. The Public Works crew charged with maintaining these mountain roads were constantly fighting one rockslide after another just to keep the road open for the steady stream of vehicles ranging from the expensive European automobiles to the two and four-wheel jalopies that plied from one hill station town to another. On a good day, the top speed was no greater than 25 miles per hour which on most normal days dropped down to 10 to 15 miles. The trip to Darjeeling from Kalimpong, all of 30 miles, would take almost three hours.

Ravi and Caitlyn were up early in the morning to give themselves a whole day to visit and explore Darjeeling and the beautiful, picturesque ride which would take them through the lush tea gardens that grew the world-famous Darjeeling tea. Dr. Pradhan had arranged for an additional team of two Gorkha fighters bringing the total to eight. Ravi and Caitlyn would ride in one of the Mountain SUV's with two Gorkhas and the other six would be in the other vehicle.

They were on the road as the sun was still rising. Their journey would take them west from Kalimpong at 4,000-foot to close to the 7,000-foot altitude of Darjeeling. The morning air was laden with dew drops that had fallen and collected over the flora and fauna and was emanating an exhilarating fresh aroma that could only come from a well nurtured mountain forest such as that which surrounded their drive. Ravi and Caitlyn, despite their recent travails, could not help but be bright eyed and bushy tailed looking forward to their first stop at a tea plantation, learning all about this ancient drink that had made its way from China to India and then the rest of the world.

At the plantation, they joined a group of other visitors. The Gorkhas had taken position near the entrance and had their hands on their weapons as they inspected the crowd for anyone who may fit the bill of *At Any Cost*. Ravi and Caitlyn were also on their guard constantly, looking over their shoulders to detect any suspicious movements by other visitors. Nothing stood out.

The tour was led by their guide and local historian, Ms. Anjana Bhowmik. She was the right person to give them an introductory lesson in the fascinating plant.

High quality tea, she began, such as the Darjeeling tea, came from evergreen bushes that grew in tropical or subtropical climate with a minimum of 50 inches of yearly rain fall. The rain needed to be scattered over the entire growing season and should ideally be followed by days of sunshine to allow the plants to flourish and provide healthy leaves. The ideal altitude for cultivating premium quality tea was between 4,000 and 5,000 feet, with the tea gardens located on the hill side to prevent water from accumulating and oversaturating plant roots, providing a natural irrigation system as the water flowed down the hill. Darjeeling and the small towns around it met all these requirements and were therefore home to many tea plantations scattered throughout the region.

The tea was harvested several times during the year, Ms. Bhowmik continued, known as flushes – in the language of the tea aficionados. The first flush was in the spring when the leaves were still nascent, tender, and small, and were considered to have a delicate and light texture. It was also the most valuable harvest.

The autumn flush, which followed the second flush of summer, was still on the plants and ready to be harvested. It would have a more mature taste to it, which was another way of saying it was somewhat darker and to non-connoisseurs bitter. The autumn or third flush, while still quite expensive, was the cheapest variety of Darjeeling tea. Ravi and Caitlyn would get a taste of the freshly picked autumn flush as part of their tour of the Tea Garden and its processing facility, located just about halfway to their destination of the day – The Buddhist Peace Pagoda temple in Darjeeling.

There were four major steps to processing the fresh leaves from the garden into the green, black, white, oolong or the myriad of other types of teas sold throughout the world. In some ways it was no different than what Ravi did in his Materials Institute where he took the basic metals and nonmetals coming out of the earth and converted them into extremely strong and durable alloys.

Ravi and Caitlyn had both grown up in a tea drinking culture and were quite familiar with the nuances of good and not so good tea. But they had never had anything close in taste and aroma to the tea made from freshly picked and processed leaves. For a moment, they both forgot the trials and tribulations of the past three months and completely immersed themselves in enjoying and savoring the famous tea from Darjeeling in Darjeeling itself. They were going to remember this experience for the rest of their lives, however long that was going to be.

Their visit to the Tea Garden passed without any incident and they were feeling bolder and upbeat. They did not see anyone following them, but in the busy traffic, it was close to impossible to know even if someone was following them. And if they were being followed, which they were almost certain of, they were dealing with professionals who knew how to remain inconspicuous. For now, they were not going to worry about it. They would be careful, but they fully intended to make this a memorable day and carry on with their visit to the town proper.

They were back on the road, with the morning sun still trying to make its way up the horizon. Their plan for the rest of the day was to spend a few hours in the hill station bustling town of Darjeeling and then make their way to the Buddhist Peace Pagoda temple on the outskirts of the town. Caitlyn was also hoping to get a glimpse of the mansion in which one of her favorite actors, Vivien Leigh – Scarlett O'Hara in the Hollywood classic movie *Gone with The Wind* - was born and spent her formative years in.

Until the British discovered it in the 19th century, Darjeeling was a small village in the lower planes of the Eastern Himalayas. It was alternately ruled by the kingdom of Nepal and the kingdom of Sikkim. The town only came to prominence when the British empire negotiated its transfer from Sikkim, the last kingdom to rule it, and made it part of what was then the East India Company. The British found its cool summer weather to be a natural escape from the searing heat of the Gangetic planes and the then capital of British India in Calcutta, the modern day megapolis of Kolkata.

They developed the town as a hill station and used the town as the seat of their summer government. The city attained an exclusive feel to it, with access limited to the high-ranking government officials and the rich and wealthy who would send their kids to the many British style public schools that the expatriate established. Most of these institutions were still in operation and had become private schools, with their rich Indian clientele coming from all over the country and some even from other Asian countries.

They were also a major draw for tourists who flocked to these schools to take in the beautiful sights of the Victorian Style buildings and the English Public-School ambiance that the British had imported from the 19th century England.

Growing up in Varanasi, about 500 miles south of Darjeeling, Dr. Ravi Kumar had heard a lot about the hill station and its many elite and expensive schools. He had never had the chance to visit the city, and the exclusive schools had not been in the cards for him. But he knew, some day, he would be visiting Darjeeling and find out for himself what this jewel of the Himalayas was all about, and why it was featured in so many of the Bollywood movies.

But he could never have imagined the circumstances he would be visiting Darjeeling - a naturalized American running for his life with his Irish Japanese wife trying to hide from professional hit teams let loose by some of the most powerful corporations in the world. All he could do now was to smile at the curve ball life had thrown at him and try to live the moment or as the ancient Romans would say, "Carpe Diem," and he fully intended to do so.

Ravi instructed his driver to take them to the Saint Joseph School, one of the oldest and by some accounts the best boarding school in the city. Dr. Pradhan had called the Headmaster of the school, whom he knew well, and had given him a heads up about their visit. They were expected and depending upon the time they arrived could even get to see some classes in progress. They would certainly be able to get a tour of the campus and the many old Victorian buildings still in use by the school.

They got to the school just as the autumn sun was making its way to its apex in the blue sky painted over the picturesque North Point where the school's rambling compound was located. The school was founded by the Jesuits more than 125 years ago and was still an active presbytery. As they were driving in, they could see many of the residents in their Jesuit outfits strolling the grounds of the school. The Victorian buildings were exactly as they had expected – stately and beautiful.

By Indian standards, it was an awfully expensive private school and still an extremely hard one to get in. Anecdotes abound that parents got in the queue for admission well before a baby was conceived, just to have an outside shot at qualifying for a place in the hallowed halls of Saint Joseph.

The headmaster had a sumptuous Indian meal prepared by the school's head chef. After lunch, aware of his guests' tight schedule, he gave them a quick tour of the campus and invited them to come back for a more leisurely visit if they happened to be in the area again.

Dr. Kumar and Dr. Mariko thanked their host and were on their way to the last stop of the day – the Buddhist Peace Pagoda temple. They still had a good part of the day left and the temple was only about an hour from the school. They should have enough time to explore the famous landmark and maybe even participate in some of the prayer services at the temple.

The day thus far had passed without any apparent incident, but both Caitlyn and Ravi were still wary and apprehensive about visiting an open-air monument where it would be relatively easy to get at them. Before starting the visit, Ravi was going to get with the leader of the Gorkha fighters – Captain Ram Bahadur Thapa – and bring him up to speed and strategize on the security plan against potential attacks from at least two or maybe three teams of professional hit men.

CHAPTER 42

DARJEELING, INDIA – ONE WEEK TO LAUNCH DATE...

Ram Bahadur Thapa, 55 years old, was a retired Captain from the Gorkha Regiment of the Indian army. He had served for 25 years starting as a non-commissioned officer, and then rose to the rank of a captain as a commissioned officer, a feat that did not frequently happen in the armed forces. He had seen action at all the border hot spots – in Kashmir against the Pakistanis, in Laddakh and Sikkim against the Chinese and the Bangladeshis, and Burmese on the eastern front of the Indian subcontinent. Towards the end of his tour with the army, he was part of the elite teams involved with covert operations aimed at keeping the country safe and secure.

He had been trained in the many interrogation techniques and was an expert in extracting information from even the most reluctant of adversaries. He had earned high honors and accolades for his bravery and saving lives of his fellow soldiers and was looked up to in his Gorkha community. He was a native of Kalimpong and knew the area like the back of his hand. He was also licensed to carry arms, a privilege not afforded to many Indians.

After retiring from the army, Captain Thapa launched a personal security company that he called VIP Security Services. He hired retired army soldiers from his Gorkha Regiment, many of whom had been in his platoon under his command. He started with a team of six ex-soldiers in a decrepit and obscure building in his hometown of Kalimpong, providing security to visiting dignitaries and the rich and famous from Kolkata who spent their summers in the hill station and needed protection from the prying eyes of the public.

Many of his clients were well-known actors from both the regional Bengali and Bollywood movies requiring personal security to maintain their privacy. Over the ten plus years that Captain Thapa and his VIP Security Services had been in business, they had acquired a reputation of being an honest and discrete outfit who could be trusted and who would be loyal to their customers. VIP Security Services had expanded to now have offices in most of the major towns in and around its headquarters of Kalimpong, with a sizeable presence in Darjeeling.

His company now had its own private fleet of fully equipped SUVs and a small private hospital that they used to provide health care for their publicity shy clients, as well as to treat his own staff discreetly. The locations of all his facilities were obscure and were closely guarded.

Captain Thapa ran his company as an army unit and strictly followed many of the army's hierarchical and disciplinary codes of conduct. He had a good working relationship with the law enforcement authorities who generally supported his and his clients' needs for privacy. Captain Thapa was an honorable member of the community and was given a lot of latitude in his operation by the local leaders. They had full faith in his operation and were confident that he would not engage in any illegal activities, although they recognized in his business at times it was necessary to work under the radar. They essentially operated on the principle of "*Don't Ask, Don't Tell.*"

Captain Thapa and one of his Gorkha fighters were riding in one of the two SUVs and the other five ex-soldiers in the second vehicle. It was close to an hour drive from the school, assuming normal traffic. It was enough time for Ravi to bring the Captain up to speed and give him a sense of what may lie ahead. He wanted Captain Thapa and his team to be fully vested in the mission, and the only way to do that was to lay out the bigger picture. He decided the best way to do that was to start from the beginning.

"Captain Thapa, I want to thank you and your team for providing us your protection and making this trip possible. You already know that this is a dangerous mission and have possibly heard some of the background to our visit here. But I think it is important that you should know a little bit more about us and what has happened over the last three months and why we are in flight for our lives," Ravi said.

"I agree, Dr. Kumar," Captain Thapa, known for not saying more than necessary, replied.

Ravi started by talking about airplanes and airplane engines and the key performance metrics for an engine – the amount of fuel it burnt per passenger mile and the emissions it created, contributing to the overall climate harming pollutions. He explained that the amount of fuel an engine burns and the pollution it created were two sides of the same coin – the lower the fuel burn, the lower were the climate harming emissions. He underlined the damaging effect airplanes and airplane engines had at high altitudes on the ozone layer that provided cover against the harmful ultraviolet rays from the sun, and how the loss of the protective ozone layer added to the greenhouse effects caused by pollution created by land-based vehicles – such as the SUV they were riding in.

Captain Thapa was intently listening to Ravi's narrative and nodding in understanding. Ravi then went on to talk about his Materials Research Institute and the work that Caitlyn and he did at the institute.

Dr. Kumar then talked about the new super alloy – MRI 297, that he, Dr. Caitlyn Mariko, and his colleagues at the Materials Research Institute had been working on for the last ten years. He talked about how this new super alloy would enable new airplanes and the engines that power them to burn less than half the fuel per passenger mile than the most modern airplane in operation today, and at the same time cutting down on the climate harming pollutants by almost three quarters.

"Imagine if you will, Captain," Ravi explained, "it will be like the SUV we are riding in could get 50 miles instead of the 25 miles per gallon it is getting now. It would not only mean we would be consuming half the gas, but also at the same time cutting down on the pollutants in the exhaust gas – CO, CO2, and Hydrocarbon particulates, our SUV produces by a whopping 75%."

Captain Thapa could certainly relate to that.

He gave Captain Thapa a thumbnail sketch of the two Industrial Juggernauts – General Technologies and United Electric, both members of the prestigious blue-chip Dow Jones Industrials Index.

Dr. Kumar then talked about the new engine designs that both United Electric and General Technologies had been working on to power the new airplanes that were on the drawing boards of the European and US airplane companies. The new airplanes were expected to go in service in five years, which meant the new engines must be designed, developed, and certified in four years – an extremely tight schedule given the step change in performance expected from these new engines.

The step jump in the performance goals for these new engines, Dr. Kumar continued, required the new super alloy that he and his team at Materials Research Institute had developed. Both United Electric and General Technologies have had detailed discussions with him to obtain the rights for this material. And although he was prepared to give them the required know-how, he would like to do so on his own terms – one of which was, it would not be exclusive. That meant both US engine manufacturers, and, indeed, any other manufacturer who was licensed by the US government to use this new alloy could get this new material.

Captain Thapa nodded again as Ravi continued.

However, the two companies, Dr. Kumar continued, made it clear that they wanted to have exclusive rights to the material and offered him very generous compensation – in the sum of tens of millions of dollars. And that they were determined to get the rights to the new material and to get it ***at any cost***. This was just about three months ago.

They were getting close to the Buddhist Peace Pagoda temple just as Dr. Kumar was beginning to wrap up his story and hopefully have Captain Thapa and his team fully understand the background and be completely vested in the mission.

Dr. Kumar continued, "Captain Thapa, we did not quite understand what 'At Any Cost' meant until Caitlyn and I were almost driven off the road into the lake in our hometown of Ithaca. We suspected the attack might have been carried out by one of the two engine companies, but we were not sure. And then the whole thing became further muddled by a note we received from one of my Chinese colleagues of the possible involvement of the Chinese government. We knew our lives were in danger and that we needed to get away for a while until we knew who was after us and why. So, for the last three months we have been on the run trying to wind down the critical launch clock. We are now just a week away from fully running down the clock and have no doubt that the hit teams are waiting for us right here in Darjeeling."

"Captain, let me finish my story by telling you about our three daughters. Our enemies have them in their crosshairs, as well, and even though we tried to keep them under the radar, they know where they are and have let us know that if we do not succumb to their demands, they will be going after them. We must therefore find out who these people are and prevent them from harming our daughters. That is why, in spite of the danger, we have decided to come out in the open and take our chances. Our attackers have called us and let us know they will be waiting for us in Darjeeling, maybe at the Tea Garden or the Peace Pagoda. We dodged them at the Tea Gardens. Now my gut tells me, it is going to happen right here at the Peace Pagoda, and I want us to be fully ready. Ready, not only to survive their attacks but to try and capture them alive," Ravi said, concluding his story.

Captain Ram Bahadur Thapa had carefully listened to the story and now fully understood the background, what was at stake, and why he and his team had been hired. Listening to Ravi talk about his girls and his family, he could not help but empathize and was determined to do all in his power to keep them safe. He did not have the same gut instinct as Dr. Kumar, but then again, he had just gotten involved with the project and had not developed the neural connections that controlled those instincts.

He deferred to Dr. Kumar and agreed that if not the Peace Pagoda, there was going to be an imminent attack and it could be much more violent and injurious than the previous ones. He wanted to be fully prepared and maybe over-prepared to ensure he and his team could tackle whatever was thrown at them and keep their precious charges from the United States safe.

He got on the phone and called for another of his company's fully equipped SUV's and another team of two Gorkha fighters to meet them at the Peace Pagoda temple. The temple was now in their sight, but before they reached the site and got out of the vehicles, Captain Thapa laid out a tactical plan for their visit.

He wanted Ravi and Caitlyn to be separated – perhaps one of them at the near end of the temple and the other at the far end. They would each be guarded by three of his fighters, and two of the fighters would be positioned between them, surveilling the area. Captain Thapa, himself, would be moving back and forth between Ravi and Caitlyn, keeping an eye on the crowd and ready to take out anyone that looked like they were going to attack one of his charges. He and his team were professionals and knew they had to be discrete and needed to mingle with the crowd and not be noticed by the perpetrators, who like them were also professionals.

Dr. Ravi Kumar and Dr. Caitlyn Mariko agreed with the plan and were ready to roll and start their visit to this world-famous Buddhist temple. However, before they began their visit, Ravi emphasized, "Captain, it is critical, that besides keeping us safe, you need to capture the hitmen alive. We need to find out who is behind these attacks and bring them to justice. I hope you understand and agree."

Captain Ram Bahadur Thapa simply nodded his head in agreement and opened the door of their SUV to begin the tour of the beautiful Japanese Buddhist temple and the Peace Pagoda, in Darjeeling, India….

CHAPTER 43

CHICAGO - 1 WEEK TO LAUNCH DATE...

Jack Stevens, the chairman of American Aviation was getting quite anxious and even angry at not having heard back from either of the engine company Chief Executives. Both Bill MacMillan, the CEO of United Electric and Dave Ward, the CEO of General Technologies had promised to get back to him within 72 hours with the status of their new engines but had not done so thus far. And a week had already gone by. The launch date was now just one week away, and he had heard nothing from anyone connected to the business – not the engine companies, the airplane companies or the trade magazines which usually had the inside track on such a big event in the aviation industry.

The new airplanes were important for his airline and to his legacy. This was going to be his parting gift to the company he had dedicated his life to and took a lot of pride in. The health of the aviation industry had been precarious for the last two decades with the dual scourge of high fuel cost and low-ticket prices.

The new airplanes would put the airline industry in general and his beloved American Aviation on a financially sound footing for the future. That would be his legacy, and he wanted to make sure he made it happen. He had the financing lined up for the biggest single airplane order in the history of commercial aviation and he was ready to sign on the dotted line.

All he needed now was a firm commitment from the airplane and engine companies guaranteeing the performance levels that he was assured could be met with the new material invented by the group in Ithaca and its leader, the well-respected Materials Engineering researcher, Dr. Ravi Kumar.

Jack Stevens was done talking to the CEOs; it was time to escalate.

Jack was well acquainted with the chairman of United Electric's board of directors and the chairwoman of General Technologies' board of directors. He was a fellow director with them on the boards of several leading US corporations.

The chairman of United Electric, Harry Daniels, was a retired chief executive and also chairman of the largest US bank, with an MBA from Harvard and renowned for his expertise in mergers and acquisitions. He was not an engineer and did not have much knowledge of the technical side of the business, but he was an astute businessman and fully understood the financial and marketing aspects of an enterprise. He also knew when an opportunity knocked at the door and how to capitalize on it. Jack was on the board with him in three major corporations and had spent many afternoons at board meetings held around the country. He had gotten to know him well during their many golf outings organized by the companies for their directors.

The chairwoman of General Technologies, Ms. Catherine Watson, was the retired chief executive and also chairwoman of a major Silicon Valley corporation. She was a graduate of Stanford with a major in Electrical Engineering and was one of the few woman leaders of a world class electronics company, a field mostly dominated by alpha males. Jack had met her several times and found her to be an extremely intelligent person with a keen interest in airplanes and the aviation industry. Jack quite enjoyed talking to her.

Jack's first call was to the chairman of United Electric,

"Harry, my friend how are you doing?" Jack asked. Harry Daniels knew this was not a social call. He had heard from his CEO about his discussions and American Aviation's interest in their new engine. But that was his extent of knowledge on the subject. His response was cautious and measured,

"Hanging in there, Jack. Hope you are doing well and keeping the airline business booming. So, what do I owe the honor of this call?" Jack got down to the reason for his call. He asked the chairman if he and the board had been briefed on his impending order for new airplanes which would be the largest in the history of commercial aviation and which would require the new engine his company was on the verge of launching.

The chairman and the board did have some knowledge of the subject. Bill MacMillan had included three slides at the last board meeting summarizing the latest status of the new engine and the potential order from American Aviation. The funding for the new engine program had already been approved at an earlier board meeting, where a convincing business case had been presented to request and secure the close to one and half billion dollars' investment required to develop and certify the new engine. The presentation to the board was heavy on tactical and strategic plans focusing on retaining and expanding their current lead supplier position of commercial engines. It was relatively sparse on the technical and engineering side and that suited the mostly finance and marketing focused directors fine.

At that meeting, held just about three months ago and around the time discussions with Dr. Kumar had begun, Bill MacMillan had included a slide that showed the key performance goals for the new engine. The goals were based on the current materials and did not include the step jump in performance achievable using the new super alloy. But with 25% reduction in the fuel consumption and the projected increase in market share, it was not a hard sell to the board to get the significant funding required to launch the new engine. Bill MacMillan had intentionally avoided talking about the new material and the meetings he had had with Dr. Kumar. He did not want to cloud his funding request and the business case he was making by throwing in the uncertainty created by this new super alloy to their new engine design.

Jack was not surprised to hear that the chairman knew nothing about his discussions with Bill MacMillan and the new goals for the engine that he had specified, which were based on the new super alloy. The chairman was not an aero engine man, so Jack took the opportunity to give him a quick layman's guide to the fundamentals of engine design without dragging him through the thickets of Brayton cycle and the laws of thermodynamics.

He gave him a quick thumbnail sketch of the new material and what it could do for aero engines and that the much higher performance goals specified by his airline were based on this new material.

He then went on to talk about the precarious finances of the airline industry. Harry Daniels already had a fairly good appreciation of that and did not need much convincing about the need for having better performing engines to help not just the airlines but the entire aviation industry.

Jack Stevens then underlined the significant reduction in the climate harming pollutions emitted by airplanes and the emission-based penalties the world community had begun levying on airlines, cutting into the already razor thin margins.

Jack took a pause and asked:

"So, Harry do you have any questions on what I have been talking about? I hope by now you understand how important it is for my company and yours – and the industry as a whole, and indeed, our planet – to bring the full force of new technology to reduce the amount of fuel our airplanes burn and the pollutions they create."

Harry Daniels, the chairman of United Electric, although not an expert in the field of aero engines, fully comprehended the criticality of what he had heard from one of his main customers and friend. He also had a good idea of the reason for Jack's call but wanted to hear it firsthand from him.

"Jack, I am fully with you and appreciate your calling me and sharing your concerns with me. Please continue and tell me how I can help," Harry Daniels said.

Jack Stevens picked up where he had left off.

Based on recommendations from independent experts in the field, Jack continued, the new engine should be able to achieve 50% reduction in fuel burn relative to the current state of the art, and it would be irresponsible for him or any other airline to accept anything less than that. The goal for the new airplane and hence the new engine that American Aviation was planning to order had therefore been set at 50%.

The 25% reduction that United Electric had thus far proposed was therefore a nonstarter and would obligate American Aviation and most likely other major airlines to look for other suppliers. Jack added, this was not a threat, but simply a statement of facts, and he would urge United Electric to get back in the game and adopt the new material in their engine design and set the goals consistent with the capabilities of this new material.

The chairman of United Electric digested all that he had heard from one of the most respected leaders in the aviation industry. He then replied that if he was in Jack's shoes, he would have done the same thing and that not only did he not consider this as a threat, but he even would go so far as to consider this call a service to his corporation which would have invested several billion dollars on a product which would have been out of date from the get-go. He thanked Jack for taking the time to talk to him and promised that he would personally get in touch with Dr. Ravi Kumar and do all in his power to obtain the rights to this new, game-changing super alloy. He would also have an in-depth discussion with his chief executive officer and the senior engineering staff in the aero engine division and get back to him within the next 48 hours. He then added,

"Jack, before I let you go, let me reiterate how much I and the board of United Electric value you and your company as our customer. Rest assured we will do all what we can and use whatever is out there to meet your goals and field a competitive engine that will not only meet but exceed your expectations."

As he got off the phone, Jack Stevens was relieved to get the commitment from the chairman of United Electric. He knew the chairman to be a straight shooter, a man of his word, and a good businessman. He also knew the chairman had the full backing of his board and would be able to control his temperamental and egotistic chief executive officer. He knew it was not going to be easy, but that was his problem.

Jack's next call was to the chairwoman of the other engine company – General Technologies. He needed her to also understand and buy into the significantly more aggressive goals demanded by the airline industry for the new engine that her company was due to launch. He wanted her to get personally involved in negotiations with Dr. Kumar and his Materials Research Institute, ensuring her company had the rights to the new super alloy. With just one week to the launch date, he needed for her to understand the urgency of this and work with her chief executive officer to redirect their design team to the new targets and incorporate the new super alloy in their new engine concept.

His discussions with the chairwoman were much easier, since as an engineer and airplane enthusiast, she already had a good understanding of the workings of an aero engine. Her board had also given a go ahead and allocated the funding required for the launch of the new engine which GT hoped would help them get back into the market they had lost to United Electric in the last major competition. Dave Ward had been keeping her and the board informed of the progress on the new engine design, but he had not yet shared with her the new goals set by American Aviation based on the use of the new material.

So, Jack's call and his message was a total surprise to her. She was disappointed to hear that her chief executive, whom she and the board had full confidence in, had decided to keep this critical make or break information from her and the board. She was grateful to Jack for bringing this to her attention and just like the chairman of United Electric, promised to talk to Dr. Kumar herself and ensure that they sign a contract for the use of the new super alloy in GT's new engine.

She had rightly guessed that the wily chairman of American Aviation had also had the same discussions with the competition and that the new super alloy would be part of their design as well. It would now be up to her designers to distinguish their new engine capabilities with that of competition using their ingenuity and inventiveness, even though the enabling materials may be same in both new engines.

And just like the chairman of United Electric, she assured Jack that she fully understood his requirements and that it was in her and her company's interest to pull out all of the stops and meet or exceed his goals. She promised to keep him abreast of the developments and would call him back within the next two days to provide an update.

Jack Stevens got off the phone feeling he had accomplished what he had set out to do and that he had the commitments from two of the well-respected leaders of his industry to advance the state of the art on delivering the ground-breaking performance of the new airplanes and the engines that powered them. Now, all he could do was wait.

CHAPTER 44

DARJEELING, INDIA - SIX DAYS TO LAUNCH DATE...

Despite the potential danger lurking at the door, Ravi and Caitlyn were excited to be visiting this peaceful and serene landmark just on the outskirts of Darjeeling, sitting in the foothills of the beautiful Himalaya mountains. The Japanese Temple and the Peace Pagoda adjacent to it were built to promote world peace and harmony by a Buddhist Sect following the atomic bomb attacks on Hiroshima and Nagasaki. Caitlyn and Ravi got into the main prayer room of the temple just as the afternoon chanting was beginning. The priest, an expatriate Japanese monk, was happy to meet Caitlyn, especially when he found out she was from a town in Japan, not far from his birthplace. He handed them a small drum and a stick and for the next 20 minutes they joined him and the assembled public in chanting the mantra of the sect:

Nam Myo Ho Ren Ge Kyo

They were not religious people but were surprised to come out of the prayer hall with a feeling of peace and calm that they had not often felt, certainly not recently. They marveled at the power of the simple chanting at the beat of that little drum and the repetition of those 6 simple words, the exact meaning of which they did not know and did not particularly care.

The Peace Pagoda, at about 100 feet in height and 75 feet in diameter, was the tallest building in Darjeeling and was in the same compound as the Japanese temple about a five minutes' walk from it. It housed a large statue of Buddha under a round dome called a *Stupa*. The life of Buddha from his early childhood to his departure from the world attaining *Nirvana*, was etched on the walls surrounding the Pagoda. Ravi and Caitlyn planned to spend the rest of the afternoon going around the Pagoda, in what would be their *Parikrama* or circling – a Buddhist and Hindu tradition – around the temple and learning about the life that Buddha lived and preached.

The backup vehicle with an additional team of two Gorkha fighters that Captain Ram Bahadur Thapa had requested was just pulling up as he was about to begin the surveillance of the perimeter. He now had a total of ten ex-army Gorkha soldiers at his command to secure the premises. It was a pleasant autumn afternoon in the hill station, and although a weekday, the place was filled with visitors of all persuasions. There were relatively few local people in the mix as most of them had either already seen it or had the "It is my backyard and I will see it tomorrow" mentality. It made the job of Captain Thapa and his team somewhat easier to try to identify suspicious characters. Based on what Ravi had told him, he was especially looking for people of European descent or Orientals. Although the majority of the Nepali population in Darjeeling also had Oriental features, Captain Thapa had a way of distinguishing Nepalis from those that came from the Far East countries like China, Japan, and Korea. It was not a foolproof system, but he had seen enough people from those regions to have a reliable feel of their origin.

On that day, there was a group of about fifteen mostly white Europeans that appeared to be part of some organized tour as he could see their guide with their tell-tale banner flag leading them through the complex. Although the hit men could join that group, he did not place high likelihood to that possibility. He was really looking for some lone person or perhaps a man and woman masquerading as a couple – the usual modus-operandi of a professional hit team. He did notice several such people in the crowd and assigned them for surveillance to one of his Gorkha fighter team members.

Then there was a relatively large group of Orientals as part of another one of those guided tours led by their tour leader with a banner flag. The recent affluence of the Chinese had started to be reflected in their becoming a major travelling group, with places like the Buddhist Temple in Darjeeling seeing more of them. Captain Thapa discretely examined the group and concluded that they were not a potential threat but still worth keeping an eye on. Once again, he was looking for loners or couples who stood out by their mannerisms, appearing anxious and restless. And he did notice several that fit the bill and asked another one of his team members to keep them under surveillance.

Captain Thapa caught up with Ravi and Caitlyn just as they were coming out of the temple and ready to walk towards the Peace Pagoda.

"So, how did you find our beautiful temple?" Captain Thapa asked.

"Better and more peaceful than we had expected," Ravi and Caitlyn replied almost in unison.

Captain Thapa briefed them on his observations and the actions he had taken thus far. He discreetly pointed out the European and Oriental visitors that he had identified as potential suspects and asked them to be vigilant and be prepared for a rapid getaway if the situation warranted.

The short walk from the temple to the Pagoda was uneventful and as they had planned, Ravi and Caitlyn separated – Ravi heading towards one end of the building and Caitlyn the other. Each of them was surrounded by a team of two Gorkhas who were discreetly following them, trying to mingle with the crowd and remain unnoticed. Captain Thapa took up a position somewhere in between the two and began slowly pacing the perimeter. His remaining team spread out along the circumference, with their hands on their hidden guns, ready to fire.

Ravi and Caitlyn spent some time inside the domed Pagoda admiring the giant, gold-plated Buddha statue in its well-known lotus position. There were also smaller statuettes of him in standing, lying, and walking positions. On the walls inside the Pagoda there were etchings of Buddha's teachings spawning from his basic belief that a life well lived was a life of moderation – avoid the extremes on either end of the spectrum, whatever aspect of life that spectrum happened to cover.

From there, it was on to the outside of the Pagoda to study the paintings on the side of the exterior walls depicting the life of Buddha. This would also be their *Parikrama* or circling of the holy monument – an important tradition for both the Buddhist/ Christian Caitlyn and Hindu Ravi. Caitlyn would start at the end where the life of Gautam Siddhartha began as the prince of a small kingdom called Kapilvastu in ancient India and Ravi from the other side where the prince had attained enlightenment becoming the Buddha and was now lying on his death bed, ready to depart this world and hopefully breaking the cycle of birth and death, attaining the ultimate goal of *Nirvana*.

They were reminded once again by Captain Thapa to be extra alert and be aware of the people near them as they were going around the Pagoda. He told them that he and his men would be there and would be closely monitoring their and the crowd's movements, but it was still critical for them to be on guard and scream at the slightest sign of impending danger.

It happened almost at the same time for Ravi and Caitlyn. She was on the fourth painting of the young prince leaving his palace and his wife and a little son to find peace and enlightenment, committing to a life of an ascetic and meditating under a Bodhi tree. Ravi was at the mural that depicted the Buddha having attained enlightenment, giving his first sermon to his disciples in a wooded lot in a place called Sarnath, just about 5 miles from Varanasi, India, the birthplace of Ravi.

Caitlyn was about to move to the next painting when she sensed a slight movement of a hand, belonging to a white European man, towards her. She was sensitive to such movements, having been already attacked in Agrigento, Sicily. Her third-degree black belt karate instincts warned her of the imminent danger, and she made a lightning fast karate chop at the Adam's apple of the man bringing him down like a termite infested stud. The other European man, next to her, who was perhaps his companion, broke into a sprint towards the exit of the temple complex. The two Gorkha fighters guarding Caitlyn were down on their knees with a choke hold on the man brought down by Caitlyn. Captain Thapa came running towards them and ordered the crowd who had gathered around them to disperse and instructed the two Gorkhas with Caitlyn to cuff the man and take him to one of their vehicles. He would have liked to have caught the other person, as well, but he needed to protect Caitlyn and could not afford to chase the running man. In any case, he reasoned, he at least had one of the perps and he had no doubt the man would sing once he was in his interrogation room.

Caitlyn was shaken but was otherwise OK and was worried about Ravi, so she began to run towards him.

Ravi was unaware of what was happening to Caitlyn as he stood there admiring the painting. There were several other visitors crowding around the painting, who just like him were fascinated by the picture of Buddha emanating a bright glow from his beautiful face.

Suddenly, the short Oriental man who had slowly positioned himself next to Ravi threw a hard punch with his righthand palm landing just below Ravi's right carotid artery. Ravi did not have the same reflexes as Caitlyn, being by his own admission somewhat of a klutz. The pain of that blow was so severe and debilitating that he could not breathe for the next few seconds and began to lose his consciousness as he crumpled down. The attacker was clearly a professional and had selected the precise location for the blow for it not to be fatal but cause temporary debilitation. Dr. Kumar did not have a chance. And as he was falling to the ground, he could hear or maybe just imagined in his state of hallucination someone whispering in his ears "***Sign the Contract – Everyone needs Electricity.***" Then he heard shots ringing out from a distance, and it all went dark.

The two Gorkha fighters guarding Ravi had seen the Oriental man deliver the unexpected and debilitating blow to him. One of them fired a shot aimed at the Oriental man's leg. They were only a few paces away and it was not a difficult shot.

Just then, a black SUV came roaring towards them. The Oriental man had been shot but had gotten up and started running towards the SUV, dragging Dr. Kumar with him. Captain Thapa was sprinting from his post and was screaming,

"Don't' let them get away!"

One of the two Gorkha fighters was already at Ravi's side and fired another shot at the Oriental man. The black SUV was speeding away from the scene with the driver firing a volley of shots towards the guards, leaving the Oriental man behind. Captain Thapa had made his way to the unconscious Ravi as had the two Gorkha fighters. One of them took out a bottle of water and started sprinkling it on his face.

The Oriental man was lying on the road. The bullet had hit just below the kneecap, exactly where the Gorkha fighter had aimed. He was heavily bleeding, screaming in pain and asking for help.

"Are you alright, Dr. Kumar?" Captain Thapa asked, his voice trembling. There was no reply except an imperceptible twitch. The Captain checked his pulse and it appeared to be normal. He was unconscious but was breathing normally.

The crowd around them had quickly scattered and did not want to get involved with what clearly appeared to be a planned attack by a mobster.

Caitlyn had by now reached them and was breathing hard as she asked worriedly,

"Is he all right, Captain Thapa?"

"Yes, I think so. But we need to get him immediate medical attention," Captain Thapa replied as he pulled out his cell phone and asked the drivers of all three SUVs to bring the vehicles over. The two Gorkha fighters guarding Caitlyn were leading the European man, now in cuffs, to the exit towards the SUVs. Captain Thapa barked at them to take the European man to their local facilities which fortuitously was only a ten-minute drive from the Peace Pagoda.

He then fashioned a tourniquet from his handkerchief and tied it around the bleeding leg of the Oriental man – he needed to keep him alive – and with the help of the two Gorkhas guarding Ravi carried him to another one of the SUVs which had just pulled up beside them. He ordered four of his fighters to take the Oriental man to the same place as the European.

In the third vehicle he, Caitlyn and the remaining two Gorkhas gently carried the unconscious Ravi to the back seat and laid him down. He was still breathing normally and appeared to be OK. They sprinkled some more water on him, and he twitched again. They all felt relieved knowing he would be all right until he got medical attention. Captain Thapa had already called for it at his establishment.

The third vehicle with Ravi, Caitlyn, and Captain Thapa quickly departed for the same complex to which the other two vehicles were heading.

The whole incident, which seemed like a lifetime, was over in three and half minutes.

Ravi's premonitions and fears had come true. They did not know how they were found out, but it was a moot point. What they did want to know, was who was behind this, and now they had two of the antagonists under their roof.

Captain Thapa could not wait to get to know them better and hear them sing.

CHAPTER 45

The three SUVs from Peace Pagoda with its mix of passengers headed to the Darjeeling offices of Captain Thapa's security company. The complex was located on the outskirts of the city, only a ten-minute drive from the Peace Pagoda. From outside it looked like a decrepit, abandoned building with peeling paint and a barely standing boundary wall. It had a rusted gate that appeared to be ready to come off its hinges. But this was all for external show and to keep it stealthy, away from curious and prying eyes. On the inside the building was equipped with the most modern security apparatus. There were two rooms on either end of the long corridor, which had been fitted with anechoic sound proofing material between the walls to keep even the shrillest of screams inaudible from outside.

These were the interrogation chambers.

In the middle of the long corridor and situated between the two interrogation rooms was the medical examination and operating room. This was the domain of Dr. Anand Johari, a partner of Captain Thapa and the resident physician and surgeon. He had been with Captain Thapa in the Indian Army and retired about the same time as him. And just like the Captain, he was involved and schooled in the art and science of covert operations and interrogation of enemies and criminals. After retirement, he was exploring opportunities, when his old friend called him and offered him a partnership in his still nascent enterprise and a chance to live, practice, and advance his profession in the beautiful hill station town of Darjeeling. Dr. Johari was somewhat of a loner and did not have a family. His work was his family, and he had a keen interest in developing new interrogation techniques which would be more humane yet yield the needed critical information from his subjects.

Dr. Johari was happy to get the offer and had no hesitation in joining his old friend in helping him establish his business. That had been more than ten years ago. He had found his calling and could not be more fulfilled with his life.

For the last five years, Dr. Johari had been working on developing new ways to interrogate and "encourage" his patients to talk without falling back on the inhumane methods used by governments and other private organizations such as his. His focus had been to understand how humans experienced pain and how he could induce pain without resorting to barbaric techniques like water boarding, electric shocks, or mechanical torture devices that crush the limbs and fingers, leaving the subject permanently scarred and damaged, both emotionally and physically.

His answer was a mini electrode planted just behind the ears that could inject electrical shocks to the part of the brain that perceived pain. He called it the truth electrode and with the help of a functional Magnetic Resonance Imaging or fMRI machine he could not only detect how the subjects were reacting to external electrical stimulus but also if they were telling the truth. He had successfully tested his new invention on animals and was looking for opportunities to try it out in real life interrogations.

As the SUV carrying Ravi and Caitlyn was pulling into the security company compound, Ravi was still somewhat groggy, but beginning to stir and make guttural sounds. Caitlyn and Captain Thapa felt relieved and stretchered him to the operating room where Dr. Johari was already waiting for them. He conducted a thorough examination of Ravi and concluded his current state was temporary and that he had sustained no permanent injuries.

"Dr. Mariko, I expect Dr. Kumar to be fully conscious in the next 30 minutes. I would like you to keep an eye on him and have him rest for the next few hours," Dr. Johari said.

"Let me take a look at you, as well, and make sure you are all right," Dr. Johari continued as he conducted a quick examination of Caitlyn and found her to be fully fit.

"If you would like to get back to Kalimpong after Dr. Kumar has regained full consciousness, I do not see any problem with that," he added, as he left the room to check on the European man who was being wheeled into one of the interrogation rooms.

The European man was still unconscious from the sharp chop that Caitlyn had delivered just below his left carotid artery, and just like Ravi, he was slowly coming out of his stupor as Dr. Johari walked into the room. He had been firmly strapped to the bed and was ready to be examined by the doctor.

"He appears to be fine and is fit to be interrogated. If you like, I can plant the truth electrode once he regains full consciousness," Dr. Johari said.

"Yes, do it," Captain Thapa instructed the doctor. "Now, please go and attend to the other man we captured. He is injured and is in the Operating Room," Captain Thapa added.

The Oriental man was lying on the gurney in the OR. The tourniquet that Captain Thapa had put on him at the Pagoda had slowed the blood flow from his wound, but he was still bleeding and was in significant pain. The bullet was still lodged in his leg. Two Gorkha soldiers were firmly restraining him onto the gurney while one of Dr. Johari's assistants administered a dose of pain killer and cleaned up his wound.

The Oriental man had caught a break. None of his leg bones were shattered from the bullet. The bullet had just missed the bones and was lodged in the flesh of the leg. It was a relatively simple procedure for Dr. Johari to remove the bullet and stitch him up under local anesthesia. The Oriental man was awake and witnessed the entire operation. This he expected and in fact was thankful to the doctor.

He did not, however, expect – and began screaming and cursing in Chinese – when Dr. Johari gave him a dose of local anesthetics near his right ear. The Oriental man did not know what was going on when the doctor inserted his miniature electrode through the small hole he had drilled just below the ear. He inserted the electrode deep enough into his skull such that it was in contact with the Thalamus. Dr. Johari confirmed the positioning of the electrode from X-Ray photographs of the area, before stitching him up, and was quite pleased with his work. Although he had practiced the procedure on the monkey, this was the first time he had inserted his home-made electrode into the skull of a live human being.

The Oriental man was wheeled out of the OR into one of the two soundproof rooms and was now ready to sing for Captain Ram Bahadur Thapa.

The European man in the other soundproof room was just coming out of his unconscious state and was looking around the room. He knew he had been captured and was now in a hostile place in a foreign country. He knew he was in for some rough time ahead, but he was a professional and accepted the risks and rewards of his job. He was waiting to see what lay ahead. He did not have to wait long.

The two Gorkha fighters guarding him wheeled his gurney to Dr. Johari's operating room as the Oriental man was being wheeled out. For a fleeting second, the two hitmen eyed each other, not knowing they were both after the same prize for their respective employers and masters.

The European man now was the second patient for Dr. Johari, and he was already feeling much more confident in the procedure. The man was completely restrained and was terrified to witness what was about to happen. He screamed and cursed in his native tongue, which sounded like an Eastern European language, but to no avail. Dr. Johari implanted another one of his home-made electrodes, confirmed its positioning with the X-Ray, and stitched him back up. The entire procedure took all of 20 minutes.

The European man was now also ready to talk and was wheeled into the other soundproof room where he waited for Captain Thapa and his associates to get to know him better.

CHAPTER 46

DARJEELING, INDIA - FIVE DAYS TO LAUNCH DATE - EARLY MORNING...

The Oriental man was still groggy from the anesthesia and was recovering in his room. It was going to be the turn of the European man first to get acquainted with Captain Thapa and his team. The Gorkha guards had already conducted a strip search of the man and found only a burn phone with no call logs, a wallet with wads of Indian Rupees and a few Ben Franklins, but no identifications. They also found a gauze soaked in what appeared to be a strong chemical with a pungent smell. Captain Thapa had come across that smell and recognized it as a tranquilizer that caused temporary debilitation of the victim. He showed it to Dr. Johari who confirmed his suspicions. He hypothesized that the European man was not alone and was working with others who were also present at the scene. They were going to sedate Caitlyn and snatch her with the expectation that in a public place such as the Peace Pagoda, their actions would cause a mass confusion, giving them enough time to get away with their victim before anyone could react. They did not count on Caitlyn's lightning fast reflexes from her training as a level three Karate black belt, and they paid for it.

The only other thing the Gorkha guards found was a cryptic note which said:

"Do the right thing for yourself and your family, everyone needs electricity."

The note did not make any sense to them but when they showed it to Caitlyn while Ravi was still unconscious, she immediately recognized it. The message was similar to the ones they had been receiving, the last one being at Agrigento by the man who had been shot and killed by some unknown assassin. Neither the police nor the security people guarding them there had been able to capture the killer and the dead man did not say anything before he was shot. So, although Ravi and Caitlyn had some idea about who the note was from, they needed to know for certain before deciding upon their course of action. They now anxiously waited for Captain Thapa to "encourage" his European captive in doing the right thing and revealing information to them.

The European man was now fully awake and conscious from his minor operation from having the "truth electrode" installed in his skull. He was a big man, maybe in his late forties or early fifties, with dirty blond hair. As he saw Captain Thapa, he began scowling and asked in clear but accented English,

"Who are you and what are you doing?"

Captain Thapa simply smiled and introduced himself,

"I am a friend of the person you were sent to capture."

He recapped the episode at the Peace Pagoda, taking special delight in reminding him of the hit he had taken from a woman that had completely knocked him out. He then asked him politely,

"Do you have anything to say to me?"

"I don't know what you are talking about," the man said, feigning complete ignorance and launching

into a rant that basically said he was a tourist and was visiting the country and that he was going to take the matter up with the authorities. He demanded to be immediately released; otherwise, he was going to call his embassy.

Captain Thapa kept smiling and signaled to one of the guards controlling the electrical panel connected to the truth electrode. The guard moved the knob, just a fraction of a turn clockwise. The Thalamus of the European man got the electrical signal simulating a moderate level of pain. It relayed the information to various parts of his brain. There was no physical or visible damage to his body, but the reaction was swift; he squirmed, screamed, and tried to move his limbs, which were all well secured to his bed. He was not going anywhere.

Dr. Johari's invention was working.

Captain Thapa asked the European man again,

"Tell me why you are in my country and if you have something to say."

The man, as expected, just uttered a lace of vulgarity. He was a professional and was not going to succumb easily. Captain Thapa was in no hurry.

Just then, Dr. Johari walked into the interrogation room. He was curious to find out if his invention were working, and if so, how well, and if he could help.

"How is he doing? Dr. Johari asked.

"Looks like it is working. I did see him react to the stimulus, but it was low level and besides squirming he has not said anything," Captain Thapa replied in Hindi, to keep their conversation private.

"I am not surprised. He needs a bigger dose. I would like him to be moved to the fMRI room where I can observe his brain activities as the stimulus is being applied," Dr. Johari replied.

The Gorkha guards transported the European man to the fMRI room, which like the two interrogation chambers had also been sound proofed for occasions like this. Once he was hooked up to the machine and fully restrained, especially his head, Dr. Johari explained to him what was in store. He told him about the lie detecting capability of the machine and that it was in his interest to tell the truth and be spared from the increasing level of pain, a sample of which he had already experienced. The European man simply scoffed and cursed.

Dr. Johari switched on the fMRI and one of his assistants applied a low-level voltage to the electrode, replicating what was done back in the interrogation room. The man screamed and tried to jump, but the straps kept him in place. The fMRI showed an increased level of activities in the Thalamus and the prefrontal lobe and two other areas of the brain – just as Dr. Johari had expected.

Captain Thapa then took over the interrogation and asked the man:

"What is your name and where are you from?"

No reply.

He asked the question again and still no reply.

He nodded to the assistant who turned the dial another two degrees. The applied voltage level increased to level two out of the possible ten levels – still low, but high enough for the man to scream louder and start cursing in his accented English. The color of the areas of higher activities in the brain became darker, signifying the increased level of fresh, oxygenated blood flow. But the man still would not give any answers.

The dial on the truth electrode was slowly increased to level four when the man screamed in agony and said:

"Please stop, I will tell you all you want to know."

Captain Thapa asked him the same questions – what his name was and where was he from.

The European man replied:

"My name is Kurt Polanski and I am from the Czech Republic."

The fMRI lit up in the area controlled by emotions. The man was telling a lie.

Dr. Johari showed "Kurt" the image on the monitor and said,

"Mr. Polanski or whatever your name is, I told you about the lie detection capability of this machine. See for yourself, the area of your brain that controls emotions is overactive. You are lying. So, try again and this time try telling the truth."

The European man insisted he was telling the truth.

Captain Thapa nodded to the assistant once again and this time the level was increased to six. The pain areas of the brain lit up brighter with a proportional increase in the decibel levels of the man's screams. He begged them to stop.

Captain Thapa repeated his questions. The man, now in perfect American English, replied:

"My name is Dick O'Connor and I am from Southington, Connecticut." The emotional area of the brain showed no activities. He was telling the truth.

Dr. Johari was gratified to see his invention working. They now they had a system where they could get critical information from a reluctant subject in a "humane" and non-hurtful manner. The machine had also proven to be a valuable tool in determining if the subject was truthful. His job with the

European man was done and he left the rest of interrogation to Captain Thapa and his team.

He needed to check on Ravi and Caitlyn, and the Oriental man, their other captive, who was going to be next on the fMRI machine. He quietly slipped out of the room while Captain Thapa continued his grilling of Dick O'Connor, the European man who turned out to be an American from Southington, Connecticut.

The pain perception felt by Dick O'Connor had now subsided and he was beginning to feel relaxed and chatty. So, when Captain Thapa asked him about his family, he told him that he was divorced and had two kids in college. He was proud of his kids, one of them majoring in engineering and the other in communications. He would have liked to have both be studying what he thought were "Hard skill majors- engineering, science, accounting, and computing" – but he was proud of them and their excellent GPAs.

He did roil about having to pay $4,000.00 for a course in Human Bonding that he thought he could have taught free of cost. But overall, he was happy and quite content with his family life.

When the Captain asked him about what he did for a living, he told him he owned a security service business providing personal security to VIPs and corporations, not unlike the business Captain Thapa was in. He went on to talk about his stint in the armed forces, his experiences in the two Gulf Wars, and the friendships and contacts he made there, and how much he cherished his time in the military.

Captain Thapa knew Dick O'Connor was telling the truth and the fMRI machine confirmed it. There were no unusual activities in Dick O'Connor's brain.

Suddenly the Captain made a pivot and asked:

"So, Mr. O'Connor, what are you doing in my country and what was your mission at the Peace Pagoda?"

Captain Thapa was using his army training as an officer of covert operations to relax the subject first and then do a hundred eighty degrees turn and ask some pointed intelligence questions. The expectation was that the subject's brain would not have had time to realign and would respond following the path of least resistance, which was to tell the truth.

But Dick O'Connor was a professional and had been through many interrogations. He was not going to be trapped. He replied:

"I am visiting your beautiful country as a tourist and was at the Peace Pagoda, like thousands of others, to see and admire the famous Buddhist temple."

He was speaking calmly and confidently to try and fool the lie detecting fMRI machine to which he was strapped and constrained. But the machine caught his lie and lit up.

Captain Thapa turned the monitor towards him and showed him the image of his brain and the portion that had lit up as he spoke. He explained to him the significance of the image and asked him the question again, getting the same response.

He turned towards his assistant and held up seven fingers, asking him to apply a level seven signal to the truth electrode. Dick O'Connor let out an animal scream and implored him to stop, signaling he was ready to talk, and this time tell the truth. The Captain nodded to the assistant and he rolled back the dial. The pain sensation slowly subsided.

And as the pain was subsiding, Dick O'Connor looked at his limbs and his torso and did not see any sign of torture. This was quite different than what he had experienced before, either while being interrogated himself or interrogating others. He was used to seeing significant physical signs of torture to inflict the type of pain he had just experienced. How did the Indian man do it? He could not contain his curiosity and had to ask. Captain Thapa simply smiled and told him to talk otherwise he would have to use that magic device again.

Dick O'Connor decided there was no point in suffering through more pain and started at the beginning.

"Alright, I can see you are going to get what you want one way or the other and you have been kind to me by not physically torturing me, as I would have done if I was in your shoes, Captain. So, let me start from the beginning."

"It was just about three months ago," Dick O'Connor continued, "that I got a call from one of my old army buddies who was now the security chief at a major industrial conglomerate, looking to hire me and my company for a surveillance job. And no, at the time he did not know the name of the conglomerate his friend worked for and did not particularly care. As you can well appreciate, in our business, we do not ask too many questions."

Captain Thapa could certainly relate to that.

"The pay was very good," Dick O'Connor continued, "and it involved chasing the subjects around the world and reporting back to the security chief on their whereabouts. Looked like a benign and interesting mission and I was happy to accept the assignment. It would help pay the steep college fees for my two kids."

"Then about six weeks ago, I got another call from the security chief," Dick continued, "telling me the mission needed to be expanded to include a few more critical tasks. The new mission required for me to recruit at least three more associates and travel abroad to a country that was still to be determined. The total contract value for the new mission was now in seven figures and all expenses would be paid."

"Now, I have been in business long enough to know that for that kind of money, this was going to be more than surveillance. The money was good, and I had several freelance ex-army friends who had occasionally worked for me and I knew should be available for the right price. Getting a team together would, therefore, not be a problem. I had rarely been to foreign countries, so an all-expenses paid trip sounded like an added incentive. My only reservation was that my team or I would intentionally not kill anyone, and I told that to the security chief as my condition for taking on the contract."

The security chief assured him, Dick O'Connor added, that neither he nor his employer were going to intentionally be involved in murder and that he fully agreed with Dick O'Connor's conditions. The security chief then gave a thumbnail sketch of background to the mission, concluding that it was important for his company to have the exclusive rights to the new material that the two doctors had developed. Thus far, the security chief continued, they had refused to do so, and it was becoming critical to the schedule of the project to get them to sign the contract. The two doctors were currently on the run and were hopping countries, the security chief had gone on to say.

Dick O'Connor's mission was to snatch the wife and get the husband, the primary inventor of the new material, to sign the contract. The signature needed to be witnessed by at least two witnesses. Finally, he was to leave a note at the scene of the abduction with wordings meant to confuse and point to their competitor.

The security chief had sent him a text with the pictures of the two doctors. He also had sent a package through FEDEX that Dick O'Connor was instructed to open only when he had the wife in his captivity and was to destroy it if for any reason the mission failed. He was not to talk to anyone about his mission and his connections. Although it was hard to believe, he still did not know who his employer was. He had an idea based on where he believed his employer's headquarters were, Cheshire, Connecticut, but he was not sure and there were several corporations with operations throughout the world who had their offices in Cheshire. Captain Thapa believed him and the fMRI machine confirmed it.

Then two weeks ago,

"I got a call from my employer, the security chief, telling me the subjects were going to be in Darjeeling, India and that my team and I were to get there and wait for them, and to complete the mission as soon as I saw an opening." Dick O'Connor said, "I have been following the two doctors ever since they got into Kalimpong. Their visit to the Peace Pagoda gave me an ideal opportunity to carry out the mission." He finished his story lamenting:

"I only wish the security chief had warned me of the martial arts expertise of the lady. I would have been much better prepared and not found myself strapped to this contraption."

Captain Thapa was beginning to like this man, and if it were under any other circumstances, they could have been good friends. They were both ex-militaries trying to make a living doing what they loved and what they were trained for. But right now, they were adversaries and he still needed to get a lot more information from him.

He asked Dick O'Connor where his associates were and if they had been with him at the Peace Pagoda. His response did not surprise him. They had all been there, one of them ready with the getaway vehicle and the other two hovering next to Caitlyn. The plan was for Dick O'Connor to administer the tranquilizer, while his two associates covered her with a hood. Meanwhile, the getaway vehicle would already have reached them and the three of them would carry her to the SUV. They were counting on the ensuing confusion and chaos to help them with their getaway.

It sounded like an amateurish and ludicrous plan fit for a Hollywood or Bollywood movie, but Dick O'Connor was confident they could pull it off. They had staked the area in advance and had timed the whole operation to less than a minute, assuming, of course, all went as per the plan.

If for whatever reason the mission failed, and one or more of the team members were captured, the instructions were for the remaining group to immediately make a run for the closest airport and get out of the country. In case they were being pursued either by law enforcement or private security forces, their instructions were to lie low in one of the neighboring towns, and when things had quieted down, to leave the country, not as a group but individually and preferably from different airports.

So, Dick O'Connor had continued, he did not really know where his associates were. He did, however, know that they would have gotten in touch with their employer, the security chief, and would have warned him of the mission's failure and the resulting fallout.

Once again, Captain Thapa knew he was telling the truth and once again, the machine confirmed it. He had been recording the interrogation and would listen to it again to see if there were any gaps that needed to be filled. He was also going to provide a transcript to Dr. Kumar, whom he was certain would be going over it carefully to chart his future course of action.

"Where is the package you got from your employer?" Captain Thapa asked.

"It is in a safe at the Darjeeling hotel where I am staying," Dick O'Connor replied.

Captain Thapa knew the manager of the hotel well.

"Very well. I know the manager of the hotel. I would like you to sign this paper authorizing me to get the package," Captain Thapa said, motioning to one of his assistants to get a memo pad and a pen as he eased off the straps restraining his subject.

Dick O'Connor hesitated just for a moment, but realized it was no use resisting. He did not want to experience the acute pain sensation administered by Dr. Johari's invention.

He signed the paper and Captain Thapa dispatched one of his Gorkha fighters to go and get the FEDEX package. He also phoned his friend at the hotel, giving him a heads up, informing him that his hotel guest Mr. Dick O'Connor was staying with him for a few days and needed to have that package. The hotel manager had known Captain Thapa for a long time and had no problem with his request. Darjeeling, after all, was Captain Thapa's town and he held chits from many of its residents, the hotel manager included.

The Gorkha fighter was back in less than an hour and had the package with him. It was still in the original FEDEX envelope. The package was posted from somewhere in Connecticut, but not from Cheshire, and had the name of a private person as the sender. There was no indication of any corporate affiliation. Captain Thapa was going to let Dr. Kumar open the envelope and examine its content. He had done his job by providing him a written transcript of his interrogation of Dick O'Connor and the envelope. Dr. Kumar should now have enough evidence and ammunition to confront at least one of the antagonists who was behind this deadly and harrowing experience.

Captain Thapa had just one more question for Dick O'Connor – how he got paid. Dick once again hesitated, but then answered, he was paid half the amount in a cashier's check drawn on a personal account. He did not know who owned the account and once again he did not care. The check was mailed to him at his office address in Southington, Connecticut.

Dick O'Connor was telling the truth. He looked at the Captain and asked:

"So, Captain Thapa, now that I have told you all what you wanted to know and have done so truthfully as confirmed by your machine, what are you planning to do with me?"

The Captain had already thought about this.

"Mr. O'Connor, you have two choices," he said. "I can turn you over to the Indian authorities and let the legal system take its due course."

"What is my other choice?" Dick O'Connor had heard about the Indian legal system and somehow knew that may not be his best choice.

"You call your employer, the security chief, and have the chief executive of his company call Dr. Kumar. He needs to first own up to the attack on him at the Peace Pagoda and others he may have orchestrated over the last three months. He then must accept Dr. Kumar's terms and conditions for the new material. You need to make sure your employer understands that if the chief executive does not call within 24 hours, a copy of the transcript of your interrogations and the content of the FEDEX package would be sent to the Indian and US authorities for appropriate legal action. I am sure it will not be a hard sell for you given what your employer's multinational corporation has been involved in," Captain Thapa said. "And if you succeed, then I will make sure you safely leave the country without having to deal with the Indian authorities. Until then, you will be our guest," he added.

For Dick O'Connor, the choice was a no brainer. He had heard and read much about the Indian legal system and how convoluted it could be. He had to convince the security chief, his employer, that it was in everyone's best interest for his boss to call and square it with Dr. Kumar.

Captain Thapa gave Dick O'Connor his unlisted burn phone number which his employer was supposed to call and left the room to check on the Kumars and his other guest, the Oriental man.

CHAPTER 47

CHESHIRE, CONNECTICUT - FIVE DAYS AND TWELVE HOURS TO LAUNCH DATE...

In Cheshire, Connecticut Dave Ward was jarred by the shrill ring from his private phone. It was early in the morning and he had gotten to his office to catch up on some paperwork. He was also expecting a call from his security chief with hopefully what would be positive news from their operation in Darjeeling. He was on the hook to get back to the chairwoman of his board with an update on the contract with Dr. Kumar. It was his security chief on the line,

"Yes, I hope you have some good news for me," he said with apprehension in his voice.

"I am afraid not. The operation has gone horribly bad and one of our men has been captured and is now in the custody of the security team guarding Dr. Kumar," the security chief answered timidly ready for a tongue lashing from his boss.

"No, I don't believe it. What happened?" Dave Ward replied trying to remain calm but not succeeding.

The General Technology security chief then went through the events at the peace Pagoda in Darjeeling and the text he had gotten from one of the two members of the three-person team sent to abduct Caitlyn and deliver the contract package, concluding with the capture of their team leader – Dick O'Connor.

The usually cool and collected chief executive of General Technologies was furious at the news and let his subordinate have it. While that helped him vent some his frustration and anger, he knew he needed to keep his wits about him and try to contain the damage.

"I am sorry to dump on you. Keep me posted and see if you can keep my name and the name of our company out of it," Dave Ward said as he hung up.

The GT chairwoman of the board, Ms. Katherine Watson, had called last night enquiring about the status of the contract with Dr. Kumar, and he had promised to get back to her this morning with the latest updates. She had sounded quite upset for not already having the contract in place and had threatened to take the matter into her own hands. He had promised to call her early in the morning and was hoping to give her a positive response and was expecting his security chief to deliver. But now he had a catastrophe on his hands, and he knew this was not going to end well. He had to talk to Dr. Kumar and try to contain the damage.

The morning had already come and gone, and he had not yet called the chairwoman. It was late afternoon in Cheshire and close to midnight in India - too late to call Dr. Kumar. He would have to wait until tomorrow to try to get in touch with him, assuming he was answering his phone and he would take his call. The last time he had talked to Dr. Kumar, it was not very friendly, and he had almost blown him off. Hopefully, with all that had happened over the last few months, he would have forgotten it and would talk to him.

Dave Ward sent out a short text to the chairwoman letting her know that he was still working on getting her an update and would be getting back to her tomorrow.

In Darjeeling India, it was already the next day. Dr. Ravi Kumar was groggy but had almost recovered from the effects of the viscous blow from the Oriental man. The blow was meant to temporarily disable him and was administered by an experienced person. It had knocked him out for longer than expected but he was awake now and was trying to get his bearings. Dr. Anand Johari had given him a full examination and had declared him to be fit to travel back to their residence in Kalimpong, whenever they were ready to do so.

Captain Thapa had finished his interrogation of Dick O'Connor and was in the room with Ravi and Caitlyn. He gave a copy of the transcript of his interrogations as well as the FEDEX package to Ravi. He then provided Ravi the gist of what he had learned from Dick O'Connor and the choices he had given to him.

"Dr. Kumar, as you would expect Dick O'Connor has chosen to call the chief executive of his employer company and you should expect a call from him anytime now."

"Which company is that?" Ravi asked.

"He does not know. And I believe him," Captain Thapa replied.

"We do have the FEDEX package that Dick was given by his employer for delivering it to you and it might provide us the name of his employer. We have not yet opened the package and have left it for you and Dr. Mariko to do so," the Captain added.

Even in his groggy state, Ravi understood everything Captain Thapa had described. He agreed with the choices given to Dick O'Connor and asked why the Captain thought Dick O'Connor was telling the truth.

"Let me explain." It was Dr. Anand Johari, who had joined the group, jumping into the conversation.

He talked about his invention of the truth electrode and the ability to administer the perception of pain without causing any physical hurt and the role of the fMRI machine in detecting the enhanced activities in the area of the brain that perceived the pain. The fMRI machine, Dr. Johari continued, could also detect if a person were telling a lie, like a polygraph, and by some account was more reliable.

"Dr. Kumar, I was present when Captain Thapa was interrogating Dick O'Connor and I can say with some certainty that the subject was telling the truth," Dr. Johari said.

The scientists in Ravi and Caitlyn were fascinated by Dr. Johari's invention and the fact that he had a way to extract information in a more humane way. They had heard about the use of fMRI as a lie detecting machine, but to actually have it used in a real-life situation affecting them was remarkable. Ravi could justify to himself the machine as a lie detector, but he was torn for it being used as a pain inducing system, even if the pain were not physical.

"I am not sure I fully subscribe to this being a more humane way of extracting information. After all, the brain still perceives it as torture," Ravi said, somewhat unconvincingly.

"Ravi, these guys were out to cause physical harm to us, and we need to find out who they are working for. Do you think they will just give us that information out of the goodness of their hearts?" It was Caitlyn who countered Ravi testily.

"We have to find out who these people are working for and we have to find it fast to protect ourselves and our family. I think this is a great invention to get the information we need without leaving permanent scars on the culprits – although after what we have been through, they probably deserve that," Caitlyn added with finality.

Ravi had to agree with her even if he was still not fully sold. They accepted Captain Thapa's conclusions that Dick O'Connor indeed did not know who his employers were, and they may be able to find that out from the content of the FEDEX package.

"Caitlyn, go ahead and open the package and see what it contains," Ravi said.

Captain Thapa handed the FEDEX package to her. It was a typical letter envelope, carefully sealed with no address. It had been delivered to Dick O'Connor's office in person by a private courier with a tang to open it at the perforations. She was just about to tug on the tang when Ravi's phone rang. It was his secretary in Ithaca. He had given strict instructions to call him only in case of emergencies; otherwise, he would call if he needed something from his office. He wanted to minimize the possibilities of his whereabouts being found out by pinging his phone.

"I am sorry, Dr. Kumar, to call you again. But the lady said she was the chairwoman of General Technologies and that she needed to speak to you urgently. She was insistent that I either give her your number or connect her to you, if you agreed to take her call," Helen said.

"She is waiting on the other line, if you would like to talk to her," Helen added.

Dr. Kumar had met the chairwoman, Katherine Watson, several times, not in a one on one meeting but in a group setting. The first time he had met her was when he was awarded the inventor of the year award at his old company, General Technologies. Ms. Watson had made the journey from her home in the Silicon Valley to be present at the ceremony and hand out the awards. It was her firm belief that a corporation was only as good as its employees, and the current but more importantly future health of the business depended upon the continuous invention and rejuvenation of its products. Dr. Kumar had received seven patents that year, with most related to the invention of new materials and coatings for the high temperature sections of modern aero engines.

Since then, he had met her several more times, at professional conferences and internal board meetings where he was invited as an expert presenter. He had always found her to be quite interested in the work they were doing, asking questions that clearly demonstrated her engineering background and a keen business sense. She was sincere and at least in his assessment a straight shooter. He had a lot of respect for her and considered it an honor to be talking to her. He gladly accepted her call.

"I am sorry, I kept you waiting Ma'am, but I and my wife are on the run and have to take precautions from several hit teams that are after us and would like to take us out." Ravi apologized to Ms. Watson.

This was news to Ms. Watson. She had no idea that Ravi was on the run for his life.

"Dr. Kumar, I had no idea you were on the run. Is it in any way related to your new invention?" she asked.

"Yes, I am quite certain it is," Ravi replied.

"Can you tell me more about it?" she asked.

Ravi told her it was a long story and she probably did not have the time to listen to it and asked her for the reason for her call. Katherine Watson was a smart and perceptive woman. She had the feeling that Ravi's story most likely was related to why General Technologies had not yet signed a contract with him for the new material and it was important for her to get the full background before she came to the reason for her call.

"Dr. Kumar, I have all the time in the world and would very much like to hear what is happening to you and your wife. I have the feeling the reason for my call may well be related to your story," Ms. Watson said.

Ravi was not sure where to begin so he thought it was best to begin at the beginning but keep the narration succinct and cover only what was relevant to her company and how it was involved in their current predicaments. Over the next five minutes, he summarized for the chairwoman the invention of the new material, what it could do for aero engines, his refusal to sign an exclusive rights contract with either of the two engine companies, and the threatening notes he had received over the last three months from professional hit teams who were chasing him and his wife, Caitlyn, through four continents as they were trying to find safe haven. The latest attempt on their life, he had added, was at their current hideout in Darjeeling, India.

"You may be wondering why we decided to run and why we did not take the matter to the authorities or to the boards of the two companies."

"You are right, I was going to ask you about that," she replied.

"For two reasons. We did not approach the boards because we had no evidence until yesterday who was behind the attacks. We had our suspicions, but until we had some concrete proof, we did not want to accuse some of the most powerful people in our industry," Ravi said.

"And the other reason?" Ms. Watson asked.

"We got calls letting us know the people who were after us also had our three daughters in their crosshairs, and for their safety we were warned to not go to the authorities. We could not risk that. Our best course was to get out of the country and run the launch clock down. We were counting on the two engine companies coming back to the negotiating table as it got closer to the launch date for the engines," Ravi said.

The chairwoman was aware of the impending launch of the new engines by both companies and knew the criticality of that date. She also knew this was a historic event in the annals of commercial aviation and that to be in the game, the two major engine companies had to have at least some piece of that market if not the whole thing.

She knew her company had to win some or all of this market as they had been an underdog and were in danger of becoming irrelevant in the lucrative commercial engine business. The punishment Wall Street would administer on the valuation of her company could well be fatal and make them a candidate for unfriendly acquisition – a prospect she and her board and the senior management at General Technologies could not accept.

Dr. Kumar finished his story recounting the events at the Peace Pagoda and how Caitlyn's black belt in Karate and the quick reflexes she had developed training for it, not only saved her but also, for the first time, delivered a perpetrator who was now in their custody. They could now finally find out who was behind these attacks and bring them to justice.

The chairwoman's ears perked up at this last comment,

"Do you know who he is and who sent him there?" she asked.

"No, we don't. But let me tell you what we do know from our interrogations so far." Ravi then recounted for her what they had learned from Dick O'Connor over the last several hours of questioning.

"We have a written confession from the man about his mission and his employer which was to kidnap Caitlyn and get me to sign a document. Dick O'Connor, the person we have under our custody, professes to not know the name of his employer. He says he was hired by one of his old military friends who was now the security chief at a major corporation. He is cooperating with us and as a condition of his release, we are waiting to hear back from the chief executive officer of the company that he is working for," Ravi added.

"Dr. Kumar, do you have that document?" the chairwoman asked.

"We just got the package with the document from his hotel room and were about to open it when you called. If you wait, we can open it now and find out about its content together," Ravi replied.

"Yes, please go ahead. I will wait."

Captain Thapa had handed the FEDEX package to Caitlyn. Ravi asked her to open it, as Ms. Watson waited on the phone. They were finally going to find out who was behind the attacks on them and even if there was more than one team after them, at least they would know who had hired Dick O'Connor.

Caitlyn slowly opened the FEDEX package. Inside it there was a letter sized sealed Manila envelope with no external markings. She carefully and deliberately opened the Manila envelope. The suspense in the room was palpable. They could even hear heavy breathing from the phone. Caitlyn finally extracted the document from the envelope. It was a thin document, no more than 4 to 5 pages, printed on plain computer paper with no identifiable company logo or letterhead.

Caitlyn began reading the document aloud for the benefit of the people in the room and Ms. Watson. It was filled with legalese with "herewith," "therefore," "parties," "forthwith" sprinkled all over. It was clearly written by lawyers for lawyers and was made as confusing and difficult to understand by lay people as most legal documents usually were. But even through the confusing language, it was clear that it was a contract document written on behalf of the company who had hired Dick O'Connor and said,

"I, the undersigned, as the director and chief executive officer of the Materials Research Institute assign exclusive rights to our patented material – MRI 297 to the General Technologies Corporation for use in their products as they see fit. The terms and conditions for the assignment of these rights are summarized in the attachments with this document."

The document was not signed by any of the company officers and only had an empty slot for Ravi's signature attested by two witnesses. The next two pages of the documents were the attachments referred to in the contract and summarized the terms and conditions which were essentially the same as what Ravi had outlined in his meetings with GT executives, including Dave Ward.

The chairwoman of General Technologies could not believe what she had just heard and asked,

"Dr. Kumar, I cannot believe what you just read. How can you be sure that the man you have in your custody is telling the truth?"

"We have ways of getting and validating information. I will be happy to go over that if you like." It was Captain Thapa who replied.

"We also have the man right here and we can put him on if you would like to speak to him personally."

"Please put him on," the chairwoman instructed.

For the next five minutes she grilled Dick O'Connor and could not find any holes in his story and had to accept that he was telling the truth.

She was livid and could not contain her anger at the hubris of her executives, especially the chief executive officer – Dave Ward. She had a lot of respect for the man and had been personally responsible for bringing him onboard when he was passed over for the top job at their competitor – United Electric. She could not understand why Dave Ward would go to such lengths and authorize actions which clearly were criminal and put the future of the entire corporation at risk. She had no plausible explanations for such amateurish behavior on the part of a highly intelligent and experienced person. If he was trying to get GT back in the commercial engine business, this was certainly not the way to do it, and he must know that. No, it had to be his personal vendetta against his former employer for being passed over for the top job.

The chairwoman could now see it clearly – Dave Ward and Bill MacMillan had made this new engine contest their personal war and they were both going to try to win it and win it at any cost….

"Dr. Kumar, I believe the man and am at loss of words except to offer our sincere apology on behalf of my company. You can rest assured that we will address this egregious behavior of our chief executive with the fullest force available at my and my board's disposal. But tell me, what are you planning to do with the man you have in your captivity?"

Dr. Kumar told her about the call, Dick O'Connor, her company's hired hand had made to his handler, the security chief. He told her Dick O'Connor was instructed to let the security chief know that the CEO of the company, whom now that they knew was Dave Ward, needed to personally call Dr. Kumar and take full responsibility for the attacks. Dave Ward was instructed to inform his board of his activities and have the chairperson contact Dr. Kumar directly to decide what should be done going forward. Dave Ward was further instructed to call Dr. Kumar within 24 hours; otherwise, the matter would be handed over to both Indian and US law enforcement authorities. He then added,

"I was actually expecting this call to be from the CEO of your company but am grateful that you called. We can now talk about where we go from here."

Except for the question she had asked about the FEDEX document and her grilling of Dick O'Connor the chairwoman of General Technologies, she had quietly listened to Dr. Kumar's story.

"Dr. Kumar, I am a grandmother myself and fully understood and laud your and your associates' noble motives for wanting to see the widest application of this new material to curb the climate harming pollutants and to preserve the precious and finite fossil fuel supply for the future generations.

"The world needs more engineers and researchers like you," she continued, "to fight these battles and put the interest of the planet and the life forms that inhabit it, before their own.

"I have absolutely no problem with the new material being used by the entire aero engine industry. I have enough confidence in the inventiveness of my design team at General Technologies that even if both engine manufacturers have the same new super alloy, they would be able to come up with an engine concept that would differentiate itself from the competition.

"A complex machine such as an airplane engine," she continued "is judged not just by its performance, but its durability, reliability, serviceability and its first cost, all of which are critical to the overall operating cost and hence the profitability of its customers - the airlines and the flying public."

"My designers are hungry, and I have full confidence that they are ready to field a product that would get our company back in the commercial engine business. They know what is at stake and have been preparing for this historic contest for the last four years. I am also certain that the men and women working on this project would be equally shocked and saddened to hear that their chief executive officer had resorted to actions fit for thugs and gangsters, because just like me, they want to win, but win it fair and square and not at any cost...." She made her case for understanding and forgiveness from Dr. Kumar, his family, and his associates at MRI.

"As soon as I am off the phone with you," she continued, "I will call an emergency meeting of the board and put forward a resolution to sign the contract with you and your institute on your terms which appear to be fair and equitable for all parties. I believe the board is fully behind me and I should have no problem in getting their buy in. Please give me the time to convene the board meeting and get the resolution through and I beg you to not approach the authorities until then and only if I am unsuccessful," Ms. Katherine Watson said, appealing to Ravi, and Caitlyn, who was also listening to their conversation.

"Dr. Kumar, do you have any other condition to accept my request for not going to the authorities?" she asked before concluding the phone call.

Dr. Kumar thought for a moment and then replied in a measured and even tone with no malice in his voice,

"Dave Ward," he said, "has been one of my mentors and friend for a long time and I have learned a lot from him during my time at General Technologies and even after I left to launch my own institute. He has been incredibly supportive, both financially and intellectually, in the formative years of our non-profit independent organization. I owe him a lot, professionally and socially. I am therefore saddened and angry to learn that my friend and mentor has been behind these physical and psychological attacks on my family and me.

"Now, I do not want to be vindictive," Dr. Kumar continued, "but I believe, he has betrayed the immense trust vested in him by his company, his employees, and his customers. Through his actions, he has put the fate of his company and the livelihood of hundreds of thousands of hard-working employees and thousands of small and large businesses that depend on them, in jeopardy. He needs to face the consequences of his actions.

"For my part," Ravi Kumar continued, "I would want the board to immediately sever all relationships with him and all those who were directly involved with these heinous attacks. Furthermore, the severance should be done with no golden handshakes and pensions of any kind. These were the minimum reparations that I would insist on. The board could then decide what other punitive or legal actions it deemed appropriate for someone who has betrayed the fiduciary responsibilities of the chief executive officer of a world-renowned corporation and put it at mortal risk."

The chairwoman of General Technologies, Ms. Katherine Watson, had carefully listened to Dr. Kumar's conditions. She had already decided that Dave Ward had to go, so Dr. Kumar's demands did not appear to be outrageous, but she needed to get buy in from her board before she could commit to him.

"I clearly understand your conditions and will bring it up to the board. I don't think there would be any problem in the board accepting them, but I do need their buy in before I can commit. Let me once again say how sorry I am for what has been wrought on you and promise to get back to you within 24 hours."

With that Ms. Watson hung up. It was going to be a long 24 hours in Cheshire, Connecticut....

CHAPTER 48

The two Gorkha fighters guarding the Oriental man wheeled him into the interrogation room equipped with the fMRI machine. Captain Ram Bahadur Thapa and Dr. Anand Johari were waiting for him there. The Oriental man was awake and staring at the ceiling. The two Gorkha fighters, with the help of Captain Thapa, moved the man onto the fMRI machine and secured him with straps on his legs and his hands. His head was also secured with another set of straps encased with foam. He was completely immobile.

Dr. Johari examined his wound. The Oriental man was lucky; the bullet had only scratched the surface of his leg. The wound was superficial and was already beginning to heal. He was otherwise healthy and in good shape with a well-built body. Dr. Johari had implanted the "truth" electrode in the man at the same time as when he was taking care of his wound. The Oriental man was ready to be interrogated by Captain Thapa.

And just like he did with Dick O'Connor, Captain Thapa started by introducing himself and describing to the Oriental man the properties of the truth electrode surgically implanted into his head and its ability to directly send electrical signals to the parts of the brain that sense and react to pain.

"You will feel the pain, exactly as it would be from a real torture device, except you will not see any external sign of that torture on your body; it will be all in your head. So, it is in your best interest to answer my questions truthfully and completely; you will save yourself a lot of pain and agony. Also, let me tell you that this fMRI machine you are strapped to can detect truth from lies and that every time you tell a lie, the severity of the pain will go one notch up," Captain Thapa said as he began his interrogation of the Oriental man.

The Oriental man was still looking at the ceiling and did not reply to the Captain when he asked if he understood what had been explained to him. The Captain had spoken slowly to him in conversational English and was certain the Oriental man comprehended the language; he would not be in India, otherwise.

He asked the Oriental man what his name was and what he was doing in India. The Oriental man just kept staring at the ceiling and did not reply. The Captain repeated his question and said,

"This is your last chance to reply to my questions. If you do not, I will have no choice but to activate the truth electrode. And I can assure you that you do not want that."

The oriental man remained silent. The Captain nodded to the Gorkha fighter operating the controller for electrode. He turned the knob to the lowest setting. The Oriental man groaned in pain, but still did not say anything and continued staring at the ceiling. Slowly the Gorkha fighter kept increasing the millivolt input to the truth electrode. The Oriental man grimaced and groaned but kept silent until the level reached seven.

"Michael Zhang." Suddenly the silence was broken.

Captain Thapa looked at the Oriental man. He said in halting, accented but clear English – "My name is Michael Zhang. I am from Beijing, China, and I am a visitor here."

The fMRI machine indicated he was telling the truth.

Captain Thapa smiled and said, "Thank you."

"Now let me formally introduce myself – I am Captain Ram Bahadur Thapa. I am a retired officer from the Indian Army. My team and I have been commissioned to ensure the safety of our guests from the United States while they are in our country. You and perhaps your associates, attacked one of our guests at the temple. He was lucky that his injuries were not life threatening and we were able to capture you, his attacker." We know that there are several organizations and large corporations that would like to intimidate our guest and have him commit to binding contracts that would make them rich and powerful at the expense of the greater good to our planet and the people who inhabit it. Our guest has refused to do so, and these greedy organizations are now trying to terrorize him into signing the contract. We already know about one of them from the other person we captured at the temple. It is critical that we know who hired you and what your motive was. Understand that one way or another, we are going to find out the truth, and you can save yourself a lot of pain and suffering by cooperating with us. You will not only be doing good for yourself, but also for the rest of us, including the people of your country."

"I want to remind you of the micro electrode implanted in you and the machine you are strapped to that lets us know if you are telling the truth" Captain Thapa continued, "The electrode will dissolve in a few weeks leaving no trace and pain, so you do not have to worry about that."

"It is in your interest," Captain Thapa continued, "that you tell us the truth and tell us who hired you. If you do so, we will make sure that you are safely escorted out of this country. You will be our guest while you heal from your injuries and can stay here as long as you wish. But, if you decide not to cooperate, we will have no choice but to turn you over to the Indian authorities and I do not think you would want that. The choice is yours."

With that, Captain Thapa stopped and gazed into Michael Zhang's eyes.

"Now tell me about yourself and what you are doing here," Captain Thapa asked.

Michael Zhang had been quietly listening to the captain. He believed what he had heard, and he knew the only realistic course of action he had was to tell the captain the truth and hope that they would release him after they had heard his story and gotten what they wanted. Michael Zhang was a practical man, and unlike make believe characters in Hollywood and Bollywood movies, he knew when to concede and live to fight another fight. He began,

"My name is Michael Zhang and I am the security chief of a major joint venture company in China. And like you, I am also a retired military man. I was in an elite Navy team, like the American Seal team and was deployed around the world with the Chinese Navy. And no, it was not fortunate that Dr. Kumar, and yes, I know his name, lived. It was intentional; we wanted to keep him alive. If we wanted to kill him, believe me, he would have been dead, and I would not be here. But we had to capture him alive and bring him as our guest to China."

Captain Thapa raised his hand and asked Michael Zhang to stop. He wanted Dr. Ravi Kumar to hear the story as well. He sent one of the Gorkha fighters to fetch Dr. Kumar and Dr. Mariko.

"We thank you for not killing Dr. Kumar, and let me tell you, as well, that if we wanted to kill you, we would also not have missed. So, I believe we are all square," Captain Thapa said to Michael Zhang as Dr. Kumar and Dr. Mariko walked into the room.

At the Buddhist Pagoda, the attack on Ravi was so quick and unexpected that he did not get a chance to see the face of his attacker. He knew it was an Oriental man, but that was it. Now, as he entered the room and saw Michael Zhang up close, his eyebrows furrowed. He had definitely seen this man somewhere, but he did not remember where and in what setting. Captain Thapa noticed that and looked at him questioningly. Ravi did not say anything and simply gestured to the Captain to continue.

Captain Thapa introduced Michael Zhang to the two doctors. He gave them a summary of what he had learned thus far from their captive and suggested they might also want to hear what he had to say. With that, he gestured to Michael to continue his story.

"Dr. Kumar, I am sorry to have caused you temporary debilitation, but I can assure you I have no personal malice against you. In fact, I am familiar with your work and have the utmost respect for what you, Dr. Mariko, and your colleagues at the Materials Research Institute are doing," Michael Zhang began.

Captain Thapa and the Kumars were surprised by Michael Zhang's lucidity and his knowledge of their work. They did not expect this from a security type person involved in kidnapping and attacks. They had also heard that he was the head of security and did not expect the head would be involved in a field action such as this. They knew Michael Zhang was no ordinary security guy and they were keen to hear what he had to say; they wanted to hear his story from the beginning. It was fortuitous that his interrogation had just begun and that they would all be hearing his story at the same time without any repetitions.

"Very well then, start from the beginning and remember we are only interested in the truth, and as I have already warned you it will be in your best interest to do so and save yourself a lot of pain and agony," Captain Thapa said.

Michael Zhang smiled and nodded. He then began,

"My Chinese name is Min-Chun Zhang, but for my western friends it is Michael Zhang. I am originally from the Chengdu province in China but have spent most of my life in Beijing and the United States. I am a mechanical engineer, having obtained my bachelor's degree from the University of Beijing and master's from Lehigh University in the US. But I have never been employed as an engineer. For the most part, my interest has always been intelligence. I retired as a Commander of the Navy, some fifteen years ago. Since then I have been working with the Chinese Aero Engine Corporation or CAEC as it is known in China. It is a quasi- government enterprise with the majority of shares held by the Chinese Government. The public holds minority shares in the company which are traded on the Beijing Stock Exchange. My responsibilities at CAEC are quite flexible. For the last five years I have been their head of securities and intelligence, but I take on special projects at the direction of my management, many of which are critical to the strategic and long-term goals of my company and by extension my country."

"Three years ago," Michael Zhang continued, "CAEC entered into an agreement with one of the major US corporations to design and manufacture commercial aero engines in China, mainly for use in the Chinese market but also for export to countries where China has exclusive bi-lateral and multi-lateral trade treaties. Many of these are in Africa. We formed a Joint Venture (JV) company with a 50/50 partnership. The JV has only a skeleton staff and draws experts from the two parent companies for most of its work. The corporate offices of the JV are in Beijing and in New York. The presidency of the company rotates between the Chinese and American every two years."

Michael Zhang paused for a moment. Captain Thapa believed him but was also monitoring the fMRI machine, which confirmed that he was telling the truth. Michael Zhang was still strapped to the machine and was lying horizontally. He asked for some water and the Captain obliged, making sure he was still in the straps as he raised him and helped him with the water bottle. Captain Thapa was aware of the lethal capabilities Navy Seals possessed and he had no doubt Michael Zhang, even in his injured state, could be dangerous if his straps were loosened. He could not take that chance, even though he had begun to respect and like the well-built and well-spoken Chinese man.

"I was assigned to the joint venture," Michael Zhang continued, "to head a special task force of about half a dozen ex-military personnel to support the broad objectives of the Joint Ventures of promoting our company and facilitating its business. In many countries, especially in Africa, it meant working with regimes and organizations that some may call dangerous and are almost always corrupt. We tailored our missions to respond to the requirements on the ground and did whatever it took to get the desired results. I also spent considerable time in the US working at our corporate office and at the plants of our JV partner to familiarize myself with their operations and to set up the required logistical and tactical infrastructure. I had gotten to know the security chief of our JV partner's company quite well and also had several meetings with its CEO. I found him to be a highly intelligent person and a savvy businessman."

The Kumars and Captain Thapa were anxiously waiting for Michael Zhang to name the US company, but he had carefully and deliberately avoided mentioning its name. They let him move along with his story, knowing full well that either voluntarily or involuntarily they were going to find out who his US employers and partners were.

"From my student days at Lehigh and then my frequent visits to the US on behalf of our JV," Michael Zhang continued, "I had gotten to know many people and the country well. I was fascinated by the ingenuity of the Americans and their free enterprise spirits. I believe this in large part is responsible for its economic and strategic dominance of the world. I also got a firsthand look at how well the three-legged stool – Government, Industry, and Academia work in your country."

"But I have also seen the forces that are keeping your country back endangering its world power status and providing opportunities for developing countries like China and India to catch up and eventually take the lead." Michael Zhang continued. "Take the insistence on diversity. I have never understood why the society forces the industry and the government and the academia to hire people who are not the best for the job."

For the next few minutes Michael Zhang went on to describe his take on what in his view ailed America, views which had been reinforced by his superior in Beijing and had been a big factor in his accepting the assignment. His arguments against diversity were impeccable as was his lucid enunciation of mindless outsourcing and the hollowing of the American industrial might.

"Mr. Zhang, it is quite interesting, and we are all fascinated by your story and your views on the American ways of life. But can we get back to the subject, which is what are you doing here and what were your motives behind attacking Dr. Kumar?"

"I am getting there and thought it was important to set the context behind our actions. I ask for your indulgence, just a little longer and I will finish giving you the background to our mission," Michael Zhang said.

Captain Thapa looked at Dr. Kumar and he nodded his approval to have Michael Zhang continue with his story. Michael Zhang resumed his narrative about his time in the US and what he had learned from his interactions with many of the citizens there from different backgrounds.

Dr. Ravi Kumar had been quietly and intently listening to this remarkable man from China. He wondered how was it that Michael Zhang's views aligned so well with those of his own. Could it be because they were both from outside the United States from rapidly developing countries who had first-hand experience and understanding of the strengths and weaknesses of the only remaining superpower on the planet? The focus on diversity at the expense of meritocracy and the hollowing out of the industrial base for short term profits had been something that had kept Ravi awake at night, worrying about the future of his three daughters. It was that reason he had left the safety of private companies to start an independent institute where he could apply himself without the constraints imposed by Wall Street and the greedy top 1% who profited from outsourcing the well-paying middle-class jobs.

He knew Michael Zhang was leading up to describing the motive for the attack. He was curious to see what else he wanted to cover as part of the background. He was not going anywhere, and in fact was quite enjoying the conversation.

Captain Thapa, on the other hand, was getting restless. He had been monitoring the fMRI and could confirm that Michael Zhang was telling the truth; there was nothing going on in the lie detecting area of the brain. He looked at Dr. Kumar, who nodded to let Michael Zhang continue.

"Take clean energy and climate change," Michael Zhang continued, "America is still debating if climate change is happening and if so what to do about it. Clean energy is one area that, even if the climate change were a hoax, would benefit our planet by preserving the precious fossil fuel for the generations to come. Solar cells, long lasting electric car batteries, wind turbines and many other clean energy products were invented by your country but were left to others to reap the benefits from their ever increasing and expanding markets all over the world."

"America lost an excellent opportunity to capitalize on what is sure to become a major wealth generating machine of the future. My country, China, was happy you did that since it helps us achieve our national goal – to become the number one nation in the world – economically, politically, and militarily – in other words the next and only remaining superpower. We, the Chinese, believe, that it is our rightful place to become the nation of inventors, thinkers, and educators once again as we were at the dawn of the human civilization. We seemed to have lost our way, but rest assured we are coming back and people like me have taken the pledge to dedicate ourselves to making it happen."

Michael Zhang paused again, took a sip of water, and continued:

"I appreciate your patience and realize it must be running thin, but I thought it was important that I tell you a little about myself and the corporations I work for. I will not keep you waiting any longer. So, let me now talk about why my team and I were here in Darjeeling and why we attacked Dr. Kumar…."

CHAPTER 49

AVIATION WEEK & SPACE TECHNOLOGY, SEPTEMBER 1 ISSUE – NEW ENGINE UPDATES

With less than a week left to the critical launch date for the new engines, AW&ST has learned from confidential sources that Dave Ward, the Chief Executive Officer of General Technologies, has decided to take early retirement effective immediately. This has come as a shock to the Aviation community since Dr. Ward is only in his early fifties and has been leading the charge on the new engine. There was no prior indication of his impending retirement and no replacement has been named by the company. AW&ST reached out to General Technologies communications and was given a terse "No Response" comment. The Chairwoman of the board, Ms. Katherine Watson has assumed the role of the CEO until replacement for Dr. Ward is announced. The company would also not confirm if it has signed a contract with Dr. Ravi Kumar for the new material and reiterated its intentions to launch the new engine on schedule, and that the new engine would meet all its design goals, including the target fuel burn and emission reductions.

Sources also tell AW&ST that the other engine company, United Electric has also not yet signed the contract for the new material and that the inventor of the new material, with his wife, is currently out of the country. Efforts by AW&ST to contact Dr. Kumar have been unsuccessful. It is not clear and a mystery as to why the two companies have not yet signed the contract with Dr. Kumar and why he has decided to be out of the country at this critical time. AW&ST will continue to follow the developments on this still breaking story and will provide updates as they become available.

On the Chinese engine program, AW&ST has nothing new to report except that the higher level of activities detected by our Beijing bureau still continues. It is clear that the Chinese are preparing to launch their own version of the new engine and would most likely be bringing it to the market on the same schedule as the two engines from the west. AW&ST will continue to monitor and report on the developments in Beijing, as well.

CHAPTER 50

DARJEELING, INDIA – FIVE DAYS TO LAUNCH DATE...

The AW&ST article about the new engine had just popped up on Ravi's phone. He did not have to hear from Ms. Watson that she and her board had already acted upon the commitments she had made to him. Although the news should have pleased him, he only felt a sense of loss and sadness at the fall of one of the most prolific and key men in his industry. He only hoped that out of this tale there would be lessons learned for future leaders of the corporate world on how they should conduct themselves and that they should fight and fight hard, but it should be a fair fight lest they would be punished and punished severely.

He was still thinking about his onetime friend and mentor, Dave Ward, as he turned his attention back to Michael Zhang who was continuing his story about his and his team's mission in Darjeeling and why he had attacked him.

"The one area China is still significantly behind is in the field of aviation. Oh, we did get some help from the Soviets and then when the Soviet Union disintegrated from the Russians, but their technology is still several generations behind. In fact, we have now overtaken them in many of the aerospace disciplines."

"My country has made large investments in aviation and has built state of the art research and development facilities that can design, develop, and test airplanes in full scale wind tunnels that can simulate the harshest environmental conditions that these airplanes could be subjected to. We have brilliant scientists and engineers from all over the country working on the latest aerodynamics design codes that fully account for the three-dimensional nature of the fluid that dictates the behavior of these high-performance aero machines. I am confident that it is only a matter of time before the airplanes designed by our Chinese engineers and scientists would be equivalent to or even superior to those from America and Europe."

"So, when I say we are behind in aviation," Michael Zhang continued, "I really mean the high-performance aero engines that power these airplanes. Without modern aero engines such as the ones currently available from the major engine manufacturers in the US and Europe, the airplanes are just a beautiful looking aerodynamically sculpted piece of aluminum which would go nowhere anytime fast."

"The engines that we currently have or even those available from our old communist partners could be thought of as the hulking V8 Detroit auto engines trying to power a high performance, fuel sipping, Toyota Prius. It just does not work. It is for this reason the commercial airplanes designed by the various design bureaus in the old Soviet Union and now Russia, as well as those designed by us, do not have many takers. Even the state-owned Russian and Chinese airlines hunger for the airplanes from the west due to their superior all around capabilities, especially when it comes to fuel burn and emissions. And it all goes back to not having the modern aero engines to power these domestically designed and manufactured aircrafts."

"Now, within the aero engines," the Chinese continued, "which is one of the most complex and technologically advanced machines conceived by man, we the Chinese have the expertise to design many of its parts. We just lack two major disciplines – advanced electronics and high temperature, high strength materials. We have made significant progress in electronics – through acquisitions and collaborations. We have, for instance, bought the PC business of IBM with its mother lode of advanced electronics know how. Our domestic electronic industry has also made great strides and is now the major manufacturing hub for some of America's household gadgets from iPhone to Smart TVs and everything in between."

"Of course, the electronics for aviation or avionics is different from consumer electronics, but the basic ingredients and the knowhow for the two are closely related and transferable over time. So, I have no doubt that we will be able to develop our homegrown avionics systems for the aircrafts and the engines of the future that will be competitive to the systems from the west."

"Materials, on the other hand, is a completely different story," Michael Zhang continued. "Now, I may be out of turn, talking about Materials Engineering in front of Dr. Kumar and Dr. Mariko, but let me just say that we have not had much success in developing high strength materials that can operate at temperatures close to their melting points."

"We have been working on alloys suitable for aero engine applications for close to 25 years, with help from our collaborators in the Soviet Union and now Russia but have not been able to achieve all the critical properties demanded by a high-performance aircraft power plant. We tried licensing the technology from the west, but the very stringent export control regulations prevented us from doing so. We even sent one of our eminent Materials Engineering researchers, whom Dr. Kumar knows well, to spend a year at his institute, but again his access to sensitive and classified information was quite restrictive. So, Dr. Xi Ping, our research scientist, had an interesting and personally rewarding time in the US, but was not able to bring back much with him that could help us resolve the problems we were facing in manufacturing these materials."

"We have attended all the technical conferences on the subject in the US and Europe. In fact, I was part of the delegation with Dr. Xi Ping at the recent Aerospace Specialists conference at which Dr. Kumar presented his ground-breaking invention of the new material MRI 297. But, as Dr. Kumar knows well, we only get extremely limited new information at these meetings, as most of the useful material is protected by the many government regulations."

Ravi now remembered where he had seen this man before. It was at the Madison Square Garden. For some unexplained reason, he had noticed him sitting next to his friend Dr. Ping and was intrigued by what he thought was a penetrating stare which he could feel even from his vantage point on the Dias, at least 50 feet away.

"Our vision of becoming the pre-eminent and most powerful country in the world was beginning to look like a dream." Michael Zhang continued, "How can a nation claim to be the most advanced and developed country in the world if it does not have superiority in aviation? Not only the commercial leadership, but also the military depends upon dominance in aviation, and unless we can design, develop, and manufacture the most powerful commercial and military airplanes, we will never be able to claim the superpower status that we as a nation deserve and hunger for."

"After much agonizing, we resorted to what any capitalist country would – we decided to buy the technology. Now, as you well know, this is not something we can buy legally in an open marketplace – your government would not allow it. But, for the right price, we found out we can buy anything, even if selling this restricted know how would be criminal and possibly treasonous since it could compromise the national security."

"The leaders at my company and I as their special project chief, were agonizing over how best to move forward with our plan to buy this restricted and controlled technology, when the way forward almost fell into our lap. In one of the lighter moments, the security chief of our joint venture partner casually mentioned to me that his CEO was in a financial bind due to large settlements arising from his messy legal battle with his wife who had filed for a divorce for carrying out a long term extra-marital affair with his young broker."

"The security chief did not know the details but had found it quite amusing and ironic that one of the highest paid executives in the country was no different than the average Joe, when it came to personal finances – only the numbers were much larger, but the end result was still the same, you fool around, you pay, and you pay through your nose until you bleed."

Michael Zhang paused again and saw his audience, the Kumars, Captain Thapa and Dr. Johari, who had joined the group, intently listening to his story. He knew they were anxious to hear who he was talking about but were being polite and considerate in not interrupting him and pressuring him to get ahead of himself. He was almost certain that with what he had already disclosed it would not be hard for them to guess the American company he was talking about, but they wanted him to confirm their suspicions. They were ready to bide their time, confident that he would get there eventually and hopefully soon. Dr. Johari was also monitoring the fMRI machine and nodded to Captain Thapa and Dr. Kumar, indicating Michael Zhang was indeed telling the truth.

"It was easy after that," Michael Zhang continued. "We approached our joint venture partner security chief and let him know we were in the market to buy the Materials Technology for aero engines and that we were prepared to pay top dollars, all under the table, no questions asked. The security chief took our offer up his chain of command and got back to us with a proposal. They were prepared to sell the know how to manufacture hot end aero engine materials that were just one generation behind the most modern materials used by the current aero engines in production."

"Now, clearly, we would have liked to have the latest materials but agreed to buy the slightly older technology since it was still far superior to anything we had, or anything we could get in the foreseeable future on our own. This was about three months ago. We deposited half the money, in the high eight figures, in a Swiss account and in return received a document detailing the complete process. It was prepared by their chief metallurgist and was closely examined by our experts to validate its authenticity before the balance of the funds were transferred."

"Due to the highly sensitive and secretive nature of this transaction," Michael Zhang continued, "the agreement was that we would get the details of the process and would have the opportunity to closely examine it and ask any questions we had through the same channels the documents were transferred. We would have a window of 2 weeks to conduct our due diligence and obtain clarifications to our queries. After that, we were on our own. There would be no follow-on support and if discovered by either government, our partner would completely deny having provided the technology."

"In any case, we had no intention of following up since we could not risk an international incident between our countries by getting caught in this clandestine and illegal operation. We had to keep it quiet, even if it meant we lost our high eight figure investments by not being able to translate the written know how into a real product."

"We, of course, had no idea and indeed no interest in knowing how the payoff was distributed, but a large part of it must have made its way to the CEO, since he had to finally authorize the sale."

"Now, over the last three months," he continued, "we have been trying to produce this hot end material in our own laboratory. We have deployed the best minds we have available, including Dr. Xi Ping, on this project but so far have not been successful in achieving all the critical properties. We can get the high temperature and high strength but not the ductility. The material is too brittle, like ceramic, and is not suitable for application in a real aero engine."

"We have tried all possible permutations and combinations varying the fraction of the components in the alloy, the rate of cooling and heating, the environment, etc. but still no success. We are clearly missing something which we have no doubt we will find out over time. We have patience and we can persevere. We, Chinese, do not give up."

"Then, unexpectedly, another opportunity fell into our lap. About three weeks ago, I got a call from the security chief of our joint venture partner with a very enticing proposal. Our JV partner was offering the know-how to the latest hot end material technology, the one flying in all the modern engines around the world and at least a generation ahead of what we had bought. This was again going to be done clandestinely and in violation of the US export control laws. And, best of all, they were not going to ask any more money for it."

"But, in return, we had to get a document signed by Dr. Kumar. They would not tell us what the document was about, only that it was extremely sensitive and time critical and that we needed to get it signed and witnessed within the next two weeks. They added, that due to the regulatory and US legal constraints, they could not do this themselves and needed a third party, preferably from a foreign country, to carry out the mission."

"They provided us the details about Dr. Kumar's movements and left the planning completely up to us. They made it clear that we needed to devise a plan that under no circumstances could be traced back to them, lest there would be severe political and legal consequences."

"We thought hard about their proposal." Michael Zhang continued, "The mission did not sound difficult and we had the resources to do it. But we were not in the business of carrying out illegal and mercenary acts, especially in an unfriendly foreign country. But in the end, the reward of obtaining the technology we so desperately needed justified the risk."

"There was also an additional bonus for us – if we could get Dr. Ravi Kumar to China, as our honored guest, of course, then perhaps he could help us solve the problem we have been having in translating the know-how we had bought and the latest one we had been promised into reality. After much deliberation, our company, CAEC, accepted the proposal from our American Joint Venture Partner."

Michael Zhang paused again and looked around. Not a word had been spoken by any of his audience who were most likely still trying to process what they had just heard. He continued.

"We knew that the Kumars would be in the Darjeeling area and as they have done at their other hideouts, would not be staying underground for long. We had a local outfit track their movements and keep us continuously informed on their whereabouts. I had a team of five of my best men with me on the mission. The plan was to kidnap Dr. Kumar and then transport him to Nepal through an almost open border crossing near Siliguri, the major Indian city at the foothills of the Himalayas and just 30 miles from here. We had scoped out the border crossing, a real quaint scene with people, cows, sheep, bicycle, rickshaws, trucks, and automobiles all sharing a dirt road that connects the two border towns."

"Border control on either side is close to non-existent and whatever there is, can be easily bought with just a few dollars. We had greased the skids amply and with the Indian Dr. Kumar and a bunch of Chinese who look just like the local Nepali Gorkhas, we did not anticipate any problem crossing the border and getting to the nearest Nepalese airport of Bhadrapur."

"We had our private jet waiting at Bhadrapur which would have flown us directly to Kathmandu. From there, we would have flown Dr. Kumar on our own CAEC airliner to Beijing where we had reserved a suite in the best five-star hotel for the duration of his stay, however long it was going to be."

"So, you can see we had no plans of harming Dr. Kumar and only wanted him to visit us as our honored guest and spend some time with us. We had planned our mission well and were confident in its success. We did anticipate some level of security around Dr. Kumar and were prepared for it. What we did not expect and did not plan for was Captain Thapa and his team and the airtight protection they provided to the Kumars. My hat's off to him. I am humiliated at being captured and have failed my company and my country and am ready to accept whatever you decide to do with me."

"I think," Michael Zhang said wrapping up his story, "I have now told you all that you wanted to know truthfully and to best of my knowledge. Go ahead and ask me any questions you may have; I do not have much to hide."

Michael Zhang was still strapped to the fMRI machine and was being continuously monitored by Dr. Anand Johari. He nodded to Captain Thapa to let him know that he was telling the truth. They all felt sorry and somewhat in awe of this sincere and brave Chinese man who had embarked on this dangerous mission not for his personal gains, but for the greater good of his company and his country.

He had considered it to be his duty and had performed it admirably, even if the results were not what he had expected. As Hindus, Dr. Kumar, and Captain Thapa could relate to that. They had both been taught and tried to practice one of the more important teachings of their sacred Hindu book – Bhagwat Gita – "One only has control on their duties and should perform it to the best of their abilities without worrying about the results which will follow as they must." Michael Zhang was not a Hindu but seemed to be following that same universal lesson from whichever book he used as his guide. And for that, he had earned the respect of his audience, even if he was their foe.

But Dr. Kumar did have a few questions for him. He had told them everything except who was behind this. He had a good idea, but he needed confirmation from him. He also was curious to find out what would they have done if he had not cooperated with them after he was abducted and whisked to China as their "honored guest." He thought that would be a good place to start with his questioning.

"Thank you, Mr. Zhang," Dr. Kumar began. "We appreciate your candor and your cooperation. We believe you have been truthful to us. You have kept your side of the bargain and we intend to do so as well. So, whenever you are ready, we will escort you to the border and make sure you are safely out of this country. In the meantime, you will be our guest and Captain Thapa and his team will try and make your stay here as comfortable as possible. But I do have a few questions for you."

"I was wondering," Dr. Kumar continued, "what would you and your colleagues in China have done if I had refused to sign the document or help you resolve your problems with the materials?"

"Well," Michael Zhang replied, "we would have encouraged you to do so. After all, we know all about you. We, of course, know about Dr. Mariko, but we also know about your daughters Lilly, Sita, and Reiko, and where they are. We know you have tried to keep them shielded in various countries, but it was quite easy for us to track them. We were certain that you would do the right thing for yourself and your family and comply with our requests."

Michael Zhang's reply was expected, but it still gave him a chill and made Dr. Kumar's and Captain Thapa's blood boil. They knew this was a war and the old saying of "All is fair in love and war" was the playbook here. They probably would have done the same if the shoe were on the other foot. Michael Zhang, once again, was being honest and forthright, which made his answer somewhat palatable.

Dr. Kumar could not wait any longer to ask that all important question.

"Mr. Zhang, could you please tell us who your joint venture partner is and who orchestrated your mission."

Michael Zhang, still strapped to the fMRI machine in a horizontal position, slowly replied,

"Dr. Kumar and Captain Thapa, you have been kind and civil in your interrogation and I have truthfully replied to all your questions. But I cannot directly respond to this question. I have given my word that I will not reveal the name of our joint venture partner or the people who are behind this mission and I ask for your understanding in not forcing me to break my word."

"Now, I know that you can use your micro-electrode and subject me to the perception of extreme pain which may force me to break my promise and lose whatever little self-respect I have left for myself. I can, however, get you your answer and still keep my word, if you were to name some potential candidate companies and I will nod yes or no to your suggestions. That way, at least in my own mind, I would have kept my word of not revealing the name of our partner company. I hope you grant me this indulgence."

Dr. Kumar and Captain Thapa looked at each other and nodded positively. Michael Zhang had been honest and cooperative with them and they had developed a great deal of respect for the man. They saw no benefit in destroying his self-esteem, which was already at its Nadir due to being captured by them and cuffed and strapped like a common criminal, which he was not by any stretch of imagination.

They were about to start dropping names of potential candidates when Dr. Kumar's unlisted burn phone rang. It was Lilly.

CHAPTER 51

TOKYO, JAPAN - FIVE DAYS TO LAUNCH DATE...

It was late in the afternoon in Tokyo, Japan. Lilly Kumar, the Kumars' eldest daughter, was all packed up for her trip back to the States. She was booked on the evening United Aviation direct flight from Tokyo to New York. Her grandparents had dropped by from their home in the suburbs to her apartment near her University in downtown Tokyo and were helping her pack. She had been in Japan for almost three months and had picked up quite a lot of her mother's native country's language and culture. She had also spent weekends and holidays at her grandparent's home and had gotten quite close to them. They were sorry and sad to see her leave, but understood her life was in the US. She had promised to visit them as often as she could and continue her education in the language – and more importantly, in the ancient and elegant Japanese culture.

Lilly was a junior at Harvard and while in Japan she was enrolled at Sofia University in an intensive Japanese language class. She was also preparing to take her MCAT exam required for attending a medical school. She was a beautiful young woman, mature beyond her years. The maturity had come from being the older sister to her twin sisters, Sita and Reiko, who although only a year younger had looked up to Lilly as their leader and mentor while they were growing up. They attended the local public schools in the town in which their parents happened to live and excelled in their studies as well as extra-curricular activities. On the weekends, they attended Hindi and Japanese classes to get some familiarity with the culture and the language of their parents' native countries. They were fortunate that in their formative years, they had had a strict disciplinarian and dedicated principle who had instilled the value of hard work, empathy, and tenacity that would serve the girls well as they transitioned from their childhood to becoming responsible young adults.

At thirteen, Lilly had represented the children of her country at the first Earth Day summit in Rio de Janeiro, Brazil where she met the then Vice President Al Gore and other leaders of the environment movement. She also visited the Favelas at the outskirts of the city and was moved by the deplorable living conditions of the residents of that suburb, right under the nose of the affluent Brazilians who tanned at the pearly white beaches of Copacabana. It deeply affected her young conscience and she came back a changed and grown up girl wanting to do something for the planet and the people who inhabited it. For quite some time, she was a lost soul, not eating much and not sure what to do. Her parents understood her emotional distress and supported her the best they could to help her overcome the sense of sadness and helplessness she felt.

But, slowly, with the help of her parents and her teachers at the school, she managed to move forward and dedicate herself to her studies and the many extra-curricular activities she was involved with. Although not fully sold, she had accepted her parent's advice to pursue a career in medicine that not only provided a decent quality of life for herself and her future family, but also gave her the skill set to help her community in a tangible and meaningful way.

Lilly graduated from her high school as the valedictorian and was admitted to many of the country's prestigious colleges. The choice eventually came down to Cornell, the alma mater of her parents, or Harvard. After much agonizing, she chose Harvard and immersed herself in the demanding premed course work maintaining a GPA of close to 4.0. The time at Harvard almost flew and before she or her parents knew, she was just a year away from graduating. She was a junior now and was scheduled to take her MCAT exams that fall when the unexpected turn of events with her parents forced her to consider rescheduling it and extend her stay in Japan. Fortunately, she had been able to prepare for this critical milestone in her life and if possible did not want to reschedule it. Although there were several other dates still available and if necessary, she could take the exams later, she wanted to take them while the material from her last three months of concentrated preparation was still fresh in her mind.

She had called her parents, the night they were attacked at the Buddhist temple,

"Hi Dad, how is it going?" she asked when Ravi answered his phone.

"Well, not so great," Ravi replied.

He then briefly summarized the incidents at the Buddhist Pagoda and the attacks on him and Caitlyn.

Lilly was horrified to hear about their experience. She was enormously proud of her parents to have accepted the significant risks in standing up to the powerful corporations and follow their convictions. They had kept her and her sisters fully in the decision-making process and she supported them whole heartedly. Nevertheless, she was worried about their safety and well-being. So, when she heard about the attacks and that her father was temporarily incapacitated, she blurted out,

"Dad, I am relieved to hear you guys are all right. But I am worried. Can I come and see you in India?"

"Lilly, we are fine now and have the people who attacked us in our custody and are currently interrogating them. We know you are scheduled to take your MCAT and we would like you to concentrate on that. Since we have the two team leaders captured, we think it would be safe for you to return to the US to take the exams. I will send a text to my friend in Westchester, Dr. Gopal, whom you have met, to pick you up. You can stay with them while in New York and getting ready to take the MCAT," Ravi said.

"Dad, I can take the MCAT later on. I really think I should come and spend some time with you and Mom," Lilly insisted.

"Listen, our run is almost over, and we would be heading back home, as well. So, don't worry about us and concentrate on your tests. Just be careful," Ravi said.

"OK, if you insist. I will call you as soon as I land at JFK tomorrow," Lilly said as she bid goodbye to her parents.

He had sent a text to his friend Dr. Gopal asking him to pick Lilly up at the airport and that he would fill him in on what was going on with him and Caitlyn when he saw him in a few days.

That was last night.

Lilly was happy to get her parents' approval to travel back to her country of birth. She arrived at Tokyo's Narita international airport well in time and bid farewell to her grandparents. It was a sad moment, but she knew her stay in Japan had brought her closer to them and she would forever cherish their time together. But now it was time to move on and she was looking forward to spending some time in the Big Apple, a city she had visited frequently from her home in Ithaca and had fallen in love with. She was also excited, albeit somewhat apprehensive about the MCAT, but was confident that with all the preparation she had done over the last three months, she should do well in these tests which weighed heavily in getting accepted to a good medical school. She also could not wait to get back with her friend Jesse, who had become a big part of her life at Harvard.

Her plane landed at the JFK international airport slightly ahead of schedule. She texted her parents as soon as the plane touched down,

"Just arrived at JFK. Will text again once I am settled in Westchester."

She also texted Jesse. He was doing a summer internship at Harvard.

"Hi, back state side. Would love to see you."

He texted back within a minute promising to come and visit her that weekend. Lilly was happy and was feeling quite upbeat as she made her way through customs and immigration and collected her bags. She joined the throng of passengers as they came out of the exit gate which was crowded with family and friends. There were also Limo and cab drivers from professional transfer services with placards bearing the names of their customers. One of those placards had the name Lilly Kumar printed on it and was carried by a smartly dressed, middle-aged Indian man.

Lilly was expecting her Dad's friend who would be her host during her stay in New York to be there at the airport to pick her up. She had only met him a couple of times and that was several years ago, so she did not quite remember what he looked like. But, when she saw her name being held by an Indian man, she assumed it was either her host or someone arranged by him to meet her and bring her over to Westchester where she would be staying. She approached the man with the placard and asked him if he was her Dad's friend or if he was sent by him. The man smiled and replied,

"Hello, Miss Kumar. Welcome back to the United States. I am sorry, he was held up in a last-minute meeting and has sent me to pick you up. He will see you back at the house."

Although Lilly was a cautious girl, and even more so due to what was happening to her parents, it all appeared to be above board to her, and she gladly handed her roller boards to the man and followed him to his car, which was waiting just outside the exit gate.

It was a black SUV like many others plying the street of the Big Apple and even Ithaca. A uniformed driver was at the wheel. Lilly found it somewhat odd that her Dad's friend would send an official looking vehicle with two people just to pick her up. She simply chalked it up to his affluence and got into the back seat of the SUV. The man who had come to meet her inside got in the front passenger seat and the car rolled off the curb and was soon on the highway to Westchester.

It all looked perfectly normal and Lilly was hungrily taken in the view of her favorite city, enjoying the gorgeous fall afternoon in the Big Apple. They had just gotten on the highway when the man in the front passenger seat who had come to greet her at the airport turned around with a small gun in his hand. Lilly's face turned white; she knew she was in big trouble, and that she was now part of the deadly drama unfolding with her parents.

"Give me your phone and do not make any noise," the man instructed Lilly in a menacing tone.

She complied, realizing that was her only safe and wise choice under the circumstances.

The man opened the window and threw it out – he did not want the GPS in the phone to track their movement. Lilly knew she was being kidnapped. The beautiful fall afternoon had suddenly lost all its charm and appeared to be dark and grey, but she reminded herself that she was a Kumar, brought up by parents who were not afraid to stand up for their beliefs even if it meant putting themselves in harm's way. Her initial fear had given way to a steely determination to keep her wits about herself and get ready to fight. She had full faith in the deep-rooted belief she had been brought up with that in the end Right will prevail and they were on the side of Right….

CHAPTER 52

MANHATTAN, NEW YORK - FOUR DAYS TO LAUNCH DATE...

In Manhattan, at the corporate headquarters of United Electric, Bill MacMillan was pacing the length of his corner suite nervously and furiously. He had just gotten off the phone with his security chief who had told him about the failed mission in Darjeeling, India. Project **At Any Cost**, the highly secretive and clandestine mission to force Dr. Ravi Kumar to sign an exclusive contract for MRI 297, had gone horribly wrong. The elite team sent to capture Dr. Kumar and bring him over to Beijing, China had miserably failed in its mission and the team leader, the decorated and extremely reliable and resourceful Michael Zhang had been captured and was now in custody of the Indians. Bill MacMillan was livid and let his security chief have it. But he knew his dumping on the security chief might help him vent his anger but would not solve anything. In fact, he needed the full cooperation of his security chief to get through this disaster and contain the far-reaching harm it could do not only to his corporation but to himself personally.

The problem was now much bigger than just forcibly getting a commercial contract signed. It now involved violating national security which bordered on being treasonous. He did not even want to think of the penalties that would be meted out if the state ever discovered what he had done. He was despondent and could feel it in his bones that his gig was up. But he reminded himself, he was Bill MacMillan, the head of one of the most powerful corporations in the world. He had worked hard to get there, and he was not going to go down without a fight. He needed to clear his head and think and come up with a plan – he always did, and he would do it again. He just needed to be calm and be the leader he was and was going to be for many years to come.

He called back his security chief,

"I am sorry Ed, for losing it this morning. I know it was not your fault and that we need to get ourselves together and strategize on out the best way forward. Can you come over to my office right away?"

"I am on my way."

Bill knew the security chief was as much in this as he was, and he had no scruples to pin it all on him, if it became a choice between saving his own hide or roping one of his trusted lieutenants. He was aware of the moniker – Ruthless Bill – a faint smile broke out on his face. He was beginning to feel better already.

Ed Malone, the security chief of United Electric, was a retired FBI agent. In his late fifties, he was built like a tank and had a full head of salt-and-pepper hair. He had been through many battles inside and outside of the bureau and had been with the company ever since he retired, some ten years ago. He had a good working relationship with his current boss, Bill MacMillan, and knew all about his reputation as a ruthless executive and that if the chips were down, the only person he would care for was Bill MacMillan. He also knew about his Contessa and her awfully expensive taste in jewelry, designer clothing, and the exclusive club hopping lifestyle of the rich and famous.

A large part of Bill MacMillan's earnings - pay and stock options – went towards keeping his Contessa living the high life of the privileged one percent. Unbeknown to Bill MacMillan, Ed Malone had meticulously kept records of all his correspondence with him. This included a detailed trace of their underhanded and illegal dealings with the Chinese and the large sums of money transferred to the personal account of Bill MacMillan. And just like Bill MacMillan, he would not hesitate to use this information to take down his boss if it ever came to that.

He arrived at the corner suite of Bill MacMillan from his office on the fourth floor in less than two minutes and took his seat at the large conference table in Bill's suite.

"Come on in, Ed. And once again, I am sorry for my outburst."

The security chief simply nodded and smiled. They were just the two of them in the large office. They were more than colleagues in a large international enterprise; they were also co-conspirators in many of the clandestine and often illegal activities that large corporations such as theirs might engage in. It could range from bribing some third world country official to securing a favorable disposition on their proposal to underbidding competition after unscrupulously obtaining insight into their bids. But it had never gone as far as it had gone with illegally transferring data on the restricted and controlled materials which could compromise national security. They had justified their actions by considering what they had sold as outdated materials technology which had already been replaced with new and more capable materials.

They had used the same justification when they offered to the Chinese the current generation of materials, flying both in commercial and military aircrafts, which will soon be superseded by MRI 297. They did not feel any remorse and simply considered it a good business deal for themselves and for the country. They were bringing in a considerable amount of money into the country for something that would have little or no value in just a few years after MRI 297 has been pressed into service. In their contorted way of thinking, they were helping reduce the trade deficit with a country that was accused of playing an unfair game.

"Ed, I think you already know this, but it looks like we have chewed off more than we can swallow, and we may be in big trouble," Bill MacMillan said as his security chief took his seat at the large conference table in Bill's office.

"I think we are. But this would not be first time we have skirted around the laws and have managed to keep the business going. We are one of the major employers in many of the congressional districts around the country and have maintained a high level of employment there. Our exports of high value-added products have significantly helped with the balance of payments in manufactured goods. We have a lot of chits from representatives both inside and outside the government and I am sure we can call upon some of those to help us get out of this mess," Ed Malone replied, trying to mollify his boss.

Bill MacMillan was well aware of all that, but it still was helpful and somewhat pacifying to hear it from his co-conspirator.

"That does make me feel better. But we have never had a situation where one of our key operatives was captured. How are we going to contain the damage from Michael Zhang's capture?" he asked rhetorically.

Bill MacMillan had met Michael Zhang several times and was extremely impressed by the well-read and well-spoken Chinese man. He knew Michael Zhang was the point man in the transactions with their Joint Venture partners involving the illegal transfer of the materials technology. He was also their special project team leader and was intricately linked to Project MRI 297. United Electric was counting on him to "convince" Dr. Kumar and get him to sign the exclusive contract. With the new engine launch date just days away, UE needed to give a go ahead to its aero engine division to move forward with this new material and fulfill its commitment to Jack Stevens, the chairman of American Aviation and other airlines to deliver an engine that would meet the game changing fuel burn and emission goals.

Instead, they had this catastrophic turn of events on their hands. He had no doubt Michael Zhang was a brave man and had been through many battles. This could not be the first time when he was interrogated by enemies and adversaries and he must have developed high pain thresholds. But they also knew that with persistence anyone could eventually be broken. They had to assume Michael Zhang would talk, and they would all be exposed. The resulting fall out would not only be disastrous for them but could also irreparably harm their venerable company. They had to find a way to prevent this from happening.

"Ed, we have got to find a way to spring Michael Zhang from the Indians. We cannot afford to let his confessions fall in the hands of any of the countries involved – India, China, and of course the United States," Bill MacMillan said with some desperation in his voice.

"I agree, Bill. Except right now I am not sure how. But let me think about it," Ed Malone said.

Just then, the private phone of the security chief rang. Only a select number of his people had this number – one of them was their Tokyo operative, tasked with the surveillance of Lilly Kumar.

"Ed, I have some important news for you."

"What is it?" Ed Malone asked impatiently. He was not happy to be disturbed during his meeting with the CEO.

"I just saw Lilly board a flight to New York. Looks like she is on her way back to the States."

UE had been keeping track of all three Kumar girls, spread out in different parts of the world. And as serendipity would have it, Lilly Kumar was on her way back to the US and was on an American Aviation flight from Tokyo to New York.

This was a gift that the two conspirators did not expect. Bill MacMillan and his security chief had considered the Kumar girls as part of a backup plan as an additional incentive to persuade Dr. Ravi Kumar to sign the exclusive rights contract. If necessary, they were going to temporarily abduct one of the girls and have her be their house guest until her father accepted their demands. They knew, if they followed through on this, they would have transitioned from a civil to a criminal act with severe punishments and recriminations. Their hope was it would not come to that and they would be able to break Dr. Kumar by their attacks on him and his wife. So far, not only had they not been successful, but they had also failed miserably, exposing them to potentially disastrous consequences.

"OK, we will take up her surveillance when she gets to New York," Ed Malone said as he hung up.

Ed Malone looked at Bill MacMillan, who had been listening their conversation. They agreed the time had come to execute the backup plan: Snatch Lilly Kumar when she lands at JFK and then use her as a hostage to demand release of Michael Zhang, destruction of all evidence linking them to the illegal transfer of the restricted and export-controlled materials technology and sign off on the exclusive rights contract for MRI 297. Dr. Kumar, they surmised, would have no choice but to agree to their demands, if he wanted to see his oldest daughter alive again.

Bill MacMillan and the security chief, for the first time in last several days, felt relieved and raised a toast with the single malt scotch that Bill MacMillan had taken out of his cabinet.

That was last night.

Bill MacMillan was once again pacing his office waiting for the word from his security chief. Lilly Kumar's plane had landed forty-five minutes ago, and she should be making her way to the exit. He was keeping his fingers firmly crossed. A lot depended on the success of their plan – either the whole nightmare with Michael Zhang would completely blow over, or he might be locked up behind bars for a long time. It was now not just a matter of selling State secrets, but he had stepped into the realm of criminal offence with the kidnapping of a young woman. He could not believe how low he had sunk down, and all that to win the heart and love of his elegant and beautiful Contessa. And he was not even sure if she was with him for his money and his power or if she really loved him. But he did not care, all he knew that he could not live without her and would do anything to keep her in his life. He did not also care that it was hard for anyone to comprehend that a man like him who had the reputation of being a calculating, ruthless, self-centered person even had a heart and would throw everything away for the sake of a woman. But that is exactly what he was doing and he himself did not understand why. Maybe it was because the Contessa made him feel young and vibrant, something his wife of thirty years did not do any longer. He had married her when he was just starting out and she had been a good partner and companion as he slowly rose through the corporate hierarchy. But now, she had become domesticated and predictable with little room for adventure and excitement. No, he needed his

Contessa and did not care what happened to him. He was ready to face whatever lay ahead. For the sake of his love. His Contessa.

He almost jumped out of his skin when his phone rang.

"The bird has been captured." It was Ed Malone.

"Where is she now?"

"She is being driven to one of our safe houses," Ed Malone replied.

"Keep her safe and keep me posted."

Bill MacMillan breathed a big sigh of relief as he slumped in his oversize executive chair. For a change, something had gone right. He was back in the game. Now, he just needed to contact Dr. Kumar and give him the "good news." He was about to get on his personal unlisted phone when the phone rang again. He was quite annoyed at his secretary to have disturbed him, but then again, he knew she would dare to do that only if it were an important call that could not wait.

He picked up the phone. It was the chairman of the board, and his titular boss, Harry Daniels. Bill MacMillan did not much care for the chairman and considered him and the entire United Electric board to be superfluous and more of a nuisance and distraction to his running the corporation. He was hoping to add the chairman's title to his name soon and was actively working towards it. But for now, he needed to keep up the pretense and treat Harry Daniels as his superior.

"Harry, I was not expecting your call," Bill MacMillan said.

"Bill, I was expecting you to get back to me with an update on the new engine, and more specifically, on the new material. Have you signed the contract?" Harry Daniel asked.

"I am still working on it. Dr. Kumar is playing hardball and is not accepting our terms and conditions which we believe are reasonable and in the best interest of all concerned," Bill MacMillan said.

He neglected to mention anything about UE insisting on an exclusive rights contract which was the reason for Dr. Kumar not signing the contract. The chairman and the board, of course, knew nothing about the illegal export of the restricted materials technology, the international manhunt that Bill MacMillan had put in action, and certainly nothing about the kidnapping of Lilly Kumar.

Harry Daniels could sense the annoyance and impatience in his CEO's voice. He knew all was not well and even if Bill MacMillan did not ask for it, he needed help.

"Look, Jack Stevens called me about the new engine and that it would meet all his requirements. He was specifically concerned about getting the new material in the engine and I promised to get back to him. I see you have your hands full, so let me call Dr. Kumar myself and see what is going on and if I can help. Do you have his contact number?"

Bill MacMillan thought for a moment and took this as another godsend opportunity. The chairman can do his dirty work to let Dr. Kumar know that he had his daughter in his captivity. He was also not sure if Ravi would even take his call, given the bad blood and threats he had made to him at their earlier encounters.

He gave the chairman Ravi's unlisted phone number and requested the chairman that when he did talk to Dr. Kumar to please ask him to call him as soon as possible and that it would be in their mutual interest to do so.

This was clearly some code language between the two men. The chairman did not ask for any clarifications from his CEO. Somehow, he felt, it may be easier and more reliable to understand the meaning behind those code words, from Dr. Kumar than from his own CEO.

Bill's phone rang again as soon as the chairman had hung up.

"Bill, you better take this phone call." It was Ed Malone, his voice trembling as he connected Bill to the man on the line.

CHAPTER 53

MANHATTAN, NEW YORK - FOUR DAYS TO LAUNCH DATE...

"Bill MacMillan here. Who am I talking to?"

"I am Michael Zhang's superior calling from Beijing." It was the gravelly voice.

A shiver went through Bill MacMillan's body when he heard that voice. He had never spoken to the man with the gravelly voice but had no doubt he was who he said he was, and that his call meant trouble. He replied apprehensively,

"What can I do for you?"

"You have the Kumar girl in your custody. I want you to make sure she is safe and is out of harm's way in a secure location. I want you to then call her father and instruct him to release Michael Zhang and travel with him to Beijing. I have our corporate jet waiting just across the border in Nepal that will bring them to Beijing. He is to stay with us for as long as it takes to help us solve the problem with getting the properties in the super alloy that we have bought from you and which we have not been able to obtain thus far. The sooner he can get us to successfully achieve the objectives, the sooner he can leave Beijing and head home. In return, you would promise him to disclose the location of his daughter and that she would be safe and unharmed," the gravelly voice said, with no preamble, in accented but clear English. The gravelly voice had undoubtedly spent time in the West.

"And I should listen to you because…" Bill MacMillan answered meekly, knowing full well what his caller's response would be. His brain was working furiously to find a way out of the very grave danger he had put himself and his entire corporation in, and he was just trying to stall.

"I think you already know the answer. But let me spell it out for you. We have foolproof evidence of the illegal transfer of highly protective and export-controlled defense technology that you have sold to us and that can put you behind bars for the rest of your life and would be catastrophic if not fatal for your storied company. If you do not comply with my instructions exactly as I have just stated, these documents will be handed over to the authorities and will also be leaked to the press. Do not ask me how and do not try to second guess me. You have no way out, Mr. MacMillan. Do you understand?" the gravelly voice asked sternly, leaving no doubt in Bill MacMillan's mind that squirm as he may he had no choice but to obey the commands just given to him by this man from China.

"I understand."

"Good. I expect to see Michael Zhang and Dr. Kumar in Beijing within the next twelve hours. And for your sake, you better not fail," the gravelly voice said as he hung up.

CHAPTER 54

DARJEELING, INDIA – FOUR DAYS TO LAUNCH DATE...

In Darjeeling, Dr. Ravi Kumar and Dr. Caitlyn Mariko were in full panic mode. Ravi had just gotten a text from his friend, Dr. Gopal, in New York telling him he had yet not connected with Lilly. It had been more than an hour since Lilly had sent Ravi a text letting him know her plane had landed at JFK. Even allowing for the delay in customs and immigration and baggage pick up, she should have already been at the exit gate. Dr. Gopal had gotten stuck in the heavy New York traffic and was fifteen minutes late getting to the airport. But that did not explain why he had not seen Lilly yet. She should have been waiting for him at the exit.

Ravi tried calling her, but it went straight to her voicemail. Ravi then called Jesse to see if he had heard from Lilly. He had and was going to see her that weekend in the city. She was going to call him once she had settled down at her host's house in Westchester. Ravi did not know what else he could do. He asked Dr. Gopal to please wait a little longer and see if she showed up. Ravi was getting a really bad feeling about it and could not stop second guessing himself having allowed her to travel to

New York while the matter with the two conglomerates had still not settled and they were still on the run.

The shrill sound of his unlisted phone brought him to the present and out of his self-recriminating state of mind. He jumped and answered it on the first ring. He was hoping to hear Lilly's voice.

"Yes," He said with anticipation and apprehension in his voice.

"This is Harry Daniels. I am the Chairman of the board of United Electric. Is this Dr. Ravi Kumar?"

Ravi had briefly met the chairman on previous occasions but barely knew him, except that he was the retired chief executive and chairman of a leading bank and that his expertise was in finance and not in engineering. Ravi had come back quite impressed with the chairman and had formed a favorable impression of him.

Now, if it were any other time, Ravi would have considered it an honor to get a direct call from someone like Harry Daniels. But these were not normal times and Ravi was in a panic state of mind. He also wanted to keep his personal unlisted phone line open.

"Yes, it is. How can I help you?" he answered, somewhat abruptly.

The chairman sensed the panic and urgency in Ravi's voice and immediately came to the point.

"Dr. Kumar, I am calling to talk to you about your new super alloy and the status of the contract with my company for using it."

"I also have a message from Bill MacMillan, our CEO, whom I believe you know. He would like you to know that both you and he are holding something that is especially important to the two of you and that you need to get in touch with him as soon as possible," Harry Daniels added.

Ravi's face went completely white. His worst fear had happened. Bill had almost certainly kidnapped Lilly and was holding her hostage. He now also knew who Michael Zhang was working for – it was, just as he had suspected all along, United Electric.

He was silent for what seemed like an eternity to the chairman patiently waiting on the other end of the line. Although he could not see Ravi's face, he knew the news was not good and that he was in a state of shock. The chairman had expected as much when he talked to Bill MacMillan. The chairman broke the silence,

"Dr. Kumar, are you all right?"

Ravi barely stammered a reply, which the chairman could not discern. He persisted and asked again if everything were all right and if he could help. Ravi could not contain himself any longer and let out what appeared to be a muffled sob. He was trying to gain his composure back, but the thought of Lilly being in harm's way was too much to bear. He begged,

"Please forgive me, Mr. Daniels, for my outburst. I am not myself right now. Tell me again the reason for your call."

The chairman of United Electric had been around the block a few times and knew that the reason for his call, to get an update on the signing of the contract for the new super alloy, must be intricately linked to whatever that had happened and that had so distressed this man of science and technology, whose profession is usually perceived to be dry and bereft of expressing outward emotions.

"Dr. Kumar," Harry Daniels said, "I called you to talk about the contract, but I sense that the news from Bill MacMillan has caused you significant pain and distress and I think it involves my company. Would you like to tell me what it is about? It may well be connected with what I called you about and if possible, I would like to help."

He then added,

"I would like you to know that I am on your side and would like to do what was right for both you and my company."

"I know a lot of people, including high level officials in the government and the law enforcement agencies and that I can bring the full weight of my contacts both inside and outside the government to right whatever wrong that might have been done to you and your family." Harry Daniels said, sounding sincere and empathetic.

Ravi was moved by the genuine sincerity in the voice of Harry Daniels. He had regained some of his composure back and had been thinking about the way forward to cope with this unexpected turn of events. He knew that as long as he had Michael Zhang and his confessions, Bill MacMillan was not going to harm Lilly. He also had full confidence in his daughter and her ability to keep her cool and not panic. She would know that it would not be long before help would arrive, and she just had to best manage the situation as it arose.

But still, Ravi could use the help and contacts from this powerful and well-connected man who had a reputation of being a fair person and a straight shooter. He needed to get him on his side and the only way to do that was to tell him his story and the pain and suffering to which his people had subjected him and his family.

"Thank you, Mr. Daniels. I do very much appreciate your concern, and yes you have guessed it right. My family and I are in considerable trouble now and can certainly use help from someone like you."

He told him the same thing he had told the chairwoman of General Technologies and that it was a long story and he was not sure if the chairman had the time or patience to hear it. Harry Daniels assured him he had all the time in the world and that it was important for him to get the complete picture so that he could be of help in addressing whatever was causing him so much distress.

Now, this would be the second or third time, Ravi had lost count, that he would be narrating the harrowing story of their hide and seek around the world. And this time he was going to try and keep it as short as possible, but he considered it important to cover the ground to give the chairman a good understanding of what had happened thus far, and why. He also knew that the chairman of United Electric was not an engineer and perhaps not as grounded in science and technology as the chairwoman of General Technologies, Ms. Watson was, to whom he had told the story just a few days ago.

Ravi then went on to narrate almost the same story as he had given to Ms. Watson, albeit keeping it less technical. He got to the point where he had begun discussions with his company and had offered the new super alloy for use in their new engine design. He said to the chairman,

"About three months ago we offered this new material to both your company and your competitor and they were both quite interested. But they both wanted exclusive use rights and offered very lucrative contracts to do so."

He then added:

"Although we at the Materials Research Institute were quite tempted, in the end we could not agree to their demand." He then went on to explain his reasoning for turning down their exclusive rights demand which was to maintain a healthy competition in the marketplace and keep the continuous advancement in the state of the art incentivized.

Harry Daniels finally understood why the contract for the new super alloy was not yet signed. His chief executive officer had not bothered to provide him or the board the conditions he had laid out for Dr. Kumar and his refusal to accept those conditions. He was not happy. But this was just the beginning; he did not yet know it, but there was a lot more to the story than what he had heard so far.

Ravi then took the chairman of United Electric through the events of the last three months starting with him and Caitlyn almost being run off the road alongside Lake Cayuga in Ithaca and their around the world flight in search of a safe haven.

His hope had been, he added, that the companies would have to back off and accept his terms once it got closer to the drop-dead date for the launch of the new engine. And they had just about succeeded and were at the last two weeks mark of the final count down. But then two days ago, right here in Darjeeling, India things went completely awry.

"We had our suspicions," Dr. Kumar continued, "but it was only when we captured two of the attackers that our suspicions were confirmed about one of the corporations behind these attacks – General Technologies, your competitor. And only today from your phone call we were finally able to connect the other attacker to your company and your Joint Venture partner in China. We now have in our custody the leader of the team sent from China and have been interrogating him for the last twenty-four hours. His name is Michael Zhang and he is right here in the room listening to our conversations. I will let you hear from him directly what your company and your leadership has been involved in and that it is much more than simply getting the contract for the new super alloy signed. It is also causally related to the events that have just unfolded in New York and for which your CEO, Bill MacMillan wants to talk to me. It involves my daughter."

With that Ravi handed his phone to Captain Thapa, who along with Dr. Caitlyn Mariko, Dr. Johari, and Michael Zhang had been listening to the call. Captain Thapa raised the fMRI bed to allow Michael Zhang to sit up, still cuffed and constrained, and speak into the mic. The chairman was on the speaker and could be heard by everyone in the room.

But before Michael Zhang began, Dr. Johari, the inventor of the truth machine, gave the chairman a quick overview of his invention and how it was used to detect if a person was telling the truth. He did not talk about the micro electrode imbedded in Michael Zhang's skull and its use in encouraging someone to talk by subjecting them to only perceived rather than real physical pain. Dr. Johari concluded his brief introduction emphasizing that whatever the chairman heard from Michael Zhang would be the truth and if at any point he was telling a lie, he would interject and spike him out.

Michael Zhang started by introducing himself as the chief of special projects at the United Electric and China Aero Engine Company Joint Venture. The chairman was familiar with this joint venture but did not know Michael Zhang and was anxious to hear his story.

Michael Zhang began by talking about his most recent mission which was to snatch Dr. Kumar and bring him over to Beijing where he was expected to sign some documents sent by United Electric. He did not know what the document was but based on what he had learned since his capture by Dr. Kumar's people, he suspected they were the exclusive rights contract documents.

This news the chairman had expected and although he was furious at his chief executive for using such strong-arm tactics, he was not completely surprised. He, like the rest of the industry, had known about the ruthless character of his CEO and to a certain extent even condoned it.

But what he heard next, gave the chairman of United Electric a chill and shudder the like of which he had never experienced in his long career. Michael Zhang was talking about illegal export of products protected by the United States Government under the National Security laws. Could his company with its illustrious past and status as an icon of the American Industrial be involved in such illegal and possibly treasonous acts? He did not want to believe it, but Michael Zhang gave convincing evidence of large amount of money being transferred to the personal accounts of the security chief and his CEO, Bill MacMillan.

Harry Daniels, the chairman of United Electric, had heard rumors about Bill MacMillan's affair with the Contessa and his large divorce settlements with his ex-wife, but had not paid much attention it. In his and his board's mind, it was his personal affair and had no bearing on his ability to lead the company. He had rationalized it by thinking in today's America it was almost a norm to have extra-marital liaisons and it was not his or his board's business to be meddling in his CEO's personal life. Based on his exemplary successes with the various divisions of the corporation, Harry Daniels had been one of the vocal supporters of Bill MacMillan and had the final say in selecting him over Dave Ward as the Chief Executive Officer of United Electric.

Now, listening to Michael Zhang, all he could do was to feel a great sense of remorse, and anger not only at his CEO but also at himself for recommending Bill MacMillan for the top job and putting the fate of the entire corporation and the hundreds of thousands of men and women that work for it at peril. Michael Zhang was finished but it was not the end of the story. There was more.

Dr. Kumar took over the narrative. He talked about his three daughters who had been hiding around the world until it was safe to come back home. He then, with his voice breaking down, told the chairman about his decision to allow his eldest daughter to come back to New York from Japan so that she could take the all-important MCAT tests for admission to medical school. With the two antagonists under their captivity and less than a week left until the expiration of the launch clock, he had considered it safe for her to return. But he was wrong. His daughter had arrived in New York about an hour ago and was supposed to be picked up by his friend. He had received a text from his daughter after her plane had landed and she was going to text him again after she had settled in his friend's place in Westchester. His friend, Dr. Kumar continued, was going to meet her at the airport and let him know when they were on their way to his house. Instead, he got a text from his friend, just before the call from the chairman, telling him his daughter was nowhere to be found and that he was getting quite worried.

"And then you called," Dr. Kumar said to the chairman, "with a message from Bill MacMillan that he has something of great value to me which can only mean he has kidnapped my daughter and now has her in his custody. He is holding her hostage, most likely to secure the release of Michael Zhang and destruction of any evidence we have against him."

At the thought of his daughter being in harm's way and a pawn in this deadly game of greed and power, Dr. Ravi Kumar, a grown man and an eminent engineer and scientist, could not contain himself and was sobbing hard as he paused to take a breath. Caitlyn had taken over the role of the stronger parent and was trying hard to console Ravi, rubbing him on his back.

The chairman of United Electric, at the other end of a five thousand miles electronic connection, could almost feel the anguish of this father. He was a father and grandfather himself and could well empathize with the plight of the man who was only trying to do the right thing. He could not believe what he had just heard and had to use all his will power and self-control to not let out his own sense of despair and raw anger at his one-time protégé.

"Dr. Kumar, to say I am sorry for what my company has done to you and your family will not even come close to the anger and remorse I am feeling at my chief executive and myself on behalf of the board. You can be rest assured that the full weight of the law will be brought upon him and all involved in this insidious and criminal act and that I am going to do all within my power to secure the release of your daughter."

"I personally know the deputy director of the FBI and am myself going to lead a task force comprising law enforcement and our own internal security team to locate and free her. I would like you and your wife to come back to New York immediately and join me and others as an integral and critical part of this task force," Harry Daniels added.

With that, the chairman bid goodbye to the Kumars, telling them he looked forward to meeting with them when they were back in the city.

The chairman's sincerity and his words somewhat assuaged the Kumars' worries about their daughter. They now had just one mission, to get back to New York and do all they could to make sure their daughter was back home safely. They called their host in India, Dr. Shiavats Pradhan, in Kalimpong and let him know that they would not be coming back and to have their belongings shipped back to the States at his convenience. Dr. Pradhan had been getting updates from Captain Thapa, so it was not a surprise to learn of the Kumars' decision. Dr. Kumar then bid his farewell to Captain Ram Bahadur Thapa and Dr. Anand Johari for all their help and support and instructed Captain Thapa to hold Michael Zhang until they had located and freed Lilly. He then thanked Michael Zhang for his truthfulness and his dedication and commitment to his company and to his country telling him that someday they might meet again in more favorable circumstances. Michael Zhang, the feisty Chinese man from Beijing, simply looked at the Kumars with sadness in his eyes and the unspoken words they communicated expressing his deep sorrow and hope their suffering will end soon.

Dr. Kumar had one more unpleasant task to do before he and Caitlyn left Darjeeling, and that was to call Bill MacMillan. He took out his cell and was about to make the call when it rang. It was Bill MacMillan.

CHAPTER 55

NEW YORK – FOUR DAYS TO LAUNCH DATE...

The black SUV carrying Lilly Kumar had left the JFK airport and the borough of Queens behind and was now making its way North, heading to the small ritzy town not far from the city. The town was home to many rich and famous from all backgrounds, affording them exclusive and private habitats. It was also the site of one of the several guest houses United Electric maintained for its customers, suppliers, government officials, and visiting company executives. Its remote and secluded location was ideal for many of the company's guests who needed to keep a discrete and low profile for conducting their business, not all of which was always legitimate.

The UE guest house, just like the others the company maintained in the region, was fully furnished with all modern conveniences, and was stocked with ample supplies. It was also fully secure. There were no house phones – most of the guests preferred to use their own personal phones or be completely away from them for the days they spent there. All windows were double pane and were fixed. The doors had electronic locks which could only be opened with special magnetic keys even from the inside. This was for additional privacy to prevent hired help from opening the doors inadvertently, if the house guest was indisposed or did not want to have any visitors or in special cases, such as that with Lilly, the guest needed to be restrained from venturing outside the house.

It was going to be the temporary home for Lilly Kumar until she was moved to yet another UE guest house. Bill MacMillan had instructed Ed Malone to make sure she was safe and secure in her temporary abode. He also wanted her to be moved from one location to another and keep her whereabouts secret and known to as few people on his team as was absolutely necessary. The warning from the Chinese man with gravelly voice was still ringing in his ears.

"Ed, we cannot screw this up. Ask your guys to be extra vigilant and text me her whereabouts confirming that she is safe and secure. I am going to personally run this operation and am counting on you to make it happen."

"I understand," Ed Malone replied, somewhat irked at his boss for having usurped his role. He was expecting to be running this delicate operation himself but had to defer to his superior even if he did not fully agree with his command.

Ed Malone did not know this, but Bill MacMillan had other plans for Lilly. He was fully expecting the law to eventually catch up and he wanted to buy as much time as possible using Lilly as his human shield.

CHAPTER 56

DARJEELING, INDIA – FOUR DAYS TO LAUNCH DATE...

"Dr. Kumar, this is Bill MacMillan here. I have your daughter. Listen very carefully to what I have to say. Your daughter's life depends upon it," Bill MacMillan said, with no preamble, when Ravi answered his phone.

"I am listening and will do whatever you want me to do. Just do not harm my daughter," Ravi said, trying hard to control his true feeling for the man whose neck he would not hesitate to wring and would have no remorse doing it.

"Good. There is a private jet waiting for you at Bhadrapur in Nepal, just about an hour drive from where you are. You will be taking that plane to Beijing. Michael Zhang will be accompanying you. In Beijing, you will help the Chinese resolve the problem they are having with the super alloy they are trying to produce. Michael Zhang can fill you in with the details. Once the Chinese have successfully produced the super alloy, they will board you on their latest Bombardier Global 7500 executive jet for non-stop flight to New York. Once the plane lands in New York and just before you disembark, the crew will give you an envelope with the address of the house where your daughter is being held. Also, before departing your current location you will destroy all physical and electronic records of your interrogation of Michael Zhang and you will do it in his presence. I assure you; your daughter is safe and will remain safe and will be waiting for you at the house if you do exactly as you are instructed to do."

"How do I know you are telling the truth and that my daughter is safe and will remain safe?" Dr. Kumar asked, his voice trembling as the shock of what he had just heard began to subside. He was being blackmailed into going to a country which was known to have autocratic rules and where people could vanish without trace. As he began to think about all the things that could go wrong and that he may be stuck in that foreign land for a long time, his face began turning white; Caitlyn watched him in horror, worrying that he may collapse again.

"You don't. You only have my word and you need to believe me for the sake of your daughter and do as I say. Do not approach the authorities and do not try to communicate with me. I will contact you if I need to with further instructions, if not it is goodbye," Bill MacMillan said menacingly.

"I will do it. Just do not hurt Lilly," Dr. Kumar said as Bill MacMillan hung up.

"Caitlyn, I have to go to Beijing with Michael Zhang," Ravi said, almost whispering. He then went on to summarize his phone call with Bill MacMillan.

"Ravi, I would like to come with you, as well."

"No, you go to New York and get with Harry Daniels and see if you can locate Lilly with the help of his contacts within the company. Warn him to not involve the authorities yet. I should be able to get the Chinese to resolve their problem with the super alloy within a day or two at the most and should be back in New York with the address of the house where they are holding Lilly, if you have not already located her. Get the authorities involved if I am not back within 48 hours. We need to keep our heads together and get through this just as we have done all our lives," Ravi said with finality.

He then went to see Michael Zhang who had been moved to the recuperation room,

"Mr. Zhang, we are going to Beijing," he said without any preamble and gave him the gist of his instructions from Bill MacMillan.

Michael Zhang should have felt elated at the news and had a good idea who was behind his sudden release from the Indians. But he could not but feel sorry and sad for the scientist and said,

"Dr. Kumar, I am terribly sorry for what has been brought upon you and your family. I give you my personal word and promise to you that you will be safe in Beijing and that you will return home safely with the address of the location where your daughter is being held captive. I also promise to you that I will use all my contacts and influence to ensure her safety while she is in the custody of her captors."

"Thank you, Mr. Zhang," Ravi said and then instructed Captain Thapa to expunge all records of their interrogation of the Chinese man while he was witnessing. The Chinese did not know and Captain Thapa did not volunteer the fact that the fMRI machine on which most of the interrogation had been conducted also had an internal recording system which could be accessed and used as evidence, if it became necessary.

CHAPTER 57

WALDORF ASTORIA HOTEL, NEW YORK -
FOUR DAYS TO LAUNCH DATE...

Caitlyn's flight landed at the JFK airport on time just after noon. She was travelling west and had gained ten hours to arrive only two hours after she had boarded her plane at Bagdogra airport. Captain Thapa and Dr. Johari had accompanied her on the ride from Darjeeling to the airport, about three hours away. Their friend Dr. Shiavats Pradhan had also come to meet her and bid her farewell and wish her the best in finding Lilly. It was a sad moment, but Caitlyn had boarded the plane strong and resolute to face whatever lay ahead to bring her daughter back home.

Their friend from Westchester, Dr. Gopal, with whom Lilly had been going to stay with, was waiting for them. Jesse was also there. He had gotten a text from Dr. Kumar about Lilly's abduction and had driven to New York to help in whatever way he could to find and free her.

The Chairman of United Electric was already in the city, having arrived yesterday from his sprawling home in Greenwich, Connecticut. He had rented a suite at the Waldorf Astoria and had been in touch with the deputy director of FBI. He had brought him up to speed and had his commitment of full cooperation. He had emphasized, and the deputy director had agreed that they needed to be extremely careful and keep their operation low key in order not to alert Bill MacMillan and force him to take some rash and harmful action against Lilly. The need to keep FBI and other law enforcement authorities below the radar had become even more critical after Harry Daniel had received a text from Ravi informing him about his phone call with Bill MacMillan and his warning to not involve the authorities. Ravi had let the chairman know that he was going to Beijing and that Caitlyn would be meeting him by herself in New York.

The deputy director promised to assign a senior agent to the case who would be part of the task force. Earlier, the chairman had tried calling Bill MacMillan, but there was no answer and his secretary did not know his whereabouts. The chairman had expected that. He had then called Ed Malone, the UE security chief, and had gotten the same response. Ed Malone was out of the office and his secretary had no idea where he was. Harry Daniels was not surprised. Michael Zhang had told him the two of them were in it together and would be colluding with each other.

The chairman also knew the US attorney for the southern district of Manhattan and had called him and appraised him of the situation. A senior staff from his office was on his way to meet the chairman and be part of the task force.

He was now waiting for Caitlyn to get back to the States and provide the detailed update from Ravi's phone call with Bill MacMillan. This would help him and the rest of the law enforcement team to map out a strategy to find and rescue Lilly and bring the rogue CEO to justice.

Ed Malone, the security chief of United Electric, a retired FBI agent, had gotten the chairman's message from his secretary and was already at the Waldorf. The chairman had heard great things about him at the FBI and was instrumental in bringing him onboard. The chairman, just as he felt with Bill MacMillan, took personal responsibility for the actions of the security chief and after his initial anger with him had subsided had decided to reason with him and bring him on their side. The senior agent from FBI had also been a colleague and friend of Ed Malone and was with the chairman, as was the senior member from the US attorney's office, when the three of them met with him in the private suite of the chairman.

Ed Malone was apprehensive about the meeting, not knowing how much the chairman knew of his involvement with the illegal export of controlled material and now the kidnapping of the Kumars' daughter.

The chairman did not pull any punches and let the security chief know how angry and disappointed he was with him and that he knew all about his participation in the events with the Kumars and the export of restricted and protected data particularly to an unfriendly and banned country. He then threw a carrot to the chief and said,

"Ed, you can do yourself and the company a lot of good by cooperating and helping us find the girl. I have the commitment from both the FBI and the Prosecutors that they will view your cooperation favorably and get you a lenient sentence if we can bring the girl back to her parents safely. I urge you to take the offer and tell us what you know about the kidnapping and where we can find Lilly."

Ed Malone had worked long enough in law enforcement to know that neither the chairman nor the authorities had any evidence linking him to the export or the kidnapping and that even with the leniency promised by the authorities, he would be facing a long prison time. He was not going to make their task any easier by admitting his involvement and helping them find the girl. Bill MacMillan had already told him about the call he had gotten from the gravelly voice man in Beijing and that Michael Zhang was on his way back to China with Dr. Kumar and that all records of his interrogation were going to be purged. Bill had convinced him that their best course of action was to stick together and hope this whole episode would blow over.

Ed Malone told the assembled group with a straight face that he had no idea where the girl was and that he was not involved with the kidnapping, assuming the girl was even kidnapped and had not in fact decided to take a few days off and gone into hiding.

It was clear to the chairman that the security chief was fully in the camp of the CEO and would be an obstruction rather than help. He dismissed him with the warning,

"Ed, I hope you are telling the truth. You have lost your chance for any favorable consideration from me or the law and if you are found to be complicit in any of the illegal and criminal acts, I will make sure that the full force of law is brought against you and you will be put away for a long time. I hope you will think about this and call me if you remember something and want to talk to me."

"Before you leave, write down the names of all our guest houses and the names and contact information for their custodians. And Ed, you will be well advised to not contact Bill MacMillan and tell him about this meeting. We will be keeping tabs on you, and if we find out you have talked to him, you will be considered fully complicit in his actions and will bear the consequences," Harry Daniel said as Ed Malone got up to leave.

Their hope now was that Caitlyn might have some new intel based on Ravi's phone call with Bill. She was due to arrive in town shortly and would be coming to the Waldorf right after that. While waiting for her, the FBI agent suggested they would like to get a head start by looking into the bank statements of Bill MacMillan over the last few years and see if they pointed to any unusual and recurring payments that may lead them to his secretly maintained hide out place. Following the money was a true and tried way of tracking criminals, and the FBI agent was hoping it would also be the case with Bill. He assured the chairman that they could do their investigations surreptitiously without raising any flags that may alarm the rogue CEO and put Lilly's life in danger.

The chairman saw no harm in getting this work started. Time was of an essence, and anything that may help with tracking down Bill MacMillan and his hostage was worth pursuing. He agreed, and the US attorney got the necessary authorization to subpoena the bank statements of Bill MacMillan for the past five years. A young agent from FBI was well into examining them as Caitlyn arrived at the Waldorf. Jesse had met her at the airport and was with her as Harry Daniels greeted them at the entrance to the hotel and led them to his suite where other members of the task force were waiting to begin the arduous but hopefully successful effort in locating and bringing Lilly safely back home and apprehending Bill MacMillan to bring him to justice.

"Dr. Mariko, welcome back and let me say again how sorry I am about your daughter. As I promised Dr. Kumar, we will do all in our power to bring her back safely to her family," Harry Daniels began as he introduced the other members of the task force.

"Thank you, and please call me Caitlyn. This is Jesse Shapiro, Lilly's friend at the university. He will be helping us find her. You already know from the text you got from my husband that he is going to Beijing as part of the deal to keep Lilly safe and get her hideout location from Bill MacMillan. He asked me to remind you of the warning from Bill MacMillan to not involve the law enforcement authorities, so we need to make sure that any help we get from them must be exceptionally low key and should be kept at the minimum. Ravi should be back within 48 hours with the address of the house where Lilly is being held. That will be our backup plan if we have not already located Lilly by then. Ravi did ask to get the authorities involved if he is not back in 48 hours."

"Understood, and we will ensure that Lilly's safety is not jeopardized in anything we do. We will begin our search with the list of guesthouses our company manages around the area. My guess is she is most likely being held in one of them," Harry Daniels said.

He took out the list of residences he had received from Ed Malone. There were four residences listed scattered around the city. One was in the midtown not far from the corporate head offices of UE, one in the Hamptons on Long Island, another one in White Plains and the fourth one in Queens near the JFK airport. Also listed were the names and contact information of the caretakers of those residences. The chairman personally called the first residence and after verifying his identity with his superiors, the caretaker told him he had no knowledge of Lilly and that no one was currently staying at the residence. He got the same responses from the other three caretakers. Harry Daniels was disappointed but not completely surprised. Bill MacMillan was much shrewder than that.

What Harry Daniels did not know was that the list was missing the name of a fifth UE guesthouse known as the "stealth house." It was in an exclusive and remote neighborhood in Westchester County and was only used sparingly to provide complete privacy to high powered decision makers from countries around the world brought to the US for lavish entertaining as part of UE's marketing effort. Only Bill MacMillan, the security chief, and a handful of trusted people at the headquarters knew about the stealth house. Harry Daniels was not one of them.

Lilly was being held at the stealth house.

CHAPTER 58

BEIJING, CHINA – THREE DAYS TO LAUNCH DATE,
24 HOURS SINCE LILLY'S ABDUCTION...

The Bombardier Global 7500 executive jet aircraft landed at the China Aero Engine Company private airport on the outskirts of Beijing just about seven hours after it had taken off from Kathmandu's spanking new airport built with Chinese money. Besides the two pilots it carried only two passengers – Michael Zhang and Dr. Ravi Kumar.

Earlier in the morning, just as the sun was beginning to peak out of the Himalayas, Captain Thapa and two of his senior security team members had whisked them from their compound in Darjeeling to the nearest Nepalese airport, Bhadrapur, just across the international border from the Himalayan foothill town of Siliguri in India. It was a short 50-mile ride from Darjeeling to Bhadrapur, but even at that time of the morning when the town was beginning to wake up and not much traffic was on the road, it had taken them more than two hours to make the journey – a bone-jarring drive. It was only 5 miles from Siliguri to Bhadrapur, but as soon as their SUV had crossed onto the Nepalese side, the blacktop road had given way to a stone and boulder filled dirt street that felt more like a ride on a roller coaster in an amusement park than a ride to the airport. The border crossing or the little culvert that separated the two countries was barely wide enough to accommodate their SUV and even at that early hour in the morning, it was crammed with Rickshaws, pedestrians, and hawkers with their loads of goods delicately balanced on their heads, going about their business as they had done for many centuries before the countries were separated and artificial international borders were created.

Captain Thapa knew the border control agents on both side and had already cleared his passengers; they were waived through as they made their way from Indian to the Nepalese side of the border to travel the final leg of their trip to Bhadrapur. Dr. Shiavats Pradhan had also driven over from Kalimpong and was there at the airport to bid farewell and wish his friend success in his mission to Beijing and secure the safe release of his daughter, back in the United States.

It was just after noon when their plane arrived in Beijing. They had gained three hours travelling east to China from India. Ravi was quickly processed by the immigration agent who had received instructions from the man with the gravelly voice and was waiting for their flight at the CAEC airport. Michael Zhang and Dr. Kumar were greeted by the CAEC Vice President of Engineering and were escorted in the company Limo for a short drive to the main conference room of the CAEC Materials Lab.

Ravi was expecting a large gathering of CAEC engineers and scientists present for the meeting and was surprised to see just three people waiting for them – the Director of the Lab, the Chief Metallurgist, and his old friend, Dr. Xi Ping.

"Ravi, welcome to China. I wish we met under different circumstances, but my colleagues and I are going to do all we can to help you complete your mission here as soon as possible and be on your way back home to reunite with your family," Dr. Xi Ping said with a tinge of sadness and regret in his voice.

"Thank you, Xi. So, tell me where you are with your super alloy and the problem you are having," Ravi said without any preamble and anxious to get on with his mission of getting the Chinese the super alloy that they had illegally bought from Bill MacMillan and thus far had been unable to produce.

"We are not getting the expected strength from our super alloy. We have followed the process exactly as specified including the chemistry, and the heating and cooling rates. We have also controlled the ambient conditions around the melt as specified and have conducted the melting in vacuum following the well-known and well-practiced vacuum induction process. We have tried everything we can think of but have not yet come up with a solution and we cannot go back to UE for any help." Dr. Xi Ping summarized the status as succinctly as he could, knowing Ravi's time was precious and that he needed to get out of there as soon as possible.

"Sounds like you have done all I can think of. Can I take a look at your set up?" Ravi said.

"Yes, of course. Let us go," Dr. Ping said as he led the entourage, including Michael Zhang, to the clean room where the super alloy manufacturing furnace was located. It was a small induction furnace primarily used for Research and Development and not for large scale manufacturing. It was about ten years old and had been extensively used by the Chinese in their effort to unsuccessfully develop their own version of the super alloy. It was a furnace almost identical to the one he had spent many days and nights tinkering with at Cornell as a graduate student. It did not take him long to find the most likely cause of the problems the Chinese were having. It was a small hole no bigger than the size of a dime at the base of the furnace on the side close to the wall and easy to miss unless someone was specifically looking for it. By serendipity, Ravi had come across the same problem with one of his experimental melts at Cornell and it had taken him and his supervisor, Dr. McQuinn, almost a month to find the source after much trial and error.

"Xi, you see that hole there," Ravi said as he pointed to the almost invisible hole in the furnace.

"Ravi, I believe you have found the problem. We had missed that hole and it must be compromising the vacuum and letting in ambient air from the room," Dr. Ping said with excitement.

"And that ambient air, even if coming from the clean room has minute traces of particulate matter which finds its way in the material as it is being processed, reducing its strength," Ravi answered. At that moment, the two of them were just two scientists and had forgotten the circumstances under which they were collaborating.

"I will get that patched up and fire up another melt. It should be ready in twelve hours. Meanwhile, you can go and take some rest. It has been a long day for you. I will call you as soon as we have the new sample and are ready to test," Dr. Xi Ping said as he led Ravi and Michael Zhang out of the lab.

It was still dark, and the sun had not yet risen when the phone in Ravi's hotel room woke him up. It was Dr. Xi Ping calling from the lab. He and his team of CAEC engineers had worked all night and gotten the latest batch of the super alloy with the furnace hole patched up.

"Ravi, sorry to wake you up, but I am sure you wanted to hear this. We successfully produced our latest batch of the super alloy and have just completed the critical strength test. It meets the specs," Dr. Ping said excitedly.

"Thanks, Xi. I will let Mr. Zhang know. I assume my mission here is now completed and I can go back home," Ravi replied, suppressing his yawn.

"I have already called him, and he tells me the Global Express is ready to fly you back to the States as soon as you are ready," Dr. Ping said.

"Let him know I will be ready in 30 minutes," Ravi replied.

"I will. And once again let me say how sorry we are to have put you through this and wish you Godspeed in getting Lilly back safely and securely. I hope we get to meet again in not too distant future under more favorable circumstances," Dr. Ping said with genuine regret in his voice as he hung up.

Just then there was a knock-on Ravi's door. It was Michael Zhang. He was staying in the same hotel and had come to drive Ravi for the short ride to the company airport where the Global Express was fully fueled up and ready to take off for the twelve-hour, non-stop flight to JFK. CAEC had already filed the flight plan with the FAA and had clearance to land at the JFK's Corporate and Business Jet air strip.

"Dr. Kumar, I hope you have a good trip back," Michael Zhang said as Ravi got out of the Limo and was walking up to the steps of Global Express.

Just then Michael Zhang's phone rang.

"Zhang, Ming-Chung." It was the man with the gravelly voice.

"Yes, Sir."

"I understand our guest was successful in resolving our issue with the super alloy."

"Yes, he was. And now he is on his way back to secure the release of his daughter as we promised. I have the address of the house where his daughter is being held and will hand it over to him just before he departs, as you have instructed," Michael Zhang said with some concern in his voice.

"Before he leaves, I want to get the name of the missing element that enabled his latest super alloy – MRI 297," the gravelly voice man said authoritatively.

"But sir, it was not what we had agreed to when we brought Dr. Kumar here. I have given him my personal commitment that once he helps us resolve the problem with the material we bought, he can go back home with the address of the house where his daughter was being held," Michael Zhang said with anger and exasperation in his voice – a tone he had never used against his superior before – a tone that could get him in some serious trouble.

"Zhang, Ming-Chung. Be careful and mindful of what you say and how you talk to me. We need the name of the missing element before our guest leaves Beijing. China must have this if we want to gain equivalency and then superiority in aviation. You have worked all your life towards that goal, and you must not fail us now. Get the name of the missing element before you give him the location of his daughter's hideout place," the man with gravelly voice said sternly as he hung up.

Michael Zhang had taken the phone call away from Ravi's earshot. Ravi could see his face turning red and knew it was not good as he approached him.

"Dr. Kumar, I am afraid I have some bad news."

"Yes," Ravi replied his heart palpitating worrying that the news may be about Lilly.

"My superiors have instructed me to get the name of the missing element in MRI 297 before we give you the address of your daughter's hideout," Michael Zhang said, almost whispering.

"Mr. Zhang, I have done all you and your superiors have asked me to do. If I reveal the name of the missing element, I will be breaking US export control laws and may be prosecuted," Ravi said, protesting, but knowing that it was not Michael Zhang and that he would have to tell the Chinese what they wanted to know.

"Yes, you have and please do understand that it is out of my control. I can only say that it will still take us a long time to successfully produce the new super alloy even if you give us the name of the missing element. I know that is small consolation, but I must have the name before I can give you the information about your daughter," Michael Zhang said.

"Erbium," Ravi replied with resignation.

"Thank you, Dr. Kumar. And here is the envelope with the address. The pilots will give you your phone back as soon as you land in New York for you to get in touch with your family and get your daughter back." Michael Zhang said as he handed Ravi a sealed envelope and bid him goodbye as the Bombardier Global Express took off for its long non-stop journey to JFK with two pilots and its lone passenger – Dr. Ravi Kumar.

CHAPTER 59

MANHATTAN, NEW YORK – TWO DAYS TO LAUNCH DATE, 48 HOURS SINCE LILLY'S ABDUCTION...

The Global Express landed at the JFK executive airport just about the same time as when it left Beijing – they had travelled West and had gained the twelve hours it had taken them to fly the close to 6000 miles. It was still early in the morning. The second officer had handed Ravi's phone back as the plane touched down and began its taxi towards the terminal. He had caught a few catnaps during the flight but was wide awake now as he called Caitlyn,

"I just landed at JFK. Did you find Lilly?" he asked apprehensively.

"No, not yet. Mr. Daniels contacted all the possible locations including the four guest houses his company maintains around the area, but no sign of Lilly yet. Did you get the address from the Chinese? And Ravi, I am relieved you are back safely," Caitlyn responded, with concern and fatigue in her voice. She, too, had not slept and had been helping the task force with their search.

"Yes, I do. She is being held at 24 Magnolia Lane in Pound Ridge," Ravi replied.

"OK, I will let the team know. Come and meet us at the Waldorf Astoria. Mr. Daniels has reserved a suite here for the task force," Caitlyn said.

"I am on my way. Good to be back. And Caitlyn, please remind the task force the need to keep the search low key and the law enforcement personnel well hidden. We cannot afford to risk Lilly's safety," Ravi said, with an audible sigh of relief.

Ravi jumped out of the Limousine as soon as it reached the Waldorf. He made his way to the fourteenth-floor suite Harry Daniels had rented for the task force. He was still out of breath as he entered the suite where Caitlyn, Harry Daniels, and the rest of the task force members were anxiously waiting to hear from him about his visit to Beijing and any more light he could shed on the kidnapping of Lilly. Caitlyn had provided the address of the house Lilly was being held and two FBI agents had already been dispatched to discreetly scope out the location.

"Thank you all, for being here." Ravi began. "I was successful in getting the Chinese resolve their problem with the super alloy they had illegally bought from Bill MacMillan. In return, they provided the location of the house where Lilly is being held and also promised to do all they can to ensure her safety," Ravi said as he heard an audible sigh of relief from the gathering. He did not, however, mention having to reveal the name of the missing element to the Chinese. He was going to inform the authorities about it after they had secured the released of Lilly and had her safely back with them.

"I suggest, Caitlyn, Jesse, and I drive up to Pound Ridge and the rest of the team follow us, keeping a safe distance. I was warned again not to involve the authorities and we cannot afford to take any risk. I will keep you constantly informed of our status and will ask for your intervention if it becomes necessary."

"Agreed," Harry Daniels said on behalf of the task force as they all left the Waldorf for their trip to Pound Ridge.

CHAPTER 60

POUND RIDGE, NEW YORK – 2 DAYS TO LAUNCH DATE, 52 HOURS SINCE LILLY'S ABDUCTION

24 Magnolia Lane was tucked away in the woods in the small town of Pound Ridge which was more of a ritzy village than a town just off the Wilbur-Cross highway on the border with Connecticut about 50 miles from Manhattan and the Waldorf Astoria Hotel. There was just one exit sign and it was easy to miss unless someone was looking for it. The town people wanted it that way. Most of the habitants of Pound Ridge were from the top 1% of the American population and valued their privacy; they did not have much to do with the average Joe and did not believe in explicitly displaying any sign of their residences.

It took Ravi, Caitlyn, and Jesse almost an hour to get to Pound Ridge and find the address. Their GPS was only of marginal help, but they did finally locate it. It was an ordinary, unremarkable, single-story bungalow from the outside, with a main entrance door and no windows, at least none that could be seen from the front of the house. But from inside, the house was anything but ordinary. It was equipped with all the modern and high-tech devices and was tastefully furnished with top of the line furniture and appliances, ready to accommodate and entertain the discriminating guests that usually occupied the house. Most of the guests were decision makers from countries around the world invited to this discrete location to be wined and dined by their host who spared no expense to curry their favor. The woods around the house were fenced and populated with wild boars providing hunting opportunities to further enhance their experience and help the guests let down their hair and feel fully relaxed as they pondered on their contractual choices. The guest house was part of a clever marketing ploy successfully employed to win many closely fought high value contracts by the corporation that owned it – United Electric. It was also UE's stealth house. Lilly was being held there.

It was late in the afternoon when Ravi, Caitlyn, and Jesse reached the guest house. Harry Daniels and the rest of the task force were just behind them. There was no sign of anyone there as Ravi asked the Limo driver to pull the car into the circular driveway. He asked Caitlyn and Jesse to wait in the car as he approached the house. His heart was pounding heavily as he rang the door chime. On the second ring the door opened with a middle-aged man dressed impeccably in a black suit standing at the door.

"Yes sir, can I help you?" he asked in a tone that said he was half expecting to see Ravi there.

"Do you have a young lady staying at the house?" Ravi almost stammered as he answered the man.

"She was, but she left with Mr. MacMillan a few hours ago," the man replied as Caitlyn and Jesse followed by Harry Daniels joined Ravi at the door.

"Good afternoon, Mr. Daniels," the man said as Harry Daniels approached.

"You know me?" Harry asked, somewhat perplexed.

"Yes, Sir. I do. You may not know me, but I am one of your employees. Would you all not come in?" he said as he stepped aside to let the group pass and get into the high-ceilinged foyer of the house. The grandeur of that ordinary looking house took them all by surprise as the man introduced himself to the chairman, telling him the house was owned by his company and that he was the caretaker manager of the property.

"I take it you are Dr. Ravi Kumar?" the man added.

"Yes, I am, and the young lady is my daughter," Ravi said.

"I know that. She had been staying with us for the last two days and only left this morning. Mr. MacMillan asked me to give you this letter," the man said.

Ravi hurriedly tore open the sealed envelope. It contained a short note which Ravi read aloud for the benefit of the group.

"Dr. Kumar, your daughter is safe, and I assure you, will remain safe with me provided you sign the exclusive rights contract for your new material with United Electric. I had warned you before that I intend to get the rights to this new material one way or another and am warning you again that if you want to get your daughter back safely, do as I instruct you. The COO of United Electric has the necessary documents. You need to get in touch with him and sign the document and let me know you have done that the old-fashioned way – a classified ad in the New York Times Personal section. That will be the only way to contact me as I will be going completely black electronically. And Dr.

Kumar, let me warn you once again, for the sake of your daughter, do not involve the authorities.

*Dr. Kumar, let me emphasize once again, I am determined not to lose and am going to win, and win **At Any Cost**."*

CHAPTER 61

POUND RIDGE, NEW YORK – 2 DAYS TO LAUNCH DATE, 54 HOURS SINCE LILLY'S ABDUCTION

It was clear that Bill MacMillan, the rogue CEO of United Electric had gone black and would be difficult to track down. But by asking to communicate through the Times, he was also giving some much-needed time – it would take at least a day to post a new classified – to the team. They now had to use that time as effectively as possible. The task force needed to move fast.

The team decided to use the Pound Ridge guest house as their new base.

Bill MacMillan's note had demanded that Ravi sign an exclusive rights contract with United Electric and against all that he had held sacred and non-negotiable, for the sake of his daughter he was prepared to accept Bill's demand. But Harry Daniels did not. He wanted to win as much as his chief executive, but not *At Any Cost*. He wanted to win it fair and square and had full confidence in his engineering team that even with the new material being available to his competition, they would be able to field an engine that would be competitive and unique. The chairman knew what he had to do to preserve the dignity and integrity of his iconic company while assuring the safety of the scientist's innocent daughter.

On behalf of United Electric, Harry Daniels signed the contract for the new material without the exclusive rights provisions. It was witnessed by the two law enforcement team members and included a clause that would override any other past or future contracts signed by the company on that subject. With that in place, Ravi called the COO of United Electric and informed him that he had decided to sign the contract with *exclusive rights* and to courier the papers to him at the Waldorf.

Ravi then called the Times and placed an ad in its classified section under Personal Announcements. The ad would be published in the paper next morning and would say:

"MRI 297 signed. Release the bird."

They were not sure how Bill would respond without being found out. If he called the Times and placed a response ad, he would need to give his contact information which would give him away. He must have someone whom he could fully trust on the outside – perhaps the Contessa acting as the go between. The turnaround time for his response was still two days away. They would find out then if he would respond and how. Lilly would be safe for at least until then. They had to smoke Bill out by then. They just could not afford to wait for his response.

Their hope was the young FBI agent pouring over Bill MacMillan's bank statements would find some clues, and he did not disappoint.

The young FBI agent had found an entry for the city of Lake Placid, New York for each of the last five years that the bank statements were available. The amounts were not large but showed a regular year over year increase. His guess was that they represented municipal tax on a relatively modest home.

"I think I found something!" The young FBI agent was quite excited at this discovery as he called out to his superior.

"What is it?" the senior agent asked as the rest of the task force gathered around the young FBI agent's laptop.

"I noticed a regular year over year payment to the municipality in Lake Placid. It could be the property tax on a house. Bill MacMillan may have a cottage there and could have taken the young lady there," he replied.

The senior FBI agent agreed with his young colleague's findings and immediately called the municipal clerk of the city of Lake Placid. In most municipalities, the property tax records are open to the public and do not require any specific request from the authorities. But it could take some time to get the records. The senior FBI agent identified himself and impressed upon the clerk the urgency of the inquiry. They had their answer within five minutes.

Bill MacMillan did own a home in Lake Placid and had owned it for many years. He gave the senior FBI agent the address.

They called up the Google map for the area and just as they had suspected it was in a remote and secluded area of the town, ideal for a hideout and keeping a low profile. It would also be a perfect venue for detaining a hostage like Lilly where she would be shielded from the prying eyes of the neighbors.

There was no time to lose now. The FBI agent on the task force called the Lake Placid local police and quickly appraised them of the situation. He emphasized the need for utmost caution and asked them to put the house under surveillance but from a distance so as to not raise any suspicions and cause the CEO to take some precipitative action. They would be, the agent added, on their way to reinforce the local police. He then called the county Sheriff's office and the State Police office and gave them the same information and instructions.

With the local police already on their way to secure the premises, the question now was how to ensure Lilly was there and that she was safe.

"I think I have an idea." It was Jesse, who had thus far only been an interested bystander.

"Let us hear it," said the senior FBI agent.

Jesse then told them about the secret sign with candles or table lamps that he and Lilly had developed when they first met at a joint outing of his fraternity and her sorority. It was part of a game they played where they had to find their partner by identifying the rapidly flashing signs from the windows of their multistory buildings and locating the room from which the sign was being flashed. The team that got it correctly the fastest won the first place, the next second place, and so on. Jesse and Lilly had gotten the first place and had been together ever since.

The task force considered Jesse's proposal carefully. They were not sure the plan would work – what if Lilly did not have access to any windows that were visible from outside, what if Bill MacMillan noticed the flashing signals, what if there was no discrete place for Jesse to stand and flash the signals, what if, what if? A lot of what ifs, but no one had any better ideas, so they all agreed it was worth a try. They would just have to deal with whatever fall outs happened when they got there. With that, the task force was on its way to Lake Placid, the site of the winter Olympic games, and now most likely the site of a cruel game being played by a ruthless and power-hungry chief executive officer of an iconic American company.

CHAPTER 62

LAKE PLACID, NEW YORK - 36 HOURS TO LAUNCH DATE...

Lake Placid, New York was a small village of some 2,500 permanent inhabitants located in the Adirondack mountains. It was the site of the 1980 winter Olympic games and was a popular ski resort on the Whiteface mountains rising some 5,000 feet above sea level. It was also a village where many of the rich and famous owned ski chalets, some of which could fetch millions of dollars. There were also more modestly priced accommodations, one of which belonged to Bill MacMillan who had bought it many years ago when he was just starting out as a young engineer with United Electric. He could have easily afforded a more upscale and exclusive residence now, but the secluded and wooded location combined with his emotional attachment to the cottage, his first country house, had made him keep the place. He had renovated it many times over the years and had it furnished with the latest accoutrements fit for someone of his stature. It afforded him the privacy that was hard to get in a village like Lake Placid. With his busy schedule, he only sparingly used the cottage now. His recent visits were all with the Contessa when he wanted to get away from the noisy din of the Big Apple and spent some quality time with her.

It took the task force two and half hours to get to Lake Placid from the city. They already had the address of the house, which was located on the outskirts, not far from the Whiteface mountain. It was in a densely wooded area with only a few other houses visible. Its discreteness was ideal for a person like Bill MacMillan seeking to keep a low profile. On the flip side, it was also ideal for setting up surveillance by law enforcement without raising any red flags. Several officers from the local village police were already in the area, at a safe and well-hidden vantage point. They had mapped out a perimeter around the house and were surveilling both the front and rear entrances. They were also watching the windows. But, over the last four hours, since they had set up their operation, they had not seen any activity. They were not sure if anyone was in the house and had been waiting for the contingent from New York to arrive and decide upon what their next move should be.

The sun was beginning to set when the contingent from New York arrived at the house. The local village police lead quickly brought them up to date and let them know that they had not observed any activity at the house. They could also see no vehicles in the driveway, but that could be because they had used the two-car garage to park the cars. Their first job was to find out if Lilly was in the house. They all agreed the best and most inconspicuous way was for Jesse to discretely position himself in line with the upstairs window, which they assumed was in the bedroom, and to flash his light signal. It did not take long for Jesse to find just a spot like that – about hundred feet from the window, well-hidden and in line with the window. They all kept their fingers firmly crossed as Jesse began his coded signal with the light flashing:

On-Off – pause, On-On-Off-Off -pause,
On-On-On-Off-Off-Off-pause

He waited after the first set. There was no response from the house.

He repeated the set two more times and still no response. They were all getting quite worried and discouraged. Perhaps, Lilly was not there. Did they just waste most of the precious day on a wild goose chase? If she were not there, where would Bill MacMillan have taken her? Were they back to square one with looking at the bank statements again to try and discern some other clue? They were all huddled behind a large oak tree, trying to stay out of sight, in case someone was looking out from the house.

It had been almost an hour since they had arrived at the scene. The sun had set now, and they were no further ahead. Ravi and Caitlyn were beginning to lose hope and were very worried. Jesse had doggedly stood at the same place, not ready to give up. And just then, he saw a faint flash of light come from the window. He nodded to the rest of the team and stood there mesmerized. The flashing was just a little brighter and was clearly in some pattern. The entire team gathered around Jesse. They were all looking at the window and the light flashing from it. And they all saw the same pattern:

On-Off-pause, On-On-Off-Off-pause,
On-On-On-Off-Off-Off-pause

They almost screamed with excitement but had to contain themselves. Lilly was there in the house. No doubt about it. Ravi, Caitlyn, and Jesse just looked at each other – relieved and happy. But it was not over yet. They had to safely get her out of there.

The senior FBI agent in charge of the operation and had been through similar situations before. He turned down the demand from the local police to immediately break in the house and not waste any more time. But that could drive Bill MacMillan into desperation and into hurting the girl. He could not take that chance.

"Look, I understand the urgency. But it is too much of a risk. We have to try and talk to him and reason with him first before taking any precipitative actions. We need to tread carefully," he said.

Bill MacMillan had warned them not to involve the authorities. They all agreed that it would be best if the FBI and the rest of the law enforcement personnel stayed in the background and let Dr. Kumar take the lead. The FBI agent handed Dr. Kumar a bullhorn that he had gotten from his car.

Dr. Kumar carefully walked towards the house. He stopped about fifty yards from the front door. The rest of the task force remained in place ready to jump into action if things went bad.

"Mr. MacMillan, this is Ravi Kumar," he said into the bullhorn, confident that he could be heard inside the house. "We know you are in there with my daughter. I have done everything you have asked of me and am begging you to do the right thing and release her. By releasing her unharmed, you will not only be helping her and her family, you will also be helping yourself. I have the commitment from the US attorney's office that your cooperation will be viewed favorably and get you a much more lenient sentence. I implore you to please let her go."

There was no response from the house. Dr. Kumar continued talking in the bull horn as he and the rest of the team slowly moved towards the house. They were now virtually at the front door. Still no response. Lilly was continuing to flash the light signals, giving hope to her rescuers that she was all right. Two of the officers from the local police force were guarding the rear entrance, ensuring no one could escape from the house.

Dr. Kumar took the last few steps to reach the door and gently knocked on it. Caitlyn, Harry Daniels, and the FBI senior agent were standing at the landing below the front door. Ravi turned the doorknob. It was not locked. He motioned to the FBI agent to come and join him. The FBI agent took out his gun and held it in his right hand; with his left hand, he pushed the door ajar. The officers from the local police had also moved next to him and were providing cover as he entered the house with Ravi and the rest of the task force team members.

The front door opened into a large foyer with rooms on both its left and right sides. The left side room looked like a family room and the right side a more formal living room leading into what looked like a dining room. The foyer lights were on as were those for the living and the family rooms. But there was no one in the house and no signs of anyone being there and having left in a hurry.

The FBI agent cupped his mouth and called out:

"Any one home?"

The only response they got was from a room on the second floor – most likely the room where Lilly was locked up. They cautiously looked around, surveying the rooms from the foyer. And that is when the FBI agent noticed something on the coffee table in the living room – it looked like a note and a credit card size object next to it. He slowly approached the coffee table with the local police still providing him cover. The rest of the team just stayed transfixed in the foyer.

367

The FBI agent picked up the note from the coffee table. It was addressed to Dr. Ravi Kumar and was handwritten in cursive letters. The FBI agent handed the note to Dr. Kumar. He slowly unfolded it, not knowing what the note would say. He read it aloud for the members of the task force, which by now included Jesse, who had joined the group in the house.

> *"Dr. Kumar, your daughter is in the bedroom upstairs. The door of the bedroom has a magnetic lock, the key for which is next to this note. Except for the torment of being kidnapped and locked up in a room, she has not been harmed. I am deeply sorry to have put you and your family through this psychological and physical trauma. All I can say, it was never my intention to hurt you or your family; I just wanted to do what I thought would be the right thing which is to use your revolutionary material in our new engine and help address the issues you are so concerned about. I truly believed that with our very significant advantage in the commercial engine market, signing the exclusive rights contract with us would have been the fastest way to get this new material into the commercial aviation fleet and achieve the step reductions in the climate harming pollutants and the precious fossil fuel consumption. I was convinced that my actions, underhanded and odious as they may seem, were well aligned with your goals that you had so eloquently articulated at our meetings.*
>
> *Unfortunately, things went awry and got tangled up with my past actions that had nothing to do with you or your new material. I had to use*

your daughter as a protective shield to buy me some time to get away and atone for my actions in some faraway land. I would rather be a fugitive than spend the rest of my time behind bars in this country. So, please do not look for me, you will not find me. By the time you get this note, I hope to have already gotten beyond the long arm of the US justice system.

Good Luck and Goodbye.
Bill MacMillan."

The FBI agent, with Ravi, Caitlyn, and Jesse right behind them, ran to the upstairs bedroom where Lilly was still banging on the door. They opened it with the magnetic key and there she was. Crying but still strong and resolute, she fell into the arms of her parents with Jesse right next to them. Her ordeal was over....

CHAPTER 63

NEW YORK - NEW ENGINE LAUNCH DATE...

Dr. Ravi Kumar, Dr. Caitlyn Mariko, Lilly, Jesse, and the chairman of United Electric took one of the Limousines back to New York. The senior FBI agent and his associates stayed behind in Lake Placid to wrap up their investigation in the kidnapping of Lilly Kumar. They opened a new criminal case against Bill MacMillan for kidnapping, exporting, and selling restricted data to foreign countries without license, and a civil case charging him with abandoning his fiduciary duties to his employer. He had been declared a fugitive and would now face the full force of the United States government to locate him and bring him back to stand trial in a federal court of law.

Dr. Kumar called the chairwoman of General Technologies and invited her to come join the chairman of United Electric for the formal signing of the contracts for the new material. It would be available to both companies for incorporation in their new engine designs, ensuring competition, the life blood of continuous improvements and advancement of the state of the art, would be alive and well. It would be now be up to the engineers and designers of the rival companies to use their ingenuity to fully leverage the capabilities of this new material while fielding engines that best the other guy's product. The new engines might have similar performance as far as fuel burn and emissions were concerned, but there could be plenty of other differentiating factors such as the cost, durability, ease of maintenance, and product and customer support, all critically important criteria used by the airlines when selecting a new engine to power their fleet of airplanes.

The new contracts would provide a steady revenue stream for Dr. Kumar's beloved institute, allowing him and his colleagues to continue working on newer and better materials without worrying about the immediate and short-term payoffs. It would also help keep America at the forefront of aero-engine technologies, thus maintaining its lead in one of the few remaining areas where the country still excelled.

The chairman of United Electric called Jack Stevens, his friend, and the CEO of American Aviation, and gave him the good news about the launch of the new engine by his company. The new engine would meet or exceed the much higher performance targets specified by his airline; he invited him to a detailed briefing at his earliest availability. Jack Stevens promised to take him up on his offer in the near future.

The chairwoman of General Technologies, Ms. Catherine Watson, flew into New York with her new chief executive officer, Dr. Cheryl Adams – the first African American woman to hold that position in a blue-chip corporation and a constituent of the Dow Jones Industrial index. They were exhilarated to hear about the safe release of Dr. Kumar's daughter and that he and his family could now cease incessantly looking over their shoulders and that their harrowing run across the world had ended.

Although Ravi did not ask about his old friend and a foe of late, Dave Ward, Ms. Watson let him know that he was no longer with the company and had accepted to sever all ties with no golden handshake or generous lifetime pension and benefits. In exchange, the company agreed to not pursue legal actions against him for his involvement in the Kumar affair and the pain and suffering he had caused the family. She knew that would be an acceptable outcome based on her lengthy conversations with the Kumars when she had called them in Darjeeling.

Stripping Dave Ward of the immense authority vested in him by the board and the incredibly significant financial rewards that went with it, would be an abject lesson to the future generations of industry leaders. They would be sending out a clear message on what the society expects from the future captains of the industry – run your business to be the best in its class but do so within the prescribed legal bounds, and more importantly do so without losing your moral compass....

United Electric and General Technologies soft launched their new engine on schedule at the Waldorf Astoria hotel. The Kumars were there for that somewhat low-key ceremony.

A week later with much fanfare, the two companies formally announced the launch of their new engines slated to power the airplanes on the drawing boards of both the major aircraft manufactures. The new airplanes would go in service in five years and would cut the climate damaging pollutants by more than three quarters and the consumption of precious fossil fuel by half. The reduction in the pollutants, both companies noted, was especially important for airplanes as they operated at altitudes where they were closer to the ozone layer and hence were a major cause of its depletion.

Jack Stevens was there at the announcements with Harry Daniels and Catherine Watson and a 50-year-old champagne bottle to celebrate the historic milestone in the annals of the aviation industry. He could now hang up his shingles knowing that his beloved airline would be financially healthy and continue to provide the flying public a reliable and affordable mode of transportation for the foreseeable future, and that he had a hand in not only doing right by his company but also his country and the planet. It was an incredibly good and satisfying feeling.

Harry Daniels and Catherine Watson had one other surprise announcement that they were happy and proud to make at the signing of the contract and the launch of their new engines. The boards of both United Electric and General Technologies had unanimously authorized a signing bonus of $5 million each to the lead inventors, Dr. Ravi Kumar and Dr. Caitlan Mariko and $10 million each to their institute with the hope that they would continue their quest for knowledge along the unbeaten path and invent new technologies that would equip mankind with tools to fight the increasingly calamitous effects of climate change.

It was a gratifying feeling, and Ravi could not help but let a faint smile break out as he affectionately looked at Caitlyn…

CHAPTER 64

MOUNT FUJI, JAPAN – THREE WEEKS AFTER LAUNCH DATE…

Dr. Ravi Kumar and Dr. Caitlyn Mariko bid goodbye to the chairman of United Electric and the chairwoman of General Technologies and caught a train back to Ithaca. Lilly stayed behind in New York to take her MCAT exams and would be going back to Harvard after that. Jesse decided to spend a few days in the city as well and would accompany Lilly on her trip back. Sita and Reiko were going to finish out their terms in Paris and London and would be back in time to resume their new semesters at their US schools.

MRI 297 – the new super alloy gave the institute much exposure and favorable press. It helped attract a large pool of engineers and scientists who wanted to come to the institute and be part of the next big breakthrough. Dr. Kumar and Dr. Mariko were gratified to get the recognition and the wherewithal to continue with their ground-breaking work. But that would all have to wait. Ravi had promised to Caitlyn when this was all over, that they would head out to Japan for a much-deserved R&R and check off an item on their bucket list – climb Mount Fuji.

The Kumars spent just a few days in Ithaca getting their house and the institute in order and were soon on their way to Hakone, Japan, the site of the beautiful and iconic Mount Fuji. They had to wait for the climb until the weather cleared, and the mountain opened for the climbers.

The days went fast with the Kumars enjoying the peaceful countryside dotted with brooks and lakes and blooming Japanese gardens. They kept in touch with the goings on back home through Google news. Two weeks into their stay in Japan, they saw a news item that immediately caught their attention. The news was about the extradition of the ex-CEO, Bill Macmillan from Canada to the US where he was going to face criminal and civil charges. Bill MacMillan had been a fugitive and was hiding in the Laurentian mountains just outside of Montreal. The FBI, working with the Royal Canadian Mounted Police, had been able to find him in record time by following the movements of his lover, the Contessa. There was a picture of him in handcuffs being led to a US Marshall van for his trip back to Manhattan where he would be tried and prosecuted for the kidnapping of Lilly Kumar and for selling restricted classified data to a foreign entity.

Dr. Kumar could not help but feel sorry for the man who had held so much promise and ran one of the storied American corporations. He had fallen from the pinnacle of the corporate hierarchy and his fall had been hard. The power of his office combined with his greed and his determination to win, and win at any cost, had blinded him from seeing right from wrong and aided in his becoming the ruthless executive that he was. And just like his nemesis at General Technologies, Dave Ward, he needed to face justice for his horrific actions and be an example for the future generations of industry captains of what not to do and recognize the heavy responsibility that goes with the authority the company and the society vested in them.

The Kumars needed to put this chapter behind them and move on. They were getting restless waiting for the weather to clear and the mountain to open. The announcement finally came during the third week of their stay in Hakone. They were ready and well rested to take on the mountain and create some indelible memories in doing so.

They trekked all day reaching the seventh stop late in the evening. After a few hours rest in a mountain dormitory, they were on their way at midnight for the last mile of the ascent to the top of the mountain. They wanted to get to the peak before sunrise and witness the sun come out as the earth transitioned from its last western stop to the east. They wanted to witness the rising sun in the land of the rising sun as it came out, a red ball of fire.

Ravi and Caitlyn reached the peak of Mount Fuji, and saw the sun just as they had imagined, a bright red ball coming out of its hiding place, a harbinger of the new day full of hope and promise. They looked at each other with tender smiles and a hint of mist in their eyes. They could see the beautiful and majestic Lake Yamanaka at the foot of the mountain beginning to shimmer in that first light.

They knew the mountain, and the lake, and the forest were all under seize from what the humans were doing, and they needed help. They needed help to be there for Lilly, Sita, and Reiko, and the generations that came after them. They felt gratified and humbled that all their lives, in their own way, they had tried to do right by their daughters, their community, their adopted country, and most importantly, their planet. But they could not rest on their laurels. The planet was still hurting.

The Kumars would be going back to Ithaca with a resolve and commitment to work on their next project, which like MRI 297 would help heal the planet, and like MRI 297 would have a greater cause and would be ***Not For Sale!***

ACKNOWLEDGEMENTS

Not For Sale! and the other two books I plan to write as part of the trilogy is based on my journey through life which has taken me from my native India to Canada and finally to the land of free and brave. It has been a long journey full of memorable events and experiences that have shaped my being and made me what I am today. Along the way, I have been mentored, friended, taught, challenged and loved by many.

I am grateful to my graduate studies advisor, thesis supervisor and the department chair at Carleton University, Ottawa, Canada – my alma mater in North America, who helped me feel at home on this continent away from my native home in India.

I thank my colleagues and associates at Pratt and Whiney Canada and Pratt & Whitney in Hartford, Connecticut for their friendship and support during the thirty-five plus years I was there and had the opportunity to work on many of the civil and military airplanes flying today.

My eight years at Rolls-Royce in Montreal and the UK, were some of the best years of my working life. I got to learn and work on land-based applications of aero-engines such as those used for producing electricity and pumping natural gas.

I thank the engineers and scientists at RR for their patience in converting an aero-engine guy into an industrial turbine professional.

I was fortunate to have the opportunity to work with some of our customers and partners, in the US and abroad and learn from them the value of collaboration and customer service. I thank the many engineers at Boeing, US Army, GE, Honeywell, MTU and MBB in Germany and Perm Motors in Russia for helping me become a better team player and supplier of our goods and services.

I will also like to thank the professional societies – American Society of Mechanical Engineers and American Helicopter Society for the maverick work they do in keeping our profession at the forefront of mechanical and aerospace engineering.

I thank my dear friends and family Yuri Agrawal, Manoj Agrawal, Ben Zaitchik, Bill Phillips, Victor Valente, Joe Manganiello, Rita Pascoe and Holly Zaitchik for taking the time to read the manuscript and provide me their valuable comments and feedbacks. I am especially thankful to my youngest daughter, Miki Agrawal for her critical but constructive suggestions to help improve the pace and the storyline.

I thank my editors Wendy Lee and Hillary Koenig for all their help in improving the story telling and taking care of those pesky grammar and copy-editing glitches. I thank my book cover designer – Richelle and the designer of my author's website – Farhan Awan.

My daughters Yuri, Radha and Miki have been an ever-present source of encouragement and love, so essential in seeing a project like this through. Thank you, girls.

And finally, I want to thank my wife and life partner, Mire Kimura Agrawal, my own Caitlyn for putting up with me for the last forty-five years through thick and thin and for being my biggest cheer leader making sure I kept going even when the going got tough. I am truly blessed for having her on my side prodding me along. Thank you.

Printed in Great Britain
by Amazon

29802516R00215